ON MY MIND

~ and in ~

MY HEART

Based on a True Story

Gabrielle A. Hunter

1st edition 2025 Printed in the United States of America

ISBN-13: 979-8-9918848-0-8

To K.D

Without you, this story would not have been possible.

Table of Contents

"I arise from dreams of thee in the first sweet sleep of night."

— Percy Shelley

"Nice to Meet You"

Nickie

Unbeknownst to me, an ordinary day altered the course of my life. Meeting him laid siege to my heart. The love was unequaled, and so too did the emotional pain claim its rightful place.

The time was 2:00 p.m. that Sunday afternoon. With the bright sunlight filling the room, the curtains were just for show. I stretched and yawned. The aroma of brewed coffee wafted through the air, mingling with the faint perfume of my favorite scented candle. I groaned, feeling the softness of the sofa beneath me, and realized I had perched my empty cup of coffee on the edge of the side table before dozing off.

My gaze perused the large, tidy, but too quiet living room, a sanctuary from the world. Three identical smiles beamed back at me—a picture of Craig, Hyuen, and myself at the Brooklyn Botanical Garden last summer. The sun shone high in the sky behind us, the sweet scent of the red and pink roses tickling my nose and making me giggle. Maybe I should switch the frame's location on the wall unit with the precious Lalique vase I received on my fifth anniversary at the company. *I love that picture.*

A shopping trip had been on my agenda today, and the thought of browsing through the shops in the mall, surrounded by the vibrant clothes and the buzz of eager shoppers, would have been great. I planned to leave my credit cards behind, try on everything, and not buy a thing—pure bliss. I couldn't believe I had undone my plans by cozying up on the sofa, lulled to sleep by the soothing music of Sade Adu on the CD player. This morning's walk, granted, had been longer. The mild and crisp air had enticed me to overdo it, the cool breeze brushing against my skin as I strolled along the tree-lined path. Frankly, I was getting too comfortable with myself since Craig moved out after college. Things had to change; there was more to life than work and rest, no matter how comfortable I was inside my four walls.

Well, there was no point in sulking. I got up. The soft carpet beneath my feet provided a comforting sensation. I was eager to venture beyond my comfort zone and explore new opportunities. Anything but laundry!

I flipped open my laptop. The click of the lid echoed, and soon, the sound of the dial-up internet connection filled the kitchen. As I waited for the laptop to boot up, I noticed a flyer for a book club on the countertop near the microwave. I had intended to go for weeks but always made excuses not to. *Next one*, I thought.

Perhaps today, though, I would find my match. I had enrolled in a month-long free trial on a dating site a few weeks ago. A new concept in the last two years, I wondered if it could help me find a meaningful connection. A work laptop brought freedom; I was no longer bound to the office on weekends. The owner's approval, with no objections, validated embracing technology. In 1998, we had to keep up with the changing times.

Three messages were waiting; the notification sounds chiming from my laptop. I researched the individual profiles first, scrolling through the descriptions. I skimmed the first two but paused at the third, intrigued.

Anon. Dekin
Distance: 1033 miles (1662 km)
Gentle, soft-spoken, with a lot of love to give

46-year-old male in Minneapolis, seeking 30 to 40-year-old female for email pen pal, activity partner, or long-term relationship.

Remember: On this day, Smile for me, Laugh, and Give warmth, for, unlike tomorrow, to-day shall never be again. It's just another muscle-bound poet looking for a heart to share. If you like a cozy evening in front of the fireplace, walking under the stars, showering with someone who would soap your back, a good book, cuddling in bed, and looking for a long-term relationship, drop me a line, and we will take the time together.

Ken

I had been at work for two hours, the fluorescent lights overhead casting a harsh white glow on my desk. The continuous shrill of the phones filled the air. But solving the same problems was uninspiring, like a monotonous melody playing on a loop. The clock on my desk seemed to move in slow motion, each tick echoing in the quiet office.

I really shouldn't be complaining about the monotony if I didn't want a repeat of last week's chaos from installing new equipment. The company had upgraded all the computers to the new Pentiums with their fancy CD drive. The monitors and keyboards remained bulky, so they had to expedite ordering new desks to accommodate them better.

At home, leaving the kitchen had been quite a task yesterday because I cooked breakfast twice. I burned the pancakes I made, distracted by Claire's drawing on the refrigerator. I smiled at the colorful artwork and how she had misspelled "daddy."

A minute later, I stood there, spatula in hand, contemplating my culinary disaster. A song I liked came on the kitchen clock radio, salvaging the moment. Sade's sultry voice had me humming along in no time while cleaning up the mess. I wanted everything in place when the children arrived in the afternoon. I couldn't wait to see the joy on Claire's face when she unwrapped her much-desired Power Rangers lunchbox.

A magnet next to Claire's drawing tucked a picture of me and the girls on the fridge. We were all laughing because Chelsea had just proclaimed that she wanted a baby brother and expected me to come up with one by next Christmas. Though I had no intention of having more children, the thought made me realize it might be time to dip my feet into the dating pool again. The divorce happened long ago. I had dozed off last night, reaching the end of my latest book on keeping depression at bay. The book was still on the side table near the couch, lying open to a page about the companionship of friends, a partner, and other social commitments that may help.

Internet access was such a novelty in the office that I often forgot about it. Only two months earlier, my employer had implemented a company-wide network for all the technical people, bringing a sense of modernity to our routines. It was a month before I started checking it during my lunch break, hoping to find something more interesting to distract myself from the tedium.

Immediately, a random instant message popped on my screen amidst emails and notifications. Alex, from Ukraine, was asking me if I played chess. I accepted the challenge, and we began a game that lasted over a week, exchanging moves and messages daily.

The monotony returned, and one day, unable to wait for lunchtime, I took a break and browsed the internet. I stumbled upon an ad for a personal dating service. I clicked on it out of sheer curiosity, hoping to find someone interesting and nice. I'd lacked adult company that didn't include talking about network connectivity troubleshooting or babysitters, teachers, and coaches for too long.

Humming softly, I began designing a profile, expecting it to be a simple and lighthearted task. However, as I started, self-examination set in: *what am I doing with my life? How long can I live like a monk? Will I ever be good enough?* Each word I typed carried weight as I strove to express the genuine desires of my heart and not the judgments in my head. Doubts crept in — *why was I even doing this? To speed up the afternoon for one! Maybe get a date and discuss theater and art. What a welcome change it would be!*

The next few days blurred into work deadlines, network crises, and mundane tasks. Then, one lazy afternoon, boredom struck again. My fingers tapped unconsciously on the keyboard. I opened the browser and logged in, and there it was—the forgotten profile.

I chuckled at the absurdity of it all. Who was I kidding? But curiosity tugged at me. What were other people putting out there? I looked through the profiles like a detective examining evidence. There was Sarah, the yoga enthusiast, Meredith, the self-proclaimed foodie, Emily, whose profile seemed to revolve around her cat's virtues. I chuckled at each one, appreciating the quirks people had. But none of them resonated with me, like characters in a play—interesting but not quite my scene, until one that stood out. I read it for the third time, feeling an inexplicable connection with the person behind the words. Gathering my thoughts and putting pen to paper, so to speak, I said hello. Little did I know the significance this profile would hold for me. Here is what inspired me:

Anon. Nickie Yes
Distance: Unknown because you are a guest.
The Best Is Yet to Come—La Vie en Rose.

40-year-old female in New York City, seeking a 38 to 52-year-old male for email pen-pal, activity partner, or long-term relationship.

I am a slim, attractive financial professional, divorced black female who enjoys reading and great conversations. I also like hiking, biking, and long walks anywhere. I am well-educated (MBA) and confident.

I may have confused having a career and having a life for too long. NO MORE! I am now ready for the finer things in life, SUCH AS YOU: If you are a man with a sense of humor, integrity, and respect for YOURSELF and OTHERS. You are also honest and sensitive and can provide love and affection.

I seem to want everything! But don't worry, you don't have to be perfect. I am not. But if you aim for something, you may as well reach for the best. Don't be surprised if you get it! Any worthwhile relationship should start with a strong friendship, so let's give it a try!

Nickie

I sat in the conference room, my open laptop in front of me. The room smelled faintly of stale coffee and printer ink. I got up, cracked the window open, and glanced at the clock on the wall, the long oval table, and the stuffy chairs around it — ten minutes until the meeting was supposed to start. My colleagues hadn't arrived yet, leaving me to prepare for the presentation alone. I had fiddled with the various cables and connections and was satisfied that I would project to the whiteboard without a hitch. It was unfortunate that my assistant was out sick for the day. To kill time, I navigated to the Match website and reread the first letter I had received after enrolling.

Subj: ***Hi!***
Date: 1/06/98 10:00:01 AM EDT

Hi Nickie,

My name is David, and I couldn't help but notice your profile on Match. As an investment banker, I dive into market trends and financial mysteries daily. But beyond the stock tickers and balance sheets, I'm also a firm believer in the power of a cup of coffee and a good chat—those are truly the best moments!

I was really drawn to your profile, and I think it's because we share a love for hiking and biking, which just so happen to be —my two favorite ways to enjoy the outdoors! Plus, I can't resist a riveting conversation—who doesn't love a good back-and-forth, right?

I'd love for this to kick off some fun communication! No pressure, just a friendly chat. We could discuss everything from the latest market volatility to our favorite travel spots. Who knows, we might discover even more we have in common beyond the boardroom. If not, no worries! I'm just hoping to brighten your day a bit. Looking forward to hearing from you!

Best regards,
David

I had replied to David, and we exchanged a few emails. With many shared interests, I thought a great friendship was developing, but no romantic feelings were involved. I wondered why there was a lack of spark. He certainly sounded great on paper. *I believe we are somewhat too similar, both in business and personal interests. Too bad!* However, yesterday's email made me feel something indescribable, like a long-dormant longing.

Subj: ***Getting to know you***
Date: 1/18/98 9:50:34 AM EDT

Hello Nickie,

I hope you're having a fantastic day. I'm Ken, currently based in Minnesota but open to travel. I noticed we have some shared interests, and I'd love to hear more about you.

I joined Mensa at a young age and was an all-state athlete in football and gymnastics (rings). I am a little shy. I get approached often, but my instincts always make me back off. I have been a workaholic, but now I would prefer to hold someone instead of something. I have a sixteen-acre patch of land surrounded by 20 acres of lake where I live with my three dogs. I finished building a corral and plan to get two horses this fall. Did you know that even horses need companionship to thrive?

I write poetry, am a stage actor (I do 4-9 plays a year), and work full-time as a Systems Engineer in the computer department of a major retailer. I've held this job for ten years. Now, I want to hold someone for the rest of my life.

I am not perfect, and I'll not claim to be, but I can still get to heaven if you come to take my hand and walk with me.

Just be,
Ken

Subj: **Re: Getting to know you**
Date: 1/18/98

Hello Ken,

Nice to meet you; I enjoyed reading about you. You are a fascinating person. I like how you are interested in so many things and are a member of Mensa, no less! Despite a satisfying career and an array of other activities, we eventually realize we are incomplete without that special someone to hold our hand.

A few more details about me: I am 5 feet 4 inches tall and weigh 120 pounds. My MBA is in accounting, and I am a Controller for a major insurance company. I am passionate about travel, but my workload limits me to twice-yearly escapes from NY. I feel self-conscious talking about myself. Why don't you ask me anything you are interested in knowing?

You mentioned being shy, so one thing puzzled me: several of your interests (gymnastics, football, and acting) involve performing in front of an audience. Is your shyness only at the one-on-one level?

Until we speak again,
Nickie

When I got home the following evening, I kicked off my shoes, sank into the plush cushions of the couch, and called my friend Linda. Since she joined a chess club and a gym near her job, we hadn't met as often as we used to. As the phone rang, I opened the takeout container for the food I purchased, and the sesame oil aroma made my mouth water.

"Hello," Linda said, picking up.

"Hey Linda, it's Nickie. How are you? Am I interrupting anything?"

"Hey Nickie, no worries! Just got off the phone with James. We're gonna grab some grub—nothing fancy. How are you? It's been so long!"

"Oh, I am fine. I just wanted to catch up."

"How come you are not working late today?"

"You know me too well, but I wanted to be home on time for once. I got some delicious Chinese food and rented the last Star Trek CD movie before the new one came out."

"Really, Nickie? When was your last date? It's not all doom and gloom out there. We could even double date on a Friday if you find someone."

"It's hardly over a year, but you are right. And it's not that I haven't thought about it. I'm not jaded. With everyone splitting up, do you think there's a Mr. Right? I haven't found mine yet, that's certain."

"You'll find him, but you've gotta be out looking. Take James, for instance; he's like the unexpected plot twist in my favorite novel, and suddenly, everything else makes perfect sense in my life. It's not like a lonely telepath is scanning the ether for someone with your spreadsheet skills and penchant for Star Trek marathons!"

"Don't be silly. I want trust, understanding, and respect. Sort of friend and partner; of course, we must have chemistry. Also, he can't be intimidated by my career. Do you know anyone like that? Ah ah!"

I could feel myself smiling as I joked with Linda about my ideal partner.

"What about true love?"

"Yes, that too! Maybe I'll write to Santa this year!"

"Good. Sounds like you're heading in the right direction! Oh, hang on, Nickie. James showed up early. Let's catch up more next week. How about lunch? I can swing by your office."

"Sounds like a plan. Go get the door, and say hi to James for me."

"Will do. Bye."

"Bye."

Ken

A smile spread across my face as I finished the letter. I leaned back in my chair. A welcome diversion, it had been a shot in the dark, the only letter I had written. Not only did I get an immediate reply, but it was also enjoyable. The real world was messy and unpredictable. But Nickie was a mystery waiting to be unraveled. *What does she look like?*

How do I tell her my story? Where do I begin? My mind drifted to my childhood as if it were yesterday, one event seared in my memory. I was eight years old, counting my marbles, on my way to see Billy. I didn't see the car bearing down on me. The driver was speeding; I learned months later that the police had detained him. I last remembered the blue sky and the thought of flying to the clouds. Almost every bone in my young body broke. I was in a coma for forty-three days, in a body cast for eighteen months, then another cast on my left leg for six months. The doctors told my parents I'd never walk again, but being alive wasn't enough for my father. Dad met and became friends with a doctor named Kioto in Korea. Kioto worked nine hours a day for six months to get me out of the wheelchair, and nine months later, I was more athletic than I had ever hoped to be. The doctors told my mother I would have been four inches taller if not for the body cast, though she swears parts of me are six feet, five inches (my large hands and feet). During the same period, I skipped two grade levels (tested out of them); age or size-wise, I didn't feel I ever quite fit in.

My musing over, anticipation building, I took a chance, and already, my fingers were dancing across the keyboard, relaying most of my childhood trauma. I rapidly drafted another email in a more upbeat tone. *I am not defined by my past but by my hope. Did I express that? Will she reply?*

Subj: ***These maladroit times***
Date: 1/19/98 11:38:33 AM EDT

Nickie,

I took an improvisation class to help with my shyness (social), and my instructor talked me into auditioning for a public television performance of Macbeth. I got the lead (he told me the camera loves me, but who wants to cuddle with a camera?), and the rest, as they say, is history.

By the way, I apologize for oversharing about my childhood. I didn't intend to write my novel just yet. (smile). I also apologize if there are any spelling errors in my missives. There is no spell checker here, and to give you a background, when I was 13, I published my first poem, which convinced me my English was perfect. Being an adolescent and having a somewhat overbearing English teacher, I snubbed her and her class, and to this day, I can't spell worth tinkers. I don't learn partly out of laziness, but also, it's a means to keep occasional arrogance in check by just writing myself a letter.

What are your favorites—food, color, morning or night person, long or short hair? What color are your eyes? When did you begin using the internet? I don't want to overwhelm you, so I won't ask intimate questions (I still will answer any you have, and I may work up the nerve to ask you later).

I am looking forward to your letter.
Ken

P.S. My childhood heroes were Dr. Savage and Sherlock Holmes (at least I didn't want to grow up to be someone unrealistic)

Nickie

How would he know what he misspelled if he is a lousy speller? I didn't see any errors, but English is my second language. Oh well.

Subj: **More**

Date: 1/19/98

Hi Ken,

You had quite a traumatic childhood. I can't imagine enduring so much at such a young age. Even the good things you mentioned seem overwhelming. You emerged from it all more than OK, which must have involved great determination from you and everyone else.

My childhood was tame in comparison. The highlight was that I got to travel because my dad worked for the World Health Organization (WHO). I lived in Zaire for a year and spent two years at a boarding school in France. I came to the States at fifteen and have lived in New York City ever since.

Regarding your questions, I am adventurous with food and will try all types of dishes at least once. I find it easier to appreciate a culture after having tasted the food. So far, Japanese food is my least favorite. My favorite colors are orange and green. In a conservative field, I primarily wear navy suits.

I am a night person. When everyone leaves the office, I get a second wind and dig into my work. The issue seems psychological, as I have no problem waking up early for a brisk walk on weekends.

My hair is short. It was a mistake on my hairdresser's part 3 weeks ago, but I have received so many compliments on the style that I'll keep it for a while. My eyes are medium brown. My friends tell me I am attractive (I won't offer my opinion since it would be biased anyway).

Before I forget, I've been using the internet for around three years; I spearheaded its adoption at work but only for research, communication with our bankers, and our main office in Milwaukee. However, I recently persuaded the Agency's owner of the various virtues of laptops for both of our roles (smile). Now, I have access from home on the weekends. As for personal use, that only started three months ago. How about you?

Please share similar personal details with me. What's your taste in music and books? Were you ever married? If yes, how long since your divorce? How many children do you have? What are their ages? What is your birth date? Have you done any traveling? If so, where to? US or abroad? Answer at your own pace.

Till we speak again,

Nickie

From the 17th floor of the famous Chrysler building, I had a view of Lexington Ave. *I wonder what he looks like.* The city's fast-beating heart was visible through yellow cabs, private cars, and pedestrians moving up and down the avenue. *Too bad the email hasn't worked out a voice note option. I can tell he has a baritone.* My ergonomic leather chair was a joy to behold, but I stared unseeing at my bulky desktop computer with a boring beige phone on the side and a blinking amber light. *Less than the six feet five inches of his mother's dream! Thank God! It'll be so nice to hug him.* A new laser printer sat across the room next to the filing cabinet. The wooden desk was spacious, but until last year, I still had to contend with a noisy dot matrix printer that I did not want too close to me. Three organized stacks of papers, reports, folders, my calculator, and a framed photograph of Craig and Hyuen were resting on the desk. A clock, a whiteboard, and my diplomas hung on the wall behind me.

The office was orderly, but my favorite view was a large, colorful framed print of a Thomas McKnight painting. It always helped to look at it after a frustrating meeting with my boss. I had noticed it in a small gallery while strolling during lunch hour one summer day and had been obsessed with it until it hung facing my desk two weeks later.

I waited eagerly for his reply until 3 p.m. the next day. The phone had been ringing when I stepped into work that morning.

"Hello, this is Nickie. How may I help you?" I said, expecting it to be my boss.

"Hi Nickie, this is Mike from Brent and Co. I'm calling to confirm our meeting for tomorrow. Is 10 a.m. still alright with you?" Mike asked.

"Uh, yes, of course. 10 a.m. is fine. I'll see you then," I replied, trying to hide my annoyance.

"Great. Thanks, Nickie. Have a nice day," Mike said and hung up.

I sighed; I had no time to check the computer. The receiver hit the phone, and my office door clicked louder than expected as I rushed down the corridor to catch the closing elevator. Thank goodness I was wearing my most comfortable pumps that morning. I didn't intend to be tardy at a meeting with my boss and the company's bankers. I had to be at their uptown offices within minutes. A yellow cab dropped someone off as I exited the lobby; I slipped into the back seat and was on my way.

Subj: *The scary stuff*
Date: 1/20/98 11:14:59 AM EDT

Nickie,

Okay, so down to it, my father was a math professor at Oxford. I was born here in the States, in a small hick town called Hazelwood (80 people); they counted the dogs at census time. At the ripe old age of 3 weeks, I moved to Teddington, England, where I lived for 17 years. My parents met while my father was doing an internship at Butler University. My mother was a student. She comes from an affluent family in Minnesota. My father was a member of the Dutch aristocracy. His parents emigrated to the US to escape the Germans in WWII. My grandparents on my mother's side thought my father was after my mother's money. It led to a big roué, and my father took the first position offered, which was as far away from my grandfather as he could get. When I was growing up, we used to take a "holiday," a three-to-four-day weekend. For about 30-60 pounds, we could go anywhere in Europe. My father died when I was fifteen, and my mother got so homesick that two years later, we came home to Minnesota in Oct 1969.

I was married for 13 years and have three daughters, Camille, 14; Chelsea, 10; and Claire, 7. I got divorced in June 1995. My ex was a good woman and a great mother, but some issues developed, a minor one was that she was somewhat paranoid; she thought I would take up someone upon one of several propositions made by the actresses in plays I had been doing and one rather insistent producer from Channel 2 (Our public TV station). Those actresses also left several embarrassing messages on our answering machine, aggravating her discomfort. To date, I can count the number of women I have been with on the fingers of one hand and have three fingers left over. A relationship is like a good meal; it is something to savor. It needs to be succulent with the right spices and full-flavored; this requires time, preparation, and work for both the chef and the diner; it is not something to take lightly or quickly. There is a difference between love and sex; once you have made love, you will never settle for just sex.

Okay, this is scary; I am an incurable romantic. Most of my poetry is sad.

Taste in music: I grew up listening to classical; my favorite is Vogner. I sing folk classics (I like to understand the lyrics). I enjoy listening to jazz when reading. My uncle Rob played horn (B flat cornet) for Duke Ellworth and married the jazz vocalist in the band. They were happily married until 1998, when my uncle died. Occasionally, I get into a mood for R&B and listen to pop with the girls.

Taste in books: I read sci-fi; currently, I am reading Melanie Rawn's The Mageborn Traitor, the sequel to Exiles. It's a romance novel without the graphic stuff. Imagination and anticipation are two critical spices to savor in a story. I was a big fan of Sir Arthur Conan Doyle when I was younger, but I also read Popular Mechanics, Time, U.S. News, and Better Homes and Gardens. My father used to say that the mind is like a muscle; sometimes, you need to work it, and sometimes you need to take it for a walk.

Most of the plays I do are Shakespeare, so my hair is longer than shoulder length, auburn, and curly. My eyes are hazel, changing from light brown to green with gray flecks, broad shoulders, a barrel chest, big hands, and feet. Still, I am vertically challenged at 5'10". I have a little American Indian on my mother's side, so people tell me that white, blues, and greens are good colors for me. Admittedly, I don't overthink what I wear, but I have had no one to dress for in almost six years (it's part of the effort that goes into a relationship).

Oh, and I don't look too bad if I say so myself outside my clothes; you must have a good foundation if you want the work to stand. (That was a joke. Sometimes what I say sounds a little pathetic, but you have a right to know that, too, which is why I didn't edit it.)

Okay, I have danced around as far as possible (one more deep breath, exhale s-l-o-w-l-y). My birthday is on 1/09; I was 27 when I lost my virginity and 30 when I married. I married the 2nd girl I dated (that was probably more than you wanted to know, sorry again, the editor). I have pulled off several Band-Aids; how is your maternal instinct? Will you kiss it and make it better? I hope to hear from you soon.

I considered sending another list of questions, but I may be pushing my luck.

Till then,
Ken

P.S. As if this letter weren't long enough (smile), I realize I neglected to answer your question about the Internet. Post college, I got my first computer. They have always fascinated me and I practically taught myself HTML and Java, thus my field of work. Using the internet regularly, however, is recent, when my employer provided access. Since we are communicating, I can see the possibilities. It's my first time trying online dating. What about you?

Subj: ***Not too scary***
Date: 1/20/98

Hello Ken,

Please send me your new list of questions; I am sure I'll answer them with no problem. Without ESP, unless we want to spend a fortune on long-distance phone charges, this communication is the only way to get to know each other.

Before I continue, could you share the first poem you published at 13 (or any other that you're comfortable with)? Poetry is one of the unique and condensed ways of expressing intense feelings, and I greatly enjoy reading it.

Well, I should continue telling you about myself. I got married at 18 and divorced at 21. I have a son, Craig, who is now 21 and recently graduated from college and got an apartment. Since my divorce, I have had three long-term relationships lasting 8, 6, and 3 years. Pursuing my career is my excuse for not being remarried yet. Deep down, I know that had any of those men been the "Mr. Right" or "soul mate" my heart wanted, no career or anything else would have kept me from further commitment. As the saying goes, "Once bitten, twice shy."

I liked your analogy about relationships being like a good meal. We live in a society where "instant gratification" reigns supreme; no one wants to let things develop and "savor" them, as you put it. We can eat a thousand apples and not remember what they taste like, or we can have one and savor it to where we can describe the taste and consistency of every particle of its makeup.

It's also my first time trying online dating. Since it's new, I'm unsure what to expect, but I'm willing to see what happens. It's more accessible than waiting to be introduced to a good man by a friend or co-worker, and I don't frequent bars. With life being so busy, this seems a promising solution.

By the way, your self-description sounded highly appealing. One other little thing (I hope you won't think me an airhead for saying this): Your birthday makes you a Capricorn, and I am a Scorpio; we should have good compatibility. Horoscopes were my teenage astrology hobby. I am at work, and interruptions have been frequent, so that's all I'll say for now.

Till then,
Nickie

Subj: **Hey, hey**
Date: 1/22/98 3:38 PM EDT

Hey there, gorgeous,

Jay here; I like your profile. If you were a vegetable, you'd be a cutecumber...

I cringed. Not this idiot again; my finger pressed the delete button. I opened the second one.

Subj: **Hello**
Date: 1/22/98 3:56 PM EDT

Hello Nickie,

Should I say Nicole? I like your name. I am Fred. I like your profile. My office is downtown by the South Street Seaport. Let's meet for a drink after work. I can tell you all about me. I play racquetball; I jog. I travel, work, and play hard, and I....

I sighed, yawned. I deleted the message and was about to navigate out of email when I heard the ping of a new message. I smiled when I saw the sender's name. Ken's emails were like a treasure hunt with fresh surprises. Yes, his last email was more than I expected, rather shocking and revealing, yet it left me with a strange mix of curiosity and delight.

I knew we were only sharing information about ourselves, but I was taken by how effortlessly it was happening. Perhaps Ken was naturally open, but I was reserved and private, but with him, that was not the case. The letters were becoming a delicious anticipation, and I was craving his words, thoughts, and stories. *Am I being foolish? If so, I don't care.* It did not differ from a secret week-long spring crush on an unsuspecting coworker. *Or is it?*

Subj: **Thinking of you**
Date: 1/22/98 4:04:30 PM EDT

Nickie,

I, too, am at work. I didn't want to overwhelm you with questions. So, what would I see if you were entwined with me and I was lost in you?

As for my first poem, please sit back and lean against my chest; I will rub your neck, sip your wine slowly, the lights dimmed, and the music haunts the shadows. The last rays of the sunset are playing with the shadows on the wall; my voice is soft, deep, and rich with a hint of an English accent I could never lose, and I am talking just above a whisper next to your ear.

"When I Was a Little Boy"

When I was a little boy,
Young and fancy-free,
I would lie in the meadow
And watch the clouds go drifting by.

When I was a little boy,
There was so much to see.
A Deer in the wood,
A rabbit in the bush,
Or a bird on the wing.

All this is gone now.
I have grown and must
Play a different game.

The world is yours, my son.
All the glories of the universe
Your imagination is free.
Play;
Just be,
Until tomorrow takes its toll.

The clouds,
Still, go drifting by.

The Sun has completely set, and the world belongs to the noises of the night; I have surrendered your neck, and you are sitting on the floor with me before the fireplace, your back against my chest, your head against my shoulder, your hair teasing my cheek, my arms enfolding you. Will you share the moisture of the wine still lingering on your lips, or shall we rest awhile and listen to the music?

I know it's sneaky putting in questions this way. I hope I have not offended you; I am nervous about your reaction. I have 8-foot-high windows, 16 across the house's south wall. Last night, I stood in the living room watching the sunset, the storm's remnants dissipating. I played some jazz softly in the background and found myself dancing with someone I couldn't describe; her smell haunts me beyond my senses. Suddenly, I realized I miss you.

So, your assignment, should you accept it? How do you feel in my arms? Is it something you are comfortable doing? I am asking not for shapes and weights but for thoughts, feelings, and sensations.

Till then,
Ken

Did my heart skip a beat? *What's happening to me?* His last letter was so intimate. *No wonder I am unsettled.* But in a good way. *Should I be honest and answer in the same vein?* I didn't think it was my imagination saying that he was interested. *Should I let my feelings lead the way for once?* I was setting myself up for disappointment, but what the heck? I liked how I felt, and I would tell him exactly that.

Subj: ***Re: Thinking of you***
Date: 1/23/98

Dearest Ken,

Curious way of asking questions. Let me see, if I saw myself entwined with you, and you were lost in my face, what would you see? If we reached that level of intimacy, you would see a woman with love in her eyes and trembling full lips filled with desire and anticipation.

You know, sitting on the floor, facing the fireplace with your arms around me and soft music playing in the background is so cozy. I am afraid to move; this seems like a perfect moment. Dreaming, I slowly turn and raise my face, searching your eyes in the semi-darkness, one hand in the hair resting on your neck, gently pulling your face to mine. You can still taste the last drops of wine lingering on my lips. The evening is young. Heaven can't be too far away.

Well, you thought you were being bold? I do not know what got into me; I know there are at least a thousand miles between us, and you cannot see me blush as I write these words.

Coming back to reality, thanks for sharing your poem with me. I delighted in reading it. My head tells me I should not send this email or write something more characteristic and proper, but I am not listening. So here goes.

Till then,
Nickie

My right hand hovered over the keyboard but fell to the desk as my smile evaporated. In the thrill of reading the first letters, I overlooked a minor detail. Ken was in Minneapolis! Not Manhattan, not even New Jersey or Connecticut. The distance wasn't drivable. *It's not practical at all.* I saved my reply, closed AOL, and with my enthusiasm wavering, I navigated to the Excel spreadsheet I had started yesterday, analyzing the cost-benefit of acquiring a new phone system to prepare for the Y2K concerns. *Ugh, I need to think.* Maybe I had been too hasty to dismiss the others as uninteresting. I should at least read the other messages from the past two days.

"More"

Ken

The cup of tea in my hands was steaming after I reheated it in the lunchroom microwave. The dark blue and ugly hallway carpet leading back to the server room didn't bother me today, and somehow, I caught myself whistling. I reread her letter, and a wide grin crossed my face.

This "Nickie" person was getting to me. I hadn't felt this good in longer than I cared to remember. Of course, it was just infatuation. *But who knows what can happen?* I felt a surge of heat (not in my head), making me smile. Was it too early to tell her that? *What if I scare her?* No. I should take it slow. I was enjoying our banter too much. The only way to find out was to write.

Subj: ***Is it getting warm in here?***
Date: 1/24/98 6:25:24 PM EDT

Hello Nickie,

My membership expired, and I was oblivious until I received my message marked "return to sender." It was the only way to reach you since we had not exchanged real email addresses, but I don't want to look further.

I'll let you in on a secret. We have already done the hard part; you see, I opened up to you, expecting nothing but hoping you would feel good, and you opened up to me even though you were, shall we say, nervous; we just made love with words.

By the way, I know people use nicknames on this site; I just wanted to tell you that I didn't, and my real name is also Ken, so just in case I have made you mad, and this will be my last chance I have to write to you. It flattered me you blushed. I thought so much trying to feel your presence I wrote you a poem (I told you I am an incurable romantic, and I refuse to take the shot if they develop a vaccine)

"Without You"

How lonely the night without you,
How cheerless the sun.
The thrill of birds
Is suddenly silenced,
As though
They had sung their fill.

How pointless life is without you,
How banal the dreary day.
Uncloaked of your lilting laughter,
The dress of my hours is gray.
My smile when it comes

Is empty.
My hand to a friend,
Is chill.
In a world where one lover
Listens,
But the voice of the other,
Is still.

Oh, I try with my heart to believe
What the poets,
And sages say.
Time heals,
Life is not hopeless,
But without you,
It seems that way.

I'd give my right arm for a fireplace, and as Dante said: "A loaf of bread, a jug of wine, and thou." To taste the breath on your lips ...

According to the computer, we are 1037 miles apart, and I am not crazy, just infatuated with you.

Till then,
Ken

Subj: ***Opening the windows won't help the heat***
Date: 1/25/98

Hi Ken,

Why would I be mad at you? The only thing I am afraid of is that we have both taken a leave from Reality and are wandering through the Land of Wishful Thinking and Unfulfilled Desires.

I knew I was in trouble when I woke up yesterday morning and spent an hour thinking of, reinventing, and embellishing the details of our "Fireplace Encounter." Our need for love may be taking us too quickly into the dwelling of our desires. One of my favorite songs is by Celine Dion. A few years ago, she recorded a song called "The Color of My Love." I played this song more than a few times yesterday while thinking of you. This may be a case of acute infatuation; I know I am acting out of character, but I don't care.

Your beautiful poem only added to my confusion. I never imagined becoming someone's muse, even for one poem. Do you realize we have only been corresponding for a week? Somehow, it feels much longer.

I don't know how far this "infatuation" will take us and if we will end up disappointing each other or growing this into enduring and lasting feelings. For now, I only know it's terrific to feel the smile on my face whenever I open my mailbox and see your notes. Have a wonderful weekend.

Till soon,
Nickie

Day and night, I was daydreaming about Nickie. She was invading my mind and capturing my imagination, all without us ever meeting or her lifting a finger (except to type.) *When did I last think of my old life with Mary Lou? I can't remember.*

Was it my long, self-imposed solitude that made me so optimistic? I had to admit, Nickie was reading me like a book, allowing me to open up page by page. She was direct without being intrusive, and I gladly gave myself to her since I had no secrets. *Hold on. I'm getting ahead of myself.*

Subj: ***When dreams dare us to grow beyond ourselves***
Date: 1/25/98 6:01:24 PM EDT

Nickie,

It sometimes feels like I have known you my whole life and my life will never be long enough. I think of us in various situations: walking down a crowded street, at work, feeding each other and the birds in the park finger food, doing mundane things about the house, and at a party with a group of people we know. I let myself flow into the scene, taking in the smell, the lighting, and the abstract sounds in the background; I concentrate on one spot of this daydream and try to make it as accurate as possible.

I couldn't sleep last night, so I walked into the living room just before it started to rain. There were some lightning flashes but no thunder, and my reflection kept appearing and disappearing in the glass. I noticed two deer out under the trees by the pond; I stood there for almost 2 hours. The deer had fled by the time the world again registered with me. It was a beautiful night, and you are a marvelous dancer. I hope someday to experience you in my arms. Once, I thought of us lying on the floor playing backgammon; I was lost in your eyes and laughter, and I could almost see you being impish; you are beautiful. By the way, you won.

On my tape deck, I have Savage Garden singing "Truly Madly Deeply," which captures the essence of my love and commitment. The song contrasts the challenges and obstacles we face in our relationship and reminds me of our bond that transcends time and space. So lifelong old friend, (figure of speech) it occurred to me, do you like baths or showers, morning or night, alone or with a partner? (It's fun to fill in the blanks; truth be told, I am blushing but still ready outside the door with soap, wine, and candles). Ask me anything. I wrote you one last poem. I feel like a child with over-indulgent parents at Christmas when I come into work and log in to my mail. I am saving the poem for later, lest I time out again.

Oh, I did try to tell you: if you go to the museum and check out Michelangelo's David, my hair is a little longer, my nose not so big, and my lower eyelids may be a little puffier, and I am a little taller, but otherwise, that's me. Now I am blushing. Oh, did you get the e-card I sent?

Till then,
Ken

P.S. I am trying to find out who we are, maybe be a bit entertaining in the discovery, who knows, even charming (you have to hear my voice for me to go for debonair). So far, I want to scream from the rooftops, but I know it's a good thing I'm a genius; this way, I am just eccentric (kidding).

Nickie

I couldn't believe how endearing I found Ken. Per my friends, I had an uncanny way of sensing people's true feelings, emotions, and motivations, and I agreed with that at least fifty percent of the time. *Okay, fine, I am proud of it.* I attributed the "gift" to being non-compromising, introspective, and brutally honest with myself; I almost always recognized when people rationalized, evaded, deflected, or lied about themselves or things. However, the "skill" was most often used one-on-one. I was doubtful it would translate into print.

But why am I over-analyzing things so much? Why can't I enjoy this brief interlude without putting it under an emotional microscope?

I exited the park further than expected. The downpour was steady, but at least there was no wind. A couple in proper rain gear passed me, intent on catching the city bus crawling up the tree-lined street two blocks away. I crossed the street without hesitation, but an unseen car splashed my jogging pants with water. *What an idiot! Where's he rushing off to on a Saturday morning?* I looked at the sky, but the sun was losing a battle. *Come on, Nickie, get a move on.* I'm sure there was a letter in my inbox. *Wait. Did I just twirl in the rain like a madwoman? Hold on, girl; you are losing your mind. But who cares?* I felt alive.

Subj: ***Let's dream on***

Date: 1/26/98

Ken,

I just returned home, drenched in the rain. I went for my morning walk and was sure I would return before it started pouring. In truth, I should have gone and been back long before I did, as has been the case the entire weekend: I wake up, get lost in a reverie of you, and lose track of time.

I'll go back to bed, anyway. There is thunder and lightning, unusual for this time of year, and it's turning out to be the kind of day you want to stay in bed cuddling with someone while watching old movies. Unfortunately, I don't have someone to cuddle with, but I rented two videos yesterday, which will occupy me for a few hours.

Until you asked, I didn't realize how much I would enjoy having someone soap my back in the shower, although I prefer to be alone for baths. If you were a good boy, I would allow you to join me with the candles, the wine, and the music. We could be silly and play with the bubbles, or I could lean against your chest, rest my head or your shoulders, and quietly enjoy the moment until the water turns cold. That could be the prelude to a slow, unhurried night of lovemaking or act as a gentle lullaby for peaceful sleep in each other's arms.

So, you look like Michelangelo's David, huh? Playing football and being a gymnast have their rewards in more ways than one. Unfortunately, there is no female equivalent of "David" to which I can compare myself. If there were, I would fall short of it. I don't know your physical preferences for a woman, but my friends tell me I am attractive, and I believe it, although I would not call myself beautiful. I am slender, with a small chest, a tiny waist, a round derriere, and lean thighs and legs. I wear a size six. I have pretty hands, and I am proud of my lips. I can wear all kinds of lipstick colors, and they all suit me!

By the way, you mentioned an e-card, but I am still waiting to receive it. Also, please send me the other poem you wrote.

It's quite an adventure! We will probably have to begin from scratch if we ever meet in person. In the meantime, I keep thinking of you and missing you.

Till then,

Nickie

Subj: ***Words***

Date: 1/27/98

Ken,

I received your greeting card, and it's lovely! So is your poem. You have a way of capturing the essence of our feelings. I don't have your gift with words, so I'll borrow from a site I found online. Here goes:

"Breathe"

*The wind dances in four directions
 and touches what it sees.
But of all the breezes I've ever felt,
 only one encircles me.
It gently slips beyond my thoughts
 and hides within my needs,
Capturing my heart inside.
Through words, you made me breathe.*

By Belladora

Frankly, I can't think of a way to improve on this or express how you make me feel. My pragmatic mind tells me this is all a dream I will soon wake from, but my emotions tell me to give it rein and see where it leads.

Yesterday's movies were Sense and Sensibility and The Piano. (Responding to your e-card question about what we were watching.) You monopolized the blankets, and my little feet were cold. It was a ploy so that I would cuddle closer to you.

On a fresh note, I have a couple more questions: What is your most outstanding quality? What would you say is your biggest flaw?

*Till then,
Nickie*

Ken

The window bench was astonishingly comfortable. On the far wall, I spotted the painting I had dragged from the hallway closet where it had been stored for the last six years. Two horses grazed joyfully in a field with bright yellow wildflowers in the distance. What a serene picture! I could not believe I had kept it hidden this long. At midday, the beauty of this piece should be even more apparent. The soft rays of an early morning bathed the room with a sense of hope that paralleled my feelings. It's as if I had lifted the shades darkening my heart, expecting a new day. On my lap was a yellow pad on which I had scribbled a reply to Nickie's last letter. I will put it in an e-mail when I get to work, which will no doubt save me some time.

Nickie understood what truly mattered. Was this a coincidence, or was I given what I needed without realizing I wanted it? How else could I explain this connection with someone I hadn't met yet?

Subj: ***The best and the worst***
Date: 1/27/98 2:22:45 PM EDT

Darling,

Please sit back, give me your feet, and I will warm them. As with most men, my most significant strength is, by definition, potentially my greatest weakness, which would be my capacity for compassion.

I am genuinely concerned for those I know and some I only know through circumstance; this makes me a true friend, a considerate partner, a good parent, and many other things only possible if you do not always place yourself first.

This concern is also my greatest weakness, as I am naïve and trusting. I believe in the essential goodness of everyone I meet and take people at face value. Sometimes, I get taken advantage of, but I have never regretted it. What we do to others will either enhance or diminish us, as the golden rule applies to how we treat others; ultimately, we will have treated ourselves. My faith is such; it is not my responsibility to judge others; that is God's job. My job is to be the best me I can be. It's your turn to answer the same questions. Are your feet still cold?

Till then,
Ken

Nickie

I was sitting cross-legged on the living room carpet, the laptop on the coffee table. I had forgotten about the phone jack on the wall behind the sofa; the laptop cord was blissfully long enough to attach with no inconvenience. *I should add a phone extension to the living room.* The cursor blinked on the screen, waiting for my decision. I'd been staring at the map for fifteen minutes, tracing the imaginary lines connecting NY to Minneapolis. The distance was daunting, with highways, cities, and time zones between us. I wavered between hope and hesitation. Our letters sparkled something unexpected. It would be nice to have someone whose laughter I could hear without the digital filter, but Ken made me feel seen and understood. Wasn't that worth the distance?

I sighed, my eyes drifting to the window. The moon hung low, witnessing my turmoil. I had never been one for impulsive decisions, preferring to weigh every possibility. Yet here I was, caught between longing and practicality.

And then there was what Ken said about putting others first, even when it meant getting taken advantage of? It was both endearing and frustrating. But what if I was always competing with others for his time and attention as he went on to sacrifice not just his but our well-being? Could I handle that in the long run? People are so complex! Maybe that's why I found dealing with my accounting ledgers and spreadsheets more enticing.

Subj: ***Re: The worst and the best***
Date: 1/28/98

Dearest Ken,

My most outstanding qualities are integrity and coherence between values, words, and actions. I can't run away from myself; liking the person in the mirror and knowing I try to be faithful to her is crucial. I make mistakes, sure, but the introspection of my motives and actions leaves no room for self-delusion. This approach brings me peace and serenity.

My worst fault is inflexibility; I have made great strides there but still have a way to go. I endeavor to make allowances. People are unique, with different histories and experiences. What's obvious to me may not make sense to them; thus, I need understanding and compassion in certain situations.

I consider myself a work in progress and make effective changes when needed.

Till then,
Nickie

Ken

I started to believe we were kindred spirits, like two sides of the same coin. One, yet we each had our unique perspectives. I visited the UN building a few years ago, took the tour, and admired the Persian rugs on the wall. The carpets were stunning, but they concealed one minor flaw: a deliberately empty space within a pattern or a color mismatch.

Only God can create perfection; we can't. If we were imperfect, that was the devil's work. The devil made us compare and contrast, judge and criticize, better, worse, beautiful, ugly, affluent, and poor instead of appreciating everything and everyone. It meant that although we had flaws individually, as a unit, those flaws might cancel out and reveal the perfection of God's work, which resonated with me.

My only question is, when we meet, will I be able to restrain myself until we are alone and I have her permission, or will they arrest me if I try stealing a kiss? That thought made me grin.

Subj: *Muse*
Date: 1/29/98 AM EDT

My Dearest Nickie

I came to work an hour early today to write this note; I was grinning, thinking of your reaction and what to say. I feel like I am 16 again. Last night, we had a special preview of one of my plays (it opens soon). The play is called Love Letters. I play Andrew Makepeace Ladd III, who, at the end of the show, after 40+ years of letter writing to Melissa and Melissa's death, realizes how deeply he loved her. Melissa's spirit was hovering, saying she did know.

As I read Andy's last letter and the potential analogy, I thought about us, and tears streamed down my face. Tammy (who plays Melissa) and I received a standing ovation at the preview; I wanted you to know you are an inspiration and a muse, and in my fantasy, you are many things to me. I won't wait 40 years.

Till then,
Ken

Nickie

I embraced the uncertainty, and the distance. I couldn't make myself ignore the other more practical options, but I wouldn't dismiss what I could have with Ken.

"You look like the cat that swallowed the canary!" my colleague said as I strolled into the office. I laughed it off, attributing it to the beautiful weather outside. Their skeptical smiles didn't go unnoticed, but they didn't press the matter any further.

I raised a few eyebrows in our management meeting when I inquired about the exact dates of our company's annual meeting. It was an event I had always objected to attending; however, my boss made it mandatory for his "team" to be present.

When I asked, I was unaware of my motivation, but somehow, I was hatching a plan in the back of my mind.

Subj: ***Will this make you panic?***
Date: 1/30/98

Dearest Ken,

I did not know you two weeks ago, and now, not hearing from you for even one day makes me feel incomplete. I have never felt such a connection with anyone else before. I spend my days missing you and the nights yearning for you.

Your last letter was beautiful. I love the words you wrote to me yesterday. It's hard to believe we experienced so much together in such a short time.

I wish I could applaud you for your play on opening night. No, I don't want to wait 40 years to meet you. I can't wait 40 days, which brings us to reality. I will be on a business trip to my company's headquarters in mid-March in Milwaukee, Wisconsin, which I know is next to Minnesota (smile). How long is the trip for you to meet me in Milwaukee?

Could you drive, or is it better to fly? Could I fly to Minneapolis after my meeting to see you? I hope you don't consider this forward; I only want us to meet, nothing else! I know we are emotionally in sync, but I don't want us to wait too long before we meet. We'll idealize each other in our heads, ultimately leading to disappointment.

I am sorry for introducing reality into our idyllic little world. Still, I'm sure, had you been in NY or I in Minneapolis, and our feelings were as they are now, we would have already had a dinner date to introduce ourselves. What do you think? Am I rushing things? To answer your questions: yes, you'll be able to keep your hands off me until we are alone, and no one will arrest you after kissing me!

I won't have the peace to write more today. The other managers are out; my office has been a revolving door of interruptions. Know you are constantly in my thoughts.

Till then,
Nickie

Ken

If my heart would stop racing, I could start typing to tell her how excited I was; frankly, I had not expected to meet her so soon. How did she manage to be shy and bold at once?

Subj: ***Milwaukee!***
Date: 2/1/98 10:34:49 AM EDT

Dear Nickie,

I am sorry I didn't write yesterday. I took a day off work and received your note today. In answer to the subject line of your last email: Yes, I will, to a slight seismic reaction to you being so near, but my response is one of anticipation. Which day will you be in Milwaukee? I am 5 hours away. Can we meet for dinner? My hours are from 5 a.m. to 1:30 pm. I can be there by 6:30, okay, seven if I stop to pay at the parking ramp and for gas.

I had this flash of us locked in an embrace; my boss wanted to know why I had the stupid grin. Usually, he sees me with a mild frown, and once the frown turns into a scowl, he sends me home, effectively curbing my workaholic tendencies. How long will you be in Milwaukee? I have too many questions; my mind is racing.

For the past two mornings, in wanting to keep dreaming of you, I have had to pry myself out of bed. Last night, there were thunderstorms and 70 mph winds; I found myself praying you were alright. When I finally did sleep, it was light; I was straining to hear the rhythm of your breathing. Four trees fell, and the power was out, but it was a good excuse to light the fireplace and relax. I may be "in love" with you; I miss you and will wait impatiently for March.

We rehearsed at Tammy's house on Saturday. Although the preview went well, we wanted to review some scenes before the official opening. Her husband applauded as we finished. I will bring a copy of the script for you in March.

Till then,
Ken

"Plans"

Nickie

I awoke, frightened and disoriented; the clock read 2:30 a.m. I wondered what had disturbed me as a bright flash lit the room, followed by a loud rumble of thunder outside my window. The rain pounded on the windowpanes. Mother Nature was in the throes of a major tantrum, and I was scared.

As a little girl in the Caribbean, my favorite thing during thunderstorms was having a hot cup of cocoa. I smiled and realized we must have gotten Ken's thunderstorms from two days ago. I hoped he was sleeping peacefully.

Suddenly, I wondered if I should have mentioned Milwaukee at all. I'd email in the morning to tell him it was from the 21st to the 25th. Dinner was doable since I'd get there by 3:00 p.m. *Did he say he only uses the computer at work*? I doubted he knew about the chat program ICQ. I found it way easier than AOL's Instant Messenger.

His play sounded terrific. Do actors rehearse even after a play opens? *How long will it run? A workaholic? He didn't sound it. I wonder what he does on his days off?* Gymnastics and football? If I keep all those questions up, we won't have anything to discuss in March.

Subj: ***Summer in Milwaukee***
Date: 2/2/98 11:06:57 AM EDT

Dearest Nickie,

I forgot to save fast enough and just lost a message from the screen timing out, so I'll summarize. I sometimes rehearse six nights a week, juggling up to three plays. Last year, I was in a play called The Chastitute. I had to step in and play a different character without rehearsing because a co-star was injured. The critics said I was better. Love Letters is planned for only one performance in a museum as part of the Stone Bridge Art Festival, but there is a chance of performing it at the dinner theater in Chanhassen.

I am a self-taught artist of primary classic-style charcoal portrait art. I used to write poetry, but while rereading some of my stuff a while ago, I realized I had repeated myself in 123 different ways. I decided I had nothing to say and stopped writing until I wrote a couple for you. I love to read, mostly sci-fi fantasy. Once in a while, I get a bee in my bonnet, and I get creative in the kitchen. I am playing around with an international translator, hopefully, to sell to a tech company. Occasionally, I will still take on a student or two and teach them karate. All that pales compared to the most significant and enjoyable parts of my days lately, fantasizing about you. In my imagination, we made love in every room in the house a dozen times, several times in the car, and once in the lake.

I am doing a Matinee of MacBeth on the 21ˢᵗ. I will be on the road by 2 p.m. and will call you at about 5 p.m., giving you a couple of hours to wrestle with cold feet (ah ah). I had a most exciting fantasy about the hotel lobby. (I envy your pillows, sheets, bath towels, perfume; you have a lovely neck, divine.)

Okay, fair is fair. Same questions, plus your favorite color and style of clothes (pajamas?). There is a delightful park in downtown Milwaukee where we can talk about flowers, allergies, coworkers, and your thoughts. We will think of something, assuming I can find a tongue to speak with.

Till then,
Ken

Subj: *(no subject)*
Date: 2/4/98

Dearest Ken,

I, too, love Sci-fi. I'm a die-hard Trekkie and have watched every Star Trek movie. I enjoy board games and comedy when I'm not nose-deep in a book. I'm always up for a good read. My other hobbies are taking long walks and hiking. I enjoy researching stuff on the computer, learning new programs, and staying abreast of the financial markets. I would frequently travel to exotic places and learn about different people and cultures if I could. Did I mention that my son is a graphic artist/designer? He is also a pretty accomplished fine artist (drawing).

I love silk pajamas, although I don't currently own a pair. Silk or satin lingerie feels better on bare skin (I don't dislike lace). The company and the hotel I am staying in are in downtown Milwaukee, making it easy to get to the park. I am curious about the hotel lobby fantasy. I hope no one was swinging from a chandelier! (Smile).

Until then,
Nickie

P.S. I am unsure how you pronounce your last name (I noticed it when you first started using your Hotmail account), but when I said it aloud, it sounded like "Candy Cane." Have you heard that one all your life?

Subj: ***Thinking of you***
Date: 2/5/98 11:03:25 AM EDT

Dearest Nickie,

My only reference point is the Milwaukee Hotel. I don't remember any chandeliers (but I am willing to hunt one down). I was in Milwaukee last year for The Acting Irish International Theatre Festival. I played Paul Keegan in John Bull's Other Island, and they nominated me for best-supporting actor. We walked around a bit over the weekend. Still, I am looking forward to "discovering" Milwaukee with you.

I am glad you didn't ask me about pajamas; mine is hard to describe (I have freckles in places I am sure I haven't seen) (caught you! I was thinking of my back). I, too, enjoy board games. Do you play chess? Cody keeps me humble. My little brother was what polite circles called challenged; his IQ was 69. Emotionally, he never matured past 6, but he was a mathematical genius; what took me seven years to master in chess, took him 45 minutes. (I am proud of him). I have always been overprotective of him, but by the time he was 15, he was already a foot taller than I was. I am rusty, not having played in, my goodness, 13 years, but I held a 1983 rating on the national circuit (Grandmaster) for 16 years. I played my father 40 games a week for almost seven years before I was good enough to beat him. Still, he played the pro circuit when school was out during the summer.

Where on the scale of forest-emerald-lime is your color green? I am picturing the way silk hangs on you, the way the light plays with the folds when you walk, and the drape of the blouse is lovely. (Yes, I am blushing again)

I look forward to seeing you. Be sure to let me know if you find a chandelier.

Till then,
Ken

Subj: ***Re: Mail test and other things***
Date: 2/6/98

Dearest Ken,

How are you today? Do you have any exciting plans for the weekend? I imagined different scenarios for our first rendez-vous. Will you drive back to Minneapolis after dinner or find accommodations for the next day? What do you intend to do after our meeting? I am both excited and apprehensive. Such a wild adventure! The next time I can't sleep, I'll imagine we are together, and I am trying to count the freckles on your body!

By the way, I would be an eager pupil if you would teach me some of the board games. My dad was a championship-class bridge player when I was growing up, and I meant to ask him to teach me to play but never got around to it, so I only know a few card games. Bridge is to cards what chess is to board games. Is your younger brother your only sibling? I have both brothers and sisters, all older except for one brother. All reside in NY except my older brother; we get together on holidays and special occasions. I am glad no one is more than a few hours' drive away. How is Cody doing these days?

I previously stayed at the Wyndham and Pfister hotels during my Milwaukee visits. The Pfister has the chandelier, so I'll ensure my company books me there!

What's your role in the IT department? Do you program, analyze systems, or process data? Is acting primary in your life, and IT secondary? How far away from the city do you live (given the deer on your property)? (In NY, I would need to drive 2 hours north before I could expect to see a deer.) I hope your day is going well.

Until then,
Nickie

Subj: ***Friends and Lovers***
Date: 2/7/98 12:20:16 PM EDT

Dearest Nickie,

Where do I begin? My schedule is to work on Sunday. I have no expectations except to meet someone who is quickly becoming important to me. Such are my plans now; ask me again Saturday Night. I admit some giddiness at the prospect.

I am the middle child of 5. Benji and Paul are my older brothers; Benji is a doctor, has been married for 27 years, and lives with his wife, Yoko, in Cambodia. Paul is married and living with his wife, Cera, in Lafayette, IN. He designs new phones for Western Electric, which sells them to the Bell companies. Billie, my only sister, who used to be a Playboy bunny and still lives in Chicago, manages an optical store, and Cody is the youngest brother. Cody lives with our mother and attends a day program that helps with independence, social interaction, and skill development. I secretly believe I am his favorite sibling because his eyes always light up with a smile whenever I visit.

My work in the computer department involves fixing what the programmer writes and integrating new technologies and applications into the existing systems. The computer work pays the bills, and the plays keep my mind flexible and recharge my heart.

I live 57 miles NW of the city on a 36-acre "farm," 20 of which were wetlands.

I have been converting into a lake, so I live on a 15-acre island. Still, you can wade across the lake (so it's not a moat; it's about 6.5 feet deep at its deepest point, and the average is about 4 feet.) It flows from Lake St. Francis, so there are fish and plenty of wildlife. Six years ago, I felt the need for solitude; now, I want to rejoin the world.

When I think of you at work, the images can be stimulating. I replay the images as slowly as possible, enjoying the quiet moments far more than the distracting bustle of the day. The day before yesterday, I purchased a body pillow. I look forward to dreaming of you. Lacking the rhythm of your breathing, the magnanimity of your smile, and the hypnosis of your eyes.

The weekend is quiet. I am trying to find a good pair of suspenders; the director for Love Letters wants me in a white shirt and tie. Still, I see the scene with sleeves rolled at the cuff, collar open, and suspenders, reminiscing in a dim kitchen. I am also hunting up a yo-yo and an old fountain pen to put in the shoebox with the love letters. It will make more sense when you see the script. It's funny, you are always with me, yet sometimes I miss you.

Till then,
Ken

Nickie

As if it weren't already too good to be true, I was thinking of him as one of those dashingly handsome heroes I used to see on the covers of the countless romance novels I devoured as a teenager. *And now he tells me he lives on some island. What next, Prince Charming, complete with a castle, drawbridge, and a moat?*

The body pillow made me smile; I got one three months ago. I put it in the middle of the bed against my back; somehow, I found this comforting. Ken mentioned feeling a need for solitude six years ago. It likely coincided with his divorce. *Is it rude to ask what tanked the marriage?* I was curious but understood this could be something he wanted to discuss later. He might still be hurting.

When did he relax? "All work and no play..." was a recipe for burnout; I should know! I was amazed that each letter brought a myriad of new questions.

I didn't know how, but I accidentally deleted the email I sent him this morning while trying to reread it. I checked the "deleted items" folder but was unsure if clicking the restore option would apply to the individual mail or all the emails in the folder. I cut my losses and gave up. I made a mental note to ask my colleagues or call the main office IT support in case of a future recurrence. That was annoying! I liked to reread my last email before opening his new one. What a bummer!

Subj: ***Life in Camelot***
Date: 2/9/98 7:04:42 AM EDT

Dearest Nickie,

You were right on the first pass. My ex-wife, Mary Lou, has Crohn's disease. The condition worsened during periods of high stress or anxiety. During our marriage, her condition went into remission. I would let her vent, knowing and understanding her pain. I did not defend myself from her rage, partly based on jealousy. She needed an outlet for her stress, anxiety, and frustration. Unfortunately, during the last six years of our marriage, her fits of rage became more violent and increased in frequency, culminating with my hospitalization. I know I can be impulsive and sometimes stubborn but I mostly gave in to keep the peace and see her happy. Her father forced her to seek mental help. She felt abandoned when I was in the hospital instead of at home during her time of need. My self-esteem hit a significant low, and one thing led to another. Many well-intentioned people became embroiled in our relationship, and we divorced. It took three years of therapy to reach a point where I wanted more from life than peace and solitude.

I have worked more than I should since the divorce, as work has become a substitute for my family. Still, it chases away the loneliness, and I haven't become too introspective, and it has afforded me some luxuries. As they say, everything happens for a reason, although not always readily apparent.

It's funny; I have envisioned you much like a princess, high in the tower of her castle, but the farm is much more romantic on paper than in real life. It's all relative to your position and your focus. It was a sanctuary once, and now, it seems empty. Where once I sought the quiet, now I seek the sounds and the creatures that invade it. Before, I did not see the walls, but now they can use a coat of paint.

I miss you constantly. The first thing I do when I arrive at work is look for your letters, and I find myself coming in early so I can read and respond to your letters before my boss gets in and try to quiet the pounding of my heart. You didn't say which color of green.

Till then,

Ken

It was midday on Saturday, and I was shopping at Syms. I usually got a couple of new work outfits for the company's annual meeting every year. Syms gave the best price and had an incredible collection of high-end merchandise. Today, however, I was looking for something more casual and flattering, a lovely dress that would keep me warm under a coat for a walk in the park or a cozy dinner date. The store was crowded and noisy, with people of all ages looking for bargains. Racks were filled with clothes of various styles, colors, sizes, brand names, and standard labels. There was the smell of fabric and the occasional whiff of perfume. Mellow but up-beat music was playing, creating a laid-back yet engaging atmosphere. The staff was busy, ignoring the customers unless we asked for help.

I spent fifteen minutes contemplating a pair of light olive-green silk pajamas and wondering if the light would reflect such an unusual color in his hazel eyes. I wondered if I had crossed a line by asking about his divorce the other day. His an-swer was sad, and after reading it, I only wanted to hold him tight against my heart and comfort him. It was a long time ago, and he was better now.

I didn't know how to handle all these emotions. I woke up unable to bear wait-ing another month to meet him, but on my way to work, I considered an approach to postpone our meeting because I couldn't abide by the thought of us not liking each other when we meet. Such confusion! But was he ready? Six years was a long time, but still. *He must be okay by now; otherwise, why would he be on a dating site?*

I was being silly, but it was hard to imagine returning to a time when I didn't have him in my thoughts every day. Lord, I missed him!

Ken

The day stretched long, from the early hours of dawn to the fading light of after-noon. Training began at 6:30 a.m., carrying me through until 3:00 p.m., each mo-ment heavier than the last. I arrived five minutes too late, forced to hurry in without the briefest greeting for Nickie, and throughout the day, her absence lingered like a shadow. Yet, there was no time for indulgence—only the quiet ache of endurance.

At work, they had upgraded the IT system, and the instructor's voice filled the room with technical details that seemed to drift in and out of focus. My mind wandered, slipping through the cracks of concentration, though enough found its way to me, allowing the instruction to leave its mark.

When the session finally drew to a close, we were detained for an additional fifteen minutes. With a tone that brooked no dissent, the manager's boss delivered the grim news of new policies: unauthorized use of the internet, a violation severe enough to bring about dismissal. Perhaps this was the cruelest part of the day, the weight of such an ultimatum settling heavily in the air.

As the day waned, I stopped by a clothing store to replace worn pants, a small, insignificant task, before continuing home. There, I made the necessary calls—first to Gateway, arranging for a PC tailored to my needs, and then to US West, securing the installation of a specific internet line. They promised it would be done by March 15.

After the calls ended, I turned to face my "home office," a space that felt more like an afterthought than a sanctuary. It occupied the farthest corner of my bedroom—a simple wooden desk, a chair that offered little comfort, and a lone bookshelf. The walls, painted a soft blue, seemed to swallow the meager light from the fixture overhead. Only the glow of the bedside lamp offered a reprieve. A small window, though tall, framed the view of the backyard, its size a pale comparison to those in the living room. The desk held few treasures—a speakerphone, an outdated headset from work, a penholder, and a stapler. The space felt hollow and incomplete, as if it were waiting for something more. I made a silent mental note to change that, to craft a space that might truly be mine.

I was eager to tell Nickie about it. If we hit it off when we met, which I hoped we would, I could say good night and good morning and perhaps not experience the anguish of missing her as acutely or worry about getting around this firewall at work to talk to her. *Should I tell her about my other surprise? No, that would spoil it!*

Subj: ***Strange day***
Date: 2/12/98

Dearest Ken,

Today was strange for me. I took the afternoon off from work, intending to take care of a few things I couldn't do on the weekend, but nothing went right. From driving in torrential rain with abysmal visibility to getting off at the wrong exit to locking my keys in the car, it was one hassle after another. Finally, I reached home with unease and irritation, having wasted half a day. I tried to listen to a new CD and read a mystery novel but found myself distracted and on edge, so I gave up and decided to write to you instead. I am better already.

By the way, are you ticklish? Did you mention being a good cook? What's your favorite dish? Do you prefer making love in the morning or at night? (where did that come from?) How naughty!

Till then,
Nickie

I hung the receiver. I had been on the phone with Mary Lou, confirming when to pick up the girls for dinner tonight. Earlier, twice, I had been startled to alertness blushing, my meanderings focused on whether the kitchen table or the bedroom would be the scene of my imaginary lovemaking sessions and whether an afternoon tryst would suit Nickie.

Subj: ***Good morning;***
Date: 2/14/98 6:34:51 AM EDT

Dearest Nickie,

First, I am unaware of being ticklish anywhere, but you are welcome to search diligently. Now, I feel like a politician. My pillows bear witness to my desire for you in the evening, and I eagerly rise early each morning, only to lose the hours in your contemplation and want. How do you feel about love in the afternoon?

Your day sounds like the kind of day I have when there are not enough hours, and my mind is reviewing the possibilities of things yet to do instead of considering the task at hand, and the world seems to conspire to slow me down. One day, I had locked my keys in my car for the second time when it dawned on me: I was at the hardware store to make a spare key to keep in my wallet to prepare for such an event. Seeing the humor in my plight, I vowed never to lock the car again. Besides, I am constantly losing things, and it would be my luck to close my keys in the car and lose my wallet simultaneously.

Oh, yes, despite my search, I haven't found the object of the surprise. I can't spill the beans till the ground is firmer under my feet.

Till then, love you in the morning,
Ken

Subj: ***Love in the afternoon***
Date: 2/15/98

Dearest Ken,

If you are not ticklish, I'll have to find another way to force you to disclose what you hold back from me. I have a great imagination and will come up with something!

How do I feel about love in the afternoon? Excellent. It is the same way I think about love in the evening, morning, and middle of the night if the feelings and desires exist. If pressed for a choice, evening is my favorite, but only because there is usually more leisurely lovemaking and cuddling afterward. If time is not a factor, then any time is a good time! And as to where all this lovemaking would be, the bedroom is not the only place I would consider. No place is safe.

Except for the first time and our first kiss in front of the fireplace, I try not to get too specific when I am lost in thoughts of you. I concentrate on your arms surrounding me, the feel of your lips on my face, never anything beyond. Doing so with all those miles between us would not be advisable.

As for being ticklish, I am, but I won't tell you where. You'll have to discover it for yourself. (By the way, I wasn't truthful before; I did allow my dreams a few times to go beyond us kissing. But that's all I'll say.) I can feel myself blushing, remembering.

Till then,
Nickie

I was at the market by 6:30 a.m. I bought a beautiful bouquet for Nickie; upon returning home, I pretended she was at the door, ready to greet me with a smile. As soon as the weather hinted at spring, I planted rose bushes by the house. Since the geese had enjoyed the ones I grew last year, I enclosed them with a trestle swing and a small picket fence this time.

Toward mid-afternoon, I made salmon, rice pilaf, and steamed carrots and had dinner staring at the lake (through the kitchen window). It had been warmer the past couple of days. There was soaking rain last night, and the clouds began rolling in again before sunset. It was gorgeous. I ventured to the barn to retrieve a box but unfortunately got caught in the rain.

Once dried, I thought of picnics in the rain and walked around with a stupid grin, particularly whenever I glanced at the lovely flowers in the vase by the foyer. *How often do I get a relaxing day like this? It's well worth telling her about.*

Subj: ***You are also on my mind***
Date: 2/18/98

Dearest Ken,

During our picnic, I could picture you asleep under a tree. Last night, I tried on a beautiful white cotton dress. I bought it in the Caribbean early this year on vacation. I have yet to wear it, but somehow, it was my chosen attire as I imagined bending to kiss you under the tree. (Did you get my naughty email, Love in the Afternoon?)

Except for my little daydreams about you, I have been in a strange mood for the last two days. I received my 3rd job offer this week. Instead of feeling wanted and happy, I felt irritated and depressed. My boss is retiring early next year, and a new person will take over this agency. For once, I want to take a few months to enjoy my personal life without dealing with these things.

On a different note, you once mentioned large hands. They should be great for massages. Do you know how to give a massage? That's what I need to relax and feel better. Should you have more computer problems at work and can only write to me once you get your own, my phone number is (718) 704-xxxx. I miss you.

Till Then,
Nickie

"Misunder-standing"

Nickie

I added a ream of paper to the laser printer, closed the tray, and stood purposefully until the monthly financials printed. Eventually, I returned to my desk to stare at my screen—no new message notifications. I clicked the refresh button, hoping something would appear, but the inbox remained stubbornly empty as it had for the past two days. My fingers drummed on the keyboard, frustration mounting. Ken was always prompt with his emails. *Is he too busy with work?*

The next day was crowded with meetings, causing me to stay in the office three hours after work to complete my report on the monthly variance analysis of the financials. I had been curt in my replies in one meeting I believed was honestly a waste of time. I wanted to be in my office to keep refreshing my inbox for Ken's reply. Yet, I drafted a memo thanking the meeting initiator for their foresight in organizing the meeting and recapping the salient points discussed. *Did Ken go to another seminar? Was his mainframe down?* Marie said I looked as if I had lost my best friend. They've gotten used to seeing me with a permanent smile. What could be wrong?

I should have attended my friend Francine's cocktail party last evening, but driving into Manhattan always made me nervous. The prospect of an hour-long subway ride had been equally unappealing. *But how will I increase my social circle if I keep refusing invitations?*

I was up by six and went for my walk. I needed to do something that would exhaust me and distract me after seeing an empty email box. I packed my maintenance gear and went to a couple of houses I owned. When I decided I wasn't ready to leave the accounting profession, even after branching out and getting a different license as a Certified Financial Planner, I still wanted to establish a second source of income. I purchased them a few years ago within a 3-year interval, with careful planning and much trepidation and anxiety, leveraging one to acquire the other. Still, all my spreadsheet numbers gave me the go-ahead, and I knew that nothing worth doing was easy.

It would be an entire morning of work. The handyman I hired must have skipped the last two weeks. I noticed the hardened snow lingering in the driveway and backyard. I already had a new tenant for this apartment, and the place had to be ready in a week.

Inside, roughly handling the equipment, I accidentally broke a piece of the bathroom vanity I had purchased. Feeling overwhelmed, I sat down and cried, realizing my frustration was more about Ken not responding. After a moment, I reminded myself I was independent and could take care of myself. Determined not to let a man dictate my mood, I started working properly, changing the lock on the front door, checking all the faucets for potential leaks, and installing the bathroom vanity. It took longer than expected, but I was proud of the result. I needed to talk to the first-floor tenant about her kids, as I had noticed some damage to the evergreens at the front of the house, which I was sure they had caused.

When things looked decent, I returned to the car and drove ten minutes to the second house. I could not get the snowblower out of the trunk, but a nice man walking his dog gave me a hand. *Once in a while, I meet a friendly New Yorker!*

This house was manageable. I had not been there for three weeks, but still, it was in good shape. These tenants had no kids and no pets. It was just blowing the snow from the backyard, and I finished in twenty minutes. When I got home, I called and fired the handyman; I was doing all the work, anyway.

It was three o'clock, and I was exhausted. I looked forward to a nice nap on the living room sofa. Trying to read would be a waste of time, as my mind would wander to Ken and the absence of mails. I had enough willpower to shower, wash my hair, and make a sandwich, but I could not proceed to the sofa without checking the computer. And there it was! His name popped up on my screen, and my heart skipped a beat. Until then, I did not realize I was close to panicking at not hearing from him.

Subj: *Big sigh of relief*
Date: 2/20/98 10:07:14 AM EDT

Dearest Nickie,

It's been a few days since I have heard from you. Today would have been the third. Admittedly, I was worried, unsure if the problem was at my end. We just implemented a new firewall. Yesterday, I figured out a way around the email problem, at least a contingency plan. But last I heard, you were considering several positions with different geographic locations, and I didn't want to add to the confusion.

I found a letter in which you wondered if I had read your views on love in the afternoon. I wish I had, but I didn't receive it. As to back massages, Sherlock Holmes would say, "I am adequate," but then I try to maintain a higher degree of modesty than Holmes. I have been looking forward to a long afternoon or evening massage, starting (your choice) at your temples or toes and working every inch to the other so I could show off. My other strong point is my voice. My eccentric second cousin says it's pure sex, and my director says it's 30% of the box office. The producer said... never mind, she's a flake. (Just kidding about the flake thing, I mean, (are you smiling?))

I think about you most of the day and all night. If it is true, "Love is of the mind, sex is of the body," I love you much, and for very long periods, admittedly, I hope and pray someday for our bodies to embrace our minds.

I, too, have been thinking about changing jobs. A corporate headhunter keeps calling, and my sister is trying to persuade me to move to Chicago. While I am the senior specialist, they mostly leave me to my own devices. Please don't get me wrong (Two big, strong hands will travel). You could take that a couple of ways because I had a mental picture different from what I originally meant. Before I bury myself, I better go. I miss you.

Till then,
Ken

P.S. Consider yourself passionately embraced for the past 5 minutes, bothered by hands and forearms shifting over your back, and a kiss I guarantee will still have you smiling during lunch. (Okay, so a guarantee is a bit presumptuous. It may even sound egotistical, but it's my dream. What can I say? I'm a hero.)

Subj: ***Missing you so much***
Date: 2/20/98

Dearest Ken,

Since I don't want you to think me nutty, I will not tell you what state I was in not hearing from you in nearly four days, but on to better things. I will attach the missing "Love in the afternoon mail" to this note. I am glad you have a sexy voice; now, I can't wait to hear it, and I can imagine how nice and soothing it will be to listen to it while you give me that excellent head-to-toe massage.

I am beginning to feel uncomfortable, and your passionate kiss and embrace will have me smiling not just through lunch but at the very least until tonight. Giving such glorious kisses is not wise unless you want to be ravished. I think I have fallen "in love" with you.

Till then,
Nickie

Subj: ***Thinking about you***
Date: 2/21/98 3:48:50 PM EDT

Dearest Nickie,

Thank you for sending the missing letter. I have read it four times. While I am glad I didn't wear jeans to work today (they are a little tight), I am particularly fond of the last paragraph.

First, you should be aware I like to take chances (with the provision that the probable outcome is desired and pleasurable). I like long, lingering kisses. Second, after four readings, I still tingle from the last "declaration." I haven't said so previously: I think I started falling "in love" with the letter before your first poem. I am monogamous by nature and choice. I wouldn't (at least it has never happened before) have as many fantasies (I lost count) about/with someone if I didn't care about them.

Your letters are unique. You are charming, witty, and shy, yet open, making me feel like I am 16 again. I see you in my dreams, and I swell with such passion (okay, maybe ardor); my pulse quickens, my breath short, and even my skin is alive with sensation.

Okay, I will concede that I have taken liberties to visualize my imagining and other abstract sensations. I am not deluding myself; it excites me more (I am talking emotionally, not physically). It is your mind, heart, and personality. I have fallen "in love" with what I see in my mind, extending what I feel in my heart. In secret, I have been working on another poem (it may give you some idea of my feelings); the last line reads like this:

I shall sit alone in the night,
When time has wreaked its vengeance upon your face,
Return to me;
I will make you beautiful,
With my eyes.

Till then,
Ken

Yesterday, I took a day off and brought the laptop home. *I wish Ken could also do that.* The delay and distance have been torture. Given a choice, though, I would rather wait to hear from him than not know him. My daily walk was a delight. The air was crisp, and the sky above a clear blue. I breathed deeply, energized by the brisk walk, feeling my calves' muscles warm up and my heart rate increase. A few playful squirrels scurried around. *Weren't they supposed to disappear in their nest or the hollow of trees in winter?*

Seeing numerous walkers, joggers, and dog owners on a weekday was surprising. I exchanged friendly greetings and smiles with a few of them. There was a sense of community, belonging, and the joy of freedom from cabin fever brought on by a spate of continuous lousy weather that kept everyone indoors.

I loved this park; it was my oasis in this busy city. After getting my much-needed exercise, I drove to one of my properties to address a minor maintenance issue, replacing a malfunctioning indoor lock. Once I completed the task, I headed back home, feeling content.

We will be meeting in less than a month! I still couldn't believe it. This morning, I decided to tone down the flirting in my mail. If I kept teasing him with naughty words, I'd be too embarrassed to look him in the eye when we met in March.

I had given little thought to job prospects. I turned down the one from Norfolk. Their need was immediate; they needed to pay more, and I could not pick up and uproot in a week without some forethought. The past year showed me a certain level of burnout, just going through the motions. *Do I need a new challenge? It's more likely I need a mental break.*

He was worried about rambling. I told him not to because I was the same way. *I am amazed at how similar we are,* although he should expect some reservations on my part when we first meet. Of course, once I got comfortable and trusting, I opened up and made a person wish I had remained reserved! *If he is too verbose when we meet, I know two lips that would love to silence him with a kiss. Did I say this to him? Maybe I should!*

Subj: ***Trying to find Poli-Sci books.***
Date: 2/23/98 11:43:12 AM EDT

Dearest Nickie,

Somewhere, I have some old political science books. I will find the longest, most boring speech in the book and maybe a backup, memorize them, and launch into a litany, a filibuster, if necessary, for I cannot think of a better or more prosperous use for words than the purchase of your kiss.

My sister called yesterday to persuade me to continue to Chicago after our meeting. My nephew's birthday is on March 27, and when she found out I was going to be so close, she decided to move Liam's party to the 24th. So, either way, you are "safe" (unless you convince me otherwise). After reading that, I realized the last sentence is open to misinterpretation. I am so maladroitly trying to say that should you desire, you now have two options to compel me away: responsibility, i.e., work, or guilt, and Liam's party.

The show was a big hit. The stage was freely accessible to the public, and we picked up 40 audience members after the play started and received a standing ovation. After the show, a rep from John Casablanca stopped and asked if I had representation (I didn't have the heart to tell him I do theater for fun). Minnesota Parent was the sponsor for the festival, and at the last minute, they decided our play may be too "adult" for children, so they moved our performance time back 90 minutes and had us on a different stage. Several people said they fought the urge to cry and thought it was great. The funny part was we had not rehearsed a curtain call, and Terri and I couldn't figure out how to get offstage at the end, so the moment became awkward. Over 100 people applauded. About half rushed up on stage the next moment, shaking our hands and patting our backs, and all tried to talk simultaneously. I could have been the mayor at that moment.

I picked up new shaving oil, all-natural, at the festival. I hope you can tell me if it makes my skin soft. I have spent several hours contemplating about you in your white cotton dress, under the tree by the lake, laying your head in my lap, dozing. I am brushing your cheek with the petals of a flower, there is a light breeze, and the sky is a pale blue with a touch of gray, the clouds drifting lazily, mostly obscured by the leaves and branches of the tree, the slight smile on your face absorbs me. I miss you.

Till then,
Ken

I was practically wearing a path into the carpet, pacing back and forth between my office door and the window. I glanced at my computer screen, where Ken's reply waited. I hoped he understood the questions in my email of the 6th and didn't think they were an invitation to stay overnight for intimacy! I hadn't even met the man, though I might be totally in love with him. I would never do that! Or at least I have never done that before! "Ouch," I cried, stubbing my foot on the chair leg. *If he thinks that's what I want... I am mortified! I'm not one to follow trends, even in the '90s. I follow my heart, and it tells me this would not suit us. What we have is too precious to rush; I want to savor it.* I bit my lip, shook my head, stopped at the desk, and sat abruptly. I reached for the keyboard. *Lord, I have to write and clarify!*

Subj: ***Milwaukee revisited***
Date: 2/24/98

Dearest Ken,

Congratulations on the success of your show. I wish I had been there to applaud you. Remember to bring the script in March. You could even read your part for me.

After your letter yesterday, I realized something I asked was open to misinterpretation (i.e., whether you would drive back home the same evening or stay overnight). My reason for asking was twofold. Can you go 10 hours with only a few hours of rest (for dinner and conversation)? If you were planning to stay overnight and depart the next day, I wanted to know if we would spend more time together in the morning. But the main reason is this: five or six thousand (their count, not mine) sales and staff from around the country converge on the city to attend the annual meeting on those dates. There is usually a shortage of hotel rooms then, so if you intend to stay overnight, you should book your reservation early because you might not find a room if you wait until you arrive.

I now realize what my question must have seemed to imply. Don't be concerned: if you don't return home the same night, it will not be because I tried to seduce you. It will most likely be because you decide to attend your nephew's birthday party.

Although we know and care for each other very much, we are still virtual strangers, which is a long way of saying that the only thing we'll have to decide is how many kisses and hugs will be enough before we say goodbye. (I must admit that the other scenario makes for more exciting fantasies, but that's all fantasies.) One more thing: I'll be rooming with a lady from my office, so this is one other reason to be sure there would be no hanky-panky going on and no expectation of such. We can relax and enjoy each other's company.

As to the new shaving oil you bought at the fair, I would have to get close to you to judge the state of your skin. Maybe that's what I was dreaming of when you saw me smiling in my sleep under that tree.

Love,
Nickie

Subj: ***Humor***
Date: 2/24/98 1:08:13 PM EDT

Dearest Nickie,

Okay, perhaps I was trying to be too cute. There's no need to fear or worry that I would drive there and be upset if you didn't share the same feelings I have or that I was harboring any preconceived expectations. I have been to Milwaukee, but I don't know it well; if you know somewhere you would like to have dinner, feel free to suggest. I will dress casually. In short, I was putting you at ease. My only expectation is to meet someone for whom, through their letters, I have developed a strong fondness. I need to be friends with someone (again, NO PRESSURE!!) I would have a long-term (i.e., permanent) relationship. Additionally, if we (excuse the expression) hit it off, and you are agreeable, I thought

I would stop back on my way home from my sister's and maybe have dinner or talk Sunday night. Two for the price of one, what a concept.

Admittedly, this is a first for me. The only extensive correspondence I had previously was playing chess with Alex in Ukraine. Additionally, I am somewhat selfish; the way I feel about you now, I will if I can spend more time with you. Who knows how soon we will have the opportunity again? I also know it may not be significant to someone else because something is important to me, which is okay. At the same time, I was looking forward to meeting you, not some kid having fun with his computer.

I was rereading this and thinking it may read like I can be some grump or something; if it does, I am sorry it was not my intention. No person should expect their "needs" to supersede another, primarily if one has implied caring for the other, because respect is not something that needs to be verbally expressed but rather shown through actions that show care. Your "needs" are as vital to me as mine. With all that said, should you FEEL like kissing me, or should you FEEL like accepting an embrace and maybe a kiss? I am not opposed to the exchange of such gifts. (Hint, hint)

Till then,
Ken

Lord! I think I upset him! God knows it's not what I wanted. Why couldn't I have left well enough alone? So, what if he misunderstood? I could have clarified when we meet, but no. *Miss "I have to be clear!" Miss "I need to make sure you know my exact meaning! I am such an idiot! But I can't help it.* I didn't like to gamble on misunderstandings, and he was too important to me to let him think of me less desirably. *This attitude is anal, no wonder I am an accountant.*

Subj: ***Did we fight?***
Date: 2/24/98

Dearest Ken,

I felt misunderstood. You sounded mad at me for saying what I did. I am clarifying I had no expectations, and I look forward to getting to know you! I did not mean to imply you had any ill will and would not be considerate of my feelings. If I did, I am sorry.

I know our acquaintance is only through email, but you are very dear and important to me now. Do you have any doubts about how I feel about you? If you do, words are indeed inadequate for their task. Like you, I don't play games and would not devote much of my time trying to get to know someone I did not care about, so don't be mad at me because it would make me quite miserable :(:(. Without knowing you, I love you.

Till then,
Nickie

Subj: *No **FIGHT!***
Date: 2/24/98 3:21:42 PM EDT

My dearest Nickie,

Oh, my goodness, I am not angry. I was worried it might read that way. Sorry, I was trying to be delicate. I am a major klutz. I was getting from your letter that you thought I was expecting you to strip off your clothes and jump me the moment you saw me. All I was trying to say was, okay, I am human, but you are too <u>important</u> to me for me to think so little of you!

By telling you about my sister, I was saying I could hang around an extra day without being underfoot, and if conditions were conducive, I could spend more time with you. Please, please, I am not mad. I am not a jerk. I am sorry (I feel so stupid).

Till then,
Ken

Subj: *Friends*
Date: 2/25/98

Dearest Ken,

I am glad to hear that you are not angry with me. I am sorry for my unclear communication. I am not upset with you at all. It was all just a misunderstanding.

On a fresh note, I need to become more familiar with Milwaukee. Although I have been there a few times, I have never taken the time to visit the city. So, for Saturday, we could find that park and walk around talking and getting to know each other. If everything works out as expected and you go to your nephew's birthday party, then on your way back, I'd be thrilled if we could spend some more time together. How persistent has that corporate headhunter been? Is it for a different job in Minneapolis or Chicago? Still,

I have gotten used to thinking about you on your island, surrounded by wildlife and nature, and I have trouble seeing you in a city of concrete and steel. Is your auburn hair closer to red than brown? Silly questions.

I love you,
Nickie

Subj: **Thinking about you;**
Date: 2/26/98 10:43:53 AM EDT

Dearest Nickie,

I spent 2 hours working on a letter only to have my session time out and lose it. The park I know is in downtown Milwaukee, so I will need to find you in Milwaukee; then, we can figure out how to get to the park from there. What is it you do in your position at work? The headhunters are not being pushy. If anything, it's my sister who is being pushy. She has several friends out looking for her, but my pay requirements have slowed her down a little (money is not an issue with me, just a convenient one for Billie's sake). The headhunters don't share the same problem. However, I have already turned down positions paying 15-20,000 more yearly than I am currently making for no particular reason. I can leave my current job. I tell people I am like a Canadian goose. It's for life when I bond, but I can't think of anything if pushed for a reason.

Last weekend, I added a screen door to the front door. Last summer, we had a lot of rain and heat. I had to leave all the windows, the back door open, and all five ceiling fans running. However, it was still clothing optional. The screen door will allow for some pleasant cross breezes this summer. I am getting ahead of the game. I am considering getting central air conditioning next year.

I admit the thought of you compensating for the heat in my chosen fashion has brought more than one smile to my face and, if dwelled on, has provoked other reactions. I wrote before about the differences between a house and a home. A home is the people who live within, not the external building. I want to build one together rather than try to fit into someone else's existing or mold someone into mine. Rather than having one personality bend to the other, they should blend, strengthening the bond rather than creating tiny cracks where they meet.

Aren't you glad I had to write the short version? You missed out on a twenty-minute flight of fantasy. I miss you.

Till then,
Ken

Subj: **Good morning**
Date: 2/27/98 8:11:22 AM EDT

Dearest Nickie,

My day started 2 hours ago, and I wrapped myself in thoughts of you; this is when I would take and share a virtual embrace and good morning kiss.

I just reread several of your emails and found I had neglected to answer about my hair color. It changes with the seasons, as do my eyes with the weather. As I am in the sun more during the summer, the red highlights are more prevalent, so in the summer, when I look in the mirror, I am redheaded and have brown hair in the winter, sometimes my eyes are green and sometimes brown and occasionally brown with a blue-green tinge.

As to my confession, I fantasize about swinging from the chandeliers; on occasion, I fantasize about meeting you in the lobby, sweeping you up in my arms, kissing, and carrying you out of the entrance. Still, I don't have a handle on where we go; I could see myself cradling you in my arms as you would carry a small child, you with your arms about my neck, and us leaving the lobby amidst the stares of those we leave behind. So, though I always try to be a gentleman, to be honest, I must admit my thoughts have strayed, so you were right to caution me. However, in my defense, I have not seen myself behaving less than honorably. I wish I were there or you here so I could hold you, feel your body pressed against mine, and begin our morning with a kiss. I hope your day goes well. Again, I am sorry for thinking you thought I expected something. Well, you know, you were right, and I am sorry. (Does this mean we can kiss and make up?) Oh, nuts, I meant after I thought you thought I did think it, but I never expected it. (Did you understand that?)

I hope I elicited a smile, a bit short of a hug and a kiss, but it will do for now if you smile.

Till then, love
Ken

Subj: *Good morning*
Date: 2/27/98

Dearest Ken,

Is there anything left to discuss when we meet? Did I mention I love auburn hair? I won't tell you everything I love about you. If I do, you'll think me hopelessly smitten and start playing hard to get!

By the way, I forgive you for thinking what you thought I expected, but you were not thinking until after you thought I had thought it! As you fantasized about that lobby kiss this morning, I turned around in bed, looking to kiss you. Some believe a strong bond enables people to sense each other's presence.

Here comes a personal question: What part of a woman's visible anatomy most appeals to you? (i.e., legs, breasts, rear). To restate the question, imagine looking at a perfect stranger: what physical attribute would make you think they are attractive or unattractive? I'll tell you about my pet peeve—enormous bellies. I don't find considerably overweight men attractive. I prefer lean muscles or a sturdy frame. (I hope this won't make you think me shallow. I am trying to find out (not so discreetly) if you'll like me when we meet.) No need to ask me the same question. Anyone who looks like Michelange-lo's David will go to the top of my list!

Till then,
Nickie

Subj*: **Good morning, my love***
Date: 3/2/98 9:31:52 AM EDT

Dearest Nickie,

You can put me in such a spot sometimes. I had hoped to keep my more bestial nature a secret until I could demonstrate some redeeming qualities; I had them here just a moment ago; let me check my pockets. I must answer your question about what catches my eye when I look at a woman. Though it may sound evasive, it deserves a fuller answer. It depends on whether she walks toward me, stands, sits, or walks away. Except for sitting, I admit to my first glimpse toward the soft curve where the hip meets the waist (caught you, this curve is on the side, where I have "love handles"). Then I look at her hair; the survey changes depending on whether she is facing me, away from me, or sitting.

There are four things about women in general. I have yet to decide which of them I find most attractive. For standing facing me, lips, eyes, standing facing away, posture, then bottom; now sitting is different. My observance has to do with angle because I can't see the face as clearly and flush and embarrass easily (I wouldn't say I like to stare). I notice the collarbone and chest area. I keep envisioning my sister with this exasperated expression, saying, "Men, you are all such animals." In my defense, I am a self-taught artist, primarily portraits (I have a thing for faces). I also am an actor, and both hobbies require me to develop observation skills. Over the years, they (the skills) may have slipped into the habit. I hope not. For several years, I have looked at people with an artistic eye; if I look too long, it is appreciation, not lust.

Okay, now it's my turn; it's springtime, and we are walking in the park. My arm is around your waist, and you notice the boys playing in the park. What do you see first, second, etc.? I forgot and was rather presumptuous. How do you feel about public displays of affection (hand holding, arm around the waist, whatever the moment ignites)?

I had this fantasy that we were in a department store where we kept coming out from the fitting rooms seeking the other's opinion regarding fit and color. It was very entertaining, especially the expression on the clerk's face when you came out one side. I came out the other with the clerk in the middle, and we were in mid-conversation. The look on the clerk's face was priceless. Of course, I wonder if they would let us back in Saks. I was so wrapped up in my dream of you this morning I was almost late for work. If we reach an intimate stage in our relationship, we will make love more often than we will brush our teeth (at least I only brush my teeth three times a day).

Till then, love,
Ken

Ken

I was rereading one of her notes for about the fourth time. It suddenly occurred to me (lucky for me) that there was a fourteen-inch drop between my chest and waist. Should I tell her, or would it sound like bragging? I have never had a beer belly, she could take my word for it, but I hoped she checked me ten to twelve times daily to keep me honest.

I was planning on checking her lips for chapping, softness, and general princi-ples or for any reason she would let me use. If I could couple a lip check with a hug, I may lose control of my knees, but I will risk it if she will.

Boy, it's good that I multi-tasked well, or my boss would get no work out of me. I hoped my letters made her smile half as much as hers did me. My father always said to smile as much at work as possible; it drove the boss crazy. I didn't appreciate that quip at the time as much as I do now while implementing it.

Subj: **We are so silly**
Date: 3/2/98

Dearest Ken,

I received two letters from you; what a treat! You have single-handedly decreased my work productivity by 90%! When I am not writing to you, I sit in my office with a stupid grin. For the last month, I have been floating.

I believe you look at people with an artistic eye, so for now, I won't join your sister (at least regarding YOU) on the many shortcomings of the male gender. I see all the re-deeming qualities you think you misplaced bulging out of your pockets, ears, and mouth everywhere. You may need to get glasses if you can't see them!

Did I tell you I wear my hair very short? It's a good style for me. I am due for a trim the day before I go to Milwaukee. It will be a breeze to endure the summer if I stick with this style. I am very self-conscious about something else. I don't want you to tease me, so I'll keep mum on the subject.

I thought you would ask me the same questions I posed regarding what I would find attractive in the opposite sex. Well, first things first, if the two of us are walking around holding hands in the park, I won't notice much since I'll only have eyes for you. However, if you are not around, and my mind is lucid for a short time, the first thing I would see in a man would be my pet peeves (or lack thereof), a general sense of proportion. I would look at the face for lovely eyes (the expression in them) and a pleasant smile. I might notice his hair, and I must admit I have more than once remarked how nice a man's pants fit, looking at his back, walking away from me.

By the way, I have no problems with public displays of affection once I am comfort-able with someone. I agree with you on our lovemaking frequency if we ever become inti-

mate. Since you are the first thing I want to reach for in the morning, and I can no longer imagine going to bed at night without wanting to feel your body against mine, we have these two times covered. Instead of comparing the number of lovemaking sessions to the number of times we brush our teeth, we should make it the yardstick we use to dictate the number of times we make love. As dentists everywhere recommend brushing after each meal, it would be wise to extend that advice to snacks. Sometimes, mainly on weekends, we may have midmorning, afternoon, and midnight snacks (even a fruit or a glass of juice at those times can qualify)! Also, since I have to keep you honest and ensure you are not suddenly developing those "love handles," I'll have to frisk you periodically... and should I find anything in your pockets, such as, God forbid, a candy bar! I'll see it as intent to have a snack necessitating brushing your teeth; therefore, it is ground for addition to the yardstick! We may only have some of those snacks over time, but we should try everything to keep the love alive and fresh, so we'll at least have two main meals daily! I hope this will keep you smiling for the day!

Till then,
Nickie

Will she have enough hair left for my fingers to run through? *Never mind, I'll hold her close and pull her to my chest, with a soft kiss on her forehead; I'll... hey, hum.* Mary and Jesse stood there, giggling like schoolgirls. Being caught smiling in the odd moment or two had been the conversation in my office more than once. Anne told me last week why Michelle, Sharon, and a couple of others had made it a habit to stop by my desk to check the LAN server several times a day. Michelle caught me daydreaming a few weeks back. Now I needed to wait for it to blow over. Truth to tell, it was already better. For a while, I thought they could have turned the Serengeti into a lush garden as a water brigade armed with Dixie cups. On the bright side, there were a lot more smiles around here. I knew my arms ached from missing her. I wouldn't tell her what happened to me during the day when I thought of the soft, round, convex portion of her spoon nestled against the concave portion of mine.

Subj: *Reading minds*

Date: 3/3/98 11:43:19 AM EDT

Dearest Nickie,

How long have you been reading minds? Just as I thought of taking up snacking, you addressed the issue. There's much catching up to do. Where were you during the last 20 years?

I bet with your hair short, your eyes must be like two beautiful whirlpools waiting to pull me in. Are your ears ticklish? What's making you self-conscious? Can it be due to short hair? If it is, and it would make you feel better, I will gladly cut mine.

I like situation comedies, like when we almost had our version of "Who's on First" going, with what I thought you thought I thought I expected. I want to cradle your head in my left hand (I need to keep it where I can see it. I am left-handed), taste your lips until our breath becomes one, and trace your curves with my right hand. As a left-hander, my right hand lacks confidence. I will have to take my time and go s-l-o-w-l-y.

Thinking of you, love,
Ken

"Wishes and Longings"

Subj: ***This and that***

Date: 3/4/98

Dearest Ken,

Although I wear my hair short right now, there is still enough of it. I admit I like Michael Jordan's shaven head, but it's not quite the look I am after. So, my current cut is not the reason for my self-consciousness. A year ago, I got it into my head that I should "improve" my smile, so my dentist recommended an orthodontist, and now I have clear porcelain braces. By the way, I asked a young couple at the dentist, who assured me they don't inter-fere with kissing, but I am not convinced. I feel ridiculous wearing braces at my age and subconsciously put my hand in front of my mouth when I smile. I am counting the months till they can come off and the days until that first hug and kiss.

Till then,
Nickie

Ken

Rain tapped against the large expanse of my living room windows, the soft rhythm lending itself more to idling the evening away than to memorizing the lines of the new script I held in my hands. I had declined the overtime offered, hoping to make headway with the play, but my concentration was off. I was relieved seeing Nancy's name on the caller ID and picked up the receiver to her familiar, warm voice.

"Ken, it's been ages! How are you?"

Nancy had been one of my anchors during my tempestuous divorce. She listened to my late-night rants and dragged me out for tea when I'd forgotten how to smile.

"Hey, Nancy." I put my feet on the ottoman and sank into the armchair. "I'm surviving. How about you?"

Her laughter tinkled through the line.

"Surviving? That's your default mode, isn't it? I'm juggling work, life, and a cat who thinks he's a philosopher."

I chuckled imagining Nancy's cat always perched on the windowsill, staring into the abyss.

"Sounds like a handful."

"Tell me about it." She paused. "Ken, I need your advice. It's about Tom."

I knew Nancy well enough to read between the lines. Tom had swept her off her feet and moved in with her three weeks ago. New beginnings, new challenges.

I glanced at the window again and wondered if Nickie had reached home by now. Did she have a pet? I didn't recall her mentioning one. It's impractical with her demanding schedule.

"Go on," I said, pushing thoughts of Nickie aside. "What's going on with Tom?"

Nancy's voice lowered as if sharing a secret.

"He's driving me crazy, Ken. He's messy, lazy, and inconsiderate. He leaves his clothes and dishes everywhere and never helps with the chores. He's always watching TV or hanging out with his friends. He barely pays attention to me. Doesn't even say "I love you' anymore. It gets to me, but he said I was nagging, overreacting, or being too sensitive."

My mind raced. Tom was a nice enough guy but clueless. He thought love meant convenience. Since my divorce, I'd seen enough of this behavior in my friends' relationships.

"Wow, that doesn't sound very good. I'm sorry to hear that. I'd offer to talk to him, but I don't think he would appreciate it. People hate interference."

"What should I do if he doesn't take this seriously?" Her frustration crackled through the phone.

I leaned forward, tapping my pen against the coffee table.

"Express your feelings calmly and assertively. Don't lose your temper. If Tom doesn't change, you'll know you tried."

"You're right. I'm emotional, but I want it to work."

"Because you care. Remember, it's a new situation for both of you, and everyone needs time to adjust."

As we talked, my gaze wandered to a charcoal sketch I was making of the Nickie I saw in my head. It lay unfinished, waiting for me to pick it up. I had completed a few others before but started over because I wasn't satisfied with the end product. *How can I explain the missing piece that is Nickie?*

"Ken?" Nancy's voice pulled me back.

"Yeah?"

"Thanks for listening. You're a good friend."

I smiled, reaching for the notepad. "Anytime, Nancy."

I gazed at the incomplete sketch and turned the page, starting a rough outline capturing Nickie and me exchanging longing glances. Wishful?

Outside, the rain persisted, and I wondered if she missed me as much as I missed her. Was my advice sound? Could I have said anything else to Nancy? I'll check in with her at the end of the week.

I wondered how long this arrangement would last. I hadn't told Nickie about my assortment of friends, ranging from eighteen to seventy-four (Terri, Nancy, Taylor, his dad Mike, and Ed). There used to be more, but I lost a few after the divorce.

I almost forgot about Anne, a coworker undergoing a significant change. She used to be Troy. She is engaged, and her relationship with her fiancé will remain intact after her transformation. I can't pretend to understand her struggles, but I would agree, as she often states that the male gender has a lot to answer for—stereotypes, toxic masculinity, and more. I promised to do my best never to leave Nickie exasperated with me.

Subj: ***Wishes and longings***
Date: 3/5/98

Dearest Ken,

Darling, I hope you'll never tire of hearing me say I love you. If you do, it would be ironic since those three small words have been challenging for me to say before you. Somehow, I can't think of you for long without wanting to utter them. It's as if I have opened a dam and can't keep the water from gushing.

Your friends sound like a curious bunch. Mine (the three closest to me) on the other end are somewhat staid, except for my friend Linda. She usually has me in stitches within five minutes of talking to her.

Please don't cut your hair, at least not until I can run my hands through it. If you have a picture of yourself with it short, bring it. All those days before our first hug seem like an eternity. Your large hands can circle my waist, failing that there are other ways of keeping them occupied, good manners prevent me from elaborating further. By the way, I blushed when I understood what you implied about other significant parts of you. I have heard the rumor about men with large feet and hands but have yet to have the opportunity to check its veracity.

I am still deciding what my feelings toward your body pillow are: envy, jealousy, or gratitude for comforting until I can replace it. I hope you'll be satiated and have more restful sleep if we ever get to that point! (I had promised not to say anything so bold until we meet, but here I go again!). I am not conscious of favoring one side to sleep on (if I press myself, I would say the right side). Another question: What color is your body hair, red or brown?

Don't worry about my knowing what you look like before I meet you. I must admit I wanted to ask for a scanned picture at first, but by now, unless you look like "The Hunchback of Notre Dame," I can't imagine being displeased. I am more concerned about our "chemistry" than anything else. I could send a scanned picture from last year, but it's unclear, and my hairstyle is quite different. I am not photogenic. I'll be staying at the Pfister. We'll find each other if it takes the whole evening! I love you.

Till then,
Nickie

Subj: ***Till the stars no longer shine***
Date: 3/5/98 1:27:00 PM EDT

Dearest Nickie,

I may have plagiarized a song, but it adequately expresses my feelings.

So now we have established you don't have Marge Simpson's hair adorned with lightning bolts. When I think of you, I see the most beautiful woman in the world because I fell in love with you, not your hair, body, or voice, but you who reside within the house the world sees. Suppose there ever comes a time when my lips do not thirst for the taste of your lips, my arms do not ache to hold you, and my body does not beg to feel your flesh pressed against it; it will be because my mind and heart no longer rule my body. If there comes a time when my eyes no longer cause my lungs to freeze when first they behold you and turn my face into a smile, my heart will have ceased beating three days gone because my heart has taught my mind and what my mind knows my body feels, what I feel is incomplete without you.

In short, if the morning comes, and I don't reach for you, kiss me quickly; I am not breathing. Sometimes, my body rises before my mind wakes. If my mind is awake, no part of my body will not want you.

Till then,
Ken

(P.S. In case I have forgotten to tell you today, I Love You)

Nickie

"So, spill the beans, girl. Who is this mystery man you've been involved with?" Linda asked, squeezing some lemon into her Kirin beer.

I smiled. "He is no mystery. His name is Ken. He's terrific and a total romantic. We have so much in common. It's eerie."

"Who told you that you were a romantic?" Linda burst out laughing.

"Shush! Linda, or I won't tell you the rest."

"Oh, okay. You left yourself wide open for that one. I couldn't resist! So, how did you meet him?"

"Well, you know I signed up for that dating website a couple of months ago, right? They match you based on your preferences and personalities. He saw my profile and emailed me. I checked his, and his letter touched me. I replied immediately, and we have been talking almost daily since."

"Oh la la la! Nickie is in love! Have you seen his picture?"

"Oh shush! He doesn't have a scanner but described himself to me. By the way, he grew up in England and lives in Minneapolis. We'll be meeting soon. He mentioned a deep voice and a cute accent. I'm so excited."

"Oh, that's great. When are you meeting him?"

"When I go to the annual meeting in Milwaukee. He'll be driving, but we are planning dinner and maybe walking around the city. Would you believe he writes me poems?"

"Wow, Nickie, this is amazing. I'm happy for you. He sounds like a keeper. You deserve this. You've been single for too long." Her eyes sparkled with genuine excitement as she leaned forward gently touching my hand.

"Thanks, Linda," I said smiling and twirling the last of the Kirin in my glass, as the last of the afternoon light was disappearing from the Thai restaurant's windows.

"One thing bothers me slightly, though. What if he turns out to be eighty years old?"

"Linda, you are incorrigible! He will not be eighty! But I thought about that, too, though I sense he is telling the truth."

"In any case, I think it's a good thing for now. I've never seen you so animated and happy. You are positively glowing."

"It's like waiting for Christmas day to open a present."

"Each day feels like forever, and you imagine what it will be like. I can't wait to hear about the meeting! The anticipation is killing me."

"Trust me, I'll fill you in on every detail. By the way, how are things going with James?"

"Same old. His wife fired her lawyers again, so there was a new delay for her to sign the divorce papers. She couldn't wait to leave him but is now dragging her feet, hoping for a larger settlement."

"He is at the finish line, although I think you should wait maybe a year before accepting his proposal. He is a bit too possessive and controlling; perhaps that's why she left."

"Wouldn't I know if there was a problem? Frankly, I love the attention." She replied defensively.

"Well," I said, searching my words carefully, "you might be enjoying it now, but it will begin to bother you later if it continues. A bit of possessiveness is flattering, but the fact that he gets on your back every time you spend time with someone else, even your sister, seems like a red flag. I know you'll get the ready-made family you want, but be careful, Lin."

"You are a worrywart; I don't listen to James. With everyone else being busy with their lives and families, I enjoy having his undivided attention. He gets cranky when I hang out with other people, but this is my life, and I won't give that up for anyone."

"Don't you forget it! By the way, how is work?"

"My boss is a creep, but I hang in there." she said agitated.

"I know you don't like him, but you didn't like the last one either. You just dislike bosses." I replied with a smirk.

"Not true! You were my boss, and I always liked you. We are friends, aren't we? You were constantly pushing me to take the initiative, I miss it now. This guy keeps everything close to the vest and only lets me do the most basic accounting stuff. He won't even let me reconcile the bank statements. Can you get any more basic?"

"Enjoy the ride. You have a decent salary, so stay put for a while. Things were different with me because I had to do things differently. As a black woman, I have to be twice as bright, twice as educated, and twice as motivated to get half of what my white male counterparts are getting. I won't ever let that stand in my way. You are not black, but still, a woman, and the odds are stacked against you in corporate America. I just pushed you to reach your potential."

"I hate to say it, but I miss working for you. Few people would have gone to bat for me the way you did. It gave me enough time to find another job, and of course, your letter of recommendation was so good; looking back, I think they were afraid I would accept a different job offer!"

"You are a great accountant, and I'd do it again. I always felt that the lay-off occurred because the Operations manager disliked you and was such good friend with the owner. I am still surprised Peter agreed; he is such a good man, and I owe him a lot. I know I pushed the envelope when I refused to fire you as my direct report and told him to do it himself since it was his company. He could have taken offense to that, but he let it slide. Frankly, there was no basis for laying you off."

"Well, I appreciate that!"

"Yes, but you are still a pain in the neck!"

Subj: ***Good morning***
Date: 3/6/98 9:41:37 AM EDT

Good morning, my love,

Would that I was holding you in my arms and kissing the sleep from your eyes? The thought I might not hear from you for three days has muted my laughter and taken the smile from my voice.

Your friend sounds terrific. My humor is dry (such is the way of the English), but my wit is quick and rapier-sharp. I usually keep a room in stitches for 45 minutes when I am in the mood.

Sorry I was so late with the news (I had to go home to check). I think my chest hair is primarily brown (I have a few freckles there, too, and in the more densely freckled areas, I am unsure if it's the freckles or the hair with the reddish tint). I am looking forward (more than I am saying) to exploring and committing to memory (I am slow, positively remedial) every inch of your body. You are welcome to reciprocate. After all, fair is fair; please understand this may take several hours each day over the years (for some things, you can't rush the research). My father always said: "To learn a subject properly, you must bring all five senses to bear: touch, sight, taste, smell, sound, and your heart." I intend to respect my father and honor his teaching.

Unfortunately, I'll be working all weekend; I open in Macbeth tonight at 7:30, then a matinee tomorrow, and 17 hours here. If my boss is lucky, she will get eight or nine hours of work out of me. I will spend an inordinate amount of time thinking about you (especially since I set myself up with that last paragraph.)

One of these days, I am going to work the kinks out of this good morning thing, a quick kiss, throw in I love you, and back to work, and if you buy that, "I have a today only once in a lifetime, have I got a deal for you unique on the Brooklyn Bridge." If we don't speak before Monday, listen for the echo: I love you.

Till then
Ken

Subj: ***You are in my thoughts***
Date: 3/6/98

Dearest Ken,

Your letters yesterday were so beautiful they brought tears of joy to my eyes. You touch me in ways I can't even describe. I wish I had your gift with words to express how you make me feel; unfortunately, you'll have to contend with the simple words I love you and the knowledge that you make me indescribably happy. I used to think the notion of a soul mate was someone's idea of a good joke, but now, every time I think of you, I consider the possibility, maybe, just maybe, there exists such a thing and fervently hope that we are it for each other.

How are you today? I am home. After writing to you, I'll go to the park for a quick walk. The weather has given us a break for the last two days. I have a few novels from the library and may rent some videos to watch later.

What would we be doing together on a beautiful day like this? I envision us at that picnic by the lake on a summer day, even taking an afternoon dip in the water if the temperature gets too high.

I plan to visit my parents on the islands for two weeks. We discussed colors that look good on you, but you have yet to tell me your favorite color or food. I reread your letters to be sure, but I could not find one instance when you told me. A picture of you flashed through my mind for no reason. You are shirtless, wearing shorts, bending down to fix some flowers in your garden. What are you wearing now? No pressure, but how is that last poem coming? Will you bring it for me in Milwaukee? Don't worry that you should be redundant in telling me you love me. I can never hear it enough, and I hope you never tire of hearing me tell you how happy you make me.

Till then,
Nickie

Subj: ***Hello***

Date: 3/6/98 1:53:31 PM EDT

Dearest Nickie,

We have an extra casual day today. I am wearing a blue denim shirt, jeans, and hiking boots. I want to remember to answer all your questions, so my favorite food will sound strange. I have many choices. I went for easy preparation, rice mixed with mushroom soup (undiluted).

Which park is near to you? I know I asked you what you have been wearing before, but I genuinely like to hear you describe yourself. Along these lines, do you wear perfume, and if so, do you have a favorite scent? (I blush to ask where you wear it). My favorite color is cobalt blue. Aside from some water glasses, I have nothing of that color, but every time I look at them, it evokes a sense of calm, and I always smile.

Which islands are home? When will you vacation there? How do you feel about flowers? What kinds of beverages do you like? What is a decent interval between when we first say hello and when I may kiss you? What is your favorite way to travel? Do your friends know anything about the bold, pushy person you correspond with?

I love you. When I read your words, I get a warm tingling throughout, and if you ever tire of telling me those words, I will know the blame is mine. I pray I never earn such a fate.

Gateway told me my PC would be here on Thursday. Soon, I will be able to kiss you goodnight. (Suddenly, audio and video communication possibilities flashed into my mind, and I shan't be able to pull my chair away from my desk for several minutes.)

Till then
Ken

Subj: ***A beautiful day***
Date: 3/6/98

Dearest Ken,

I spent almost the entire day outdoors, running errands and enjoying my walk in the park. I read some, occasionally glancing at the various teens on rollerblades or younger kids on their bicycles. The park across the street from me is called "Alley Pond," it's lovely and frequented mainly by families. Today, I picked a perfect spot to have picnics in the spring, lay in the shade, and watch the world go by while we engaged in idle conversation. We tried to find several good excuses for you to not go to work for the next few days.

By the way, I wholeheartedly agree with your father's idea of learning a subject properly. I'll greatly encourage you to adhere to that concept for your intended task, and of course, I shall endeavor to follow suit in my explorations of you. Don't worry if you can't tell whether it's your freckles or the hair on your body with the reddish tint. I intend to conduct my investigation and make a definite determination, no matter how many years it takes. (You see, I too used to be a fan of Sherlock H., but along with that, I was a great admirer of Inspector Clouseau of the Pink Panther fame, that is why, most likely, my investigation will take all these years!) I am also glad to hear you have a good sense of humor because if you can both love me and make me laugh, then you'll have my heart locked away and can throw away the keys, for it will not want to be anywhere else but in your care.

Today, my outfit for the errands was a denim skirt and a light wool top. Yes, I do wear perfume. I started wearing "Arpege" by Lanvin a year and a half ago. I wear some other scents occasionally, but this one has been my favorite. I wear it behind my ears, at the nape of my neck, wrists, elbows, knees, and ankles. (Sometimes, for some unexplainable reason, I put it around my navel, the inside of my thighs, below my waist on each buttock)! (There! I am telling you all my secrets!) Boy, I hope you are blushing beet-red! You should know better than to ask such intimate questions!

I have caused you enough embarrassment for the day. I'll continue this in the morning. I hope you have learned your lesson! I love you.

Till then,
Nickie

Subj: ***Still blushing;***
Date: 3/7/98 10:18:04 AM EDT

Dearest Nickie,

We almost said navel simultaneously. Yes, I am still blushing. After work yesterday, I stopped and bought a new pair of pants, and though I didn't think it was possible, you just convinced me they were too small. Funny, they fit fine 5 minutes ago. I shall look forward to experiencing the scent of you.

You are right, I work too much. I can't wait for an excuse to play hooky. I wish I could lie here and hold you all day. How do you like your eggs? I love you. It's going to be a long day. When it's safe to move around, I start thinking about your perfume, and I am stuck with my keyboard in my lap and blushing again. I love you. Oh, you still need to answer the decent interval question. As Holmes would say, "It is not always what we say but what we don't." Which novels did you pick up? Is your navel an innie or an outie?

Till then,
All my love, Ken

How is he this morning? I hope his opening went well last night. Was he still blushing from my answers yesterday? Gee, now I was feeling embarrassed!

Cobalt blue is a beautiful color. I must tell him visiting my parents is not certain, as they might come to NY themselves. I can arrange a real vacation after they depart in September. I need to get to it seriously. I won't risk losing my accumulated vacation time if I can't carry it over to next year.

Did I have a favorite way of traveling and getting around? I was still determining. I liked flying because it was fast and convenient. I only took the train once to Canada, and it was a pleasant experience. I have never been on a cruise; my sisters and friends rave about it. My primary concern has always been that I would get seasick and spoil everything. Long car trips were fun as long as I didn't have to drive too much; the car motion made me sleepy.

Will we have "chemistry"? Am I cautious or insecure? It was a sorry way of keeping my heart in check whenever I felt too elated about our upcoming meeting. Speaking of which, I didn't know when we meet how long we should wait to have our first kiss. Suddenly, I felt shy. *Should we wait until we are alone? Or in the park? Could we let our hearts decide? His heart matters as much as mine. What does it say?*

I spent an hour daydreaming about him looking good in those sexy blue-gray shorts. He passed by the kitchen table where I was writing, and I could not stop from grabbing and giving him a giant peck on the lips. It startled him, but he quickly got into the spirit of things. I had to ask him to be a good boy until I could finish his letter! *I hope his day is as good as my dream.*

Ken

The opening last night went smoothly. The audience was a little thin, but many activities were competing for attention, not to mention about sixty other plays in production.

The sun was out; the sky was pale blue, and the fluffy and carefree clouds drifted lazily with no place to go. I took a break for brunch. I needed time away from the office and ringing phones.

I strolled along the sidewalk and found a quaint café with a chalkboard sign. I surprised the waitress when I stepped inside and ordered an ice cream sandwich with chewy cookies, hugging a generous scoop of vanilla. The wooden chair creaked under my weight as I settled into a corner booth. With a silly smile, I wondered what desserts or sweets were among her favorites. I liked sherbet, daiquiri ice, sandwiches, and homemade ice cream with fresh fruit. Every time I thought about eating, I thought about her. (Lately, the act of breathing made me think about Nickie.) Did she enjoy the park yesterday? Which movies did she rent? (The truth is, I knew why when I thought of food, she came to mind. I would always hope to get a stupid grin whenever I got the munchies).

Subj: *Ice cream*
Date: 3/7/98

Dearest Ken,

I assure you I have answered all your previous questions, especially regarding the appropriate time between seeing each other and our first kiss. (This is not one I could have disregarded anyway!).

After all the lovemaking this morning, you got your excuse for playing hooky from work. We are still in bed, awakened from a relaxing nap. How did you manage that melting ice cream you had today? You brought it back to bed. It was dripping over my belly. I heard you say it would take too long to get a cup, and this was better than a cup and easier to drink from anyway. (I won't trust you any more to get a snack for us; there are too many ulterior motives!) By the way, I am fond of homemade ice cream, but when that's not available, my favorite sweet is Haagen-Dazs ice cream. Their rum raisin flavor is my favorite.

I picked up the two novels Until You and Acts of Love. They are silly romance novels that do not fit my tastes, but they are all my mind wants to process these days. A couple of weeks ago, I read one of the latest John Grisham books, The Partner. It amazed me that it kept my attention, but he is an excellent writer, and the storyline involved a sideline love situation). I still read my business magazines, so there is hope. The movies I rented are light entertainment: Star Trek First Contact and a romantic comedy, While You Were Sleeping.

Till then,
Nickie

Subj: ***Hum***
Date: 3/8/98 12:52:26 PM EDT

Good morning, Nickie,

After reading your letter, I went to the car this morning, reclined my seat, and spent an hour contemplating chasing ice cream (rum raisin) around your body with my tongue.

I cannot think of an increment of time (without inventing a name) smaller than a microsecond. I believe that is the proper time (we must allow for decorum) past hello that I can handle before the pain of emptiness in my arms becomes unbearable. There is no measurement minute enough to describe how long my desire wants me to wait to taste your lips. It will be some time after the act before my head clears enough to recognize where and if there was any other person in the world when we first kissed.

Till then, all my love
Ken

Subj: ***Ribbons and bows***

Date: 3/8/98 1:20:13 PM EDT

Dearest Nickie,

You have set me an impossible task; first, I blush easily; second, I feel like a kid of 18 again. Thinking about you, your body, and our bodies together — giddy, laughing, playing, relaxing, and loving — occupies 95% of my breathing time. Everything else must weave into my consciousness. I will tell you a secret. I once spent 2 hours trying to catch the play of light in one of your dimples (I won't say where the dimple was) in water beads. I was towel-drying you one body part at a time as you rested after emerging from your shower. Nickie, how can I help you stop making me blush? I can't stop myself.

I'm a gentleman, but I can't help my passion for you. I hope it's not boring for you, but it feels good to let it out occasionally and feed it. I think of it as an old steam engine. Someone stokes the coals, and the machine goes. There is a pleasant warmth inside and a gentle rocking motion as we travel the rails, and if the timing and place are suitable for an intersection and we meet (now I am blushing again), we will make a big bang. The trick is to keep the train going; even if we don't intersect, we still have a warm glow, a nice rocking motion, and beautiful scenery. The longer we travel together, the more inevitable the intersection.

Part of my dreams has been to have a big bang and make echoes that reverberate forever. (Please tell me you are smiling cause right now I am nervous.) Anyway, now you know I have some culture and brains, but I am also a bit of a barbarian. As I recall putting on my artist hat, men usually find art beautiful and emotionally stimulating and see considerably more art in the female than in the male form. (I am digging a real hole here, am I? I think I better close my mouth before I try arguing the merits of both feet in the mouth).

Please remind me to pack a bow with the growing list of things to bring. I love you. I am trying to discipline myself not to think about your body constantly. I am almost up to 5 minutes an hour.

If you are trying to fill in the blanks, I will give you a hint: I have been looking for a pair of emerald green Kimono-style pajamas to bring you as a present. Think necessity, spooning, and are you blushing yet? I love you.

Till then, love

Ken

Subj: *Steam engine and such*
Date: 3/8/98

Dearest Ken,

Reading your letter, I offer a word of caution on our first meeting; we should at least firmly establish our identities before kissing. Imagine me catching a glance of you, walking over to greet you, and suddenly seeing you take hold of and passionately embrace a perfect stranger whose sole mistake was to smile and say hello back to you! Imagine the confusion!

Before I forget, save me a seat on your old steam engine. Better yet, I would like to reserve the whole train with an option to buy. Can we draw a pleasant contract, or will this have to be a hostile takeover? While we are at it, I want to buy a dozen coal mines (to ensure we never run out of power), the engineer who drives the train, the rails, and everything remotely connected to this steam engine. After I finish this, Bill Gates will write to me for advice on an absolute monopoly!

By the way, I was smiling; I could not chastise you for anything since I long ago crossed the line of what is proper to say to an amour one has yet to meet. If we ever run out of things to say to each other, it would be fascinating to hear you argue the merits of putting both feet in the mouth! It will give me something interesting to think about the next time I can't leave a boring work meeting.

It's so sweet to think of bringing me those pajamas. I am touched. It would be best not to trouble yourself; I don't want to cause you any embarrassment in going to a lingerie store. Meeting you in Milwaukee will be present enough! I love you.

Missing you,

Nickie

Subj: *Schedule change*
Date: 3/8/98 4:41:40 PM EDT

Dear Nickie,

I am staying till 4:30 this afternoon, so there is no rush; sit back, let me get you something cool to drink, and then you can put your feet up. How was shopping? Food, fun, or window? I wish I had been there.

Now give me your feet; I will start your massage now; you can talk about whatever comes to mind or nothing if you like. The music is R&B today on low. It will take about an hour for me to work my way over that soft spot on the front of your shin. If we take our time, even a good massage is making love; oh, the muscles in your toes are tight; just a moment, let me warm the lotion in my hands first. There, that's better. Do you want a pillow?

What movies do you prefer? I like romantic comedies and sci-fi. Did you see the Fifth Element? I found it gratifying to see someone saying love was the necessary element to save the world.

I wanted to take a quick break from giddiness; this doesn't mean my head isn't full of giddiness. I wish I were there with you; it's just my 5-minute hiatus.

Sorry, I was off wool-gathering again. Whenever I work my way to the muscle behind the knee, my mind explodes in this diffusion of color. I love you.

Till then, missing you,
Ken

Subj: ***Good morning, my love***
Date: 3/9/98 7:49:58 AM EDT

Dearest Nickie,

I can't wait to get to work in the mornings. The first thing I do is check the mail; it's also the last thing I do before going home (I won't mention the 50 or so times in between). I always keep the last three letters from you in my in-basket; my electronic daytimer displays a box with a message reading "Nickie's Mail," which coincides with your last letter's time-stamp. That's not to say I think about you all the time (but then, if I didn't say it, my nose would reach Milwaukee 3 days before the rest of me, and a sneeze would be hazardous to the country), so for the sake of the nation I must tell you this, I love you.

The thought of kissing the wrong woman had occurred to me. Still, if I stopped when the last woman kissed didn't slap me, I would have found the right woman by elimination, which, as we all know, is an excellent mathematical process but potentially painful. I thought it was Milwaukee; how many beautiful women can there be? I will only embrace the beautiful women I see and stop when some man doesn't punch me, but that sounds painful; it was a dilemma. Now I see you are both wise and beautiful; indeed, I am twice blessed. As to this cooking thing, is the inability limited to food preparation? It could be an area where we complement each other. I can prepare food.

On the other hand, I have never made love in the kitchen (frankly, I am looking forward to the day I am relieved of the burden of having to admit to that). Making love to you will be like Chinese food; you can eat your fill, but an hour later, you will be hungry again. So, when you say you can't cook, are you talking about food or you?

When you went shopping yesterday, what did you purchase for supper? The movie sounds delightful; thank you for sharing your laughter. I can picture you all snuggled in, watching the picture, and I can't help but smile. I love you. I miss you.

Till then,
Ken

Subj: ***Gloomy day outside;***
Date: 3/9/98 12:48:03 PM EDT

Dearest Nickie,

The weather outside is gray and overcast. However, I have that giddy feeling of a child waiting to unwrap my special Christmas present. The only difference in my life is you; you make me feel so good; not even the weather can depress me through logical deduction.

By the way, I would like to volunteer to clean up any sticky buns found in your bed. (So much for a lucid moment.) I love you.

Thinking about you, till unveiling,
Ken

Subj: ***Shopping and cooking***
Date: 3/9/98

Dearest Ken,

After much internal arguing, I forgot about the craziness at work (there are two mid-size crises I am trying to resolve) and closed my office door to write to you. It was clothes shopping I went to yesterday. Of course, I bought things I didn't need but couldn't pass up. I purchased a cotton skirt, a top for weekend wear, and a nice pair of flat casual shoes (you loved everything). I spent the entire afternoon in the stores to purchase only those three minor items, but it was fun doing it because I got to try dozens of outfits. Your massage was heavenly, especially after being on my feet for so long. For me, it's food shopping that takes no time at all. Before leaving the house, I usually make a list to know exactly where to go when I get to the supermarket.

By the way, rest assured that my cooking deficiencies only pertain to food. After searching my memory, I could not recall engaging in any other form of "cooking" in the kitchen. Still, I have often read about various recipes involving the kitchen table, chairs, etc. We should do our field research in this area and draw our conclusions! Nothing can beat good old hands-on knowledge!

I can imagine how you felt in that Victoria's Secret shop; I would greatly discourage you from another foray into that store (but for selfish reasons). It's funny, though, because I went in to get gift certificates for my sisters for Christmas a couple of years ago. The store had so many men that I almost had to go outside to check the sign, ensuring I was in the right place. They all looked cheerful, like little boys with so much candy they did not know what to pick. They were all buying for their spouses and girlfriends and getting as much pleasure as possible. (This is one instance where the saying, "It's better to give than to receive" would get no objections from anyone!)

Regarding sleepwear, I have always worn something to bed, be it pajamas, nightgowns, etc., but I don't see them as essentials or "must-have" items of my trousseau. With you around, I suspect that if I were to insist on wearing them "to" bed, I would not be wearing them "in bed," so having them may just become part of a lovemaking ritual where it would be fun to have you take them off. Your opinion is that if we engage in any eating or dishwashing activities in bed, those annoying bedclothes would be in the way of your doing a good job (and we both know how intent you are on doing a good job!) I believe in always striving for excellence, and I will only rest when I see shiny surfaces when it's my turn to do the dishes! (You do believe in reciprocity, don't you?)

I have missed spending most of my day contemplating you, but not for one second, however, the thought of you left my mind. I love you.

Till then,
Nickie

Subj: ***Reciprocity***

Date: 3/10/98 12:48:36 PM EDT

Dearest Nickie,

Let's say, yes, yes, yes, I will be a dish for you. I believe what is good for one is suitable for another; otherwise, it would belittle the gift, for instead of an "us," I would be thinking mine. To provide pleasure is a gift to me; I want you to have that same gift as often as possible. I can't wait to sample your best culinary skills.

As I woke this morning, I wanted to tell you many things about foreplay and the difference between love and sex, which ended with "I intend to make love (underline that word) to you repeatedly."

Despite the emphasis on communication, most communication concerning love-making is non-verbal until after the loving. A person will touch their partner, and if the partner is attentive and responsive, the lovemaking pleasure will reach a climax, not a conclusion. Yes, I want to touch, taste, and explore, and it pleases me you feel the same, and I welcome the experience. I have never eaten ice cream from my lover's belly nor followed the traces of a sweet confection as it traveled in rivulets over the curves and valleys of my lover's body. Still, I would find it all the sweeter combined with your taste as you react to my touch by hand, body, and probing tongue before rushing off to work (as a hopeful prelude to the day to come).

Till then, love,
Ken

P.S. I wanted to get a note to you; I will write more later. I love you. I hope your day is much better today. On this day, wherever you are in my heart, I will be.

"The Feeling Is Mutual"

Subj: ***Good morning***

Date: 3/11/98 3:58:32 AM EDT

Dearest Nickie,

The new PC is here. It came yesterday, and I assembled it last night. After 27 years of working with computers, my sole motivation for owning one is to talk to you. I did it. I am home talking to you, my attire somewhat relaxed; I am sitting in my bedroom, looking over at a bed not built for two, wishing you were here. Soon we would be lying as close as one. When I say good night, you will be with me in my heart and mind.

I did a self-portrait with a haiku-style pencil. I will scan it and send it to you (so we blaze a new frontier). I love you.

I am off to an early start. I was about to go to bed when suddenly I realized the alarm would sound in 10 minutes. I have spent the night trying to understand the home PC. My darling Nickie, I shall steal a kiss. I am a bit late showering this morning; I just wanted to say I love you.

Till then, come spoon with me,
Ken

Subj: *Good morning, dearest*
Date: 3/11/98

Dearest Ken,

Good morning, darling. I woke up this morning feeling that you had already left for work; I did not feel your embrace, nor could I remember your kiss. I was confused and disoriented. I must have been in deep sleep when you left for work; you should have awakened me.

Yesterday was immensely improved from Monday morning. I still have some loose ends, but the big crisis is over. I was yet to learn how I could influence purchasing computer components. I'll keep it a secret since I don't want the tech stocks to get more volatile than they already are.

I got home early last evening and drove to a marina where I had hoped to spend 1/2 hour reading in the car while glancing at the water and the nice boats anchored there. Instead, I spent forty-five minutes imagining what you look like, tracing your features with my fingers! I need to think of you in concrete ways at least a few times a day; otherwise, I may believe you to be a figment of my imagination despite our frequent communications.

I have been remiss in the times I told you I love you in the past two days. Even if I don't say it often enough, I want you to know that I love you, I LOVE YOU, I love you, I love you...

Till then,
Nickie

Subj: *Missing you and wanting you*
Date: 3/11/98

Dearest Ken,

I read your letters this morning and could not wait to write again. First, let me say that I am happy you have your system functioning at home. (I copied you on the Hotmail address in my last letter. I'll do that from now on.)

No wonder I did not feel you in my arms this morning! You weren't in bed with me last night! This bond is uncanny. I woke up missing your presence, and now you tell me you were up figuring out the computer all night! You must be exhausted, and I hope you'll get some rest tonight. By the way, I like that you don't wear anything to bed.

I, too, believe that foreplay is essential to great lovemaking. The better the partners know each other's bodies and what pleases them, the more pleasurable the experience will be. What I did not expect this morning was my physical reaction to what you wrote. A soft moan escaped from my lips, and only after the sound reached my ears did I remember where I was. It's a good thing no one was passing by my office then! (By the way, kudos for trying my favorite Haagen-Dazs ice cream flavor; that little thing spoke volumes. It's no wonder I have trouble believing you to be real!) I love you. I must stop my thoughts; you have distracted me from my intended task this morning.

Missing you,
Nickie

Subj: ***Thinking of you***
Date: 3/12/98 12:54:05 AM EDT

Dearest Nickie,

Thank you for emailing both addresses. Your letters are the best part of my day at work, and while I don't expect us to talk constantly, I light up like a Roman candle when I find one.

Thank you for the beautiful card. I hope you enjoy the one I sent you; tonight, I must sleep. On my way home yesterday, I almost drove off the road several times; I kept nodding off at the wheel.

Yesterday I went shopping to search for your scent, "Arpege." You have exquisite taste. I am looking forward to getting into trouble at work because I was making love to you in the morning, afternoon, and evening; it seems there is no time in my day except for loving you.

How was your day? I answered 129 calls yesterday and solved 100s of their problems, yet I can't remember much aside from my dreams; You are always in my heart.

Till then,
Love Ken

Subj: *Missing you too*
Date: 3/12/98

Dearest Ken,

Since we "met," no matter what craziness is going on at work, everything stays in its proper perspective because you are always with me. Thanks for the beautiful card.

I may let you sleep alone if being together is causing you to get to work late. The alternative may be to go to bed earlier, so we'll have time to lose ourselves in each other and still enable you to have a good night's sleep. I am glad you like Arpege; I hope you'll want to pull and cuddle me whenever you smell it. Do you use any cologne or aftershave? If so, which? I love you.

Till then,
Nickie

Subj: *Hi!*
Date: 3/12/98 2:06:36 PM EDT

Dearest Nickie,

I have been wearing "Dune" for Men by Christian Dior; I don't know if I'd like to sleep alone again. My heart sank when you said perhaps, we should not sleep together. I will work on my restraint.

One of the unique aspects of our relationship is the ingenuity we use to accomplish little things that we would have taken for granted if the circumstances were "normal. I assure you I don't take you for granted, as happens in some relationships where couples see each other daily. I love you.

Till then,
Ken

Subj: *You are always on my mind*
Date: 3/12/98

Dearest Ken,

How could I not notice the song's title attached to your e-card? It reminded me of your love and made me feel very much wanted. If I have sounded more somber in the last couple of emails, I must have been trying to rush my notes to you to attend to some stupid work project. You brighten my day and make coming to work a lesser chore than it has been for the last year and a half. I don't intend to let anything stand in the way of us always being happy with each other. You are always on my mind.

Till then,
Nickie

Subj: ***Lunch***
Date: 3/13/98 9:37:47 AM EDT

Dearest Nickie,

Good morning, my love. How has your day been thus far today? It's 179 hours (give or take) until I can hold you in my arms (but who is counting). I love you. I received a call last night asking if I wanted to step into the leading role for "A Midsummer Night's Dream," but I turned it down. Under other circumstances, it would have been fun, but it is a bawdy play, and I didn't want to consider making sexual overtures to another woman (even pretend).

Till then, love
Ken

Subj: ***Snuggling***
Date: 3/13/98

Dearest Ken,

Thanks for the pretty card. If my memory serves me well, this is your weekend with the girls. You won't spend any time on the computer tonight. I'll check my buddy list anyway to make sure.

I came home a couple of hours ago, changed, and walked for an hour. I have not walked the whole week, explaining why I felt stressed the last two days. We have had spectacular weather lately with very low humidity.

I have an early appointment with the orthodontist tomorrow morning and miscellaneous errands. If this glorious weather holds up, I'll walk for over an hour. I'll also go to the store to research Dune. You have me at a disadvantage there.

I am sorry you refused that part in "A Midsummer Night's Dreams." I know the theater is significant to you and is part of what makes you the wonderful person I have fallen in love with. I don't want your knowing me to interfere with that. How do you stay in such great shape with your work schedule? A quality gene pool is not enough to maintain your measurements. (Confess! How long do you spend exercising?)

I will shower now and join you in bed to snuggle and watch comedies on TV (I doubt we'll see much of the shows, but at least the intent is there). Good night, my love.

Until then,
Nickie

Subj: ***Missing you***
Date: 3/14/98 11:00:05 PM EDT

Dearest Nickie,

Sorry, I have temporarily overrun. I have some friends who have become homeless (a long story,) but the short version is Tim's father had let him stay in his summer house with Tim's girlfriend. Tim and Michelle had a baby five weeks ago. His father lost his job last week, had to give up his new house, and wanted the summer house. So, the three of them couldn't stay there. It would all be too close quarters with Tim's father, his wife, and Tim's brother. Since I have three bedrooms and two baths, they'll be comfortable here. Tim thinks he can get everything together in two or three months. (Did I mention I can be a pushover?)

After taking the girls home, I stopped at the computer supply store this afternoon; I found a camera video link capable of live audio-video feeds. I have become self-conscious. It's funny that I have not given much consideration to my appearance for about six years, and now I find myself checking myself out in the mirror; all I know is I love you and miss you.

Till then,
Ken

Subj: *Ears burning?*
Date: 3/15/98 7:37:35 AM EDT

Dearest Nickie,

Yesterday was different, to say the least. You/we were quite the topic of conversation. I have tried to be open about my feelings about you, and during the past three weeks, you and I have been the topic of more than one conversation between my daughters and me.

Tim and Michelle moved in with their child yesterday. Camille was trying to find her friend in Florida. I had our Messenger running, and one thing led to another.

Tim (well, I won't go into what Tim said then) kept trying to read all my saved emails (sometimes I am not proud of my friends). Michelle didn't think that people thought about certain things once they reached my age and was hilariously not complimentary when she described us as being affectionate with one another. When I left to take the girls home, Tim and Michelle commandeered the computer, and their antics were amusing rather than exasperating. I didn't hook up the camera yesterday, not because I was afraid you'd find me as unattractive as Michelle made me feel, but more out of a sense of comedic timing. When I retired for the night, I was half-jokingly ready to offer them rent and grocery money for two months just to get some peace and quiet again. But honestly, that's not the way you help friends out, is it?

Today, I am working from 5 a.m. to 10 a.m. I pick up the girls at 11 a.m., and we go to the rodeo until three; then, I will take them home. Hopefully, Tim's curiosity will have lessened when I get home.

I shouldn't have become so agitated. I have spent considerable time wool-gathering about us in intimate situations, so okay, I am feeling guilty. At the same time, I see nothing wrong with loving the person you are in love with, even with a great deal left to the imagination. With the proximity of the computer, I could eliminate some of the creative processes. Do you think of me like some electronic peeping Tom and find me revolting?

I am so confused; I have been on cloud nine, feeling more vibrant now than I have in a long time. Now, I am worried you may secretly think I am some pervert. Nuts! I am running in circles; I love you very much. I apologize for yesterday's mix-up; I pray you are still talking to me. I can't find the words to describe how much I wish I were holding you. I am sorry if I have been a jerk; it was not my intention. I just wanted to be as close to you as circumstances would allow.

Till then, I love you,
Ken

P.S. Thank you for the card. It was most timely; I needed all your hugs and kisses and will enjoy returning each in person.

Nickie

What on earth? How could this couple and their children, who were homeless and in need of his help, be so rude? *How can they invade his privacy?* I was incensed on all levels. I admired him for his generosity, but there was no way he should accept their behavior! *Why is he tolerating this? I might sound harsh, but good manners and behavior are essential.*

I shook my head in disbelief as I read his email. I slammed my laptop shut and paced around the room. I would never open my home to any mere "acquaintance." I picked up the framed group photo of me and my siblings from the wall unit and smiled. My house was only for my family or dear friends. I would have given them money to situate themselves and sent them on their way. I valued my privacy and dignity too much. I never understood entering or staying in a detrimental situation to accommodate ungrateful and disrespectful people. I felt my blood boiling, but I calmed down with a walk and then wrote a sensible reply to his last email. I took a deep breath and hit send.

Subj: *Re ears burning?*
Date: 3/15/98

Dearest Ken,

I arose early this morning and felt a little down, trying to get a new perspective on certain things. After church, I went to the park, hoping my walk and the fantastic weather would cheer me up.

I am sorry you had such a hard time yesterday, and please vent all you want; I feel lucky to help even in the minutest way,

You may behave in whichever way you choose if it makes you happy and does not hurt anyone. You can spend however long you want to do whatever you choose in your own house. If spending 24 hours writing sexy emails to me is what you desire, you are entitled to do that, and if anyone should judge that, it should be the two people involved (i.e., you and I). I love to hear from you, and with the distance between us and how we feel about each other, I know we have exercised considerable restraint in what we have said to each other. Know that I love you, and that is what matters. Your friends' opinions should not matter much in that regard. All I ask you, in terms of you and me, is to follow your heart. If we need to straighten out something, I'll bring it up. I hope you'll do the same too.

We can discuss much else; I didn't contact you again yesterday because I felt I may have been intrusive. Anyway, I'll log on today at around 7:00 p.m. Eastern time. If you want us to chat on Messenger and have some privacy, send me a note to tell me when to contact you. Please don't feel awkward talking to me. Have fun with the girls and tell them I said hello. I love you.

Till then,
Nickie

Subj: ***MISSING YOU... WHAT HAPPENED?***
Date: 3/15/98

Dearest Ken,

What happened to our chat? One minute, we were talking, and the next, you disappeared? Was it the program, or were you interrupted by the company? I hope this is a technical problem with your computer. Please use email if Messenger is out. Let me know what's going on. I love you.

Till then,
Nickie

Subj: ***Suddenly gone***
Date: 3/15/98 11:24:50 PM EDT

My darling Nickie,

Sorry I dropped out like that. Tim and Michelle moved furniture into the next room, and the line disconnected. The house is an old farmhouse; the phone wire snakes through all the spaces around the baseboards, with junctions in the bedrooms. Simply put, the wire accidentally broke. US West will come out on Thursday to string a dedicated line for the computer, and then I set the desktop up on Tuesday. I saw no need for the extra line, so, poor planning. I'm sorry. I fixed it as soon as possible and will call US West from work in the morning.

Before the interruption, I was saying that the thought had occurred to me that we both had a camera setup. The cameras are easy to install and uninstall. Plug the camera into the printer port on the PC, run the software, and there you are, audio and video on the Internet. Despite our distance, we could have dinner together. The look on your face sharing a glass of wine, how music affects your body—sometimes words between two people cannot convey the mind's vision (a picture is worth 1,000 words)

Did you find the film The Truth About Cats and Dogs? Imagine the scene between the two as yet unmet lovers taking place while they could see and hear each other's reactions. One thing that leaped to mind was imagining you applying perfume and getting ready for a quiet dinner alone, hearing your voice as we shared our day, propping our pillows to mimic the other's position as you sat with me as your backrest. We spoke of quiet things as you moved against me. In acting class, we called it a mirror exercise; it is an exercise to heighten communication, attention, and anticipation.

I have been writing this, hoping you would come back online. With your mental image fresh from your shower, I will make mine a cold shower.

I love you. Someday, I'd love to share skinny-dipping in the lake with you (in private) and a leisurely lunch in the shade of the trees fresh from the lake; yes, I better make it a cold shower.

Till then, love
Ken

Subj: ***Line Issue***
Date: 3/16/98 9:11:55 AM EDT

Dearest Nickie,

I tried to reach you when I fixed the phone line and stayed until 1 a.m. your time. I am sorry; it was an accident, and I should have been a better host.

Which certain things need a new perspective? I hope it's not about the email reading incident I relayed to you yesterday, and I have not given the impression that I am anything less than bursting with pride in you and flattered to view our relationship as the most crucial thing in my life.

I had a speech impediment (I stuttered). I taught myself how to use the expression and a portion of the brain typically used to sing for everyday speech. I had to use the phone to practice talking. I am self-conscious, and sometimes, when people poke fun like Tim and Michele did the other night, I revert to that frightened child, learning to talk to strangers on the phone. Because you are essential and unique to me, I am self-conscious about having others read over my shoulder at home. I am as open with you as anyone would be talking to their best friend, but to someone looking for chinks, I am exposing many tempting cracks in my armor. Showing them to you seems natural. I want to be intimate with you, with hopes, fears, dreams, frustrations, winning, losing, body, heart, and soul, and I want you to feel free to be intimate with me; I want to walk beside you in every way, complementing strengths and weaknesses.

Sometimes, I am embarrassed by and for my friends, but I believe they don't mean harm; they don't know any better. By example and conviction, we teach, and with love, we dispel ignorance, for only love can give us the courage to try the path less traveled.

I want to know you so that you accompany each new thought. I want you not only to hear in my voice or see in my actions but to know deep in your heart that I love you; I want to fill you again and again, forever. Still, I never want to consume you; I want you to hunger for me as I yearn for you. Have a wonderful day today.

Till then,
Ken

Subj: *Good morning, my love*
Date: 3/16/98

Dearest Ken,

I am glad to learn that your disappearance from our chat last night was a technical problem. Mishaps happen, so we need to be patient. This morning, for instance, my system froze while retrieving your mail, and I had to reboot. You may be missing one of my letters. I am glad I am copying you at both addresses. I loved your morning letter; reading it did strange things to me.

I found your scent "Dune" in the store yesterday. The sales clerk gave me some samples. I close my eyes and imagine that you are here and that I am touching and tasting your skin; it feels so real sometimes that I have to watch that I don't think of it when other people are near me.

Let's chat again soon. I don't bring the laptop home daily, but I will if we intend to talk.

Till then,
Nickie

Subj: ***Can't get you off my mind;***
Date: 3/16/98 1:41:40 PM EDT

Dearest Nickie;

You have yet to say what happened at the stylist. What will you need to consider differently? As you know, I, too, have quite a reaction when I think about you (perpetually, I am still without intent drawing a small crowd and grins, and if they are in groups, giggles). I have gotten a sliding shelf to keep my keyboard. It sits in my lap almost all day; I love you.

Thank you for every letter; seeing them on the screen makes me feel 25 years younger. How do you say soar at my age? Did you get the last card I sent?

Till then, Love
Ken

Subj: ***The feeling is mutual***
Date: 3/16/98

Dearest Ken,

Thanks for the lovely card; it's both suggestive and funny. Sorry I am still causing you discomfort at work. I have been watching what I write, but it is equally hard to control my reactions whenever I think of you. I have an advantage in what's visible.

I am not happy with my visit to the hairdresser. There is no style to the cut. The hair should fall into place with minimum effort when that short. Instead, I have to try to make it look acceptable to me.

I have been thinking about my career, work, and personal choices. I don't know how to proceed career-wise, which is distressing to me. I also have some real estate that I am debating whether to sell. I have worked very hard to achieve some of my goals, but now I have reached a point where they don't mean what they used to, and I want to simplify my life to have more leisure time without a negative financial impact, and I haven't come up with a satisfactory solution yet. Nothing bothers me more than indecision; I am rather goal-oriented. When I decide on something, I plan and focus on a course of action until I finish. Now, I want to think about my personal life, and I resent dealing with those other things. (I should be grateful to God that I have choices; I wish I did not have to make those decisions right now!)

If it's not the weekend and I send you an e-mail late in the day, I will still be in the office (like now). I used to take it home every night; I developed an elbow and shoulder problem for two months; the doctor told me I was doing the same repetitive movements associated with carrying it back and forth. I stopped doing that, and the "tennis elbow" problem is gone. I take it home every weekend, if I stay home during the week on a day off, whenever I need to bring work home, or if I have a reason to (if we want to chat). I'll buy my laptop by the year's end. (Once I start talking to you before bedtime, I'll not want to skip a day without seeing you!)

I visited the computer store during lunchtime, and the clerk recommended a Quick-cam camera; he said it's easy to install by plugging it into the parallel port and running the program. I'll also need to get a mic, but those are inexpensive. By the way, I won't be taking the laptop to Milwaukee, so we'll have to use the phone while there. Before I forget, I'll stay at the Pfister Hotel (414) 273-xxxx. If they have the reservation under my room-mate's name, it's Beth Hurley.

Darling, it's getting a little late; I'll head home now. Keep my side of the bed warm till I get out of the shower. I'll be back. I love you.

Till then,
Nickie

Subj: ***Strange things??***

Date: 3/16/98 7:31:35 PM EDT

Dearest Nickie,

In this morning's mail, you should have told me what strange effects my mail had on you, and without that information, guessing which portions of my mail affected you is challenging. Additionally, I need to determine whether that effect was pleasurable to you or to what degree. I need that information to decide whether to pursue similar lines of imagination/ communication in the future and leave me wide open to either the sin of neglect or indulging in an activity that ultimately could drive you away. Neither condition could I bear, for my feelings for you are such that were the number not obscene (434,100), give or take, I could tell you the number of seconds until I hold you in my arms. I love you.

Till then,
Ken

P.S. If you have similar strange things haunting your mind, PLEASE feel free to engage in reciprocity.

Subj: ***Missing letters***

Date: 3/17/98 1:33:46 PM EDT

Dearest Nickie,

This letter is the third I have composed today; the emulator session keeps timing out on me. I love you. You are always in my mind and my heart. I write what I imagine at that moment, which is why it is so disturbing when the session ends. I have told you some great stuff, some suggestive things (sometimes VERY evocative), and a few pearls of wisdom passed on by my father that you have never had the opportunity to read; I am sorry. Today, you may receive several quick notes. I love you.

I will try again to impart a philosophy. I hope I word it well. God loves us, and as repayment, God commands we love one another. Aside from the obvious, there is a reason for this; the Bible tells us God made man and woman as helpmates for one another. Through pain, we define pleasure; through sorrow, we define joy. We express our highs by their relationship and distance as opposed to our lows, much the same as we know how glorious heaven must be by how terrible hell must be (but that's another story). In your touch is my pleasure. Your kiss holds my joy; loving you is my strength (hopefully vice versa). However, we are together; these times renew us, sharing love and God's gift; we share creator and creation.

You are always in my mind and heart; whatever the world offers when we are apart can never hope to defeat us because it assails only a part, and our strength comes from two as one. (This isn't as good as the first or second time I wrote it; I am worried I will lose it again, and I am sorry for my inability.) I want to give all of me to you in every way you can imagine, in every way I can imagine, and however we can imagine together, and I want you to feel free to do the same with me.

I want the expression of my love to be as authentic as possible; I have to accomplish this with words. There is a difference between love and sex. How do we know the difference? We will share whenever we can. Even in our words, we make love.

I love getting letters from you. I check my email twenty times a day; my recent work ethic impresses my boss (I didn't have the heart to tell her I was looking for NC @l....c...) Before we started writing, I sometimes only checked my mail every other week. Tell me about anything.

When we are on Messenger together, I see it as dessert (of course, I can't think of dessert without thinking about you; I already threw out the spoons and the bowls.)

Till then, Love
Ken

Subj: *345,600 seconds and counting*
Date: 3/17/98

Dearest Ken,

I hope you realize you are not the only one checking the passage of time. I check my e-mail around 50 times daily, hoping for a message from you. Today, I took two breaks from my meetings to check my voicemail, but instead, I logged on and searched for an e-mail from you! I love you. It's been an eternity since I last told you so. It is incomprehensible that people expect me to work rather than write to you or read your love letters. The nerve of them!

As far as those "strange things" are concerned, we are too close to the day of our first meeting to tell you explicitly what physical reactions some of your letters produce in me. I need to keep a close watch on my words. I want to look at you without blushing to the roots of my hair.

It is not my intent to keep anything from you. I am shy about this first meeting, but that's all. I want to share everything with you: my wants, hopes, needs, likes, dislikes, desires, moods, faults, qualities, and total, complete, unconditional love. I want to know you the same way (in a sense, I almost do already)! I have dreamed of it all my life but found it elusive; I was guarded, so afraid to be hurt. Until you, I never thought I would be so open with my feelings, let anyone inside my heart, and give total rein to my emotions. You declared your feelings and showed me you cared, and at first, it was hard for me to believe; somehow, you opened the door to a heart bursting with decades of unexpressed feelings and emotions. Maybe I was waiting for you. I love you. I can't wait to hear your voice, see, feel, touch, smell, and experience you. I am reserved, but please don't read more into it than initial shyness. I won't discuss some things with you through e-mail because I don't want to bore you, and other things might be more fun to talk about when we "chat." I love you.

I'll take the laptop home on Friday. I'll also have it Thursday evening if you want to chat. I am leaving the office soon. I am writing now in case tomorrow is a hectic day, but mostly because I have missed you.

Till then,
Nickie

Subj: ***Good morning***
Date: 3/18/98 1:54:26 PM EDT

Dearest Nickie,

My Love, you could not bore me. (I have never thought of you when you have not left me wanting more, and still more of you.) I know you have a hectic schedule, but I hope you smile today. I am glad you won't be taking your laptop to Milwaukee; I was under the impression everything BUT work went on at a convention, and you did tell me you were trying to give up that workaholic thing.

I was thinking of a nickname. When I was younger, my friends called me Dekin, "the lawgiver and protector." Do you have any ideas for a nickname?

Till then,
Ken

Subj: *Nicknames*
Date: 3/18/98

Dearest Ken,

The office is unusually peaceful today, the quietest day this week. I might go out for lunch (searching for that Jasmine-scented oil!) I came back to find a message on my voicemail from Linda. She is the only one I told of meeting you in Milwaukee; she called, told me to have a pleasant trip, and added some other things about our meeting that I do not dare tell you. One minute, she tells me to keep my feet on the ground; the next, she is naughty. I'll deal with her when I get back!

Dekin is a good nickname. I can think of others that would be very private, only for me to say to you. (Don't ask! I won't tell you now, but I assure you, you'll hear them often when we are together.)

You are right about my company's annual meeting; whenever I go, I suffer through a few lengthy, boring meetings, but other than that, it's primarily outings, dinners, and company parties. Last year, I regarded it as a mini-vacation because I found an excuse not to attend most meetings. I'll be thinking of you for the rest of the day.

Till then,
Nickie

Subj: *Good morning, dearest*
Date: 3/19/98

Dearest Ken,

Thanks for the beautiful e-card. Nothing else (even the most robust cup of pure caffeine) can put a spring in my step the way you do. I pulled down my suitcase last night; I'll have to think of what to pack for the trip. There are only two days left; in a way, it's scary. I can't believe we are finally going to meet. It's strange; after all the lovemaking last night, I don't feel tired at all, more rejuvenated than anything else. I love you.

Till then,
Nickie

Subj: *Good morning*

Date: 3/19/98 10:08:01 AM EDT

Dearest Nickie,

It's 208,800 seconds and dropping. The time is running slower with each clock tick. I got ICQ working last night. Did you receive your card? Our lovemaking woke me at one this morning, and I haven't stopped smiling yet. I love you.

Till then,

Ken

I logged on after 5 p.m. to send my mail, and there, on the screen, was the familiar icon of my instant messenger. And among the contacts list, his name stood out like a beacon. He was online!

Chat 1—3/19/98

DK: Good afternoon, my love. My heart almost stopped when I saw your name pop up.

NC: Finally! I didn't think we would be able to do this chat thing before we met. HI!

NC: How are you today?

DK: I am well, and you? Did you get everything packed?

NC: I added a few small things.

DK: What are you wearing? You still need to say what the stylist did.

NC: It's a simple cut. The hair does not cover my ears.

Did you get the card?

You probably didn't get a chance to look; I am sorry for assailing you like this.

DK: I have been waiting long enough for you to THROW yourself in my direction. I can stand a little pressure.

I will bring you, among other things (nothing big, don't worry), my publicity photo from the Guthrie. I am also taking my prop box, complete with the script from Love Letters.

NC: You love hair, don't you? Most men do, but I have concluded that I look a lot better with a short hairstyle

DK: Men love everything about a beautiful woman (okay, maybe we lust after most of it). A face is not complete without a frame; a face's frame is its hair.

So, my love, are backsides what most women prefer?

NC: I don't know about most women, but I like lips, smiles, eyes, and a reasonably flat belly. I also appreciate a full head of hair.

DK: Most women cut their hair short and tell everyone, "It makes me look younger." In truth, beauty radiates from a woman's face after a certain age, especially when she smiles; there is so much more expression when she cuts her hair, and you can see her face and beauty in a greater degree.

What makes any of us look young is love. When you are in love, your energy is up, you smile more, and your posture improves. I know I feel like a kid again. I love you and a lot more than I have said

NC: I love you too! A lot!

DK: I read in one of those old dusty books a human requires eight hugs for maintenance and 12 to grow; no one has put a limit on I love you or qualified how many times you need to make love?

NC: So, what else do you like about women?

DK: Sneaky. How are your legs?

NC: Nice legs, slender

DK: Somehow, I suspected as much

NC: Talking about body parts, I am self-conscious about something else. I have tiny breasts.

DK: Here we go again; it is not your breasts I am aching to hold in my arms

NC: I understand, but everyone has preferences. I want to warn you about my deficiencies. The rest of me is okay.

DK: Besides, have I failed to mention how the thought of your nipples brushing against my chest has felt like an electric shock and sent waves of pleasure throughout my body and made my toes curl?

NC: You hinted at it, not in so many words.

DK: Of course, the thought of your round bottom pressed against me as we spooned, was no slouch either

Are you still at work?

NC: Yes, I could take the laptop and restart it from home again.

DK: Let's take a break; I'll fix something to eat and see if I can get the camera working. I love you, and that's how I knew you were beautiful

NC: Thanks; I love you too.

DK: XOXOXOXOXOXOXOXOX

Chat 2—3/19/98

DK: Yes, my love

I experimented with the phone app. What are you wearing?

NC: A skimpy nighty

DK: I did get you something you can wear to bed when we are together.

NC: So, you went back to Victoria's Secret?

DK: I think by the time I can get you out of it, you will appreciate my perspective

Oh! Can you describe your ensemble?

NC: It's a darker color than lavender, almost purple

It has spaghetti straps to hold it up

It's satin, open; it has a little ribbon and a slight bow in front and some lace

DK: I was mixing satin and silk, and I am the one getting hot

NC: The texture is almost the same; I think you would like it because there is nothing to it

DK: How long has it been since someone has carried you to bed?

NC: So long I don't remember. Not everyone is romantic. And although I am small, it may be difficult for someone. I wouldn't want anyone to drop me on the floor. (smile)

DK: If you are under 500 lbs. It won't be a problem.

NC: 120, last time I checked.

DK: You have no worries about me dropping you. It's extracting yourself from my grasp that might prove difficult

NC: That I can deal with

DK: I was afraid of that

NC: You may get to work late many a morning

So tell me about yourself

DK: Mostly, what you see is what you get; at this moment, that would be everything

NC: okay, but what would I do with it to make you happy?

DK: In the past four weeks, you have made me laugh more than I have in the past six years

NC: If that's true, then I am happy

DK: There is the way you like to talk. Communication has become a dying art.

I am a big fan of cuddling

NC: I like that too, very much so

DK: I studied martial arts for 18 years, and I am a total pacifist

NC: that's great, but my line of thinking was in a different direction

DK: I like to draw. I tell jokes to cover my nerves; I enjoy Sci-fi Fantasy, whew, please do. I was beginning to feel like I was running downhill.

NC: So, you are a lover, not a fighter, as Michael would say in the song

DK: Importantly, I love you

NC: Essential to me

I didn't find the jasmine-scented oil

But I'll redeem my coupon at the first opportunity

DK: I may put my whole body into the massage, though

NC: a new concept in massages. I am open to new ideas.

DK: Let's spend time together when you return from the islands.

NC: Yes, I'd like to know you better. (I already know a lot.)

DK: I am looking forward to it, intimately

That's another thing I like about you

NC: New ideas?

Able to get into the spirit of things

DK: being open-minded. There are too many closed ones in this world.

NC: My open-mindedness is recent

DK: the trouble is, when you close your mind, you close your heart

better late than never

NC: I agree. Sometimes, people close their hearts because they don't want to be hurt.

DK: Can I keep the nighty too?

NC: This one is too easy. I should get a long-sleeve full-length cotton nighty for you to take off

I want to see how inventive you get

DK: You forget I have been alone for six years

NC: Your imagination got so fertile you need a machete to get through it

DK: Time had nothing to do with that; it was fertile before I quit writing a long time ago, you sparked me in more ways than one

NC: tell me one way

DK: your realness in my heart? How the most challenging thing I will have to do this year is to behave like a gentleman this weekend. Don't you believe me?

NC: I believe you.

DK: Of course, I may look like Quasimodo!!

NC: I have many vacation weeks I need to take before year-end so as not to lose them. I would like us to spend more time together.

I am sure I could find a decent plastic surgeon to fix you up

As long as what's inside is real

DK: That's all I need: a little nip and tuck

I should warn you my hands are not as soft as I suspect you are

NC: I'll bring a nice hand cream

DK: I still have four days of vacation. I had toyed with the idea of taking Monday off so that I could follow you around

NC: I think I have stupid meetings to go to on Monday and dinner that night

DK: I used to be athletic, so they are a bit big

Wide, instead of long

NC: You think they'll fit perfectly around me they should be perfect for massages.

DK: let's say I can get a good grip

NC: Okay, another reason you won't drop me on the floor

DK: Not unless I make the floor first

besides, I would strip rather than tear such a beautiful nighty

NC: You must get up earlier than me, but I'll join you

DK: Come here. I will carry you to bed

NC: Okay

DK: I love you

NC: I love you too, dearest. Have a good night.

DK: On the morrow, my love

Chat 3—3/20/98

DK: Hi

NC: Hi, I just got home.

DK: I wondered if that was you. I am sitting with Anne right now; she is resting. She had her surgery this morning and is not supposed to be alone for the first 24 hours. Her computer was up and running. It's a good thing she has the same chat program.

NC: How are you? What are you wearing?

DK: White tux shirt, denim pants, suspenders, much the same as tomorrow

And you?

NC: So I'll know how to recognize you

Still in work clothes, a red/maroon suit and soft cream Blouse with some embroidery in front.

DK: Sounds lovely.

NC: I am sure you will behave like a choir boy tomorrow.

DK: If I am a choir boy, turn on or off?

NC: Neither. I would keep my distance. I would not want to tempt you

DK: I love you. Don't forget my nighty

NC: Okay, I won't forget it. Around what time do you think you might get to Milwaukee? I'll order room service and have dinner while waiting for you.

DK: about 7. I think if it goes much one way or the other, I will call

If I don't make it to your arms, it will be because Wisconsin and MN are at nuclear war, and I was on ground zero even that's no guarantee

NC: I have reliable sources that those two states are at peace.

DK: 93600 seconds to kiss. Do you require time to practice?

NC: I'll wear casual clothes tomorrow, but I still need to figure out what. So, I can't tell you what to look out for.

DK: I love you, don't be too much of a lady on my account, (crushing hugs)

NC: Okay, I have a comment, but I won't say it

DK: why?

NC: I would blush (not that anyone can see it), but I feel it

DK: That's okay. I often blush, especially when people notice I am thinking about you.

NC: that's because you have naughty thoughts, just like my comment

DK: it depends on your definitions of the word;

NC: Well, food for thought... I was going to tell you that there will be times when we are together when I won't behave much like a lady

DK: Promises, promises. I love you.

NC: I love you too

Subj: ***Good morning***
Date: 3/21/98

Dearest Ken,

Good morning. I'll be leaving home in about two hours. I can't stay logged on because I expect a call from the taxi service and don't want them to find a busy line. I'll check my mail at least once or twice before leaving the house. If I don't hear from you, you know the Pfister's number for this afternoon is 414-273xxx. Have a good morning. I love you.

Till then,
Nickie

Subj: ***Good morning***
Date: 3/21/98 10:08:55 AM EDT

Dearest Nickie,

Sorry if this does not reach you on time. I was on the Internet, which is a dismissible offense for me here, and wouldn't you know my manager picked that moment to walk by my desk not once but twice? The mainframe is down, and I couldn't reach you through Hotmail; it has been a nightmare.

I miss you. 36,000 and closing, I feel like opening night jitters. Safe journeys, my love.

Till then,
Ken

Nickie

The taxi came, and I threw my suitcase in the trunk. As we sped toward LaGuardia Airport, I worried I didn't receive any last-minute messages from Ken. I sighed and looked out the window, trying to calm my nerves. What if we had nothing to discuss?

"Hey, Nickie!" A familiar voice snapped me out of my reverie. Mary was attending the conference in Milwaukee too. She waved at me from the next cab over. Traffic had slowed to a halt. I peeked around the driver's head and saw Highway Patrol clearing out the remnants of a minor accident. Soon, we were on our way again, and ten minutes later, our taxis were at the terminal.

"Are you excited about the reception tonight?" Mary asked, as she held out some cash for the driver and shut the passenger door.

I forced a smile and replied. "I didn't register for it; I thought last year's was uninteresting. You?"

"Yeah, sure." She shrugged, looking the other way, slightly disappointed from what I could tell.

I smiled to soften the blow and we stepped into the bustling airport terminal. The hum of chatter, clacking of heels, and whirring of luggage wheels blended into a chaotic hum. We chatted about airline food and many other trivial things. I barely listened to what she said, my mind wandering to my upcoming meeting with Ken. *Is he as handsome as I see him in my mind? Will we have chemistry?* My head was whirling.

I followed Mary to the check-in counter, where we met our boss and his wife. They had returned from a vacation in Aspen and couldn't stop gushing about their new townhouse. They showed us pictures and asked us what we thought of the decor.

"It's lovely," I said without really looking.

"It's stunning," Mary agreed with more enthusiasm.

They announced boarding, and we separated into our respective seats. I found mine in the economy class, next to a snoring man who overdid the aftershave. I put on my headphones and closed my eyes, hoping to catch a nap before landing. It amazed me I could carry a conversation and supply answers to questions, yet I had no clue a few minutes later about the specifics of the discussion. Today, I was functioning at a whole different level.

We landed in Milwaukee at 1:45 p.m., and I shared a cab to the hotel with Mary. Forty-five minutes later, I was tipping the porter who had helped me to the room with my luggage. It was a sizeable space with delicate cream and gold wallpaper, two double beds, elegant cherry wood nightstands, and a dresser. The empty closet confirmed my roommate had yet to arrive. I hoped she was not a snorer or a chatterbox.

I unpacked and hung the several outfits I had brought for the occasion, yet undecided on what to wear for my date with Ken. Opting to deal with that later, I headed downstairs to the concession stand in the lobby, seeking a distraction from my nerves. I selected a copy of Cosmopolitan. The cover story promised tips on enlivening one's love life. Despite a skeptical eye roll, I purchased it anyway.

I headed back to my room, flopped on the bed, and read. It was full of clichés and nonsense. I read the same paragraph for the third time, then gave up and set it aside.

I glanced at the clock and grimaced. It was merely 5:30 p.m. *How am I supposed to kill another hour before meeting Ken?* The door opened and jolted me back to reality.

"Hey there! I'm Beth. The taxi driver didn't know his way from the airport, so I got delayed. He made two wrong turns and missed one exit. He seemed to think "shortcut" meant "detour through the Twilight Zone." We drove through some unsavory blocks where I felt unsafe until we emerged onto the main road again. I wonder whether I should complain to the taxi company. And you won't believe this, I even considered giving him suggestions myself! One thing I know for sure: the next time I go to an unknown city, I'll print the route from the airport using MapQuest. Have you heard of it?" The bubbly young woman exclaimed. Her shoulder-length, curly brown hair bounced with every step as she entered the room. She wore casual slacks and a jacket of a deep shade of red.

"Oh, hi, Beth. Nice to meet you. I'm Nickie," I replied, smiling and almost chuckling at the whirlwind of words. She'd probably narrate her grocery shopping trips like epic quests.

"It's great to meet you too! So, Nickie, what's your plan for the evening? I am ready to conquer this conference," she replied without missing a beat.

"I'm trying to kill some time before I meet a friend."

"Ah, got it. I'm just dropping my carry-on and heading out for dinner with coworkers. You're welcome to join us."

"Thanks for the offer, Beth, but I'll pass. I appreciate it, though."

"No worries! We'll be at the Milwaukee Ale House if you change your mind. Hope to see you later, then."

"Sounds good. Enjoy!" And she was out of the door as swiftly as she entered, in a whirlwind of vibrant energy and the faint scent of a floral perfume.

I called room service and ordered soup and salad. Not long after, a knock on the door revealed the waiter with a tray of food. I sat at the desk, ate the soup, and pushed the salad aside. Once finished, I checked the time and got ready. I walked to the closet and chose a butterscotch knit dress I had gotten compliments for. I slipped it on and looked at myself in the mirror, smoothing the fabric and adjusting the neckline.

The clock struck seven; a surge of adrenaline shot through me as the phone rang. I leaped out of the chair and snatched it up, my heart hammering. A deep, soothing voice said,

"Good evening, ma'am. This is room service calling; was your meal satisfactory?" Relief and disappointment flooded me as I answered,

"Yes, quite satisfactory, thank you."

Before I could end the call, he spoke.

"I am happy your start to this evening has been pleasant. I am downstairs in the lobby. Are you ready to come down?"

My breath caught in my throat. When I didn't answer, the voice said, "Nickie, this is Ken." I giggled and stopped immediately and in a serious voice, said,

"Sure, I'll be there soon," and laughed again after hanging up.

I grabbed my purse and glanced at myself in the mirror. A wave of doubt washed over me; should I have worn something else? No time to change now. I threw on my coat, checked for the key, grabbed Ken's gift, and pulled the door behind me. My fingers trembled as I pressed the elevator button. Was it going up or down? I didn't care; it arrived in a flash. I stepped in and pushed the lobby button. The elevator descended with a whoosh; I felt like I was falling too. I couldn't believe I was meeting him in person! I reached the lobby in the blink of an eye.

Excitement and nervousness were competing within me as I walked toward the entrance. I felt a lump form in my throat as I scanned the unfamiliar lobby crowd for Ken. My eyes darted from person to person, searching for an unknown yet familiar face while trying to steady my steps. I spotted him, and as our eyes met, we recognized each other instantly. He rose, swung a leather jacket over his arm, and walked toward me with a warm smile that melted my heart. His brown hair had a hint of red that caught my eye. I had no clue why I focused on that. He was shorter than I imagined, but his shoulders were broad and strong. My stomach twisted into knots as I approached him. I tried to keep my composure, but my body betrayed me. My hands shook, and my knees wobbled as I greeted him with a nervous "hi" and wondered what to do next. He didn't hesitate to open his arms and pull me into a hug. I felt his heartbeat against my chest and then quickly let go. He handed me a package and said, "This is for you." I gave him mine, and we both said thank you, and laughed, breaking the ice. I felt a wave of relief and happiness. This moment was wonderful.

I realized I had flashed my braces and felt embarrassed. *What if he changes his mind about me?*

As we stepped out of the hotel lobby, the crisp air hit my cheeks, and I had a sense of excitement and nervousness in equal measure. We headed to the park, and I attempted to make small talk about his drive to Milwaukee, but I felt like I was babbling. *Can he notice how uneasy I am?*

Soon, we reached the park. Evergreens were everywhere, and the silvery lake was motionless, serene, and peaceful; I couldn't help but feel grateful for the moment. He stopped, extended his hand, and I slipped mine into his. As he pulled me closer, I felt the contrast between his large, rough palm and my small, smooth one. He smiled, and my heart swelled with happiness.

His arms wrapped around me, his lips met mine, and the world faded away as if it were just us two left standing. My heart raced, and I felt his chest rise and fall with every breath. We kissed until we were breathless, neither wanting to let go.

Our walk continued hand in hand. I snapped pictures of the scenery with a disposable camera from my purse to capture the surrounding beauty, but I wanted to hear his voice. His British accent was charming.

"So, will a nip and tuck be in order? He asked as if he had read my mind.

"Nip and tuck?" I questioned, thinking I had lost part of what he had said in the haze of my euphoria, or that maybe there was another British meaning to the words.

"You said two nights ago, in our chat, that if I turned out to be Quasimodo, you will happily send me for a little nip and tuck."

"From simple visual inspection, I believe you are safe from that concern," I said, smiling boldly, feeling my cheeks warm.

"I want you to be sure," he said, pulling me in his arms again for another kiss.

We sat on a bench, and he held me on his lap, spending minutes cuddling, kissing, touching, and whispering sweet nothings. The gifts sat beside us, two wrapped packages, one sporting a blue ribbon and the smaller one a delicately tied red silk ribbon.

"Shall we open our gifts?" he murmured.

"Sure," I replied, loathing to pull away from his arms even briefly. He reached across my back to grab them, his fingers brushing the tip of my left ear. The touch was electric, and I smiled, feeling my cheeks flushed with anticipation and uncertainty.

"Something I hope you'll love," he said.

I traced the edges of the paper, savoring the moment. What was inside? A piece of his heart, perhaps? *You are a total idiot, Nickie!* That, too, provoked another smile. I didn't know what to expect, but when I tore the paper, I saw a much-welcomed bottle of my favorite French perfume, Arpege by Lanvin. My heart melted. He paid attention and got me something I said I liked. I leaned into him, my lips brushing against his cheek.

"Thank you," I whispered. "It's perfect."

And then it was his turn. He picked up his gift and removed the ribbon and the wrapping paper. He was as enthusiastic as a child, and I found that endearing.

"Open it," I urged, my heart pounding. His broad smile was genuine when he unfolded the soft cashmere royal blue V-necked sweater I had gotten him.

"I searched high and low but found nothing in cobalt blue. I hope royal blue is okay," I said.

With the sweater between us, he leaned over and kissed me tenderly.

"I love it," he said," not only because it's beautiful but because it means so much more as you personally selected it for me. I love you."

"I...I love you too." I heard myself say.

I felt unique, beautiful, and loved, as if I had found my soulmate. It wasn't just our eyes that had recognized each other but our hearts.

"In my wildest imaginings, I would have never seen myself so looking forward to Milwaukee as much as I have been these past few weeks. No disrespect to Milwaukeeans; besides all the local breweries and the summer festivals, there isn't much more to be very excited about. Being here with you now makes it amazing."

"Thank you. I feel the same," I replied, not looking at him, trying to hide the blush creeping up my neck.

"How long is the drive from Milwaukee to Chicago? I am concerned about all the driving you'll be doing within such a short time," I managed to change the subject.

"The simple part is that Chicago is only about 70-80 miles southeast of Milwaukee, depending on traffic, one to a one-and-a-half hour, putting Milwaukee between home and Billie."

"I have never been to Chicago; I hear it's lovely. By the way, is your sister your closest sibling?"

"Billie did not marry Liam's father. Thus far, I have been the primary male figure in my nephew's life. While I am close to my family, there's not much difference between one member than another, and the circumstances differ. Benji lives in Cambodia and Paul is in England, making Billie and I the most accessible to one another.

As time passed, we lost track of it all. He still had to drive to Chicago.

"Were you fishing for compliments before about the nip and tuck?" I asked.

"Truth be told, I was apprehensive. But seeing you here, talking about it face-to-face, feels surreal."

"You hide your apprehension well. I have to agree with you, though. Our late-night chats, and sharing so much in emails—it all feels like a dream. You're not just a screen name anymore. There's something magical about meeting someone you've shared secrets with, someone who knows your late-night thoughts and favorite songs."

"If it weren't for the fear of disappointing Liam, I would stay in Milwaukee tonight even if I had to sleep in my car for lack of a hotel room. Nickie, can I see you tomorrow on my way back?" he whispered.

"If you don't, I'll have to fly to Minneapolis," I breathed.

We walked back to the hotel, kissing every few steps, and in those stolen moments, the world ceased to exist until we reached the silhouette of his car waiting by the curb. His arms were strong and protective, and they felt like home. My heart raced once more; kissing him was urgent and consuming, and I didn't want to let go now or ever. Finally, we pulled back, breathless and disoriented, and I looked up into his eyes. His touch lingered, and a subtle cologne scent clung to my coat. For a moment, we just stood there, taking each other in. Then, he leaned down and kissed me.

Outside the hotel, a doorman helped a guest into a town car. As we said our goodbyes, I felt a pang of sadness, life humming around us, impervious to our fragile connection. Our fingers refused to disentangle themselves, our eyes reflecting desire and longing. However, he assured me he would call tomorrow around four, and we agreed to meet for an early dinner at 5:30 p.m. I watched the car drive away, fading into the evening, the ache settling into my arms. I missed him already.

As I returned to my room, the anticipation for tomorrow rose within me; the sadness morphed into joy, and I couldn't stop smiling. His lips, warm and insistent, had left their imprint on mine. I collapsed on the bed and closed my eyes, reliving our shared moments and tenderness. I drifted into a blissful sleep, dreaming of Ken. When I woke up, the sun was shining through the curtains. Happiness and excitement jolted me out of bed. I jumped into the shower, dressed, and went to church. It was drizzling when mass ended, but I didn't mind. I skipped back to the hotel, humming a song in my heart.

I waited by the phone, hoping to hear his voice. Four o'clock came and went, but the phone stayed silent. I felt a knot in my stomach and a lump in my throat. Was he okay? Did he forget about me? Did he change his mind? I tried to push away the doubts, but they kept creeping back. I lay down on the bed, clutching the pillow. Tears streamed down my face as I drifted into a restless sleep. I didn't care what my roommate would think when she saw me sleeping in my clothes for the second day.

I went through the motions of attending Monday and Tuesday morning's meetings, but my mind wasn't there. I turned down a two-hour luncheon hosted by my boss, pleading an upset stomach. I usually attended because it showed "Team Unity" and allowed us to hobnob with the main office's higher management. None of that mattered to me then. I couldn't focus on anything but him.

I skipped the afternoon sessions and spent hours on the bench by the lake, where we kissed passionately. I closed my eyes and imagined his lips on mine, his arms around me, his voice in my ear. He had handed me a bag from his car before he left and said it contained the script of Love Letters. I opened the bag and carried the prop box from Love Letters with me. It also included a large print of his publicity picture and the Playbill. I took out the script and read the entire thing twice. He had also placed in there, handwritten, the finished last poem composed for me:

"Your Own Path"

Though the trees bow to you,
The heavens weep at your passing,
   And the mountains,
        Prostrate themselves at your feet,
             Your path is firm.
        I shall sit alone in the night,
When time has wreaked its vengeance upon your face,
        Return to me;
             I will make you beautiful,
                  With my eyes.

Just be,
Ken

When the tears continued, I retreated to my room, called Southwest Airlines, and booked an early flight for Wednesday morning. The days had felt hazy and indistinct, except for the ache of his absence. It wasn't until I arrived back home and sat before my computer that a glimmer of optimism emerged. Perhaps he would clarify things. Maybe he would say he loved me. But alas, no message arrived.

Subj: *Closure*
Date: 3/25/98

Ken,

I apologize for writing this note; I can't help but wonder what happened. You wanted to see me on your way back, and as needy as this may sound, I had been looking forward to it ever since you uttered those words. All I can think about is whether I did something to turn you off, and I can't help but be annoyed that you would leave without saying goodbye, even if that is true. Whatever the reason, I would like to know. We spent two months saying 'I love you' to each other, so please write back and tell me why. What about me didn't you like? I am disappointed and confused, but my feelings have not changed.

Thanks,
Nickie

Subj: *Closure*
Date: 3/25/98

Ken,

I just sent you a note asking for clarification. Upon arriving home, I checked my e-mail before all else. I want to emphasize how much I am hurting now. Despite how you have treated me, I still believe you are a good and kind person. Your absence already causes pain, so your words cannot make it worse. If you need more time to write, at least for now, let me know if you received my notes, and will reply later.

Nickie

Subj: *?????*
Date: 3/25/98 12:21:35 PM EDT

Dearest Nickie,

I am sorry I am so dense, but why what? I don't know where to begin. I am sorry I didn't contact you on Sunday; my sister washed my shirt, and the phone number was in the pocket; then, I didn't leave Billie's until six; by then, it was too late to detour to Milwaukee, and still be back to work by 5:00 a.m. As it was I arrived in Minneapolis at 1:40 a.m. and only got 20 minutes of sleep before getting up for work. It has been tearing me up not to write, but your letter stated you would be in Milwaukee until today, and you told me you didn't bring a PC, so I didn't email.

What did I do to make you think I didn't want to talk to you? Whatever it was, I am sorry.

Till then, Love
Ken

Subj: *?????2*
Date: 3/25/98 12:53:59 PM EDT

Dearest Nickie,

I received your second note and have already replied to the first. I need help to understand. You said you were going to the garden party on Sunday if you did not hear from me by 4:30; I found out at 9:00 I didn't have any way to contact you until I got back home. I have been waiting around like a lost puppy for three days to hear you say I dumped you, which couldn't be further from the truth if it were in outer space somewhere. I don't understand.

Till then, Love
Ken

Subj: *Re: ?????1&2*
Date: 3/25/98

Dear Ken,

Thanks for replying; I am relieved there might be another explanation for your silence. Anyone in my situation would have come to the same conclusions. I understand what happened, but if you had cared enough, you would have e-mailed me explaining about Sunday. Upon my return, I would have seen it and felt much better (I expect some consideration of my feelings). After feeling tremendous relief, I realize I am now angry with you for causing unnecessary emotional upset. I hope you are having a good day and have been able to catch up on your sleep by now. Sorry if I sounded hysterical in those letters; I was overwrought. I don't recall telling you I was going to the garden party; I remember I told you I might not be in the room when you called and to leave a message. (The party was not mandatory, and I did not mind forgoing it for the opportunity to see you again. As it turned out, I did not go and did not see you either) Thanks again for replying quickly; it helps a lot.

Till then,
Nickie

Subj: *????*
Date: 3/25/98 1:39:08 PM EDT

Dearest Nickie,

I don't want to come off as being mad or anything. Still, after mulling over your notes and doing the chess thing in my head, I wanted you to know a couple of things: first, if there was a lesson for me to learn, so be it, but don't think I was sporting fun with you or that I ever saw you as less than beautiful. I may be naïve, and my emotions may be close to the surface, but I am not stupid.

Playing with someone's emotions isn't my style, and I definitely wouldn't shell out $4,000 for a computer to do it.

Till then, Love
Ken

Subj: *Why are you mad at me?*
Date: 3/25/98

Dearest Ken,

Why are you angry with me? I said nothing to upset you; I thought you were inconsiderate for not letting me know what happened to you on Sunday. — I know you didn't mean to play with my emotions, and that's fine, but you could have contacted the Pfister hotel. In Chicago, your sister would not have had access to the Yellow Pages for Milwaukee, but failing that, the long-distance operator could have assisted. This comes with a cost, but I don't think it would have deterred you. At the very least, upon returning to work on Monday morning, a quick explanation via email would have spared me further worry when I returned home. Did you misunderstand me? A lack of consideration and not intentional neglect are what I am referring to. I still love you immensely, and that may be the problem. I don't understand it now. All I know is that I missed you, and I was distressed at the thought that you may no longer love me. Why are you mad at me?

Till then
Nickie

Subj: *E-Mail*
Date: 3/25/98 1:55:57 PM EDT

Dearest Nickie,

I did tell you I hover over this thing, waiting to hear from you, didn't I? Again, I am sorry for any emotional distress; I didn't think I could talk with you until tonight, and I thought we would do it by chat. Who would have remembered to leave a note on the fridge, as it were? And almost the last thing you said to me (as a matter of fact, I had left, and I turned back to respond, you said you wanted to go to that party, and I said it was important to network, if you didn't hear from me by 4:30 you should go to the party, and you said you would.)

It may seem that I am grasping at straws and making excuses, but now I realize I could have handled things better. In the excitement of being with my sister and celebrating Liam's birthday, I may have made assumptions and not considered the impact of my silence on you. For that, I apologize.

Till then, Love
Ken

I rubbed my temples and sighed. I am not kidding when I say I am drained. I can continue this argument with Ken about what was said before we parted, but it's the last thing I care to do. I glanced at my previous email and felt the frustration again. *I am right in my expectations. Did I misunderstand because of my excitement at being with him? Is it male cluelessness that he could not at first understand how I would feel even if I misunderstood him?* I wrote the first line of a new email, then backspaced and deleted it, stood up, and sat back down. *At least he apologized for not informing me. He is doubtlessly exhausted from all the driving and lack of sleep, and as stressed and sad as I have been, I think it best to table the whole thing and move on.* I reached for my cup of cocoa, took a sip, and felt the immediate comfort of the liquid's warmth.

Subj: **Misunderstandings**
Date: 3/25/98

Dearest Ken,

We are getting our wires crossed today. I am sorry I started this round of e-mails. I don't want to fight with you. I feel emotionally exhausted; I don't want you to dislike me. I won't say anything further about our meeting last weekend. We could start all over, and you can tell me how your visit to your sister went, if your nephew was happy to see you, and how you have been since Sunday. I love your gifts; I read the script and wish you could have read some of it for me. I'll think of you every time I put on perfume or save the bottle you gave me until I can wear it for you. You'll be the last face I see before sleep and the first upon waking, with your picture on my nightstand or dresser. I miss you more now that I know how it feels to be in your arms.

Till then,
Nickie

Subj: *Hello*
Date: 3/26/98

Dearest Ken,

A day has gone by; it feels like an eternity without you. I miss you. What will you have for dinner tonight? Did you make it to the dentist on Monday? How is your friend Anne doing? You have become such an integral part of my life that nothing works unless I have you with me, even if only in my mind. I got your morning note, and of course, it warmed my heart. I wish I had your white shirt to wrap around me. I miss you a great deal.

Till then,
Nickie

Subj: *Missing you*
Date: 3/27/98 6:52:58 AM EDT

Dearest Nickie,

I hope we can continue to communicate openly and honestly. Thanks for sharing your feelings with me. I missed you yesterday. What a mess! The company installed a new version of our call monitoring system, and it was a fiasco keeping track of everything. Sarah and Taylor borrowed my car and had a blowout of the right front tire. Thank God no one was hurt, but I had to get two new tires after work. When I got home, Michelle told me the police had stopped her, and she had no proof of insurance; she needed my car to pick Tim up from work. When I tried to log on to chat, the system couldn't reconcile my password. There is a problem in my DCU file; whatever that is, I spent three hours reloading Windows 98 and Netscape Navigator. However, I still can't access the net; I will call Gateway to see if they can help me find and fix the corrupted file tonight. We have two shows tomorrow, one Sunday, and then three next week. I am free for six days before starting on I Do Not Like Thee, Dr. Fell.

I started a half dozen letters to you yesterday, but I kept getting interrupted, or my session would time out. How was your day? Did you pamper yourself? The busier my day became, the more my mind wandered to thoughts of you and serenity. I miss you; I love you. Welcome back to work. It's nice when you start your week on Friday.

Quick update, my brakes were chirping this morning, so I'll drop by the garage on my way home to replace the front brakes. Between that and calling Gateway, I am not sure when I will be on, but whether I reach you by chat or e-mail, I will let you know when I arrive.

I started 45-minute workouts this week and am already feeling the tightening in my stomach; I expect to return to fighting shape in 3 weeks and competition shape in 6. (When I was teaching Karate, I did a few competitions and won a few, too (I even beat Chuck Nordan once in 1976.) You are always in my heart.

Till then,
Ken

Subj: ***Good morning, dearest***
Date: 3/27/98

Dearest Ken,

I hope you are having a better day than yesterday. It sounded trying. I am happy no one got hurt in that tire blowout. Murphy's Law never fails.

Does your theater schedule get busier at any time of the year? What is the storyline in I Do Not Like Thee, Dr. Fell? I was reading the playbill for Love Letters the other day, and it said that you had just returned to the theater after a 12-year hiatus. I thought you had been acting all the time. I also wanted to ask you about one prop in the box. It's a ring present, and I couldn't find any reference in the play. Is it a prop or did it end there accidentally?

Everyone is stopping by my office with questions; they functioned well when I was away, so I wonder why I am constantly interrupted.

Great news about establishing a new workout routine. Will you compete, though? If so, will it be complete contact? I hope it's for exercise (though having once defeated Chuck Nordan is one more thing about you I am proud of). Did I mention I love your voice and agree with your cousin about its sexiness? And I love your accent.

Yesterday was quite relaxing for me. I spent it all thinking of you. I still marvel I have entirely fallen in love with you.

Till then,
Nickie

Subj: *Nothing special*
Date: 3/27/98 12:32:05 PM EDT

Dearest Nickie,

Your day sounded like the remnants of my yesterday. Fortunately, no one was hurt, although Taylor told me my car would do 140 mph, which, in my mind, leaves little doubt about why the brakes are squealing today. At the theater the winter is busier; they compiled a 3-year-old press release announcement because I didn't submit one in time for that play. When the two characters were younger and off and on during the 50-year relationship, they played with the idea of marriage. Still, when one was ready, the other wasn't, so the ring was a focus memento (a prop). I am not planning on competing again; I dropped out of that scene in 1982. I wanted to be as firm as your lean body felt through your dress. I want you to be as proud to be seen with me as I am parading with you.

Till then, Love
Ken

Subj: *Hello again*
Date: 3/27/98

Dearest Ken,

I just returned from a refreshing afternoon walk. The sun was going down, and a slight breeze blew through the trees; being outdoors was delightful. How are you, dearest? I got the computer camera and the mic today, but I was too busy to go out at lunchtime.

Can the car brakes be fixed, or will you have to get new ones? I need to take my car for service as well.

Will you be working tomorrow? You mentioned having two shows; they must be matinees and evenings. Thanks for the compliment on the firmness of my body. I am glad you thought so. It's good to exercise, in your case for the health benefits, because from what I could see and feel, your body is solid (all parts of it)! I have no complaints and am proud of the way you look. I would have loved to open your shirt, run my hands over your chest, and feel your skin under my fingers. It's a shame we had little privacy, and I felt too shy even to tell you what I wanted to do.

I also just remembered that I love your dimples. They are the cutest thing! Well, I better stop here before you become conceited.

Till then
Nickie

Subj: *E-mail*
Date: 3/28/98 7:22:52 AM EDT

Dearest Nickie,

I got online last night at 12:35 your time, but it was too late for a chat. I will be looking for you tonight after the play. I will need two rotors and brakes; Midas will fix the car Monday after work.

Fortunately, yesterday was tame by comparison; work is a little crazy; it's been open season on the help desk. And my co-workers are at my desk, thinking I know something they don't (I don't).

So, tell me about this table (color, texture, height, and whether it supports 2). I love you.

Till then,
Ken

I clenched my jaw and stared at the ceiling. *What's happening with these "friends" of his? They have no boundaries, calling him "gross" because he should not be thinking about sex with his girlfriend. After all, he is so "old." They took his car without permission and destroyed the brakes, driving at 140 miles per hour without a license! That's wild! What are they going to do next? Change the locks and kick him out? Plus, it's costing him more money!* I bit my lip and folded my arms. *I am sure it's not about Midwestern hospitality. These people are ill-mannered. It's uncharitable to think so, but I can't help it. I won't say anything in my letters this time. Ken as an adult should know the difference between being kind and being used.* I threw the cushion on the carpet.

Subj: *Re: E-mail*
Date: 3/28/98

Dearest Ken,

I am glad you finally got the computer working. You sound so busy. I am surprised you even found time to write; I appreciate it all the more.

I woke up an hour ago to go for my walk, and then I'll go check out the house before the morning ends. From there, I'll play it by ear. Craig wants me to look over some work papers before he signs them. He also wants to borrow my car next Thursday to pick up his girlfriend from the airport.

I need a pretty frame for your picture. Since you asked, I should tell you, the kitchen table is lovely; it's a natural wood color, smooth, and has white ceramic tiles on top. I bought it five months ago, so it's new and sturdy, not lengthy, maybe only 5 feet, but quite capable of supporting two ordinary people. I will have some naughty thoughts every time I look at it now. I am sending you a picture since you have already seen me in person. I miss you.

Till then,
Nickie

Subj: *Good morning*
Date: 3/30/98 8:24:46 AM EDT

Dearest Nickie,

Good morning, my love. I am sorry I didn't get to chat this weekend; both phone lines at my house are down. Only after arriving home at around 7:30 on Saturday night did I realize they were out. Unfortunately, I had to take Sunday off and couldn't write.

The weekend was eventful in a good way; I had the girls, and they watched the matinee and enjoyed it. I missed you; I kept thinking about your kitchen table and the showers. How was the drive? The park? And your friend? I love you.

Till then, love,
Ken

Subj: *Good morning, dearest*
Date: 3/30/98

Dearest Ken,

Good to hear from you again. I missed you a great deal. (I feel very insecure right now). After being in the habit of hearing from you several times a day, not finding a note from you last Wednesday led me to jump to unreasonable conclusions. I love you.

Till then,
Nickie

Subj: *Finally*
Date: 3/31/98 7:38:55 PM EDT

Dearest Nickie,

I love you; I LOVE you; I love YOU, I LOVE YOU! Repeat as required.

I finally (this is my third attempt) can take a moment and write; hopefully, it won't time out again. The problem was that the calipers jammed, and the pads had become so hot they cracked and broke into several pieces. I took the news well; I drove to Duluth to give my last frayed nerve a chance to mend. I walked along Lake Superior and saw a couple feeding the gulls popcorn. We sat wrapped in a blanket and watched the setting sun, the rhythm of the surf in my ears. You nestled to me, and I don't remember exactly when it became dark; I remember the texture of your skin in my hands, the glimmer in your eyes, and the taste of your mouth on my lips.

US West promises I will have a phone again sometime today; you can only pin them down to a 24-hour window. I can't wait to receive your picture; I figured out what was incorrect with the drivers for my web camera. I hope to think of something suitably provocative for tonight. They were selling flowers to support the food shelves; I bought you one long-stemmed deep red rose (I have it in the bottle I use to replenish the water fountain on my desk). I love you.

Till then,
Ken

Subj: *Re: Finally*
Date: 3/31/98

Dearest Ken,

Thanks for your letter today. I was starving for news from you, and I can't tell you how good it feels to know everything is fine with us. I hope you forgive my insecurity now and then; it only happens because I care deeply. I gather from your letter that you haven't yet received my picture. When they restore your lines, you'll find it in a previously sent mail to your Hotmail address. You missed some of my letters, but most were brief notes.

I brought my laptop home, hoping U.S. West would fix your lines. I installed the camera software but have yet to make a call on the computer. Today, I submitted a vacation request for the next five Mondays off. I have six weeks of vacation accumulated. I have made no plans yet, but it's better than not taking them. I wish you could read that little novel I picked up at the library yesterday; every word makes me envision you and me.

I will have dinner now (chicken, rice, beans, and a small salad). What did you have for dinner? I am relieved you fixed the brakes; now, the car is safer. I love you.

Till then,
Nickie

Subj: *Good morning*
Date: 4/1/98 8:59:37AM EDT

Dearest Nickie,

Good morning, my love. I took a half-day today because I have a terrible headache (I needed to catch my breath). I just sent a rather racy message to TGF@aol.com (I didn't notice until I received a successfully sent message, oops!). I may need some sleep.

The phones came up late last night; sorry I missed you. I will try to send you a video message.

Till then, love
Ken

Subj: *Pictures.*
Date: 4/1/98

Dearest Ken,

Between glitches in the servers, computers, modems, phone lines, cameras, and audio, I am surprised we are getting any messages. I know you are missing some of mine, and I missed some of yours. Here are two pictures from last year with longer hair and a different style.

I hope your headache is gone and you feel better. Your voice message didn't come through, but I'll be looking for the video one.

Till then,
Nickie

Subj: *Sleeping*
Date: 4/2/98 8:44:03 AM EDT

Dearest Nickie,

Good morning, my love; I was out on the Messenger after nine last night and looked for you this morning before coming to work. Did you try your camera yesterday? I still have some problems; it tells me to delete extra audio drivers.

My headache is still intense; I have had migraines since I was 4. I don't get them often, but sometimes, they can hang around for three weeks. Not to worry; I don't get crotchety or anything. I move a little slower, and my speech is more deliberate (it takes a lot of effort to focus my thoughts.) Sometimes, after I recover, if they have lasted more than a week, I feel anxious and frustrated, but, a day or so of alone time brings me back to normal.

I love you (I need to tell you more often; (it makes me feel good to say it)). I am still determining if I'll stay the whole day at work today. I will last as long as possible; I can't get much sleep at home during the day.

It felt terrific holding you last night (I got a new pillowcase and spritzed it with the sampler of your perfume from the store before). I love you; I want you wrapped around me as I am around you.

Till then, love

Ken

Subj: *Thinking of you*
Date: 4/2/98

Dearest Ken,

I am sorry you still have that headache; I also suffered from migraines as a child. I only get sinus headaches these days, when the humidity is high.

I am returning the camera to the store for the upgraded version today. I miss you a lot. And I love you; I don't know what to do with all those feelings except tell you about them. Even without the video, I would like to have a chat. I miss you so much.

Till then,
Nickie

Subj: *Trying again*
Date: 4/2/98

Dearest Ken,

I'll have the laptop at home. I am still looking for that jasmine-scented massage oil. Maybe I can redeem the massage coupon on Monday when I stay home—I'm looking forward to chatting with you tonight. I love you.

By the way, you mentioned that you only had four days of vacation left. Can you get advanced vacation time? I am asking because the owner of my company (my boss) gave all the administrative staff travel bonuses (our profitability came way over budget, and he is fulfilling a promise to us). Anyway, a friend (Francine) planned a trip to Amsterdam and asked me to come along. Since you haven't been back in Europe for a while, it would be romantic for us to go together if you could. Because of work, it's a free vacation for me. I wonder if you can spare the time or afford the unexpected expense after buying the computer. I got so excited that I figured it did not hurt to ask. (smile)

Till then,
Nickie

Chat 6—4/2/98

DK: Are you still there?

NC: what happened?

DK: My PC went wild and logged me off;

NC: So, how is your headache?

DK: My head is pounding.

NC: Why are you letting me keep you up?

DK: You are keeping more than my mind up

NC: You can't see me; how can I do that?

DK: In my mind, I can more than see you, but if you have some details to fill in for me. I am all eyes.

NC: I'll describe myself tonight since we don't have the camera

I am by the kitchen table with the curtains drawn

I am wearing black panties and nothing else

DK: My mind isn't on my headache anymore

NC: What are you wearing? Your birthday suit?

DK: Well, the keyboard is in my lap; if you were sitting on my lap right now, I would be wearing a smile; as it is, I have nothing at all

NC: That's a rather lovely thought for bedtime tonight

DK: Okay, a grin thinking about you in my lap without the panties

There is much of you I want to explore; I have been saving up.

NC: Just in case, you should make sure you are in top shape, run a few miles, lift some weights, take some vitamins, get lots of rest, eat lots

you may need all that and more

I want to know the little things about you, not necessarily physical

DK: what little things?

NC: I want to look at you sleeping and eating; get used to your voice

NC: little things like do you put both your socks on before you put on your shoes, or do you put one sock, then one shoe, another sock, and the other shoe? Silly things like that.

DK: I want to feel you as you sleep, the rise and fall of your chest, the softness of your flesh, the ruffled the air makes as you breathe, both socks first, left-handed

NC: you see, I could not have guessed those things

Do you drag yourself out of bed, or do you leave bed eagerly with a purpose?

What side of the bed do you favor?

DK: When I fall asleep, it is quick. When I rise, it is quickly,

The left I sleep on my right side, leaving my left hand free to appreciate you as we spoon

NC: How would you react to someone waking you up in the middle of the night with slow, lingering caresses, tender kisses, soft touches?

DK: in kind

NC: brilliant answer

I am looking forward to spooning with you someday

Falling asleep like that would make me feel secure and happy.

DK: And I am with you. I never thought of myself as drawn to bottoms, but yours has had a magnetic influence on my mind and a stimulating effect on another part of my body

NC: well, I am glad any part of me can do that to you

I think our bodies should fit together very nicely

DK: There is not a part of you that doesn't arouse me, but you felt perfect in my lap

NC: Thanks. I was a little concerned that I was making you uncomfortable

DK: The only thing making me uncomfortable was fighting the desire to reach under your clothes to feel all of you

NC: I might have let you if we had been in a more secluded or private setting

I enjoyed your hands stroking my thighs

DK: It is late for you, later than for me; I want to caress your nakedness, and gently remove your panties, lift you in my arms, and carry you to the bedroom and spend an hour tasting every part of you

NC: And afterward, it would be my turn to caress you.

run my lips and tongue all over you

making sure there is not the tiniest part left neglected...

until you moan with pleasure...

And ask me never to stop...

and tell me you like it so muchhhhhhhh......

DK: Your curves haunt me; I love the taste of your neck and your lips; I want to taste your thighs, lick ice cream from your navel, and explore your inner secrets with my tongue

NC: You are making it hard for me to breathe...

would you enjoy what I said I would do to you?

DK: Yes, oh yes!

NC: I NEED a cold shower!

DK: That is another place I want to love you, to lather your body, to soap you all over, cup your breasts and rinse them in my mouth, and make love standing in the stream

NC: Now I can't even go in the shower! I am going to have visions of the two of us.

I will need more walks to use this unspent energy. If I don't I am liable to get cranky and snappy at work

and I can't sit still in my chair...

If you don't stop, you will have me moaning alone in my kitchen.

DK: I wish I could see you now... I better get to bed, but I must let something calm down. Sometimes, I think for too long, which can be a painful experience; it will be hard to get anything other than loving done when we are alone.

NC: If you can make me feel this way with words, I can't wait for the real thing. Love and kisses. Sleep well. I love you.

DK: I love you, good night XOXOXOXOXOXOX

"Girls' Trip"

Nickie

No! I forgot to ask if he had received my last note about a possible joint vacation. I couldn't stop replaying the scenes he described in my imaginary vacation the previous night. It got so bad that this evening, after taking Craig and his girlfriend home and driving back, I thought about having a steamy shower together instead of focusing on the road ahead, causing me to take the wrong exit twice!

We couldn't chat the next two nights because the automatic maintenance program on his computer kicked in each night, and the drive defragging took forever. He assured me he found the auto.exe and changed the maintenance time to Sunday nights.

Then, in an email, he mentioned he couldn't go on vacation with me. He said he'd be on that plane in a heartbeat if he hadn't just bought the computer. The orthodontist would fit his middle daughter for non-insurance-covered braces next month, and he needed to come up with a hefty 50% deposit. It disappointed me, although I knew it was a long shot. We agreed to revisit the subject upon my return from vacation.

We perfected our cyber connections the following days through email, chat, and audio snippets to ease this frustrating situation. We tried to get the computer to do our will, but it didn't know how to tell us its limitations except for our frustration. Little and big things helped us get acquainted; Ken downloaded a picture I sent and was over the moon about it. However, he thought I had too many clothes on! There were days when he drove 130 miles round trip so that he could spend an hour chatting with me before having to report to the theater for his plays. That was complete lunacy! I felt guilty and worried he would be overly tired and have an accident.

I am grateful for his ability with words that launched us into such a flight of fancy. When I wake alone in the morning, I still want him, needing to feel the touch of his hand and the feel of him inside me as if not imaginary. It's not wise to keep doing this to ourselves, but it feels good. This is a classic case of folie à deux.

It amazed me that amid the headiness, I had been talking to Francine and completing the details of our vacation. We bought the tickets to spend two days in Amsterdam and then go to Hamburg. Francine mentioned talking to a travel agent who convinced her to change her itinerary. Since I have never been to Holland or Germany, I was open to changes and followed her plan. It was too taxing to think of anything besides Ken, and since he could not join me on the trip, it did not matter where we went. I had faith that Francine would pick somewhere worthwhile.

I looked at the calendar on my wall and felt excited. The days flew by, and I almost panicked when, in a chat session with Ken on the eve of vacation, I realized we would be out of contact for a week. I typed frantically, asking him how we could stay in touch. Ken wisely noted that I was going to Europe, not the other side of the world. He also noted that reputable hotels typically provide an internet café for guests. He sent me a smiley face and a wink, trying to reassure me. That was also logical, so I calmed down. I leaned back on my chair and smiled, feeling his warmth through the screen. We were chatting till about two o'clock when I realized I was selfish about keeping him up so late. I would fly tomorrow and could rest on the plane, whereas Ken had to get up in a little over three hours and be alert and ready for a long drive and a productive day tomorrow. We said our chat goodbye. I crawled into my bed, hugged my pillow, and dreamed of him.

Four hours later, I met Francine at the United Airlines terminal at JFK Airport. I heard bits of conversations in different languages - Spanish, French, Mandarin.

The clatter of suitcases echoed through the terminal as travelers rushed to catch their flights. Despite the chaos, I felt a sense of excitement and anticipation. Check-in was swift. They sat us in 6a and 6c, but 6b was empty, so we could spread out and get comfortable. After take-off, I reclined my seat immediately, wrapped a blanket around me, and asked Francine not to wake me until they served breakfast or lunch. In-flight movie: *Waiting to Exhale*. I fell asleep in under five minutes. I needed more than the two hours of sleep I got last night.

We hailed a cab from Schiphol Airport and set off for the Ambassade Hotel. The sights of charming canals, with picturesque houseboats and early tulip buds, filled our eyes. Bicycles whizzing by, and occasional chimes of church bells serenaded us with bright urban life. The air carried a hint of fresh rain and the smell of Dutch waffles prepared nearby. The anticipation of fun had started.

Adjacent rooms awaited us, identical in all aspects, with soft lighting creating a cozy atmosphere, and the beds were plush and inviting. The window view showcased the charming canals of Amsterdam and the city's picturesque beauty.

The following two days were a whirlwind of activities! We explored The Van Gogh Museum, immersing ourselves in its masterpieces. We strolled through the rose garden in Vondelpark, marveling at the towering three-meter statue of the Dutch poet Vondel. In the distance, melodies of the music dome echoed, adding a touch of whimsy to the atmosphere. We took a boat tour through the waterways of Amsterdam, passing charming canal houses and graceful bridges.

Landmarks were plentiful; the Anne Frank House left a profound impact with its silence and preserved memories. The streets of the Jordaan Neighborhood buzzed with the chatter of locals and the clinking of glasses in cozy cafes. Dam Square was magnificent, with its impressive architecture and lively street performers. The Royal Palace Amsterdam's opulent interiors and intricate details awed us. The ancient Oude Kerk and Nieuwe Kerk were silent witnesses of the city's rich history with their towering spires.

In the shopping street of Kalverstraat, the smell of coffee and fresh pastries forced us into a quick treat. We handpicked souvenirs, wanting to remember this vibrant city. We had more to see, but on the third day, with a bittersweet feeling, we headed for Schiphol and caught a train to Hamburg, Germany. I could not be mad at Francine, as I had told her to run with the itinerary since I had wrapped myself entirely in my romance with Ken.

Francine had been on the phone at least four times since landing in Amsterdam. I found it curious —like she was juggling secrets or orchestrating a covert mission, so I asked:

"You've been on the phone each time I've gone to your room. Who have you been talking to?"

"Oh, that often, uh? I didn't realize it." She grinned, her eyes dancing with mischief.

"I've been talking to Mauro. He lives in Hamburg."

"Mauro?" I leaned in, intrigued. "Who is he?"

She averted her eyes, smiled, and fiddled with the edge of her scarf.

"Well, he's my cousin Mitch's best buddy. I called Mitch a year ago, and Mauro picked up. We've kept in touch and speak at least weekly."

"Wait, wait," I interrupted, leaning even closer. "Tell me more! How did it all start? Was it a dramatic wrong number moment? Or did he accidentally reveal his secret salsa recipe, and you bonded over that?"

Francine laughed, her eyes crinkling at the corners.

"Oh, it's not that dramatic. I was calling to ask Mitch about his travel plans, and Mauro answered. His voice—Nickie, it was like warm caramel. Smooth and sweet."

"And then?" I nudged.

"And then," Francine continued, "we chatted about everything—music, food, life. It felt like catching up with an old friend. And somehow, we just...clicked."

"Clicked?" I wiggled my eyebrows. "Like, 'Oops, accidentally sent you a smiley face.' clicked?"

She swatted my arm. "No, smarty pants! We discovered we both work in marketing and love comedies and funny cartoons. It turned out I forgot to ask him to put Mitch on the phone afterward, so I had to call back to speak to Mitch."

"Comedy and cartoons? A match made in heaven!" I teased. "So, isn't Mitch in London now?"

"Yeah, he moved there recently. But I am going to Germany to meet Mauro in person, not to catch up with Mitch."

"Is he a New Yorker?"

"No, he is Brazilian but lived in the States for four years in college. Anyway, I'm excited to meet him in person. And you're coming along for the ride!"

We laughed, our voices echoing on the train. Amsterdam retreated beyond the window.

We met Mauro at the train station in Hamburg. He was gorgeous, with dark blond curly locks, two deep dimples (must be the season for dimples, ha-ha!), and the most unusual jade eyes; Francine was thrilled. She introduced me, and he invited us to dinner before settling. It was a chic, hip place, and the food was tasty. Mauro said there was extra room in his apartment. I dragged Francine to the lady's room with me and told her I would go to my hotel instead, but she could do whatever she thought was suitable. Francine reminded me that Mauro had been her cousin's friend since college, and Mitch assured her he was trustworthy. She offered to call Mitch in London when we got to Mauro's if that would ease my fears. This suggestion reassured me, and I followed the plan. There was indeed a guest bedroom for Francine and me. I said good night to them while they chatted in the living room. The following morning, Francine slept peacefully in the twin bed beside mine.

After breakfast, Francine told me they discussed what would be fun to do for the next three days. Mauro suggested we take a car trip to a resort on the Baltic Sea. I had envisioned this vacation as sightseeing only. A resort vacation differed from what I foresaw, but again, I reminded myself that it was my fault for not actively participating in our vacation destination choice. We drove for a few hours and got to the Weissenhäuser Strand. It was one of Germany's most popular year-round holiday and leisure parks on the beautiful north coast of Ostholstein. Francine roomed with Mauro, which did not surprise me, given their flirty banter during the drive. I, of course, was on my own.

Feeling like a third wheel, I did my own thing during our stay at the Strandhotel. I took advantage of its swimming pools and Dünenbad saunas, where they put your health and wellness first, whatever the weather. I took step aerobics classes in one of the fitness studios. I met Francine and Mauro for dinner in the restaurant with a winter garden and also for an excellent breakfast buffet in the mornings. I thought I would feel lost in a place where the primary language was neither English nor French, but this reminded me that almost everyone in Europe was bilingual or trilingual. On the second day, I asked the concierge about the internet café, where I emailed Ken about Amsterdam and what we had seen of Germany.

Francine was glowing. She seemed pretty pleased with herself, which made me wonder if she'd discovered a secret stash of unicorn glitter.

"Hey, Francine! You look great this morning. Why are you so happy?" I asked, meeting her in the breakfast room.

"Oh, you won't believe it!" her eyes wide with excitement. "I've been practicing *tantra*."

"What's that?" I asked, picking up a container of yogurt and a banana.

"Something Mauro learned during a retreat in India with an old girlfriend," she explained. "It's an ancient Indian practice combining the body and spirit; it increases intimacy and improves the entire experience. There's a lot more to it, but that's the extent of my understanding for now."

"Interesting," I said, trying to wrap my head around Francine and Mauro engaging in ancient spiritual practices. "And how's it been?"

"It's been amazing!" she said, eyes sparkling. "I feel so connected, like a whole new level of self-discovery."

"It suits you!" I grinned. "You are making me feel like the customer answering the waitress in the delicatessen from the movie When Harry Met Sally. We have to talk more when we get back home. I want details!

"Mauro suggested the name of a book; I'll buy it when we return. I like him, Nickie. He is so easygoing and has a great sense of humor."

"And let's not forget," I added, winking, "he's quite the looker."

Francine blushed, her smile widening. "Yes, indeed. He has it all."

Mauro, who had been retrieving the car from the resort's valet, joined us for the rest of breakfast. Francine and I quickly changed the topic to the unusually brilliant weather and our expected timing for the return trip. Life was interesting with Francine around.

While heading back to Hamburg, Mauro regaled us with amusing anecdotes about his observations upon arriving in Germany.

"So, how hard was it for you to adjust? I asked.

"Well, not as hard as I expected, except for dating," Mauro replied.

"Really? " Why is that?"

"I met this girl named Inga and, after a few tries, got her interested in me. But then, whenever we hung out, she'd whip out her "calendar." Mind you, it wasn't a mere calendar; it was color-coded with work, gym, and social life sections." Answered Mauro.

"And where did you fit in?" I asked, raising an eyebrow.

"Oh, I had my special section: "Mauro Time." Seriously, it was like I was a recurring appointment. She'd say, "Mauro, I've penciled you in for Friday at 7 p.m. I have a gym class at 9 p.m., so don't be late," he imitated, his eyes rolling.

"That's... efficient?" I chuckled

"Efficient? Let me tell you ladies, she had a "Mauro Evaluation" every month! Like a performance review. She'd grade my punctuality, conversation skills, and overall date experience. I half-expected her to hand me a certificate: "Congratulations, Mauro! You've achieved Gold-Level Boyfriend Efficiency."

"And how did you react? I asked, wiping tears from laughter.

"I played along, of course. I'd show up with my own presentation: "Why Mauro Deserves Extra Dessert Points." But the best part is that she'd give me stickers! Gold star for good listening, smiley face for witty banter."

"Did you ever rebel?" Both Francine and I were snorting by now.

"Oh, you bet. One day, I showed up with a kazoo. She looked at me, puzzled. I said, 'It's Mauro Time, baby! Let's make some noise!' She didn't find it as hilarious as I did."

"And did you last long with Inga, the calendar queen?" I asked, wiping my eyes.

"Nah. Turns out I'm not successful at sticking to schedules. I missed a "Mauro Time" appointment once because I got lost in a pretzel shop. She downgraded me to Silver-Level Boyfriend Efficiency. Heartbreaking".

"Let's hear it for spontaneity! May you never be penciled into anyone's calendar again!"I said, smiling and winking at Francine.

I knew Mauro was exaggerating or fabricating the story, but we all had a good laugh. I wondered how such a "Latin" man could adjust and seem happy in this structured German environment. We returned to his apartment late; I said good night to the two of them and headed to bed. A taxi was arranged for us in the morning. Mauro had a marketing show for work. He said he would visit Francine in the States in the fall.

Ken

It had been only one day, but I missed "us" already, and I was at a loss, not writing to her every morning or chatting in the evening. I worked a few more hours every night. I couldn't believe it, but last evening, I accidentally came up with an idea that might benefit the company. The next day, I played with the codes at lunchtime and in the evening and got identical results. I could hardly sleep last night, and first thing this morning, charged into my manager's office:

"Good morning, George. Do you have a moment?" I asked.

"Of course; good morning, Ken, come, sit," he said, gesturing to the plush chairs in front of his desk.

"I have some ideas to help us save costs and increase productivity."

"That's great. Let's hear what you've got."

"We could streamline the response process by reducing the steps that we currently take. I've researched this, and doing that would reduce costs by up to 15%."

"That sounds very promising. Can you give me more details?"

"Yes, we could automate some of the manual tasks. I wrote a routine where clients could describe the problems they encountered and the level of urgency; if a task is not urgent, we relegate working on it during downtime, freeing us to attend to more urgent matters. It's more efficient than responding immediately to all requests and wasting precious hours attending non-urgent situations during peak times, resulting in additional overtime to resolve critical issues. Alternatively, we could rotate dedicated team members to less urgent tasks, leading to more thorough reviews and faster resolutions. Not only would this save time, but also reduce the risk of errors."

"I see. That's very innovative, Ken. I'm impressed. Please email me the file. I'll verify the logic, and if it's okay, I'll present it to the executive team."

"That's great! I'm glad you like the idea."

" Of course, good job!"

"Thanks. Happy to contribute."

Two days later, I stared incomprehensively at a layoff notice. I put down my still-steaming cup of tea and headed for George's office. Three other coworkers were already in line, and one more followed. George stood up, waved us in, and closed the door.

"I am so sorry I didn't get to warn you guys in person first. HR ran with the emails before I could talk to you," said George.

"But is the company in trouble? I just presented you with some time and cost-cutting options. Why get rid of us?" I said.

"Well, that was a blessing and a problem all at once. You are the senior programmer here, Ken, and you are well respected. Your idea was brilliant. Although the company is not in trouble, things are tight, and we have been looking for ways to cut expenses."

"You are responsible for this?" asked Anne, looking at me, incredulous.

George continued, "Your idea gave us exactly what we sought. Once implemented, we can do without the 4 of you. Anne can stay for now as we evaluate the potential savings. It's just a temporary layoff. You will be able to collect unemployment pay in the meantime."

"Are you kidding me? Unemployment is not even one-third of our pay. How do we survive on that?" asked Justin.

"I save the company money and get rewarded with a layoff?" I was more confused than ever.

"I am sorry, Ken," said George.

"Why couldn't you keep your f_____g mouth shut? Who asked you to do this anyway? No f______gbody," Mark spat at me as he stormed out of George's office to clear his desk.

I was speechless, and the weight of guilt was like a boulder tied around my neck. I followed Mark out to clean my cubicle. There was suppressed anger talk all around the office, and it was all my fault.

I went through the day without really thinking, numb to the irritated glances and words directed at me. When I got home in the middle of the day, there was a message on my answering machine. Unfortunately, it was Mark shouting obscenities at me. I had only wanted to help the company save money and improve operations. I had not anticipated those consequences.

I spent the next day in my bedroom, not eating nor sleeping, just endlessly thinking about how to make things right for my coworkers. The following day, I left the bed, walked to the computer, updated my resume on Monster.com, and perused the newspaper's help wanted section. I contacted some headhunters I knew about my position and any IT opportunities they may have. By late afternoon, I had heard back from three of them with contacts for possible interviews. I called my coworkers and left messages with the same info I received. No one answered their phones to talk to me. I was disappointed, but I understood their anger. Despite my efforts to help the company, I felt I had created trouble for everyone.

By the end of the fourth day, I had to drag myself out of bed bleary-eyed from restless nights. I obsessively checked my e-mail for headhunter responses and refreshed my Monster.com profile. If I found something, I immediately forwarded it to my co-workers. I knew Mark didn't have a home computer, but he must have access at the library. I asked some friends to check on their job bulletin boards or ask their HR departments if they had any IT openings. I had to force myself to wait at least two days before contacting them again to avoid being annoying. None of my laid-off co-workers were getting back to me, but I learned through Anne, who was still talking to me, that, after further review, George informed her that her position was secure. Through Anne, I also learned that all three laid-off co-workers had secured interviews for the following week. This news gave me a bit of relief and helped me concentrate on my situation. Two employment agencies called me, with three interviews set for the following week. My spirit lifted some; however, I spent the weekend curled up in bed, the covers over my head, imagining all sorts of delays. The phone rang. I removed the cover from my head and reached for the receiver, grateful for the long cord.

"Hi Ken, it's me," said Mary Lou.

"Oh, hi." I sat up.

"I wanted to talk to you about Claire misbehaving in school again, but when I called your job, they told me you had been laid off. Don't think you are going to skip any child support payments. I don't trust you with this."

"When have I ever missed a payment?"

"Well, I heard the complete story, and you should have thought about that before getting into this mess."

"I don't need a lecture. I am doing the best I can."

"You know I'll take legal action."

"It won't come to it. Anyway, why are we discussing a hypothetical situation? Let's stick to Claire, would you?

After hanging up, I felt my mood spiral downward and the grip of depression tug at my elbow again. Only knowing that others depended on my efforts kept me afloat. Even though Nickie contacted me multiple times via email, I was too consumed by sadness to muster a response. I wanted to open up more but thought it was too soon to bare my soul that way. After going to my first three interviews and hearing from Anne that Justin had been made an offer on the spot at his first interview, my spirits rose, and I answered Nickie's letters.

Nickie

Back in my apt in NY, I rushed to my laptop but was disappointed to see no messages from Ken; I was sure I told him in an email from the resort when I would be back. I figured it was the internet and his system acting up again, and I sent two messages telling him of my arrival, but there was still silence, and I began to panic. I called him, but he didn't answer. Sleep and food were out of the question, and I barely functioned at work. I continued sending two emails a day, anyway. After five days and nights of crying, I woke up one morning to find a message from him explaining the terrible week he had had. I was horrified by how troubled he would have been, but I was also relieved to hear from him again.

We resumed our emails; they weren't daily, which was understandable. I didn't suggest chat sessions. Instead, I asked about his job search and encouraged Ken to continue his plays to feel better. Although he did not mention it much except for the first time, I could feel his concern despite his attempt at lightheartedness and declarations that the thought of me kept him going. The part stressing him out the most was his daughters' weekend custody, as he was unsure how it would work out. I felt a certain reluctance from him when discussing the situation. I reasoned it wasn't right to press. After another week, he received an offer from the first job he had interviewed for, and he learned that all his laid-off co-workers were now employed again.

I was so happy for him! And, of course, for myself, because once he settled into his new position, I would mention coming to see him at my first opportunity. As it turned out, he told me he had made a reservation to visit me on an extended long weekend a week before his lay-off. He had been about to cancel, but he received his new job offer, which allowed him to keep the reservations. He had wanted to surprise me and hadn't mentioned it before. The best part was his new employer closing on the days before and after the holiday. With the weekend, we'd have five full days together.

April was speeding by, but the slower months at work were now busier. The agency owner I worked for was approaching sixty-two early next year. According to his contract, he must return his stake to the central corporate entity and retire. To prepare for this event, several additional issues needed addressing. Of course, as the company's controller, I had to ensure that we thoroughly valued the agency. I had assembled a team and put different employees in charge of things. They would update physical assets' valuation to determine obsolescence and triaging, shipping, and investigating costs of certain items, such as artwork that the current owner would buy from the corporation for his private collection and use. It was a detailed and time-consuming process, requiring weekly meetings for updates and modifications.

One morning, the owner informed me he had arranged a two-week training class he wanted me to take for a Series 8 securities licensing exam in case I assumed a different role than being the Controller with his successor. I was unhappy about this disturbance in my routine until I found out the training was in Milwaukee. I rushed to the computer that night to share the news with Ken, and we discussed our plans.

When I arrived at the Milwaukee airport on a cold, cloudy Sunday evening, the wind whistled loudly through the streets. The classes started at 8:30 every day in the conference center. We learned for nine hours daily, and the instructor's voice occasionally interrupted the lectures with slides and exercises.

Ken

It was Friday morning, and I had kept the kids from school to everyone's delight except maybe Camille, who worried about her math test next week.

It was a cloudy day outside, but the kitchen was bright and warm. I was at the stove, making their all-time favorite breakfast again, flipping pancakes with practiced ease. Camille, Chelsea, and Claire—gathered around the worn wooden table, their laughter filling the room. They had seen their mother yesterday after school and spoken to her on the phone this morning at the hospital. They knew she would be alright, so they were enjoying their unexpected stay with me as a mini-vacation, somehow knowing they had me wrapped around their fingers.

"Alright, ladies, who's ready for the fluffiest pancakes in town?"

"Dad, you say that every time," Camille replied, rolling her eyes.

"And every time, it's true."

Chelsea and Claire scrambled onto stools, their feet swinging above the floor. The kitchen smelled of vanilla and maple syrup.

"Dad, can I add chocolate chips to mine?" asked Chelsea.

"Absolutely, Chels. You're the official pancake decorator."

Camille left the table and leaned against the counter, watching me with a soft expression.

"You know, Dad, I used to think pancakes were just pancakes. But yours... they're like magic," she said.

"Well, sweetheart, magic runs in the family."

Claire was now tugging at my sleeve.

"Daddy, can we have a pancake picnic in the living room?" she asked

"You bet, Claire Bear. Plates, syrup, and all."

We settled on the living room floor, a mismatched assortment of plates and pillows, giggling as they drizzled syrup and piled whipped cream.

"You're the best pancake eaters ever," I said, drizzling more syrup on their plates.

As they devoured their breakfast, I stole glances at my daughters. Since the divorce, these were our best times —no lawyers, no paperwork, just love. But my joy had a slight damper after my call with Nickie and the bad news I had given her. She didn't make me feel guilty; she was very understanding, and I loved her even more. Camille pulled me from my thoughts as she asked:

"Dad, can we do this every Saturday?"

"Absolutely. Pancakes and all, as long as you can convince your mom to allow it."

Nickie

I liked what I was studying, but the material was complex, so most evenings, I ordered room service while I went over the day's subject and prepared. The days flew by, and on the second Thursday evening, I received a call from Ken saying he wouldn't make it. His ex-wife was in the hospital, and he had to care for his daughters. The unexpected change in plans reminded me of one of my mom's favorite quotes: "Man proposes, but God disposes."

I left the room and walked down the four flights of stairs, ignoring the elevator. I sat in the reception area but only for a minute before going to the hotel's computer room, which was empty. Besides disappointment, sadness and restlessness alternated, pushing themselves around in my mind. I stood by a window staring at the quiet parking lot, frowning and ruminating, when a fellow student entered and said, "Hi." *What now?* Although annoyed, I didn't show it.

I raised my eyes to look at him, and my body seemed to receive an electric shock. I knew I was not making it up as I saw the same spark of surprise in his eyes. Jack Healy smiled, held out his hand, and introduced himself. He could have been anyone except for his eyes, the color of the vibrant tropical sky on a sunny day, and perfect, well-defined lips that made him stand out in the most captivating way. I could not tear my eyes from those lips, and in a few seconds, the pictures that flashed through my mind made me shake my head and wonder if I had lost my sanity. How could I be in love with one man and have such a violent physical reaction to another, almost a perfect stranger? I hardly paid attention to anyone in the class, mainly concentrating on the instructor.

Something was going on that I didn't understand. My mind wandered when I heard Jack say, "What do you think?" I smiled and shook my head, having heard nothing of what he said. He smiled and pointed to his books, saying I needed nothing else, as he had all his notes and the most important textbook. I realized that he had proposed studying and quizzing each other on the course material for the exam the next day. I agreed, and we sat there, reviewing the material while feeling 10,000 volts of electricity in the air. Everything was automatic, and I supplied the answers on the mock exam and could verify his answers from the back of the book. We studied for three hours, and then I excused myself, citing the need for a good night's sleep before tomorrow's exam. I declined when he asked if I felt like a nightcap at the bar.

The sex was intense; the cascading orgasms that shook my body went on for many seconds before my head collapsed on the pillow, drenched in sweat, and my eyes flew open. The room was semi-dark, and the nightstand alarm was beeping softly but insistently. I was lost for a moment, not fully understanding my surroundings, until I realized I had just woken up from the most intense wet dream I had ever experienced. In shock, I still looked around, searching for Jack, whose ghostly body I had so passionately entwined in my dream seconds ago. Was I going mad? I blushed, remembering that I hardly knew the man and had only spent three hours studying with him. Why would my subconscious drag him up in this most intimate dream? I deduced that as my period was due any day, I must have been experiencing a surge of premenstrual hormones, and he was the last person I spoke to last evening.

At eight o'clock sharp, I arrived at the exam room and chose a desk. Some other students had come before me, and I was sure they were too nervous to linger at breakfast and eager to put the test behind them.

While checking my watch, somebody sat at the table next to me and said, "Good morning." I replied automatically before raising my head to see that it was Jack. "Ready?" he said.

"As ready as I'll be," I replied. "It was a good idea to study together yesterday."

"Yes, we covered the material in record time, and I could go to my room and watch a show for the first time in two weeks."

When I finished, Jack looked up, smiled, and waved as I left the table. Smiling, I waved back and handed my test to the proctor.

I packed quickly and caught a flight back home, disappointed about not seeing Ken.

"Drama Galore"

Nickie

I had started reading a book on Tantra that Francine was enthusiastic about finishing and had recommended to me during our trip. I had read a third of it, which was exciting—the new concepts and different perspectives were fascinating. I often got distracted thinking about what I read and imagining its implementation in the dream future for Ken and me.

It occurred to me I had heard little from Francine lately. She had been happy since our return from Europe, but I was having trouble remembering if it had been one or two weeks since we spoke. It was 10 a.m. Monday, and I wanted to see if we could grab lunch today. My hand was hovering above the receiver when the phone rang. Other than hello, I heard uncontrolled sobs: "Francine, what's going on? Why are you crying? I was about to call you to suggest lunch today. Are you ok?" She sobbed a few more times, then told me she was not at work and did not go in today; she was in a phone booth downstairs in the lobby. I tried again to figure out the issue but finally decided against it. I picked up my purse, closed my office door, and stopped by Marie, the operations manager, to tell her I was stepping out because of a personal issue. Marie was alarmed. I assured her it wasn't serious, but something urgent required my presence. I informed her I would take the rest of the day off. I advised the receptionist to forward my calls via voice mail or reach me through Marie.

Francine had stopped crying, but her eyes were red, and she looked miserable.

"Let's go get some coffee, and you can tell me what's going on," I said.

"I am sorry for disturbing you at work, but you were the first person I thought of," she replied, sniffling.

"No problem, it's Monday, and nothing was urgent on my schedule."

We walked three blocks up Lexington Avenue and found a near-empty Starbucks. I got us two freshly brewed cups of coffee. Mauro had visited earlier than expected and had been in town for the last two weeks. He left two days ago; she hadn't heard from him since, which was unusual, according to Francine. She decided to email him and discovered that Mauro had been communicating with her roommate, Lauren. Based on the email Francine found, she thought they slept together the last two days he was in NY. She had been devastated since and wanted to confront Lauren.

Although I knew it was not the first thing I should have said, I heard myself ask Francine:

"Hey, wait a second. Why didn't you tell me Mauro was in New York?"

"Oh, I'm sorry. I didn't want to upset you," Francine replied.

"Upset me? Why would I be upset?" I asked.

"I thought you might have liked him too much in Germany, and I didn't want to cause any drama," she explained.

"What? Francine, that's ridiculous. First, you are my friend; second, you know I'm in love with Ken. Besides, I thought Mauro was good-looking, but I have no romantic attraction to him."

"I'm so sorry, Nickie. I was just jealous. I shouldn't have kept it a secret," she said as her eyes widened in tears again.

We spent the morning and afternoon together, and then I took her home. We timed it so Lauren would be home so the two could talk it out. When confronted,

Lauren did not deny the affair; she apologized and admitted she had fallen hard for Mauro and intended to move to Germany to be with him. The revelation was too much for Francine. She threw the glass of water she was holding dangerously close to Lauren's feet, and I was glad to have been beside her to restrain her as she lunged at Lauren, screaming, "Get out! Get the f. out! I am going to claw your f. g eyes out if you don't leave this place right now! Right now! Get out, you backstabbing B... ch!" Lauren backed away and tripped on the dining table leg but got caught in one of the chairs. She put her head in her hands and continued apologizing, trying to convey that it wasn't intentional, but she loved him and wasn't giving him up. With that, she ran to her room, packed a few things, and left the apartment. At the door, she turned back to me as I held Francine, sobbing in my arms, "I'll send my brother to pick up the rest of my stuff tomorrow."

I stayed with Francine for the night and gave her something to help her sleep. When she was out, I bought a complete change of clothes, including underwear, all within three blocks. Thank God for Manhattan! I called in sick to work the next day to be with her. I used the same computer to give Ken a synopsis of the unfolding drama.

I returned to work Wednesday morning as Francine had passed the crisis point. She held my arm on the threshold of her apartment as I was leaving, and I turned around.

"Nickie, thank you for being there; I wouldn't have made it these last two days without your help. Not only were you here for me, but you kept me from making things worse by hitting Lauren. Nothing good could have come of that. Mauro's behavior was equally bad; he should have at least ended things with me before jumping into bed with her."

"If he is so easily distracted, you might have dodged a bullet."

"Yeah, I thought about that last night. Anyway, I'll work hard to make the next marketing bonus. Then, we can go on a Caribbean trip to thank you for your support."

"You don't need to do that. That's what real friends are for. But I'd happily go on vacation with you next summer. We'll laugh at the whole thing while sipping rum and coke in the shade of an umbrella."

"I'll hold you to that!"

"You bet!"

I hugged her and walked out to the elevator. Though Francine seemed unsure, she still smiled.

"Through the Night"

Nickie

The phone rang, piercing the silence. I leaped to my feet and grabbed the receiver, pressing it to my ear.

"Hello?" I croaked, hoping it was him. A familiar voice greeted me, making me smile.

"Hi, it's me. How are you?" Ken asked, sounding nervous.

I tried to be casual, but I felt a rush of excitement. "I'm fine, how about you?" I said. He cleared his throat and said, "Listen, Nickie, I am around the corner. I asked the cab driver to stop at the phone booth to warn you."

I gasped, feeling a mix of shock and joy. My cheeks flushed, and my heart skipped a beat. "Sure, great … I am home."

He laughed and said, "I'm so happy to hear that. I love you so much. I'll be over in a few minutes. Bye for now."

I nodded, even though he couldn't see me. "Bye."

What a silly thing for me to say. Of course, I was home; I answered the phone, for God's sake! I meant to hang up softly, but the receiver slipped from my fingers and slammed to the floor. I winced at the noise and quickly picked it up. I should have been over the moon, but I stood there paralyzed, barely breathing and feeling my heart race like a runaway train.

I pushed the kitchen chair back and surveyed the room in a strange fog. It was neat. I glanced toward the living room and saw that all was in order. I ran in and turned on one lamp. Simultaneously hot and cold, my body and mind were in shock, but I was moving. The day before, I had cleaned the place, thinking it was for exercise. Ken wouldn't come, just like the last time he had to care for his daughters when his ex-wife fell ill. My disappointment lasted for days afterward. Two nights ago, he left me a phone message telling me he would be out of touch during an intense new IT system training at his company's headquarters in Boston. The best part was that he successfully exchanged the purchased tickets before losing his old job, to take the extended long weekend visit he had promised me. This time, I prepared myself, not believing he would come, despite being ready, looking fresh and casual in a brand-new outfit. It was Saturday evening, and I had returned from 5 p.m. Mass an hour ago.

The doorbell rang, and my heart jumped; Ken was here! *Lord, what do I do? Should I run to the door? Why are my legs not moving? Why am I looking at this door and doing nothing?*

Ding dong! I came out of my daze and walked toward the front door. Ken was standing there, smiling. He was wearing a light jacket but too heavy for our current NY temperatures, doubtless perfect for Minneapolis. His soft reddish-brown hair brushed his collar, his eyes were smiling shyly, and I noticed a fine mist hugging the air above him. I hadn't realized it had drizzled. Again, I marveled at how wide he was, his shoulders filling the entire door frame so I could not see behind him. His five feet ten inches frame and handsome, kind face were the only things preventing his powerful physique from being intimidating. I smiled, invited him in, and closed the door as I heard the faint but approaching sound of my next-door neighbor's voice.

"How was your flight?" I led the way from the small foyer into the living room; instead of answering, he grabbed my arm and slowly turned me around to face him.

"Nickie, I can't believe I am here with you..." he said.

"Nor can I believe I am looking at you. You are here, and I am not dreaming," I said.

I didn't finish my sentence as he pulled me in his arms, and everything that wasn't him fell into oblivion. His lips were soft, warm, and yielding; mine were passionate and impatient. It felt as if the deepest recesses of my heart had opened to welcome him in. I breathed the light scent of his hair, savored the heat of his lips enfolded in his arms, and relished his quick breath's caress. His fingertips on my sleeveless arms thrilled me; they were both eager and hesitant. My arms came up to circle his neck, and I heard a soft sound escape from one of us; he lifted me effortlessly and moved towards the couch; my lips left him long enough to say, "No, bedroom, hallway." He turned around without ever letting go of me, somehow entered the bedroom, and put me gently on the bed.

My eyes were closed, and when ten seconds elapsed, and he wasn't in my arms again, I looked. He had removed his jacket and a heavy sweater, leaving my eyes to feast on his broad chest, seductively clothed in a tight white undershirt. I rose to a seating position and gently touched his shoulder as his face broke into a smile. I reclined once again and brought him with me; his eyes never strayed from my face as if he was looking and committing every detail to memory, even though the only illumination in the room was the faint glow of a night light. My right hand slipped into the soft hair; soon, my fingers traced the contour of his jawline, the gentle curves of his lips moving up to the tip of his nose.

"How I have dreamed of your lips," he said, once again touching mine.

Unlike a moment ago, the kisses now were soft and fluttering on my lips, cheeks, nose, eyes, and forehead. It had taken great willpower for my body to understand the steps of this slow dance we were engaged in when I heard a moan escape my lips, and a second later, his lips joined mine again, but with a passion and insistence that would have surprised me, had I not responded in kind. Our hands and arms were everywhere, pulling at t-shirts, unbuckling belts, and ripping out my panties. I resented even the fewest seconds of separation when he would pull away to remove an article of clothing. During one of those moments, I reached into the nightstand and pushed a condom into his hands.

Ken

Watching Nickie sleep, feeling her rhythmic breath and pressure, I couldn't help but thank God for blessing me. *I love her.*

Last night was beautiful; my resolve almost faltered when she molded herself to me, insisting she could no longer wait. Despite her pleading, I scooped her up and sat her on the dresser. The moments flew by until her breath and soft cries became indistinguishable, and I felt the tensing and the push of her thighs around my head for the second time. Her body trembled; she moaned, pulled my hair as I supped until she leaned back, her arms barely supporting her weight. I carried her to the bed. She tore at my t-shirt as I removed my last restraints. I moved between her beautiful legs, my chest along her belly across her chest, and as our lips met, we joined. Through the night, side by side, the last eruption came, and she inhaled in quick gasps, our hearts pounding as drums, the bed stripped bare from our love. She used my arm as a pillow, and I kissed her neck.

She was a small package with a slender body that I could have easily lifted with one arm. I didn't realize how petite she was, perched on my lap that afternoon in the park in Milwaukee, a memory imbued with two hours of intoxicating kissing. She was full of passion and a surprising sexual delight. Last night, we were two bodies with one soul, and our union was as potent as the connection of our hearts; I was so moved that I wanted to cry.

Nickie

Smiling, though a little disappointed not to find Ken next to me, I slid into the space indentation on the mattress, still warm with the heat of his body and the faint smell of Dune. I noticed a soft noise before realizing it was coming from the shower. Fully awake now, I wondered why Ken was up so early and then picked up his watch on the bedside table. Wow, it was already 11:00 a.m., and the shadows in the room were only the result of the closed curtains.

Taking a few steps toward the door, I paused, realizing I was stark naked. Blushing, I burst out laughing, feeling self-conscious as last night's events started replaying in my mind. I quickly picked a robe from my closet and ventured to the bathroom. The shower had stopped, and the bathroom door opened as I paused for a knock. Ken stood with a towel around his waist, water droplets sliding down his hair.

What a sight for sore eyes! An impish smile lit up his face as he caught my embarrassment at the apparent desire in my eyes:

"Good morning, sleepyhead," he said. "I wanted to give you a few more moments of rest while I showered because I don't want you overtired for our road trip."

I could not remember telling him about booking two days at a B&B two and a half hours from the city. I must have blurted it out as we crashed and fell into a deep sleep, exhausted from our nighttime revelries. I blushed again at that thought, and knew he felt my embarrassment as my eyes quickly lowered to his neck. His large hands cupped my face, and he kissed me sweetly.

"Breakfast will be ready once Milady is bathed." I opened my mouth to protest that I was the hostess. Still, another kiss sealed my protest. "Go on now; it's nearly eleven-thirty, and I don't want to lose another minute starting our adventure!"

Breakfast was delicious: eggs Benedict, toast with French marmalade with which I occasionally spoiled myself, a small glass of apple juice, and a robust and delightful cup of coffee. He had a steaming cup of tea for my coffee; I was glad I had purchased tea should he still adhere to his childhood British sensibilities. Ken had had no issues making himself at home in the kitchen. The only misstep was the milk in my coffee, but I drank and enjoyed it as I didn't have the heart to tell him I took my coffee black, and frankly, anything he did was perfect in my eyes.

I handed him the keys when we got to my car.

"You are the designated driver; I'll be the navigator."

Raising an eyebrow and a corner of his lips, he said,

"It's a good thing I like to drive, and of course, your wish is my command!"

We arrived at the B&B three hours later, and they assigned us to our cabin. We unpacked our weekender, where we had crammed our stuff, primarily toiletries, for the next two days. Our stay was all-inclusive, but if we preferred, dining options were just a short distance from our secluded locale. They served breakfast in the main house's dining room, and delivery to the cabin was workable when requested before 11 a.m.

We were still full from breakfast and skipped lunch, opting for dinner later. We busied ourselves by exploring the beautiful grounds. We found a lovely garden, a pond, and a forest of Coastal oak-holly. Fortunately, the air was cool but not cold. We stumbled upon a larger cabin labeled "Fitness Center" with some gym equipment for the guests. Inside was an array of treadmills, weights, and bikes. The cabin was empty, and Ken had fun pretending to be a bodybuilder: flexing his muscles, making funny faces, and giving a mock speech about winning the "World's Greatest Bodybuilder Award." We were both cracking up, grateful that none of the other guests were interested in a workout.

Dinner was at the lighthouse near the beach. We admired God's handy work. There wasn't a cloud in the night sky, and there were more stars than we could count in three lifetimes, though we made a bold start. He seemed impatient to get to the cabin, and I was eager to relieve him of his confining clothes to fill my arms with him.

A covered basket awaited us in front of the door. Ken picked it up, and we went inside. A card under the white napkin cover said, "With our compliments, The Management." This card accompanied a bottle of champagne, two crystal glasses, two bottles of Perrier Spring water, an assortment of cheese and crackers, and two small dishes of warm crème brûlée. "Wow! I said; they must think everyone here is on a honeymoon or trying to make it impossible not to return." "Or both," said Ken. He pulled me gently in his arms and gave me a sweet kiss. "While Milady is getting ready for bed, I'll pour us a glass of bubbly."

I quickly showered and donned my "special "nightgown and robe ensemble. One of my nighttime routines was to slather my skin with a lightly scented, rich body cream. Of course, I ensured I finished the ritual by dabbing a drop of *"Arpege"* in all the strategic places like ears, neck, navel, knees, buttocks, and ankles. Ready, I squeezed open the door and told Ken he could now have the bathroom, but I wanted him to come to the door and keep his eyes closed until I sat at our small table, where he set our "complimentary gifts" from the kitchen's B&B.

"Can I have one little peek?" he asked.

"No, not even one. I need your promise. I don't want to spoil the surprise." I pouted.

"Okay, okay, you twisted my arm, but you have my word, not a peek!"

Twenty minutes later, Ken exited the bathroom door, and for the third time in two days, I felt my heart skip a beat and a quick, warm flush at the sight of his magnificent body. His hair looked slightly damp, although I had heard the buzz of the hairdryer a few minutes ago. The skin on his face was bare and soft, and I realized he must have used the time to shave rather than fully dry his hair. His well-defined chest was naked, and his six-packs were competing for my attention over the cobalt blue pair of silk pajama pants draped around his hips and legs. He was flashing his too-endearing smile, walking toward me.

"If you aren't a sight for sore eyes, I don't know what is," I said.

"My thoughts exactly, looking at you," he said.

He hugged me and gently pulled me back, untying the small lace bow at the top of my robe; it fell straight to the floor. He took my hand and helped me step around the small pile. Still holding my hand, he slowly turned me around, and when I was again facing him, he drew me into his arms and murmured in my ears,

"Nickie, I love you so much. You are beautiful, and I will never forget this emerald-green vision!"

His lips were coursing my neck, trailing after his hand as he slowly brushed the straps from my shoulders, and through the slight barrier of our silk nightwear, I could feel the fast beating of our hearts and his hardness pressed against me.

I don't know how, but I pulled away from his tight embrace. I was so emotionally overwrought that I did not trust myself to speak.

Still, I heard myself whisper, "And what elixir has my knight prepared for his lady? Surely, he would not let her thirst in his presence?"

His lips curled up again, saying, "Not if he can help it."

In one fell swoop, Ken bent quickly and carried me to the bed with his arms under my knees and shoulders, propping me up against the pillows. He was back at the small table in two strides and picked up a tray containing a small dish of crème brûlée, a napkin holding two small spoons, and two full glasses of champagne. He settled himself precariously next to me, and I relieved him of the tray.

"Allow me," I said as I spoon-fed him a teaspoon of crème brûlée.

I then fed myself one, and we both exclaimed, "Mum, this is delicious!" almost simultaneously.

I held the glass of champagne to his lips; he drank a long sip, staring at me with an inscrutable expression. He placed his right hand over mine, holding the glass stem, and inquired with a raised eyebrow:

"Has Milady taken over said Knight's duties?"

"No, I answered, but her Ladyship prefers to drink straight from thy lips!"

He said nothing and moved the small tray from our down comforter to the nightstand. He pulled me into his embrace, and nothing moved for at least one minute. My head rested on his shoulder, but I slowly moved, turned around, and kissed his lips.

"I love you," I said.

"And I love you beyond reason," he said as his lips responded to mine.

I closed my eyes and could feel his hands on my body like they felt on my thighs in Milwaukee. I kissed his face, little kisses on his forehead, eyes, nose, lips, and cheeks. I nibbled on his earlobe, down his neck, down his chest, teased his nipples with my tongue, slid my tongue to his navel, and let it linger there a little while. I let my lips go back up to his shoulders and, with a slight pressure there, turned him around and started on the back of his neck, nibbled longer on his ears, back to his nape, little kisses on his back, used my tongue to trace his spine down to his buttocks where I nibbled again inflicting little bites and kisses.

I turned him around, started at his navel again, continued down his thighs, nibbled on his pubic hair, and lightly tasted him. I started with very tiny licks and kisses. I slowly worked my way from the base of his penis to the top and finally took him into my mouth until there was no more to handle. I withdrew my lips while applying firm pressure and keeping a solid grip; I reached the tip and started over again. I was tasting the moisture from him, and it was delightful.

"I love you, I love you, I love you," he kept repeating,

"I love you too," I responded. As I started the process a third time, I heard him say haltingly.

"Nickie, I can't; you are driving me mad."

His hands encircled my waist, pulling me to him until I lay entirely on him. He then rolled with me until he was lying on top of me. I felt his hard body against mine, but he pulled up his chest slowly and started kissing my forehead, eyes, nose, lips, cheeks, and ears. His tongue explored my mouth as if it was the last thing left to taste on this earth; I slowly moved my body, showing that I wanted him within me, and he obliged. We started slowly, rocking, and the pace gradually picked up. We were now on our sides, and he was caressing my thighs and waist and cupping my small breasts while murmuring "I love you" incessantly. There were no words to describe how good he felt inside me, and I hoped it would never end. My words became incoherent: love, intermingled with hard, strong, and more. We were now in a frenzy. He held my shoulders, and I grabbed his buttocks, pulling him into me. And then, out of nowhere, we felt it coming; this incredible, extraordinary wave of fire and sensations overtook us, and we held each other as if our lives depended on it and screamed each other's name as we went over the peak of our passion. We held on to each other until our bodies quieted down and the spasms subsided, and then we slept blissfully to the morning light.

Ken

My momentary confusion as I tried to place the décor evaporated when a warm body moved against me. I was the happiest man on earth!

"Good morning to you! Pray, tell the reason for your smile," Nickie said.

"Good morning, my love; waking up next to you is why I smile."

"Did you sleep well?" I asked.

"It's impossible not to when I slept in your arms all night. I love you."

She raised her head from my shoulder and gently kissed my neck. My desire was apparent as I pressed against her, but she chided me.

"Let's not get any ideas; remember our plans." Sighing, we disentangled from each other and headed for the bathroom.

"You first," Nickie said. "If we go in the shower together, I can't guarantee I'll be able to keep myself from ravishing you."

"If I promise not to resist, will you please ravish me?"

"Naughty boy, go on now; we have a full day of activities ahead of us."

Nickie

We left the cabin forty-five minutes later, donning jeans, light sweaters, and hiking boots. It was only 9:30 a.m., so we stopped at the main dining room for breakfast. The room was bright and spacious, with large windows overlooking the grounds and the lake. Two other couples also had breakfast and acknowledged us with quick nods and smiles. We both had butter croissants, a handful of grapes, and a glass of orange juice. I chose a strong cup of coffee, and Ken opted for a hot cup of Earl Grey tea. Armed with a colorful hiking trail map, we stepped out into the day and headed to the tourist village. The ground was dry, the path well-kept, and the air was fresh. We walked along the lake, admiring the reflections of the trees and the sky on the water. A slight breeze whistled through the branches. We felt relaxed and happy, lost in the beauty of the ordinary, enjoying the scenery and each other's company.

We held a brisk pace and arrived almost precisely two hours later. They decorated the setting beautifully, reminding us of those old postcards, which was the intent. We strolled through the village, looking, touching, and commenting. Ken purchased souvenirs for his daughters, and I bought a village replica of an old-fashioned snow globe.

We continued around the place, dodging in and out of festive shops. We found an empty playground and spent at least a half-hour giggling while flying on the swings and going down the slides. I could not remember the last time my heart was so full of joy, love, and playfulness. Exhausted, we found a line forming at a small café/pastry shop and investigated. We waited ten minutes, but the large slice of pumpkin pie and the steaming cups of green tea were worth it. Stomach and hearts satiated, we started our trek back again, keeping a reasonably brisk pace on the trail. We packed our weekender at the cabin, freshened up, and headed for the dining room. We had an early light dinner; I had a citrus shrimp and avocado salad while Ken chose the spinach and avocado. We followed that with a bowl of Manhattan clam chowder and a soft roll. Everything was delicious, so we had no issue skipping dessert. We savored our second cup of tea while holding hands on the table and gazing at the dining room fireplace with the soft sound of very mellow music coming through the surround sound speakers.

We decided to head back after our afternoon meal and go home early in the evening instead of staying overnight.

"I want to look around to ensure we are not forgetting anything."

"I'll go to the office while you do that. I lost the brochure I picked up this morning, and I want something to remember about this place."

"I'll be here," I said with a broad smile.

He was back a few minutes later with his booklet and a smile. He joined me on the edge of the bed where I was sitting, staring at the fireplace, pulled me close, and sweetly kissed my lips; I rested my head in the crook of his shoulder, my hand resting on his chest, eyes closed, enfolded in the warmth of his embrace, never parting. We spoke no words; none were necessary, sharing our softest, tenderest moment since we first reunited. When I finally opened my eyes to look at him, tucking a beautiful brown curl around his ear, he was again looking at me in this profoundly mysterious way.

"Thank you, my love; you have given me the most wonderful and happy time of my life. I feel more joy than I can ever express or explain."

"The feeling is mutual," I answered, above a whisper.

The desk clerk told Ken we could leave our keys in the room. We put the weekender in the car and said goodbye to our little paradise. Ken drove again, and I was in the passenger seat with the map, barely paying attention. His memory was exceptional, and the trip was quick.

"So, how's Craig doing? You mentioned that he's quite the artist."

"Yes, he's talented. He completed a new piece that he's incredibly proud of. Did I tell you he's been dating this wonderful girl named Hyuen? I think you'd like her."

"That's great. I'm glad he's doing well. It's always nice when our kids are happy.

Speaking of which, I've been feeling down. I miss having my girls and hearing their giggles and voices fill the house daily."

"I can imagine how tough that must be. Claire is the youngest, right? Seven-year-old, she's quite a character, isn't she?"

"Oh. Claire is something else. She's so willful and unconventional. It's challenging to keep up with her, but I wouldn't change a thing."

"She keeps you on your toes. But it must be beautiful to see her growing into her person."

"Out of nowhere, she asked me when we were getting married and if she could visit New York. Then Chelsea asked if you were pretty and if we would have more children. Chelsea is dead set on a baby brother."

"Children say the darndest things. Honest and direct. You have to give them that. How did you answer them?"

"I told Claire that we were still figuring things out. As for visiting New York, we'll plan something special for her. I told Chelsea we are satisfied with our number of children, but the future is unpredictable."

"Did Camille say anything at all?"

"Oh yes. She said I seemed the happiest she had seen me in as long as she could remember. She also asked if she could live with us if we got married. I said we were proceeding slowly. But we will discuss everything as a family if the time comes.

"And she's right. I have been happy. But that hasn't always been the case with me. I've had bouts of depression in the past, but I'm working on it and trying to focus on the positive things in life, like meeting you."

"Sorry you've been struggling, but I'm glad you're taking steps to address it. Remember, you're not alone. You have caring and supportive people by your side."

"Thanks, I appreciate that."

We were quiet, concentrating on the road signs because Ken thought he might have taken the wrong exit.

"Hey, despite the traffic, we got home in two and a half hours. That's better than the three hours it took before!" Ken exclaimed.

"We got lucky with the timing. I am glad we talked, though. I feel like I know your girls better."

"It's nice to have someone to talk to. Thanks for being there and for listening."

"Anytime, sweetie. I am here for you." I realized what I had called him and felt self-conscious.

We were one block from home, but he turned his eyes from the road to smile at me for a second. He then pulled into a parking spot, and before I could ask him why, he unbuckled his seatbelt, leaned over my seat, and kissed me.

"Are you hungry?" I asked.

"I could have something light, but not a meal."

"Same here. Let's order from the Chinese takeout place. What do you think?"

"Sounds good. How about some sweet and sour soup with noodles and two egg rolls?"

"Perfect."

The food arrived in ten minutes as we were setting the kitchen table.

His plane was to depart at noon, and I decided I would call in sick tomorrow to drive him to the airport. We wanted to be together as long as possible; having him sit for an hour alone in a cab to the airport was unacceptable.

After dinner, we cuddled on the couch and watched *The Fifth Element*. I remember he once mentioned it to be his favorite movie. I nested on his side as he played with the wisps of my hair. I found him staring happily at me more than once. After the movie, Ken carried me to bed (which had become a pattern) and gently undressed me; when done, he took a moment to do the same, leaving on his briefs and undershirt. He then removed a small container of jasmine-scented oil from his carry-on and began the slowest, most enjoyable, relaxing massage I had ever had. I felt like I had died and gone to heaven. I felt sensuously delighted and relaxed; the bed had become this airy, soft cloud I was floating on. It was a testament to his skill that I fell asleep, as my consciousness did not return until the very early morning hours of the following day.

As it had become our habit, he enfolded me in his arms with my head resting on his shoulder while I slept. Though awake, my consciousness was slow to return fully. My body, particularly my right hand, slowly slid against his thigh and gently explored his intimate part, electrifying him.

I heard him murmur against my ear, "You are awake; I love you."

"Hmm," I replied.

Lovemaking was slow, unhurried, and tender; neither wanted it to end, and we slowly rocked ourselves as if hoping this pace would lengthen our synchronized dance. The warm heat that engulfed our beings surprised us as I felt rocked by one, then two, then three waves of indescribable pleasure coursing through my body;

I could feel every spasm gripping him. I heard the strangled, guttural sound of his breath in my ear.

We got into the shower together, spending a couple of minutes just letting the warm water cascade over our bodies, hugging. Then we lathered, shampooed each other's hair, and shared a few indulgent moments as he worked conditioner through my natural curls. It was probably more enjoyable than the shaving lesson I'd requested earlier.

Ken stepped out of the tub first and quickly dried himself; he then turned around and handed me a towel for my hair.

"Here you go, Love."

"Thanks, Sweetie."

Without a word, he grabbed another one, wrapped it around me, and lifted me off my feet.

"What are you doing? I said, surprised. "You are making me feel like an invalid!"

He grinned and gently stood me up in the bedroom, opened the middle dresser door, removed my favorite body cream, and stroked every inch of me in the frothy lotion without a word.

"I don't remember agreeing to this."

"Shuhhh....... don't interrupt a chef concentrating in his kitchen."

I giggled and attempted to dry off my hair but had to stop when he would interrupt his ministrations to kiss and suck playfully on my now perky nipples. I thought we satiated our bodies from our early morning activities. Still, the warm current cursing from my nipples to my vagina and the visual hardness of his manhood arguably proved me wrong. I closed my eyes and thought: *God, I could get used to this*; the intimacy was effortless! Good sense prevailed as I, with both hands, gently turned his face from my nipples and said,

"Dearest, I don't think this would be the wisest choice now unless you can call the pilot and ask him to stay grounded; you may miss your flight."

"You are right, but so you know, we will need to have a bonus lovemaking session at our next meeting," he replied with a grin.

"I'll hold you to it," I quipped, smiling.

We dressed, and I spent fifteen minutes blowing out my hair and giving it a few soft curls. We each had a bowl of cereal with strawberries and sliced bananas and made two cups of tea in covered containers to drink in the car. I was anxious that we wouldn't arrive on time, but luckily, traffic was light, and we made it to JFK with ten minutes to spare. We got out of the car for a last long hug and a kiss that only ended when an attendant cleared his throat to ask us to move the vehicle from the drop-off zone or get a ticket.

Ken kissed me once more and murmured, "I'll call or e-mail as soon as I get home from the airport. I love you."

"I love you more!" I replied in a choked voice.

I got into the car, pulled away, and caught a look of pure misery on Ken's face as he stood on the sidewalk, his carry-on forgotten by his side, waving goodbye. A tear went down my cheek, and I hoped Ken did not see it.

The following day, I walked into work with what I was sure was a lackluster attitude. I passed through the central accounting office where a clerk was at her desk, shuffling two piles of papers next to a heavy-duty hole puncher and a waiting three-ring binder. I wondered if they were copies of the month's preliminary General Ledger. As I made my way to my office, I realized the indifference accompanying that thought. Even my favorite receptionist's bright "Good morning" could not lift my mood. I gave her a small smile and proceeded to my office. I got in, dropped my laptop on the desk, locked the door, and sat there with my eyes closed.

After saying goodbye to Ken yesterday, I changed into sweats and headed to the park. I walked for a while and then sat on a bench, reliving every moment of our weekend; the pain of his absence felt almost physical.

Subj: *You*
Date: 7/1/98 04:53:20 PM EDT

Dearest Nickie,

I love you; I love you; I loooooove you! I arrived safely. I am heading to the office; some servers came down overnight. A few messages on my answering machine asked for my immediate help. The thought of you haunts me every minute, everywhere I go, and in every way. I LOVE YOU, and I miss you so much already!

Till then, Love,
Ken

I finished the pizza, brushed my teeth, and went to bed at 6:30 p.m. I turned on the news but fell asleep quickly because of the weekend's activities and the two-hour afternoon walk. I woke at 4:30 this morning feeling exhausted from a long but fitful sleep. I was almost as tired now as when I went to bed. *Lord, I miss him so!*

My respite lasted only fifteen minutes. Soon, there was a knock on my office door, and I had no choice but to open it.

"Ah, Lu-Jay! Come on in."

"Good morning, Ma'am. Here are the updates for the retirement move project."

"Lu-Jay, have a seat, please."

I took a few minutes to peruse the report.

"This is a quick review, but I can already see it's excellent work. You've done a thorough job on this. I appreciate your effort."

"Thank you, Ma'am. I tried to cover all the necessary details".

"Well, you've certainly succeeded. I'll study this further and make sure every-thing is in order. If any changes are needed, I'll let you know."

"In case you require additional information. I kept my notes."

"Perfect. Keep up the good work."

"Thank you, Ma'am."

I noticed the blinking message light on my desk phone as he exited. I picked up the receiver to see if it was from my boss; the recording told me I had twelve waiting messages.

The rest of the day was a blur of returned calls, two unnecessary meetings, and only one helpful conference call with the owner and our company banker. The whole place annoyed me. I tried sending a brief note to Ken during a twenty-minute lunch break, but the secretary came to my office door asking about a report she was collating. I usually saved the email draft when people walked in, but my phone rang simultaneously. Once the smoke cleared, AOL timed out and automatically logged me off, and I lost my letter. Each time I took a day off, I returned to tons of aggravation; it seemed few people could think for themselves!

At 5:30 p.m., I packed my laptop, grabbed my jacket, and left the office. I caught the number six train at Grand Central, changed for the F at 53rd St, and made it to Queens in no time. I even found a seat. As luck would have it, a bus pulled in as I exited the subway station. When I logged on at home, Ken's quick note indicated he had just worked almost twenty-four hours straight. He would nap and write more later.

"Lunch Is Not the Problem"

Ken

I woke up at four the following day and felt better, although I could have slept for five or six hours more. I panicked as soon as I remembered I had promised Nickie to write or chat the previous night, but exhaustion had gotten the best of me.

I couldn't believe the mess I had found at home. Michelle and Tim allowed Sara, Michelle's sister, and her boyfriend, Taylor, to move into the house and sleep in my bedroom!

I was so tired when I returned from work that I could barely stay awake. I sent Nickie a quick note, made a strong cup of tea, and was on my way again. Sara and Taylor had slept on the living room sofas last night, but I knew there was no room for them to stick around, especially when my daughters would come over. I gave them a ride to a motel near Taylor's work and handed them the last two hundred dollars remaining in my wallet from the trip. Getting home again, I slept like a rock.

It was 4:45 a.m., and I could relax by starting my drive to work. With that came the immeasurable loneliness and longing of not having Nickie next to me. My mind replayed the beautiful moments of our weekend together. My heart was overflowing. It was simply not possible to love someone so much.

Subj: *Good morning*
Date: 7/05/98 10:33:01 AM EDT

Dearest Nickie,

Good morning, my love. I am sorry I did not write last night. I will explain later. I miss you terribly.

This morning, though, I daydreamed of you as I always do on my way to work, but my dreams were different. I remember enjoying the feel of your shoulders and the play of light on your face. As you slept, I rested my chin on your shoulder and rolled my head to kiss your cheek and neck. Meanwhile, I gently caressed your bottom, breathing deeply and smiling. I bent over you for no apparent reason, still sleeping, with a contented smile on your face, and kissed your buttocks. I toyed with giving you a hickey there. I remembered thinking, just in case you didn't get your butt kissed at work, at least I could kiss it at home.

Had anyone asked me a week ago, I would have said I could not love you more, but now that our minds, hearts, and bodies have united, every moment without your presence is torture!

You looked so restful sleeping there. I did not have the heart to wake you before leaving. I hope you have a wonderful day. I love you. I will talk to you later.

Till then beloved
Ken

Nickie

Not hearing from him last night disappointed me, but his note this morning fixed that, so I was in a fantastic mood all day at work. It didn't matter why he could not write. He said he would tell me later.

After dinner and reading the snail mail, I reached for the phone receiver and dialed. A woman's voice picked up on the third ring.

"Good evening, Montauk B&B; how may I direct your call?"

"Hello, my name is Nickie G. I am calling about my credit card bill. I didn't see any charges from you for the weekend I booked two weeks ago. I was informed that the charge would go through as soon as I checked in. Can you please help me with that?"

"Our billing staff has left for the day, but I can check that for you. Give me a minute, please…. Ah, it seems your fiancé, Ken, paid the bill in cash and asked us to reverse your credit card charges."

"Really? Ken paid in cash? That's unexpected."

"He came in person right before you checked out and paid the bill in cash."

"Oh, I see. That's quite thoughtful of him. Thank you for letting me know."

"You're welcome! If you have questions, please get in touch with us. Have a great evening!"

"Thank you. Same to you."

Although the gesture was very nice, I had everything covered. I paid in advance, so Ken could not do so. I knew he made decent money as an IT person, but paying child support for three children must not be a walk in the park, and he should use his money constructively, not toward romantic weekend getaways.

When he came online fifteen minutes later, my heart fluttered as usual, and nothing else mattered other than telling him how much I loved and missed him.

Ken

I smiled as I noticed Nickie waiting for me in the chat window. Of course, it wasn't as gratifying as leaning over and pulling her into my arms, but it was the next best thing. I picked up the phone and tried to surprise her with a call, but my regular line was dead. It didn't spoil my mood. I just hung up and went to the computer. I'm glad I had US WEST install that dedicated T1 line for computer use. I hoped Nickie wouldn't ask me about the cause of all the delays and issues I had at home.

We spent the next hour in a blissful chat and did a poor job of pulling each other away to go to bed. The following two evenings were the same. The third evening started the same, but Nickie brought up the skipped chat two nights ago, admonishing me for overworking and burning myself out. I had to be honest with her and tell her that it was not just work but also my home situation with Tim and

Michelle. She listened to me patiently and then told me she felt they had crossed a line as uninvited guests.

She wrote: "I once heard an old Yiddish proverb, and I believe it should be taught to all children to encourage self-sufficiency in adulthood. It said: If you ever need a helping hand, you'll find one at the end of your arm."

"I heard that one too. But did you know that the helping hand at the end of your arm is not for you? It's to help others. It's like the Christian Golden Rule: 'Do unto others as you would have them do unto you.' Life would be balanced if we practiced either rule as intended. I am fond of "We are one.""

It took Nickie a minute to type. "Kindness is important, but so is self-reliance. We need to help ourselves before we can help others. Self-reliance builds confidence, self-esteem, and empowerment. It also helps us cope with failures and challenges. Power and control are lost when we depend on others to solve our problems. We may become bitter, entitled, and dissatisfied. We are enabled by others but empowered by ourselves. It's like the story of the butterfly during metamorphosis: if we cut away the cocoon to 'help' it get 'free,' the butterfly will never fly. The struggle to get out of the cocoon pushes the fluid out of its body and into its wings. Without it, it's impaired for life."

I saw some truth in what Nickie was saying. I marveled again at how we had the same end but different methods. I thought we complemented each other well.

Nickie

These people were ungrateful freeloaders. If their father kicked them out, no one should expect more from him. Despite what I said to Ken, part of me admired his patience, tolerance, and kindness, and though I believed in the soundness of what I said to him, I also wondered if, somehow, I had become a so-called jaded New Yorker. Our chat soon reverted to our playful banter as we tried to determine when our next meeting would be and if we would lose our minds before holding each other again.

Chat 11—7/6/98

NC: When we meet again, tell me all your fantasies.

DK: You owe me 4.

NC: I told you I am shy about that

DK: Most of the time, I play the priest. I am a good listener.

Besides, it feeds my fantasies

Tonight, I will kiss you as you haven't been kissed before

NC: and I'll do the same for you

DK: I love you. Let me know where you want my tongue, and it will be there.

NC: You don't know what you just did to me.

DK: Maybe I do

I will wait for you to tell me. For now, I will lick you everywhere and spend more time there than on the rest of you

NC: So, then you know where I want your tongue

DK: I will kiss you deeply. Good night, beloved

NC: Good night, my love

Subj: ***Good morning, dearest***
Date: 7/7/ 98 10:33:01 AM EDT

Dearest Ken,

I slept well last night in your arms, and someday, I'll demonstrate the night's lovemaking session again. Doing it will be more pleasurable than the virtual sex we had.

I am constantly aching for you and your touch (maybe that's why I am so short-tempered at work today). I tried to save last night's chat but can't open the file, not even in Word. If I succeed, I'll send you a copy through e-mail. The thought of you is helping with a most stressful day at work.

I love you, and I miss you. I don't know what I am doing at this keyboard rather than being in your arms. That's all I ever want to do now.

Till then,
Nickie

Subj: ***Thinking of you***
Date: 7/7/98 3:17:42 PM EDT

Dearest Nickie,

I am sorry your day is so hectic. I wish I were there to give you a massage tonight (and that hickey I neglected to provide you with this morning; every time you sat down, you would remember last night).

I have received 130 calls today and lost three letters. I know how infuriating it can be. The main problem is when I struggle to find the perfect wording for a paragraph and write several sections afterward. If I lose it, I remember the gist, but that oomph feeling I got from the one that was just right is gone.

What did you do for lunch? The thought of tasting you sidetracked me, and it's a good thing I am wearing dark pants. I love you.

Till then beloved
Ken

Subj: ***Bedtime***
Date: 7/7/98

Dearest Ken,

I was hoping to see you log on. It's now 11. While waiting, I made sexy videos to send you. (Walking down an imaginary catwalk, wearing satin underwear).

At least I now know how to make a video on the machine. I need to read up on the file compression issue. Sleep well, dearest. It doesn't feel good going to bed without talking to you. I wish I could beep you on the computer. I love you.

Till then,
Nickie

Subj: ***Trying to get this letter out.***
Date: 7/8/98 2:31:09 PM EDT

Dearest Nickie,

Good morning, my love. Laying here next to you, I remind myself how lucky I am to have found you. I missed talking with you last night. I logged on and sent a hello when I arrived home. I thought AOL would notify me when you came online. I went to lie down. The next thing I knew, it was 11 o'clock, and when I tried to access AOL, I received a message that you had gone to sleep. I am sorry I missed you.

Did you get all the fires put out yesterday? I received a couple of e-mails from you while composing this letter. I wish you had sent the pictures. It would have been a signif-icant inducement to hook up my printer.

Till then, love
Ken

Subj: ***Lunch???***
Date: 7/9/98 2:11:57 PM EDT

Dearest Nickie,

I have yet to hear from you today, and if you didn't take the PC home last night, I might be writing to the breeze. Or you are busier than a one-arm paper hanger in a room of fast-drying paste. You aren't taking care of yourself by eating so late, in which case, S L O W D O W N!! Whatever the fire is, it can wait; turn on some relaxing music, close your door, lean back, watch out the window, and have lunch. I love you.

Till then, love
Ken

Subj: ***Lunch is not the problem; I love you, maybe too much***
Date: 7/9/98

Dearest Ken,

I tried to contact you last night via instant messenger. Since you are not the only one ac-cessing your computer, someone may have intercepted them. (I remembered you have the girls on Wednesday, but I figured you would check later.)

I am frustrated. I have a lot of feelings FOR YOU that I don't know how to handle. We haven't been able to chat lately, and you only get maybe 1 out of every three e-mails I send. I knew the distance would be a problem, but I didn't expect so many obstacles.

You are doing your best through considerable expense to enable us to communicate. I also realize that you had a life before we met. I still wish we could occasionally have some uninterrupted quality time so the sadness doesn't take over. I had planned to discuss this with you in a chat since Monday, but I am now resorting to mail.

Chat 13—7/9/98

NC: Hello, Darling. Can you chat?

DK: For a few minutes, how are you? Did you get the e-mails from today?

NC: Yes. I have been writing to you for the last 1/2 hour. I need to talk to you.

DK: AOL canceled my internet subscription. It took almost an hour to re-establish my link

DK: I usually get a bell when you send. Now, there is no sound

it's frustrating. I don't know how to look at the screen.

NC: me neither. I have no bell.

DK: Wonder what's up? How was your day? I missed you.

NC: I missed you too. When may we chat?

DK: I have to give Sara a ride.

What are you doing now?

NC: When can we CHAT?

DK: I should be back in a couple of hours

What's up? You are uncharacteristically QUIET!

NC: No, I wrote many things to you; I don't think you'll be able to return on time, and I don't want to disrupt your life. I'll send you the e-mail

DK: Are you mad at me?

NC: not mad, but EXTREMELY FRUSTRATED

DK: Do you want me to stop writing to you?

Okay, got the message

NC: How would that solve my frustration?

I DON'T NEED LESS OF YOU; I NEED MORE!

Subj: *?*
Date: 7/9/98

Ken,

KEN, HOW CAN YOU LOG OFF ON ME LIKE THAT? I am trying to tell you it hurts me so much not to spend time with you, and you log off instant messenger, like slamming the door in my face. Words are cheap. What you did speaks for itself.

Nickie

"Mail in Cyberspace"

Subj: ***Misunderstanding????***
Date: 7/9/98 9:58:51 PM EDT

Dearest Nickie,

My instant messenger was on last night because I have it set to turn on automatically when I access the net to talk with you as much as possible. AOL canceled my Net connection. I fixed the problem and went to pick up the girls. I was anxious about the time, and when I knew it was coming up, I ran out the door and left for Maple Grove. I didn't check the computer. You said you didn't plan on bringing the laptop home because you knew I would be out with the girls. The sound wasn't working, so there was no ding to alert me that someone was trying to contact me. I only bought the thing to talk with you; it's not like I always sit in front of it. I do that all day at work.

I left abruptly, uncertain if you still wanted to talk to me. Your silence after my question hurt a lot.

I strive to help people, and have personal needs, including you. That's why I was only gone for 2 hours. We had to reach the motel before 6 PM, leaving little time for explanations. I hoped to have 3 hours to talk; 20 minutes vs. 3 hours - who is more important to me?

I don't understand women at times. Someone burned me before; I would rather be alone than go through it again. I still love you.

Just be,
Ken

Chat 14—7/9/98

DK: Yes

NC: I got your letter and was replying to it

I am sorry to have confused you

DK: oh

NC: I will send it, anyway... I have to learn not to be so intense.

DK: I still don't understand what I did

NC: You did nothing. What I was doing in my letter was sharing with you all the things that were going on inside me

DK: then why did I upset you?

NC: you only upset me this afternoon when you abruptly left the chat, I added that part to the e-mail.

DK: you didn't reply to my question. Silence is also an answer.

NC: What question?

Are we talking about the same thing?

DK: When I asked you if you wanted me to stop writing you

NC: yes, I answered you, but you left the chat before you got my answer

I save all our conversations, and I can send them to you if you want

DK: Sorry

NC: What I said was THAT I DID NOT NEED LESS BUT MORE OF YOU

DK: I thought you didn't want me to write to you anymore; that's why I said I understood your silence

NC: I was upset after that because I couldn't believe that you would not wait 2 seconds for me to type my answer

DK: I had to get my act together before I could go out and greet a house full of people looking to me for answers

NC: remember that the computer was strange, with no sound and slow

DK: yes, I am sorry my emotions got the better of me

NC: I LOVE YOU MORE THAN I CAN EXPRESS

And this is what is causing the problem

DK: I love you too! If you haven't noticed, I have tried to tell you.

NC: I have always had a problem with being too intense

that's why I try not to describe my feelings in too many details

DK: it helps in the business world, I suppose

NC: Because it's like opening the floodgates

And then I could scare someone away

so, I spent most of my adult life so far learning self- control

DK: I am a little impulsive

NC: I don't ever dare lose control

DK: but I mean, well

NC: I think I'll lose myself because I am so intense.

There is nothing wrong with being impulsive

it adds sparks to life

DK: maybe that is where you will find yourself

letting go a little

NC: I have let go with you of all my emotions and see all the problems they created

DK: I won't let you lose yourself, then I would be alone

NC: I will only be alone if you no longer want me

DK: you are always with me, sometimes embarrassingly so

NC: I can't get enough of you; that's my problem

I want to clarify something. In your letter, you mentioned having been burned in a previous relationship.

DK: Yes and...

NC: Hold on, please let me finish. I am Nickie, and I am NOW, not "Women you don't understand". I try my best to be clear. I will always tell you what's on my mind when it's important, how I feel and why, and NOT play guessing games, so chances are you WILL understand me. I would not confuse you with anyone else, do the same for me. In the letter, you were defensive, trying to pull back rather than being receptive to my feelings; plus, I had no way of knowing what was happening in your household, so leaving the chat so abruptly seemed rude.

DK: I am so sorry Nickie. I love you.

NC: I would like to ask a very personal question.

DK: yes

NC: you don't have to answer; it's none of my business. I am only curious.

DK: go-ahead

NC: What used to cause your ex-wife to be so mad at you?

DK: Most of the time, she was not mad at me (according to her). She was angry about how other people treated her or something at work, but as her husband, she felt it was my job to allow her to express her anger when she did not have a socially acceptable avenue of expression

NC: It's sad but true that we hurt the ones we love the most and only they can hurt us

I used to come home very stressed from work and yell at my son Craig for any minor little thing

DK: in fairness, I let her do it for a long time at first because I thought it was good for her to let the anger off and later because I felt I deserved it, so I am as much to blame as anyone

NC: You deserved it even if you had nothing to do with the cause?

DK: Now I wish I would have been able to think of a better way of letting her vent without the hitting

NC: she would hit you?

DK: it's a self-esteem thing after six years; mine was pretty low

NC: That is why people have to seek help as soon as a situation turns sour otherwise, it becomes very unhealthy for both parties

DK: We were married for 12 years; it didn't start the way it ended. First, you think you can control it or feel guilty immediately. It took almost four years before I started feeling guilty for things I hadn't done

NC: Did anyone ever suggest therapy?

DK: I suggested it the first time, but she convinced me we could work it out ourselves; after all, we were both intelligent

NC: intelligence sometimes goes out of the window when emotions walk through the door.

DK: I thought if I did more or were more understanding, it would be enough.

NC: We all make those mistakes in one area or another

DK: So, fair is fair. What happened between you and your ex-husband?

NC: I never talk about him much because I don't like him as a person

My only excuse for marrying him is that I was young and stupid, at 18 I thought he was handsome

NC: I wanted to know about sex, and all my girlfriends were getting married early in our college years.

Darling, I don't want to let you go, but it's your bedtime

DK: I love you and miss you already. Goodnight.

NC: I love you more. Good night

I wrote this before we started chatting again last night. I have not changed anything.

Subj: *Re: Misunderstanding????*
Date: 7/10/98

Dearest Ken,

I love you very much, and that may be the problem. I am frustrated because I can never tell you even one-tenth of what I want to say each time I get a chance to chat with you.

Don't get me wrong; you are doing nothing wrong, and I am sorry if it sounds like I am trying to consume you. I miss you so intensely that although we spend a fair amount of time chatting, it isn't enough. You are doing your best. I don't want to interfere with your life or friends, and I don't want to lose you or your love. You make me feel things I didn't think I could ever feel again, and I prevented myself from feeling for anyone for a long time.

I am sorry if I have been too demanding. If you find that my attitude exasperates you too often and I am too much trouble to deal with, and you would rather be by yourself, I'll understand that too and back off. I promise you I will only ask for what you can give. I understand your needs and circumstances are as important as mine. So, I'll curtail my constant chat requests. I love you, which is all that's important to me now.

Till then,
Nickie

Subj: *Good morning;*
Date 7/10/98 7:28:27 AM EDT

Dearest Nickie,

I wasn't mad but hurt. Thank you for the pictures; they mean a lot to me. I wanted to kiss you good morning. I love you. I hope your day is better today; at least you have a 3-day weekend.

Till then, love
Ken

P.S. I was glad we chatted too. I knew you were there when I logged on, but you said nothing. At first, I was a little nervous, like walking out on the ice of a winter's lake in late fall before winter set in. I am happy we talked. I miss you and think about you a lot, waking and sleeping. Your intensity doesn't scare me; as a matter of fact, it's heady to feel the strength of your love surrounding me. I didn't mean to sound defensive in my letter. Doubtless, it was an automatic reaction from past trauma, and I similarly feel powerless with our distance situation.

Last night, I dreamed we made love in the shower. I woke up in the middle of our passion. I was trying to stay asleep, finish our lovemaking, and get up all simultaneously (I fell out of bed).

Subj: ***Good morning***
Date: 7/10/98

Dearest Ken,

Good morning, dearest. I hope you didn't hurt yourself falling out of bed; you should have awakened me. Sleeping in your arms and feeling that you still love me was good. I love you so much.

This morning, the mail engine returned my video message. It said the file was too big. I was looking forward to your comments on my first "movie."

One of the many things I love about you is that you don't hide your emotions and tell me when you are sad, happy, or hurt. It's a very unusual trait to find in a man. It makes me feel all mushy inside, and I love you more. I'll try to have a good day and hope you do the same. Don't worry about the spelling mistakes; I have not even been running my spellchecker of late. I am only concerned with what you say. I thank God for finding you. I love you.

Till then,
Nickie

Subj: *Mail*

Date: 7/11/98 7:10:09 AM EDT

Dearest Nickie,

How was your walk? Again, there is a problem with the phone lines; I can't dial outside of the exchange (612). I can't call my girls; it's more frustrating than not having a phone.

We had violent electrical storms yesterday. I got in, but the driveway became im-passable at 3:30. Three large trees fell, and the driveway flooded north of the bridge. I had to exit the back way today. I will write more later.

Till then, love
Ken

Subj: *Mail in cyberspace*

Date: 7/11/98

Dearest Ken,

I am sorry for all the trouble you are having with the storms and trees. Here, we've had beautiful weather since last weekend.

Linda called me yesterday complaining about wasting her summer waiting for her boyfriend (James) to take a week off. I asked her to accompany me on a mini-getaway since I dislike vacationing alone. I suggested Quebec in Canada, and she liked that. I know James will be mad when she proposes going without him.

I need to plan an itinerary of places to visit for the next few weekends. A bed and breakfast on the Jersey Shore is appealing, but I'll be lonely without you. I miss you a lot. We need patience until this crazy technology works smoothly together.

Till then,
Nickie

Subj: **Good morning, my love**
Date: 7/12/98 8:37:02 AM EDT

Dearest Nickie,

I arrived home at about six from my day with the girls and spent a couple of hours fixing the bridge. Your friend's boyfriend sounds a little insecure. I envy your long weekend excursions. Take lots of pictures.

We have several B&Bs around here, most are in towns with historical landmarks. This fall, we could try a weekend. There are a lot of sugar maple trees; the leaves turn such gorgeous colors in the fall, and there is a walking path that passes a small waterfall in the woods that is quite beautiful around sunset.

Till then, love,
Ken

Subj: **Re: Good morning, my love**
Date: 7/12/98

Dearest Ken,

I am glad you received at least one of my emails. Yesterday, Craig called and invited me to go with him and Hyeun (his girlfriend) to the Bronx Zoo or the Statue of Liberty

Are the weekends slower at work? Are you still following your exercise routine? Please eat well so my physical demands won't wear you out. I am now convinced to give you the job of applying lotion to my body permanently. I asked the orthodontist how much longer I would have to wear my braces, and he said that if I kept wearing the rubber bands regularly, it would only be six months.

The place you described in Bayport sounds terrific. Let's keep it on our radar for the future. I am going to treat myself to breakfast. Hearing from you put me in a better frame of mind. It scares me how much I love you.

Till then,
Nickie

Subj: *Thinking about you*
Date: 7/13/98 12:33:29 PM EDT

Dearest Nickie,

Aside from what comes through work, I haven't been able to access mail; I enjoy your letters so much that I reread them several times. Tonight, we should meet in bed early. I should slow our lovemaking down a little; I have been too impatient.

Have you heard from your son yet? It's a beautiful day here today. The sun is out, and the breeze is gentle. I will have dinner tonight under the elm trees by the lake. Is there something special you would care to have for dinner?

Till then, love
Ken

Subj: *Thinking about you too*
Date: 7/13/98

Dearest Ken,

I was out for my daily walk. I have yet to hear from my son; I presume they were out late last night and are still sleeping or making love. Frankly, I envy them!

Anyway, I did some heavy-duty thinking about my career and what I want to do with the rest of my professional life.

Is there any phone news from US West? Dinner by the lake this evening is a splendid idea. Anything you cook will be perfect if I can have YOU for dessert.

Till then,
Nickie

Chat 15—7/13/98

NC: Hi

DK: Hi. Did your son call?

NC: No, he didn't, but I was busy enough.

How was rehearsal?

DK: We need to find a new Joe. Lane won't be able to do the play

       BTW, what decisions did you come to about your job?

NC: I made considerable progress, at least in defining what was causing me such anxiety each time I thought of my future job situation.

       I was so anxious every time because I hate staying in corporate America. I'm not fond of office politics. I have never been good at compromising.

       I have begun to set new goals and objectives to pursue. It's nice to have things in focus once more. I have already started investigating something of interest.

       I still love accounting, finance, etc. I can't stand how I have to practice it.

       I thought of buying a franchise. When you own your own business, you work ten times as hard, and I want time for my personal life.

DK: Can't you do accounting and finance for individuals? Or work as an investment broker?

NC: That has its problems. I have a small financial planning/tax Practice for select people referred to me by this lady I know.

       Although I have my license for everything. The industry is highly regulated; it would be too complicated for me to do it independently.

       These serious thoughts are likely dull to you, but you are my first sympathetic ear since yesterday's newfound clarity.

       Are you there?

       ??????

Chat 16—7/13/98

DK: We are back, but what were we saying?

NC: just talking about business.

NC: by the way, this afternoon, I watched a movie that made me cry.

DK: which movie?

NC: Madame Butterfly. I didn't know it was so sad.

DK: When the heroine dies, it's heartbreaking every time

Cary Grant made a movie where he was supposed to meet his love at the top of the Statue of Liberty, which had the same premise.

NC: What was the movie?

DK: North by Northwest

the first movie I walked out of at the end crying because I was happy. Go figure

NC: you are very sensitive, unusual in men

I love you for being you

DK: One of my most significant chinks is that I am an incurable romantic

it's so natural to say to you what comes to mind as it comes

NC: It makes me feel all mushy inside,

my heart melts, and I want to hold you and kiss you and tell you how lucky I am for having met you

DK: Thank you. You make me feel wonderful when I am near you

NC: Did you get my last email?

DK: I got the one where I left you unsatisfied. That won't happen again, if I have anything to say about it.

NC: I said I wanted more

Maybe you do your work too well, so I can't get enough

DK: The feeling is mutual

NC: Being in your arms in NY felt very natural

and our bodies are perfect for cuddling after lovemaking

DK: Like you were a part of me too long absent

NC: And you felt the same way to me

EVEN if I did not say it

DK: we have much in common, my love

NC: Before you, I could count on one hand the number of times I said I love you to anyone, including my family.

with you, I have no control over it

I am sure more people love me than I think, but besides my mother and my son, the only people who ever made me feel loved are my first best friend Michelle and the person I dated for eight years after my divorce

DK: Excuse my curiosity, not that I would bring him back, but what happened to the eight-year person?

NC: essentially, I refused to marry him

It was a very messy, painful breakup

DK: Oh, I thought he was crazy and broke it off

NC: much worse than my divorce

I always feel that although we never lived together

He was my real first husband

It wasn't easy, with different personalities and emotional baggage he could not resolve

He was EXTREMELY JEALOUS AND POSSESSIVE and drove me insane

DK: That was simpler than you thought.

NC: what?

DK: Explaining about him

NC: There was another important reason as well. I felt that marrying him would curtail my career. I have worked very hard to move up professionally, and until recently, I enjoyed the challenge and the satisfaction of seeing hard work pay off.

NC: It has been both terrifying and exhilarating. Not easily achieved when there are others and their needs to consider. Now, I am ready and want those "others" in my life.

DK: One of the first things I noticed about you was independence

NC: How did you see that?

DK: I love that you can think for yourself; it adds a lot to a conversation

It's in the mannerisms of your speech

the diversity of your interests

NC: thanks. I have always taken care of myself, and if I could not think for myself, I would be in big trouble

DK: and you took a step beyond writing an ad; you responded to a letter

NC: I liked your letter

DK: I am indeed most fortunate

NC: You said something at the end that touched me

DK: I only responded to one ad, but don't tell anyone

NC: something about taking your hand and walking with you. I liked that; it was tender.

DK: I want to be with someone, not possess them. I don't mind; I rather like the idea of being owned, but I like equality

if each person is allowed their individuality, they complement each other. I felt secure when I held you, complete when we kissed, and I shared your breath.

NC: I feel a kinship between us that I can't quite describe

I was trying to explain my feelings for you to Linda, but I couldn't quite find the right words

DK: I have a hard time finding the words myself; the closest I can come is to say you are my best friend.

DK: There is more to love than sex. One is just the body, and the other is the body, the mind, and the heart together comprising the soul, and when two souls unite, there is an indescribable power

NC: Our souls are moving in harmony. Our hearts have done a great job.

DK: amen :)

NC: amen :)

Subj: *Good afternoon*
Date: 7/14/98 7:00:09 PM EDT

Dearest Nickie,

How is your day proceeding, my love? I have two store conferences with each other on my phone so that no one can ring in. It is the first time I have had to catch my breath all day. I wanted to tell you I love you.

I haven't been able to concentrate on silly things like work all day. I keep grinning; people have to ask me questions 2 and 3 times, and I forget what they ask me halfway through the question. Mostly, it has happened to Paul; he has gotten to where he writes his question down and hands it to me, and then he stands there staring until I explain the answer. I think it has turned into a game.

Till then,
Ken

Subj: *Good morning*
Date: 7/15/98

Dearest Ken,

Thanks for the beautiful voicemail last night. It's so good to hear your voice! I have listened to it ten times already! It was so unexpected and made me very happy. I sent you a brief message to that effect, but once again, with all your phone traumas, I am not sure you received it. They always say that all manners of communication go awry during a Mercury retrograde, and from what I read on the net, we are in the middle of one. Take heart; it's supposed to end soon.

Yesterday was a good day, not because I wasn't busy or irritated, but because I was so happy I let nothing get to me. I have you to thank. I took the laptop home, wanting to update my resume and chat with you, but I didn't get far. I spent most of the evening thinking of the night before. I was in such a great mood I cooked for myself (granted, it was only pasta and a salad). What you told me about people having to ask you questions 2 or 3 times yesterday was very funny. I wish I had been there to see their puzzled faces. I love you. I hope the phones behave themselves tonight, and we can chat for a while.

Till then,
Nickie

Subj: ***Good morning***
Date: 07/15/98 8:39:20 AM EDT

Dearest Nickie,

What did you do yesterday? Were you swamped with work? I will be busy tonight, but unless the computer goes wild again, I should be on between 9:30 and 9:45 (10:30 and 10:45 your time). I am going to South St. Paul to look at a duplex after work, then I pick up the girls at six and drop them off at 8:30. It takes about an hour to get home from Maple Grove. Traffic dependent. I am going to send this before I lose it again.

Till then, all my love,
Ken

"Missing You"

NC: I am back

NC: I rebooted the computer, but I kept losing audio

NC: How was your day?

DK: Not bad. I picked up the girls, and we went to a social at the church. They had a juggler and music, and the girls all sang with the choir

NC: sounds nice.

NC: So, did you think about me today?

DK: Didn't you get my message about stopping by with dessert? I had sliced strawberries, cantaloupe, and whipped cream. I won't tell you what we did with the whipped cream.

NC: No wonder those papers on my desk were in such a state!

DK: so, it was a little sticky, but it was fun

DK: I forgot about the dark chocolate sauce for dipping the strawberries.

NC: Can I ask you anything?

DK: of course.

NC: What is the craziest place you have ever made love in?

DK: outside of my mind

DK: Mary Lou was very conservative; we only made love in one place

DK: with the light off

DK: and as a good catholic girl, birth control was abstinence, and our daughters are three years apart

NC: I kind of like the lights off, too, but not pitch black, sort of a semi-darkness

NC: You mean you only had sex every three years?

DK: I have fancied candles

DK: It was over six years till our weekend in N.Y.

NC: yes, but then?

DK: I did much imagining

NC: Six years is a lot of abstinence

NC: You deserve a break today (and it's not McDonald's)

DK: now you have me blushing, so it's my turn. What is the most outrageous place and way you have made love?

NC: Remember my eight-year relationship?

DK: yes

NC: When we started dating, we were still in our early twenties, so, crazy with the hormones

NC: I was in grad school, and he was still finishing undergrad and working full time.

DK: It makes sense

NC: We used to go to a movie every Friday; the theater had student discounts, and once, we lost control at the theater and did it right there. It's a good thing we were way up on the balcony, and the place was almost empty.

NC: We laughed about it for years

DK: no wonder he was possessive. Do you think the other students were watching the show on the screen?

NC: we were the only ones in the balcony section. No one saw us

DK: We will have to try that sometime; we can go to the drive-in they still have a few around here. We will park in the back row so no one will bother us going for popcorn

NC: Darling, I need to let you get to bed. You only have 3 hours.

DK: yes, I know. I love you

NC: Will we chat tomorrow?

DK: wild horses and balking PC wouldn't stop me

NC: Hug and kisses. I love you a lot!

DK: good night. Xoxoxo

Subj: ***Good morning, dearest***
Date: 7/16/98

Dearest Ken,

Good morning, darling. I will work at a different location this morning without internet access. I hope to be back in my office by 1:00 p.m. at the latest, but in case of a delay, you'll understand why you haven't heard from me.

I am looking forward to our chat tonight. I love you.

Till then,
Nickie

Subj: *Hello*
Date: 7/16/98

Dearest Ken,

Darling, I am back in my office. As expected, having been away all morning, my phone is ringing off the hook. I hope your day is going well. I love you.

Till then,
Nickie

Subj: *Missing in action*
Date: 7/17/98

Dearest Ken,

I miss hearing from you. It occurred to me that your work server could be down, there is a spike in your workload, your phone lines at home are down, your computer at home crashed, you are at a meeting, you are in class. Etc. Which is it? I love you.

Till then,
Nickie

Subj: *Can you explain?*
Date: 7/18/98

Dearest Ken,

After a sleepless night and no mail from you, I am concerned. Why have I not heard from you for the last three days?

Can your home and work computer be out of commission for so long simultaneously? What's happening? It's tough for me to have no news. I am lost without you. It even crossed my mind that you may be sick or one of your daughters may have a problem (which I hope is not the case). You have my home number if we cannot communicate with electronic media. I misplaced your home number; otherwise, I would have called to ensure you weren't sick. I love you.

Till then,
Nickie

Subj: *Good Morning*
Date: 7/18/98

Dearest Ken,

Thinking of a zillion reasons for your silence, even some unreasonable ones. It doesn't mean that I have any doubts or mistrust of your feelings toward me, but I am grabbing at straws now and letting my anxiety get the best of me. In the meantime, I miss you.

Till then,
Nickie

Subj: *Here I am again*
Date: 7/18/98

Dearest Ken,

Each time I open the mail icon, it's with utter disbelief that I stare at the screen, not see-ing anything from you. Uncertainty is the worst form of torture for me. I would rather know that you don't want to have anything to do with me than this silence that causes me to imagine things. I should relax and see what happens in a couple of days. Still, my logical mind telling my heart what is wise to do concerning you is as ludicrous as trying to teach nuclear physics to a monkey. I love you; that's all I know. This silence from you is as big a mystery as the creation of the universe. If you misplaced my home phone, it's (718) 742-xxxx. I would call, but I lost your number. I hope all is well with you and your girls. I LOVE YOU.

Thinking of you,
Nickie

Subj: *Good morning, dearest*
Date:7/19/98

Dearest Ken,

This morning, in church, I prayed to God to protect and keep you safe wherever you are. I hope you are not ill or injured while I am here wallowing in self-pity.

I have often doubted that I could find such love as ours and that I am worthy of it. Tomorrow is another anniversary of the start of our correspondence. I have gone over our last conversation a million times and can't come up with anything amiss. At the end of our previous chat, I asked if we would speak again tomorrow, and you answered that "barking PCs couldn't keep you from it." So, our last words were pleasant.

Till then,
Nickie

Subj: ***I am lonely***
Date:7/19/98

Dearest Ken,

I am lonely. I thought of how happy I was last Sunday, secure in feeling your love, not knowing how fragile that feeling was. I have loved no one as I do you. It's logically incomprehensible, but I don't want to be logical.

"Wherefore art thou, my Romeo?" I only live when I open my email, hoping to see your words. If you are not getting any of my mail because you cannot, you will forgive me, but you must understand my anxiety. I dislike even stopping writing because I'll want to write again and spend my time arguing about the number of hours that must elapse without annoying you too much. I go from extreme worry about your physical well-being to extreme despair at the thought that you are fine and don't love me anymore.

Missing you,
Nickie

I browsed through the week's TV Guide issue for the third time, wondering if the line-up of shows on the page would change the next time I looked. I flipped on the TV twice before. The only worthwhile thing playing was an episode of the X-Files I had seen already and a new episode of The Simpsons, in which I had no interest. The phone rang, and I was glad, for once, happy to talk to anyone.

"Allo"

"Hi, Netty."

"How did you know it was me?"

"Come on, Netty, I thought you upgraded all your phones?"

"Yes, but the kitchen extension is malfunctioning; I've been too busy to return it to the store. Anyway, I am having a barbecue next Sunday for Nadine's birthday. Can you make it?"

"Of course! For my only Goddaughter, I wouldn't miss it for anything. I already bought her a birthday gift!"

"Good, so I'll see you then. By the way, how are you? Still, working crazy hours? I called you last Friday evening but didn't leave a message."

"Oh! I went out with some co-workers. It was my office clerk's birthday. He is such a nice young man; he turned twenty-two, and we took him to TGIF after work."

"That's nice, as long as you are doing something social. I'd rather hear you say you were on a date, but this is good too. I called Mom long-distance two days ago because I was thinking of her, and she spent five minutes preaching to me about encouraging you to remarry! As if I had anything to do with it! Macy told me she had an almost identical conversation with her. Now that Craig has graduated and moved out, she is even more concerned about your living alone.

"I know. I talked to her, too. When I last called them, I could even hear her in the background urging Dad to ask me about my plans for remarriage. I just told them I was working on it. How are you doing? Everything good?"

"Yep! We can't decide on the next family vacation, but that's a good problem to have!"

"You said it!"

"Nickie, I got to go; I have something in the oven. I'll see you next Sunday, Bye."

"Bye"

Contrary to what I told Netty, I had chosen Nadine's gift but hadn't purchased it yet. I drove to the mall where they had opened a new Southwestern store. Everything was handmade in that part of the country or Mexico. I had put a deposit on a delicate sterling silver and turquoise bracelet for her. Her favorite colors were blue and green, so I was hoping she would like it. I spent some hours browsing through various stores before returning home.

I was driving myself up the wall. Besides attending church that morning, I had already gone for my walk and stopped at Keyfoods for groceries I didn't need. I turned on the stereo and then turned it off. I knew better than even to open a book. Finally, I picked up the phone and called Linda, hoping she wasn't sleeping late and that this would not be an intrusion. She sounded bright and perky when she answered, so I was relieved. In no time, I talked her into meeting me at the cozy coffee shop around the corner from her.

"It's been ages! I've missed our coffee chats," I started.

"I know, right? Life can be a whirlwind. These days, though, you can't blame me. First, you blew off my request because of work and didn't reply the next time I asked. Remember how we laughed and criticized those women who dropped their girlfriends the minute a man walked into their lives? But tell me, what's up with Ken? You said he's been MIA?" Linda replied.

"I am sorry, Linda; I have taken you for granted. You may be a pain in the neck, but I care for you. I am not my typical self these days; call me out on it right away if it happens again."

"You bet! So, what's going on?"

"I don't know what's happening, and it's unpleasant. Honestly, I'm worried. Our online relationship sometimes feels like a delicate thread. Is it even viable?"

"Nickie, listen to me. You're the strongest woman I know. But right now, your insecurity is making you weak. You've got to get a hold of yourself. Trust Ken. Trust your connection. Love isn't always about physical presence. I can see how happy you've been since meeting him."

"Linda, have you ever been in love? Are you in love now?"

"Shockingly, yes. I never thought it'd happen to me. But there I was, heart tangled in a web of emotions. Love's unpredictable, Nickie. It sneaks up on you when you least expect it."

"How did you handle it?

"Oh, I fought it hard. But love is relentless. So, I surrendered. And you know what? It was beautiful chaos. Vulnerability, laughter, tears—the complete package."

"I want that. I get it, but fall apart when we don't communicate. I want to feel alive, even if it's through a screen. Linda, I need to prove that I can function well, even when Ken's not physically here."

"Then you're coming to my dinner party tonight. I've already prepped every-thing. That's what you caught me doing when you called. I didn't invite you earlier because you've been refusing invitations to avoid missing your "chat time" on the computer with Ken in the evenings. We'll celebrate love, friendship, and life. Plus, I've invited a hilarious friend—Eric. He's like a stand-up comedian trapped in an accountant's body."

"I'll be there. For friendship and Eric's jokes! I need this."

I started the car with a smile, thinking that I couldn't wait to relate this to Ken, and then remembered I hadn't heard from him. My smile faltered, and the anxiety returned.

Subj: *Sorry, I was AWOL*
Date: 7/20/98 6:52:52 AM EDT

Dearest Nickie,

I am sorry I haven't been able to write since Thursday. I have missed you a lot. My nephew Liam fell two flights of stairs. My sister called Thursday night; Liam was in the hospital, and she was hysterical. I tried to write before I left, but I was upset, too, because the computer frustrated the daylights out of me. It's no excuse for letting you hang like this since you told me how troubled you get when it happens; please forgive me. I haven't even read your letters yet. I came straight to work and returned to Minnesota at 4:33 this morning. Liam will be okay. He fractured his collarbone, broke his right wrist, and had a concussion, but it could have been worse.

I would ask what you have been doing, but I will read your mail first. I am starving for want of you. I love you. Enjoy your day off; I will write more later.

Till then, love
Ken

Subj: *Re: Sorry I was AWOL*
Date: 7/20/98

Dearest Ken,

I am so glad you are back and are OK! I opened my email before stepping out with no hope of seeing anything more in my box except junk mail, and I was so gratified and relieved to see your letter there. I have been sprinting out of bed the last few days to see if you had written. Today is the first time I forced myself to wait until now, trying to delay the disappointment of an empty email box.

I love you. I am sure you have no doubts about it now after all the million letters I sent you. I am sorry to hear about Liam's accident; at least the damage caused by the fall is not permanent, and he is recovering. I can't imagine how worried your sister must have been.

If you haven't slept since yesterday and drove directly to work, please go home and to bed after work. Should you feel sleepy, have some coffee. I don't want you driving off the road from fatigue. (You must reply: yes, Mother.) and please skip any rehearsal today. I am leaving now and will return in 2 or 3 hours.

Till then,
Nickie

Subj: *It's later*
Date:7/20/98 9:28:03 AM EDT

Dearest Nickie,

As you may have guessed, I have been at work for over two hours and have only read my mail and written you letters. My boss might get suspicious soon; so far today, I have not taken even one call, and I have had my phone set to after-call work so that no one can call me.

In your letters, I felt the worry I caused. I am sorry. However, you said nothing about what you were doing. So, did you get my phone number? A list of reasons I would not stop writing to you or my pleadings for you to write me? Did you understand how much I respect and trust you? I hope it is mutual. You know the golden rule. It is essential, given the circumstances of our relationship.

Till then, love
Ken

Subj: *Re: Just my luck*
Date: 7/20/98

Dearest Ken,

If my life depended on it, I could not tell you my daily routine for the last few days. It's all a blur. The only thing I can tell you is that I spent a lot of time checking for an e-mail from you. The only productive thing I have done and am still doing is go to one house to show an apartment to prospective tenants. It's the third apartment that will be vacant. The tenant only gave me notice last week. He is, however, allowing me to show the place while still in occupancy.

My weekend was bland, except for Linda's dinner party, but I didn't attend the work party Saturday evening (I am not sure I mentioned that invitation to you.) I have another for my best friend Wayne's daughter's birthday this Saturday.

I sit in the kitchen, clad only in my panties, writing this! I just sent you another picture with a blue and gray top; it's my favorite yet. I hope you get it.

I got your phone number from your voicemail. I have missed you so much! Imagine having no one to be naughty with for all five days (it feels like forty)! Unacceptable! Hope we can chat tonight.

Till then
Nickie

Chat 18—7/20/98

NC: Hi, how was your day?

DK: Pretend work today, I couldn't wait to talk to you.

NC: Yeah, it's tough to concentrate when your head won't cooperate. I miss you all the time, but we need to talk.

DK: What's up?

NC: This long-distance thing... It's weighing on me. I thought I could handle it, but now... it's like an ache, Ken. I miss you so much.

DK: You know how much I love you.

NC: That's it. We both care a whole lot but we haven't discussed anything more. Technology is proving more challenging than we expected, so maybe we should consider doing more. At least consider some options for the future.

DK: I think of us being together night and day, but it's not that simple

NC: I get it. We both have kids, jobs, and responsibilities. But this distance—it's eating at me. I can't sleep, can't focus. And I'm tired of pretending it's okay.

DK: Nickie, it's not that I don't want to, but I'm not ready for that kind of commitment. Moving nearer each other would be the best solution but it means uprooting our present lives. I will move when needed, but I was thinking of the future.

NC: Even so, shouldn't we be talking about it? Devise a plan or talk about possibilities to resolve future obstacles? What if we're meant to be together? I need more than late-night calls and virtual hugs.

DK: What if we ruin what we have? Nickie, I'm scared. Scared of losing you, scared of messing up. my anxiety—

NC: Ken, I'm not asking for forever. I want to make sure we are on the same page.

DK: We are.

NC: I don't always feel certain despite what we say to each other. Maybe we handle things differently due to our personalities, I don't know. Anyway, it's past both our bed time. Get some rest. Good night, dearest.

DK: I know we can work through it together. I love you. Good night.

There was no letter from Ken that morning when I arrived at work. Most of the day, I was busy writing performance reviews for two of the senior accountants on my staff and making my final recommendation to the owner regarding our capital expenditure on the proposed Y2K—compliant phone system. As I was turning off my desktop, I saw and clicked on an unread message.

Subj: *Time*
Date: 7/21/98 2:26:53 PM EDT

Dearest,

I was thinking of you. I am unsure if you were mad at me last night as your goodbye seemed abrupt, but it's my perception.

I don't intend to be a pest. I hope your morning went well. How is the office? Where is the strangest place you have ever contemplated making love? I remember the movie, but I am not talking about reality; you have already done that. I miss you.

Till then,
Ken

I sat on the edge of my bed, fingers tracing patterns on the light quilt. I purposefully left the laptop in the office. I needed to think. I hope I didn't appear needy in our chat last night; I just wanted to be sure we were on the same wavelength. *Our emotions are getting serious. Are we both ready to improve our situation?* The status quo wasn't a permanent option. *But should we drift apart because our situation is inconvenient?*

Subj: *Re: Time*
Date 7/21/98

Dearest Ken,

You could never be a pest, and after so many days of your absence, I wouldn't mind if you spent the next 30 years writing me a message every 5 minutes. I had some scheduled showings for the apartments.

Did I tell you I was practically naked when writing you the second e-mail? Well, I was. Darling, I can't wait for those hickeys!

Believe it or not, the strangest place I have contemplated making love is on an airplane. I don't think such a thing is possible, though I read about it in novels and think the writers took liberties. Now tell me about your strangest place.

I am thrilled you are back. I love you.

Till then,
Nickie

Subj: *Good morning, my love*
Date: 7/22/98 7:14:50 AM EDT

Dearest Nickie,

Good morning, my love. I lost the letter I wrote to you this morning. The video card is out on my PC. It will be 3-5 days before Gateway sends me another one.

I did not sleep well, and I could not talk with you. I thought of little else since Liam woke up around 4 Saturday afternoon. I miss you terribly.

Till then,
Ken

Subj: *Missing you*
Date:7/22/98

Dearest Ken,

I dreamed about us making love last night. I woke up afterward at 3:53 and couldn't fall back asleep. I arrived at work an hour ago, and it looks like it will be another crazy day based on what has happened. I am off to a meeting for the next 2 hours. I have to take care of something with the plumber at the house tonight. I plan to finish by 9:00 p.m. Would you be online at around 9:30 or 10:00 p.m.? Let me know. I love you.

Till then,
Nickie

Subj: *Missing you*
Date: 7/22/98 8:16:05 AM EDT

Dearest Nickie,

By now, you know I couldn't sleep without talking to you. So, I tried to tinker with the old video card last night. Of course, my computer was down. Tim, Michelle, and Alisa were trying to watch Liar Liar on DVD when it started acting up for no apparent reason. I went to bed at about 11 p.m. If I had the image of you sitting in your kitchen in my mind, you would never have been able to complete your letter. Would you have made your afternoon appointments?

As I was writing this to you, I saw your new message. My heart leaped to my throat, and for a moment, I couldn't decide whether to read or write; I wanted to read. I love you.

Till then,
Ken

"Surprise"

Ken

I was drumming my fingers on the desk after answering a question from Eve. I hardly slept these last few nights, worried Nickie was upset with me and worried the lousy video card situation would add to her frustration. It certainly added to mine. Tim's problems with his father and his expectation of me to pick sides were not part of the plan. Spending two hours working on the corral late yesterday gave me a feeling of accomplishment and relieved my mounting anxiety. Thank God Nickie's tone in her last letter seemed back to normal.

Soon, I was dealing with the strangest work situation. My productivity had increased by thirty percent, so my manager constantly asked me if I wanted to work additional overtime. At least two or three complimentary messages daily from my "stack of clients praised my skills and helpfulness on their behalf." It puzzled me because I could hardly recall any of the details of resolved problems at the end of the workday. Yet, I was breezing through them with such ease and speed that I worried my co-workers would look bad. It was a good thing they liked me, and I knew they wondered how I went from a constant dreamy state to supercharged productivity while still having this absolute happiness in my eyes. My co-workers didn't know any details, but they all concluded that I was having sex regularly. Nothing could be further from the truth, but what I had was better than sex; I had love.

At least twice a week, when I didn't have my girls or was not rushing home to chat with Nickie, I accepted two or three hours of overtime for extra money I was saving with a particular goal in mind. I could never keep a secret and came close several times to telling Nickie about my new "project."

Nickie

I spun around in a little celebratory dance, my bare feet gliding across the ceramic tiles of the kitchen floor. Arms outstretched, I twirled like a child, infused with energy. But I sobered soon, however, realizing that even in video, meeting his girls would be significant. Our cameras were behaving, and Ken had the girls with him on Tuesday and Wednesday. Nervous excitement replaced my dance when I processed Ken's words: "Would you be able to take a couple of days off so I could introduce you to the girls?" I took a deep breath, ready but trying not to jump the gun.

I had all the necessary ingredients for some bundt cake, set the weekend before, and I picked some family movies for us to watch together with the girls, as Ken had suggested. I just hoped he had arranged for the gadget he mentioned to allow us to have our video date seamlessly. And on schedule, an envelope arrived from Ken. But when I opened it, I found a handwritten note and a plane ticket inside!

> *Dearest Nickie,*
>
> *I can't keep a secret! I warned you. I have been planning for us to spend a few days together. I hope you can make it. I love you. Meet me Friday morning on the 7th at the United Airlines gate in Bridgetown, Barbados, and we will take it from there! Do you believe this? I am taking a chance and hope you can make it; please say yes. I Love YOU!*
>
> *Till then,*
> *Ken*

My heart was beating so hard that I had to sit down. I reread the note and the ticket word for word at least three times.

The room seemed to come alive, matching my excitement. The late afternoon sun shone brightly through the glass over the kitchen tiles. I could feel the warmth, and the gentle breeze that flowed through the open window carried the sweet scent of flowers.

I picked up the kitchen phone and dialed his number. When the answering machine picked up, I remembered he had a play rehearsal that evening. I did a little jig that extended into the living room. I turned on the stereo, danced, and sat down with a stupid grin; nothing could bring me down. I stood up, ran to the hallway closet, pulled out my carry-on, and started rummaging for "summer outfits." I knew I had a week and a half, but I giggled, thinking it was irrelevant.

I threw in two pairs of shorts, bathing suits, bras, panties, sample-size shampoo, toothpaste, a comb, Band-Aids, and other toiletries. I could not find any bug spray, so I swapped my blouse for a tee shirt and walked six blocks to the drugstore. I heard traffic from the main street two blocks away and hoped I wouldn't have to go there for spray and sunscreen lotion. The fluorescent lights in the store illuminated the aisles filled with various products, and I had no problem locating what I needed. The air had cooled off when I stepped out a moment later; a slight breeze blew through the trees as I walked briskly from the drugstore. I packed an extra toothbrush, body lotion, "the nightie" he liked, etc. Doing this so early felt strange, but it was the only productive thing I could do with my joy. I rummaged in a closet for both a sun hat and a visor. I placed my passport and the plane ticket in the purse I intended to travel with. I returned to the living room, put on a Michael Bolton record, poured myself a sweet vermouth on the rocks, and settled with a pillow on the rug, eyes closed, passing the hour till I could chat with him.

Later, I reached for the phone. We spoke excitedly for a half-hour, like children on a sugar high before bedtime. When I woke up the following morning, as I recorded my basal temperature on the chart, I felt a bit of trepidation; *what if we had to use condoms throughout our vacation?* It wouldn't be ideal. I calculated, and our luck continued; right after ovulation, there would be no risk of pregnancy. I used the rhythm method for birth control, and even though I had seen no one for the past year before Ken, I had continued to record everything. It was nice not to worry about birth control during our vacation.

I reached work on Monday and promptly emailed my boss about my upcoming leave. I realized I had a mid-year tax planning meeting with the auditors on Wednesday when I would be away. I called the senior contact on the account right away:

"Hey Mike, it's Nickie from the Hunt Agency. I won't be able to meet with you on the 15th as planned due to an unexpected issue. I'll book the conference room for you and leave the schedules in the credenza. Mary will provide you with the keys. I'll address all issues related to the new tax laws. Please leave me your recommendations, and I'll call after my return."

«Thanks for letting me know. Your schedules are always impeccable. We can have lunch when I come with my associates for the annual audit."

"Sounds great, Mike. Thanks for your understanding."

Typically, I would have completed most of the work by now. I hadn't even started; so "very unproductive" I had become since falling in love with Ken.

The next week and a half, I arrived early and left late, asking the receptionist to pick up my lunch daily. I even skipped one management meeting, claiming the worst sinus headache. Considering the tax law changes, I retrieved last year's easy schedules and tasked two of my senior accountants to update them. I would review them once I finished my work. Saturday's quietness allowed me to accomplish a lot. Sunday, I packed properly after church, went to the hairdresser, and chatted with Ken that evening. Monday morning, I asked the receptionist to forward any calls to voice mail. The rest of the week flew by, and I was interrupted only once by my intern, Lu-Jay, who brought in several substantial checks for signatures. I had trained him well, and all backup documents were attached.

This young man had been on Craig's track team, so I saw him grow up. There was no hesitation in hiring him when he needed to pursue an internship. He already had two offers, including sign-on bonuses from top accounting firms. He could start with them when he got his CPA exam results. I'd be very sorry to see him go, and I doubted I'd get another intern as capable as he was.

"Barbados"

On Friday, I met Ken at 10:40 a.m. at the United Airlines arrival gate in the Grantley Adams International Airport of Bridgetown. The airport comprised two terminals joined via a "membrane tent," which appeared like a single building. I walked around and noticed about twenty-two gates and realized they had direct flights to the U.S., Canada, and Europe. I had arrived forty-five minutes earlier and had time to check out the duty-free shops and the information desks, use the restroom, and visit the car kiosk. I rented nothing since I needed the details of our accommodations. The smell of coffee wafted from a nearby coffee shop, mingling with baked croissants. I sipped my coffee while watching two planes land, their luggage removed and loaded into cargo areas. When his flight landed, my heartbeat increased, and seeing him walk toward me was all I needed to drop my carry-on and fly into his arms. They closed around me.

"I missed you so much."

"Me too, more than words can say," I replied

We kissed like we hadn't seen each other for ten years. When our subconscious registered, someone was repeatedly clearing their throat. "Will you need a taxi?" His voice was deep and gravelly, as if he had been smoking for years.

"Well, will we?" I asked.

"Will we what?"

"The man is asking if we'll need a taxi."

"Oh," said Ken, turning to the porter. "There is a shuttle to our hotel, but thank you."

He grabbed my carry-on handle, which the man was holding, fished in his pocket, and gave him a few dollars.

"Thanks," we both said.

We boarded an almost empty shuttle to the hotel. Ken and I held hands, and he gazed out the window with wonder. Even though it was my first time in Barbados, I felt like I had come home as soon as we touched down.

"So, what do you think so far?" I asked.

"We have seen little, but I like what I feel. Most people are smiling, which gives me a welcoming feeling."

"It's the Caribbean, I answered. The smiles are free."

He leaned slightly, kissed me on the cheek, and whispered, "I love you."

"I love you more," I replied.

We checked in at the front desk. The concierge greeted us warmly. He assigned a room on the third floor and directed us to the elevator. As soon as we stepped inside, I headed straight to the sliding doors and onto the enclosed balcony. I felt so grateful to be experiencing this moment with Ken. With an unobstructed view of the sand, water, and waves right from our balcony, the ocean looked like a sparkling sapphire jewel in the sunlight. Ken joined me on the balcony, put his arms around me, and kissed my neck and ear. Then he turned me around to face him, and our lips met again. He said with a ragged breath,

"Nickie, if we keep this up, we might not leave this room until tomorrow."

"I agree. Let's unpack, change, and see what's happening."

We changed into shorts, t-shirts, and sneakers and headed downstairs to grab some lemonade from the bar before strolling around the grounds. A mile down the road, we stumbled upon a cluster of chain hotels popular with the surfing crowd.

Several small shops were catering to all things beachy and fun. We inquired about the restaurants with the best foods and noted their positions on the area map we picked up from the outdoor hotel bar.

I wore my sun hat, and Ken reluctantly donned the visor I'd given him. I leaned in for a quick peck on the lips. Sunscreen forgotten, we wandered for hours. I devoured a crab sandwich at a local eatery, and Ken opted for a seafood salad. The flavors were so delicious that I couldn't help but moan in delight. Ken, in his sexy voice, teased, "I thought I was the only one who could make you moan like this?" His unexpected comment made me laugh, and he had to pat my back to prevent choking. I ordered papaya juice, and Ken chose pineapple. We walked back to the hotel, holding hands. I would pull my hand back and wrap my arms around his waist, and each time, he would pull me to him and hug me.

When we arrived at the hotel, we moved two lawn chairs side by side into the shade of palm trees. Though we spent the last couple of hours strolling around, I felt the need for a long stretch before settling in my chaise. Our fingers brushed against each other.

"Ken, I've been thinking."

"About?"

"About the future."

"Remember, we're here to relax. To forget about deadlines and responsibilities."

"Did I tell you I heard about the franchise opportunity? The business in Pennsylvania?"

"You may have mentioned it. It's just paperwork, right?

"For now, yes, but it's more than that. It's a chance to be my own boss. My concern is this: should I consider other places besides NY if it's viable? Minneapolis, maybe? I need to put things in motion. What do you think?"

"It can't hurt, but for now, I only want you to consider our time together in Barbados."

Procrastination is not my thing. However, this was a vacation; I smiled and returned my attention to the pool.

"This place is fantastic. The pool is so inviting that I feel like jumping in, clothes and all. By the way, the green T-shirt compliments your eyes and hair. You look pretty hot!" I teased. I smiled and noticed a slight flush on his face.

"Did I embarrass you? I didn't mean to."

"No, I thought of you stretching like a lynx a moment ago. That was very sexy."

Before I knew what I was doing, I leaned over his chair, bent my face towards his ear, gave his earlobe a small bite, and murmured: "As long as you can make me purr tonight, I'll be the best kitty cat in the world!" I quickly leaned back in my chair and turned an innocent face toward him.

Ken was turning all shades of red and did not know how to hide his embarrassment. I knew this was wicked, but I was enjoying the sight. Taking pity on him, I changed the subject.

"I love your sunglasses; they suit you. I noticed them when you tried them on in the room. It a shame we forget them on the dresser."

"Thanks. I got them for this occasion. I wanted to impress you."

"You don't need to impress me. You already have. You're the most wonderful person I've ever met."

"Ditto, you make me happy. I don't know if I mentioned it, but though I claimed the opposite, I was nervous about meeting you for the first time in Milwaukee. After all the letters we exchanged, I was likely as nervous as you were."

"You know what? I feel more comfortable with you in person than in writing. I smile constantly."

"I'm the lucky one."

We intended to shower and decide on a restaurant for dinner. After the plane trip and the day outdoors, I felt hot and sweaty and preceded Ken in the shower. I slathered my skin in our favorite body lotion, wrapped myself in the plush robe, and left the bathroom. I was only there for fifteen minutes, but when I walked into the room, I noticed Ken dosing off the balcony chaise lounge; I wasn't surprised, as the Caribbean sun had that effect on people. I gently touched his arm, and he opened his eyes and smiled.

"Does Milady need any help?"

"Her ladyship is all done, and she would like her Knight to follow suit; she will patiently wait for his return."

Ken gave me an exaggerated bow and said, "Thy wish is my command." He gave me a sweet peck on the lips and headed for the shower.

A warm, gentle breeze was blowing on my face; it felt nice, and I wondered where it was coming from. I raised my hand to touch my face and woke up from my nap. The "breeze" was Ken's rhythmic breath on my cheek as he slept with his head on the pillow and his chin resting on my forehead. He enfolded me entirely in the cocoon of his body. One arm underneath my torso, the hand resting on my waist, the other draped over my chest as if holding me close to him. It felt nice and comfy, and I disliked moving. I looked around the room and noticed the locked sliding doors. I had pulled them shut before turning on the AC, and the room was comfortably cool. Ken must have drawn the curtains. I had slipped between the sheets, intending to review the restaurant map while waiting for Ken to finish showering. When he entered the bedroom, he found me fast asleep and decided I must be tired. Instead of waking me up to discuss dinner, he slipped beside me in bed, gathered me into his arms, and fell asleep. What a thoughtful thing to do! Every time I thought of how considerate he was with his feelings and attention, my heart melted anew, and what I felt for this man was indescribable; who knew thoughtfulness could be so sexy? This wave of emotions not only swept my heart, but my head lost clarity and set my body aflame with desire.

I eased a reddish-brown curl from his cheek and pressed a kiss there. My index finger slid down the side of his neck, barely touching him; he murmured something and turned on his back, still sleeping. He was in top physical shape, and admiring his body produced the usual feelings in my belly. Before I knew it, my lips had replaced my index finger on his neck, large shoulders, and chest, and I sweetly licked his nipples. He came awake almost immediately, and like answering a curtain call, his manhood rose to the occasion. My mouth slid down the length of his belly and, without warning, made a prisoner of him. "Nickie." He was murmuring something, but I couldn't hear him because nothing could distract my attention or my immense arousal from touching and tasting him. It hadn't gone on for long as I pulled my lips to the tip; his penis jumped rigidly, pointing straight north on his stomach as if reaching for his belly button. My lips touched the end again and caused a geyser eruption of his seed. Somewhere above me, I heard my name, a grunt, and love all mixed up. I held him in my mouth until the tremors subsided.

I reached for a box of tissues lying on the nightstand and cleaned my face and his belly as best as possible. Ken lifted my hand, embarrassed and not wanting me to continue, but with slight pressure, I indicated he should let me finish.

"I am sorry," he said. It took me by surprise; I thought I was dreaming. It was incredible; I don't know what to say."

He pulled me up on the bed beside him, facing each other. We smiled at each other in unison as if rehearsed.

I turned around on my side, slid myself to my previous cocoon position, and said with a smile,

"Go back to sleep, dearest. I love you."

"I love you more."

Ken

I didn't know what time it was but I was still holding Nickie tight against me, as if afraid she would escape from me in our slumber. I was conscious of my rock-hard erection pressed against the back of her thigh. I bent my head and kissed her nape; I felt terrible for not restraining my impulse and possibly waking her. I immediately pulled my mouth away, but to my surprise, she moaned and said," Please don't stop." It was all the encouragement I needed, and my lips found their way to her neck again, kissing, nibbling, and blowing on her skin, getting more and more excited by her little cries of pleasure. She had pushed her lower back against me, and I could feel her round, firm buttocks moving and rubbing themselves mercilessly against my penis. I pulled myself apart with difficulty while moving my right hand against her thighs and buttocks. I slid down to their level, turning her on her back while gently opening her thighs. Little kisses starting at her knees, trailed along the inside of her thighs toward her center. My large hands clasped her buttocks. I brought my face to her center and closed my lips around her clitoris. My tongue barely flicked against the sensitive and erect part while my lips gripped its sides. I would release the pressure occasionally and engulf the whole thing in my mouth as if sucking on the juiciest fruits.

Nickie was moaning and thrashing, trying to pull away from me or pushing herself against my mouth. Her little cries were distressed, and

"Ken, please, please, please," she repeated. She was pulling at my hair, releasing it, and grabbing a fistful of the sheets.

"I can't, please, Ken. I want you, please, please."

I let go of her buttocks and slid my lips up on her stomach without ever lifting them, took possession of her hard nipples, sucked hard on the right one, then slid to the left one while my hands with fingers entwined with hers were trying to keep them flat on the bed. When my lips slid to the corner of her mouth, she took possession of them as if she wanted to swallow me whole. She freed up one hand, slid it between our bodies to grab my penis, positioned the tip against her vagina, and thrusted herself against me. She wrapped her legs around me and thrusted herself a few times more before her body became rigid, and she screamed my name. I lost control of the situation, not knowing how or no longer caring how or when. I lost a sense of time, only hearing her name and barely recognizing my voice as I had the biggest orgasm I could ever remember experiencing, electrifying my body. I lifted myself off Nickie, lying on my side, and gathered her in my arms.

"Thank you, my love; I cannot find the words." Nickie didn't answer, and I raised her chin slightly to peer at her face; she had two large tears running down her face. I sat up abruptly.

"Did I hurt you? I'm sorry, Nickie. I'm sorry. I love you."

"Shhh, shhh," she said. "These are tears of joy; I love you so much that it's indescribable. I will never stop loving you. I will love no one the way I love you. Thank you."

The knot in my throat would not let me speak, and all I could muster was, "Me too."

Nickie

We missed the hot breakfast the following day and barely made it downstairs before the kitchen closed. Thankfully, I had called the desk to confirm the schedule. Getting out of the room had been hard. The shower had stopped when I was on the phone; I knocked and entered the bathroom before getting permission; we only had a brief window. Ken was combing back his wet hair. I attempted to pass by him to get into the shower, but he grabbed me by the waist and gave me a noisy kiss on the cheek.

"Good morning, my love."

"Good morning, dearest, I love you."

Glancing down at his wrapped towel, I knew he had more than breakfast on his mind, but I deflected by smiling and saying,

"We have only half an hour left, darling. Be a good boy and get dressed; I'll be there in ten minutes."

We arrived in the breakfast room fifteen minutes before closing time, which was plenty to pile up some pastries, fruits, and a glass of orange juice and head for the pool area. I left Ken at the chairs and returned to the breakfast room to get him a cup of Earl Grey tea and a steaming cup of coffee for me.

I noticed he had placed the tray on a small white metal stool between the chairs and was sitting uncomfortably, talking to a woman standing too close to him.

"Hi," I said, smiling at her.

"I got you, Earl Grey. Is that okay? I know it's your favorite," I said to Ken.

"Of course. Nickie, this is Carol. Carol, Nickie, my girlfriend. Carol was asking if we wanted to join the volleyball game on the beach, which is about to start in a moment."

I detected a slight disappointment on her face as Ken spoke because she hadn't invited "us"; she had asked "him." I gave her my most radiant smile and said,

"I am going to pass on that because I am famished, plus I am still tired from a long night."

"Did you guys go dancing last night? My friends and I were partying at the Riu. We had a blast. Where did you go? We didn't see you."

"No, we came in late yesterday morning, walked around for hours, had a delicious lunch, spent an hour and a half here, and intended to go out to dinner. Unfortunately, we never left the room, but we have a few days to catch up on the parties."

I turned to smile at Ken, but he had turned beet red and was now staring unblinkingly at something in the pool water. Carol realized the implication of my statement, and two spots of red appeared on her cheeks.

"Oh, if you guys should change your minds, you are welcome to join us; see you!" She departed in a hurry.

I could not believe I had been so naughty. Poor Ken was still beet red but turned to me with a devilish smirk.

"Nickie, you astound me every day!"

"I am sorry for embarrassing you, dearest, but she had it coming, trying to flirt with my man. I overheard her swooning over you and your British accent when I was bringing the drinks back. I also noticed her checking you out twice yesterday when we sat here. I suppose she passed by your chair a few times, hoping to catch your attention."

"Really? I hadn't noticed!"

"I know," I said, "though she is quite attractive, judging by the looks that followed her around the pool deck. That's one more reason I am crazy in love with you!"

Ken turned halfway, lifted me without trouble, and placed me on his lap like a little girl. He wrapped his powerful and defined arms around me, buried his head on my shoulder, and whispered,

"I only have eyes for you, Nickie. I love you so much!"

"I love you more!" I replied, bathed in the warm glow of the vibrant bougainvillea vines wound around wooden pergolas, providing bursts of fuchsia and coral. Tall coconut palms swayed, their fronds casting dappled shadows on the pool deck. A thatched-roof bar stood at one end of the pool, where a bartender mixed cocktails.

We ate and talked about the latest John Grisham novel I had started on the airplane.

"Hey, have you ever seen *"The Exorcist?"*

"No, I'm too scared to watch it."

"What? Are you kidding me?"

"I'm serious. I don't think I can handle it".

"Oh! I found a chink in my Knight's armor," I said with a wink.

"It's not exactly a chink, I just don't like horror movies."

"Well, you're missing out. It's a classic," I responded with a smile.

We dipped in the pool, and Ken attempted to teach me how to swim. I made good progress in being able to float but did not master the swimming part. After about an hour, I returned to the chaise, dried off, and watched Ken get drafted by some teenagers into a water polo game. He smiled when he returned to his seat; his team had won the match. I told him there was something I wanted to show him, and we picked up the towels from the chairs and put them in the bin.

"Where are we going?" he asked.

"We are almost there," I replied.

With hands entwined, we returned indoors, crossing the large lobby to a barely noticeable door on the other side.

"I booked a couple's massage this morning while you were showering. I thought it would be an excellent bonding experience. What do you think?"

He didn't answer; he just pulled me over and squeezed me in his arms. Our masseuse directed us to follow her. They set the room up with two separate massage tables so we would have simultaneous massages, and another masseuse was already there. They offered us two robes to undress and left the room; we were each offered a glass of champagne. When they returned, we spent the next hour in complete relaxation and bliss, with dim lighting, soft Asian music in the background, and a light, ethereal perfume from a diffuser. I could have stayed at that table forever, but we had to get up when the hour was over. I stood up, unsure I would stay up, my body so mellow and loose. We thanked the therapists and left.

"The massage was wonderful," Ken said. "I can't remember the last time I felt so relaxed."

"That was the intent," I said, "although I can remember exactly the last time I was so relaxed. When you gave me such a wonderful massage on your last visit, I fell asleep until the morning."

We reached the lobby and stopped at the gift shop. We were there for about half an hour, and I saw some exciting craft items, but I reasoned they were likely overpriced and that we would do better getting them at a local shop. We headed upstairs to shower and change for dinner.

I wore my favorite billowy white cotton dress and strappy white sandals. I spent fifteen minutes making sure that, with the help of a pick and setting gel, my natural curls perfectly framed my face the way I expected. I bought this hair gel for a small fortune from my hairdresser. I must say the results did not disappoint. My skin was glowing from spending two days outdoors, and after contouring, filling in my eyebrows, and adding a gorgeous shade of lipstick and a slight blush to my cheeks, I was ready to go. I also wore small dangling earrings with a delicate matching necklace. Of course, the *pièce de résistance* was to finish it with a few short bursts of *Arpege* perfume around my neck, decolletage, wrists, the inside of my elbows, and the back of my knees. Ken stepped out of the dressing room wearing a nice pair of chino pants and natural-colored loafers. He had on a white cotton shirt rolled up at the sleeves. The top button was open, but I walked over, opened two more, and smiled, saying,

"Now you look scrumptious!"

"So do you!" he said, giving me a noisy kiss on the forehead, most likely not wanting to disturb my lipstick. His thoughtfulness was so overwhelming that it often moved me to swoon.

The doorman signaled to one of the waiting taxis and gave the driver our destination, which he had inquired about as soon as he saw us. I found it silly to be taking a cab to a place hardly a mile away, but Ken insisted he would not let me walk in my pretty sandals, so my choices were I allow him to carry me to the restaurant or we use the cab. I pretended to be defeated, gave him a wink, and agreed to the cab.

Although on the busiest part of the tourists' strip, the restaurant was a stand-alone, romantically illuminated with strings of white lights. We sat in the back on a lighted, open-air patio with soft steel band music piping through the invisible speakers. There was a medium-sized pink, peach, and white arrangement of lilies on each table and two small unlit candles. The restaurant was almost full without being crowded. We had arrived for the first seating of the evening. The closest table to us was empty, to both our delights. Our waiter, a very handsome Bajan young man with glowing ebony skin and high cheekbones that would make anyone green with envy, greeted us, lit our candles, and elaborated a bit on the various menu choices.

After telling the waiter I was interested in authentic cuisine, I opted for Bajan pan-seared Mahi Mahi served with seasoned rice, lentils, and a fresh salad. Ken chose chicken curry with signature Bajan seasoning, fried sweet plantains, and a salad. We requested sparkling water and went with his recommendation of blush wine. I had a piece of Jamaican rum cake for dessert, and Ken had coconut rum cheesecake. Everything was delicious, and we both cleaned our plates and declared ourselves stuffed. I asked the waiter about beach access, and he told us to walk to the end of the strip where there would be a beach entrance; if we turned left, we could walk on the sand till we arrived at our hotel. Ken left a nice tip as we thanked him and left.

It was a beautiful night; everyone was about, and the atmosphere was very festive—a band played in a small square in the middle of the strip. We sat and listened for about half an hour while soaking in the fun atmosphere. The singer hit a few off-key notes, but no one minded, and the crowd applauded after each song. I felt pretty mellow but wasn't sure whether it resulted from the delicious meal, the two glasses of wine at dinner, or a residue of the couple's massage, maybe all three combined. I could stay there forever, but when Ken asked if we should head back, I said yes and we headed toward the beach access. He asked again if I was sure we should not get a cab, and I replied by removing my sandals and hooking the straps through my fingers while lifting the hem of the pretty white dress to my knees.

"Unless you would rather not walk, dearest, I would prefer we walk back," I said.

"I have no objections, and I would enjoy a moonlit stroll before bedtime." Ken removed his shoes, rolled up the cuffs of his pants, and took my hand in his.

We walked to the edge of the sand, the water lapping at our feet, the giant moon overhead, and a very gentle breeze accompanying us to our hotel. We were standing in the sand, almost facing our room's balcony, when Ken dropped his shoes and pulled me to him. His hug was tender rather than tight; his lips kissed my temple, and he murmured,

"Let's stand here for a minute, Nickie; it's not a moment I'll ever have in Minneapolis. I love you so much and never want to forget it."

I raised my head, and our lips met in a tender kiss. I rested my head on his shoulders, and we held each other without a word, facing the water and taking in the beauty of this moonlight-drenched ocean. When another couple appeared from that direction, we parted and headed to the front hotel lobby, crossing it toward the outdoor pool showers, where we rinsed the sand off our feet before putting on our shoes and heading upstairs.

The room was cool enough. I turned off the AC and opened the sliding doors to let in the cool sea breeze, which, combined with the surf, should be nice enough to lure us to sleep. Ken had gone to the dressing room and came out clothed only in blue-gray silk pajama shorts. The shorts showed the incredible V-shaped muscle from his hip bones to his pelvis, always evoking admiration and a twinge of desire magnified by the unawareness of his potent sexual attraction. He headed for the mini-fridge.

"I am getting a wine cooler, love. Would you like anything?"

"Get me one as well, sweetie. I'll join you on the balcony in a minute."

I exchanged the dress for my lavender babydoll and joined him on the terrace, wrapping my arms around his waist from the back. He removed my hands and pulled me by his side, both of us leaning against the railing, looking at the undulating waters of the ocean.

"We hardly spoke on our way back tonight. What were you thinking about?" I asked.

"You, me, us mostly, and how lucky we are to be here on this vacation. If you had told me four months ago that I would be here today on a beach in Barbados with this incredible woman who has made me happier than I have any right to be, I would have told you to stop dreaming. Yet here we are, and my heart is so full I can't describe the feeling."

"I have gone to heaven without dying and am not worthy of so much happiness. Forgive me if I get biblical on you, but this brings to mind a phrase in the Song of Solomon: 'I found him whom my soul loveth.' I am sorry, but everything I read, see, and think of invariably brings you to mind. I love you so much, Ken, that it scares me."

"Not as much as loving you makse me happy, Nickie."

"You know you can always talk to me, right?"

"Yes, I know."

"A while back, I believe it was when you were in NY, you mentioned dealing with some emotional issues. Would you like to elaborate?"

"Not really, I am alright. It's in the past, and I am okay now."

'No matter what it is, your daughters, Mary Lou, the job, your friends, or anything else, I am ready to listen without comments. What was weighing on your heart?"

"Things are good right now, and I can handle all you mentioned. Maybe I put more pressure on myself than anyone else, but sometimes, I worry about my daughters, caught between Mary Lou and me because of the divorce. I also don't think I am doing enough to help my friends, and my work is endless. Until you came along, acting in the theater was my main lifeline. You have made me so happy that I'm scared. Scared of failing, of losing everything."

"You won't. But you have to let me in. Share your burdens. We won't sink."

"Did I ever tell you about Guy, a college friend I had?"

"No, not that I recall."

"Anyway, he wasn't a close friend. Four of us worked at the college library and had decided on a Friday afternoon to attend a free music concert in Central Park.

He talked incessantly and was very hyper, but we were used to him. We considered him eccentric but a good sort. A train was leaving the platform. It wasn't the one we needed. For no apparent reason, Guy took off running down the subway platform and tried unsuccessfully to jump onto the last car of the departing train and fell. Someone was screaming, and it took an older woman's hand on my shoulder to make me realize it was me. They called an ambulance, and two men jumped on the tracks to rescue him. Guy was severely hurt, and took more than a year to recover from his injuries. We found out later that he had bipolar disorder and had stopped taking his medication during a manic stage. None of us knew he had mental health issues and thus didn't know to look out for unusual behavior. His family knew of his struggles, but they were from a culture where mental health wasn't discussed and was shameful, so no one knew of Guy's issues. The remaining three of us were traumatized, feeling that somehow, we should have known and been of more help. It took me months of talking to the school counselor before I could manage the guilt of not knowing."

"That's a sad story."

"Yes, I only brought it up to let you know I am ready to listen should you ever need an ear."

"Don't worry. I am fine; I feel pressured at times. Thanks for the offer. I love you."

"I love you more."

Before I knew what was happening, Ken put his arm under my knee, lifted and carried me to the bed, where he gently put me down. I had rolled down the bed-spread, and once he slipped in next to me, I pulled up the top sheet to our waists. Ken pulled me to him on the bed with my head resting on his shoulder and my arms lying across his chest. He had his other arm loosely draped around my waist; all I could think about was how comfortable it felt.

"Night, Sweetie."

"Good night, my Love," he answered, kissing my lips.

Ken

I was great at giving massages, but I had never received one in return, so I didn't know how good one would be. Thinking about it, I felt terrific. The clock radio pro-claimed it was 6:04 a.m.; I thought only minutes had elapsed. Nickie stirred from sleep and raised her head to look at me. She presumed I was asleep, carefully pulled away to close the balcony sliding doors, and turned on the AC.

When I heard her finish brushing and slide open the shower door, I got out of bed and joined her in the bathroom. I brushed my teeth. She hadn't started lather-ing when I entered the shower. She stood with her eyes closed, letting the water run down her body. She knew I was there, though, because as soon as I stood in the tub, we reached out for each other simultaneously. We stood there for a few seconds, and then she opened her eyes, reached behind me for the soap, and started lather-ing me, beginning with my neck and working her way down, at first avoiding my genitals in favor of my thighs and legs. On her way back up my body, her hands so softly soaped and massaged my penis and testicles. My breath caught as she ran her fingers over my erect manhood. I was about to declare the situation unfair when she removed her hand, grabbed the shower hose, and sprayed the suds off my body. Without finishing, she asked me to please kneel while opening the small shampoo bottle to start on my hair. I closed my eyes for a moment, partly because of the suds but mostly to fully enjoy the delicious scalp massage her soft yet firm hands gave me. Once the shampoo rinsed off my head, she directed the jet flow to the rest of my body. I got up, gently grabbed her wrist, and murmured, "My turn, love."

I grabbed her shampoo, but she stopped me. "Only the conditioner, for now; I shampooed last night, and another one this morning would be too harsh on my hair. I squirted the conditioner in my palm and massaged it into her scalp and hair. She was still standing as I was taller; she didn't need to kneel. Her eyes were closed, and from her faint smile, I could feel her enjoyment of my fingers on her scalp. Any moment now, I expected her to purr. When the first sound escaped her lips, I quickly rinsed out the conditioner, grabbed the soap, and started lathering her body. The water was cool, not cold, but her perky nipples and breasts conveyed a message that I was happy to understand. My hands continued to her hips and thighs; she slightly parted them, but as she did to me, my hands avoided her center until they returned on the way up her thighs. I could hear her breath catch as my fingers gently touched that part of her. Seeing and touching her beautiful, lithe, sinewy little body made my erection almost painful. I somehow lathered and rinsed her back and buttocks without going crazy and losing all control from wanting her. I bent my head to kiss her when she opened her eyes and exclaimed, "Ken, if you don't start making love to me soon, I will explode!" I pulled her to me, and my lips met hers before she could finish the sentence. I had put the shower nozzle back on its cradle, and the water was hitting the back of my neck and running down our entwined bodies. My lips were going down the side of her neck and alternatively going lower where my tongue gently flicked around her very erect nipples and sucked them into my mouth. Her head leaned back; she held my shoulders as if her life depended on it. Her legs faltered slightly when I kneeled before her, buried my head in her center, and grabbed her buttock.

I pulled myself to a standing position with her back leaning against the shower wall. Her thighs and legs on my shoulders loosely encircled my head. She was whimpering, and the sounds from her made me realize how much of a challenge I had to control my body.

"Are you ready, love?"

"Yes, please."

Her legs went from my shoulders to wrap themselves around my waist. Although I was bursting with desire, I let her decide how much of me she was ready to have. She took hold of me and slightly inserted the tip of my penis into herself. It was a slow back-and-forth cadence that soon progressed into having more than half of me in her and fully embracing my manhood with a vigorous push and a firm tightening of her legs around me. She then relaxed and said, "Now, please." I started an awkward back-and-forth movement, with Nickie firmly pressing against me and her back resting on the wall. It took no time for us to find the right rhythm, and as movements became more frantic, the glass door wholly fogged up. Still, we were oblivious to all that, consumed by our mutual passion as if we could defy the rules of nature and physics and merge our two bodies into one being. I felt her weight shift, her back arch, and her knees clench, the extra tightness like a vise around my penis as her spasms started. Still, before I could finish entertaining that thought, I felt myself erupt inside her as if every drop of liquid, not just my sperm, wanted to find its way within and claim her forever.

As we exited the bathroom, the front desk called to inform us that our rental car was ready at the kiosk for pickup after 8 a.m. We were still determining our itinerary for the day but planned on keeping busy. We used a canvas bag I had bought for some unexplainable reason. We threw in our bathing suits, two new pairs of flip-flops, beach towels, sunscreen, lip gloss, an island map, sunglasses, hat, and visor, two disposable cameras, wallets, room key, and some cash.

"Don't forget the kitchen sink, love!" I quipped with a smile and a wink.

"Any more wisecrack, dearest, I will put you in the trunk!" she replied.

"This, love, is why we rented a Jeep without a trunk; plus, since you dislike driving, how would we go about it?"

"It's a good thing I love you. I forgive you for mocking my thoroughness."

"I love you," I said as I picked up the bag from the bed, and took her hand.

Nickie

For once, we arrived on time for a hot breakfast. I had a Western omelet and coffee while Ken piled on poached eggs, English muffins, mango juice, pastries, and tea.

"Someone worked up an appetite this morning," I said with a smile.

"We were two chefs in the kitchen, if I recall," answered Ken.

He gave me his cute, lopsided smile, and a wink. I looked at him and smiled back, grateful that he could not see the warm blush I felt on my face. We ate leisurely, our left hands intertwined on the white tablecloth as we sipped coffee and tea.

As a former British colony, they drive on the left in Barbados; there was no way I could have managed that, so I was very grateful that it came as second nature to Ken. We consulted the map and made our stop in Bridgetown. Bridgetown is on the southwestern coast of Barbados. It's the capital and largest city of Barbados, its major port, and commercial center, and has a rich colonial and cultural heritage. I had researched most of it before the trip, anticipating that we would visit the town, and was glad I had done so.

We parked on a side street and browsed through the colorful stores on Broad Street and Swan Street. Our next stop was the Barbados Garrison, a complex of military and civic buildings from the 17th to 19th centuries. About four miles south of Bridgetown is the Barbados Boardwalk, and we walked a mile across the coast, connecting the Accra and Camelot beaches. They had benches to rest on and enjoy some splendid ocean views. We didn't stop at any of the many cafés, bars, or restaurants along the way since the distance was too short for needing rest. I wore my large-brim sun hat and sunglasses and felt like a movie star.

Afterward, we headed for a couple of old plantation houses where they produced sugar in the seventeenth and eighteenth centuries. St. Nicholas Abbey in St. Paul's showcased the history and culture of Barbados, filled with antiques, paintings, and artifacts about the lives of the owners, the enslaved people, and the workers who lived and worked there. It had become a museum, and the rum distillery had the most tourists and visitors of all the sites. There was also a beautiful garden, a cafe, and a gift shop. Our last stop was the Sunbury Plantation House, which has mahogany antiques. The house was open to the public, and we saw all its rooms and a unique collection of horse-drawn carriages.

We returned to the hotel in the late afternoon. We were tired but happy with our active day. After turning in the car at the rental kiosk, we looked forward to a light dinner and stargazing on the balcony. The pretty young Bajan woman with a million-watt smile at the booth asked us if we had already been to Oistins. We told her we had heard the name before but hadn't been there. She informed us it was the one place not to miss and that leaving Barbados without going there would be unthinkable. Her enthusiasm was contagious. We thanked her and headed upstairs to change for this unexpected adventure. I dressed in a yellow and white sundress with flats, and Ken wore khaki shorts and a polo shirt. We stopped at the desk to ask the concierge about the distance. There was another couple there and, on hearing our question, interrupted, saying,

"Hi, that's where we are going as well, and if you like, we could share a taxi. I am Helen, and this is my husband, Thierry." Thierry offered his hand and an enormous smile.

"We have been there before, but tonight is our last night in Barbados. We had so much fun last week when we went there that we could not imagine returning to Canada without experiencing it again."

They seemed to be in their early thirties with broad smiles and positive energies. I looked at Ken and asked,

"What do you think?"

"Seems like a good idea to me!"

He turned to Thierry and Helen and said, "I am Ken, and this is my girlfriend, Nickie!"

"Nice to meet you," we all said at once and burst out laughing; then, we headed for the lobby's front door.

That Oistins was a fun place was an understatement, as it seemed like all the island inhabitants and tourists alike came to enjoy this legendary fish fry party. No other island could match this fish fry in Barbados. The beauty is that all you needed was beer, food, and delightful music. There were dozens of little booths offering fresh fish, lobster, pork chops, chicken, and the island's favorite macaroni pie. Lively music from competing sound systems ensured the mood stayed festive through the evening. The party area extended from Welches Beach to Miami Beach on the south coast. We were lucky to score a table from which six party-goers moved for a larger one. Helen assured us we had one of the best spots for the food kiosks, and Thierry agreed. We had no clue, so we went along. I volunteered to stay and guard the table while the three of them headed for the food booths. I trusted Ken to get me what I would enjoy, and everything seemed delicious from the look of things. They returned a few minutes later. Ken loaded with two full plates, and Thierry and Helen each held a plate and two beers.

Thierry and Helen were a lovely couple, thirty-three and thirty-one. There was positive energy around them, as if they were always on the verge of laughter, expecting something fun to happen around each corner. They were from the province of Saskatchewan in Canada. He was an engineer for a big oil company, and she was a junior college professor. We had a good laugh about how they presumed Ken was British, and he had to explain that he was American but spent the first seventeen years of his life in England, thus the accent. They thought I was thirty-one, figured Ken to be around thirty-six, and refused to believe we were older. I was used to people assuming I was younger than my age, but it never failed to please me. Ken beamed. They thought he was ten years younger and did not protest too much when they refused to believe him. Looking at him, I could see why anyone would consider him younger. His physique would be the envy of even a twenty-year-old. He told me he didn't go to the gym and had no time between all the extra hours he worked and spending most of his leisure time with his daughters and the theater. Instead, the constant yard work and physical labor he engaged in while maintaining the woods and lake around his property were solely responsible for his staying in good physical shape. His face was unlined, only with a barely visible crease at the corner of his eyes when he smiled his endearing, lopsided, dimple-rich smile. Right now, with the golden hue beginning a tan, the hazel of his eyes in the late afternoon, and the deep red highlights in his brownish curls, I thought Michaelangelo's *David* honestly had nothing on him. But again, I was biased, and this man sent cascades of heat through my body from only looking at him!

We left the party around 11:30 p.m. after having a good time. Helen and Thierry had a competition going on in the beer-drinking department. I bowed out after my first one, and Ken managed two but stopped after that. I had a second serving of flying fish. Thierry regaled us with stories that cracked us up, although Helen winked at us whenever she thought he was embellishing the facts. People around us got up and danced any time the music moved them, and I dragged Ken up for several pieces when they played Bob Marley's reggae songs and an old Trinidadian calypso that got everybody jumping. Thierry and Helen also had fun moving to the music, although calling their movements dancing would be a stretch. We laughed at everything but mostly at ourselves.

"Hey guys, I just remembered. As soon as I finish grading my students' papers, we plan a three-week trip to Cape Verde in June. Our travel agent found us the perfect package, and we're so excited! Maybe you guys could come with us! Our agent could find a similar package for you," exclaimed Helen as we got into a taxi.

"That's a generous offer, thank you. Unfortunately, I won't be able to make it due to my daughters' custodial arrangements," said Ken.

"Me neither, although it sounds fantastic! I have some work obligations that I can't get out of."

"Aw, that's too bad. But we understand. Let's keep in touch and plan a trip together for another time when we're all available," offered Helen.

"That's a great idea!" said Ken.

It crossed my mind that they were likely financially comfortable, but working in the oil industry was lucrative regardless of the country or the company.

We said our goodbyes as we got off the elevator on the third floor, and they continued to the sixth. They had insisted on exchanging phone numbers in case "we changed our minds" about the June vacation.

I stretched my arms blissfully, eyes closed, before I realized Ken wasn't beside me. My eyes flew open in panic before his lips kissed my forehead.

"Good morning, Love. I watched you sleep, debating whether to wake you or succumb to my desire to have my way with you."

Before I could reply, there was a knock on the door and a voice announced,

"Room service."

"Too bad," said Ken as he rose from sitting on my side of the bed and went to open the door. I noticed he had already showered and dressed in shorts and a white t-shirt. His hair still looked damp. I slipped under the covers as he opened the door, accepted the breakfast tray, and thanked the server with a tip. Ken opened the sliding doors and deposited the tray on the small balcony table.

"Breakfast is served, Milady."

"Pour yourself a cup of tea, and I'll be right there, sweetie."

Reaching for the robe at the foot of the bed, I emerged from the covers. I entered the bathroom, brushed my teeth, and joined Ken on the terrace. He had his cup of tea and poured me a cup of coffee.

"Thank you, Sweetie," I said while kissing his waiting lips.

We sat at the small table facing the sea and fed each other delicious bites of *Chausson aux Pommes* and *Pain au chocolat,* which he had fallen in love with since our first day's breakfast buffet. We each had a serving of sliced bananas and blueberries and a second cup of tea and coffee. We left the room an hour later, dressed in shorts, T-shirts, flip-flops, sunglasses, and hats.

We still had Ken's canvas bag full of necessities and headed for Bottom Bay Beach. After navigating a set of stairs cut into the cliff, we reached the top. The setting was spectacular, with majestic cliffs on three sides and giant palm trees framing the back of it. We found a spot and settled for a languorous morning of sun and sand, sporadic reading and napping, delicious stolen kisses and hugs, lazy conversation, an enjoyable lunch picked up on the way, periodic dips in the water, and admiring the majesty and beauty of the turquoise sea. In the early afternoon, we visited a large cave extending into the rock face at the north end of the beach. On our way out, someone indicated a path to the right of the car park that enabled us to reach the cliffs, where we took incredible coastline pictures. When we got back in the car to return to the hotel, we felt blessed, happy, and grateful. It had been a perfect day so far.

After a delicious dinner at the hotel, we strolled to the tourist strip, hand in hand. The sound of a different band playing on the square caught our attention, and we ordered two rum and Coke to sip while listening to the music. The atmosphere was festive and inviting, and the Caribbean night was beautiful. As we walked back, our arms around each other's waists, we occasionally stopped for a hug and kisses. We marveled at the night sky's glorious beauty, where all existing stars seemed to shine to help us enjoy our last evening of fun on the island. Our pace slowed down as we got closer to the hotel. We stopped at the desk to request a wake-up call, although our return flight wasn't due to leave till mid-morning. It took us about fifteen minutes to pack our suitcases, including the bathing suits we had used, rinsed, and hung out to dry on the balcony when we returned from the beach. It had been a beautiful, balmy evening, and they were already dry. Our mood was subdued. I had my head in the crook of his neck and shoulder, my hand resting on the skin of his upper arm. We hardly spoke, maybe neither of us trusting ourselves not to choke up from the fear of separation, enjoying and savoring the intimacy of our last vacation evening together.

Ken

I knew we would be sore in the morning if we slept on the chaise all night. Nickie had fallen asleep on my chest, my arms enfolding her; I could still feel the small wet spot where her tears had dropped silently. I had to make a valiant effort not to let mine flow, at least not until after she fell asleep. We had hardly spoken, holding on to each other, not wanting these few days in paradise ever to end.

Real life intruded, and we had obligations in the States. I laid there with her for another ten minutes, then carefully put her in bed without waking her up. I thought I had succeeded when she became agitated, grabbed my arm, and murmured, "I love you, Ken; I love you so much."

"I love you more," I replied and glanced at her only to realize she had spoken in her sleep, no doubt talking to me in her dream. I removed my t-shirt and briefs, softly slipped into the bed, and pulled her into my arms.

"Ken, don't leave, Ken, don't."

I came awake, not realizing I had dozed off. Nickie was moving in her sleep again. She had grabbed and tightly squeezed a pillow to her chest. I pulled her to me, kissing her temple gently and murmuring,

"I am here, not going anywhere. I love you."

"Ken?"

"Yes, my love."

"Where are you going?"

"Nowhere, Love, you were dreaming. I am here."

She raised her chin, and kissed me. I responded to her in what I thought would be a reassuring kiss, but within a few seconds, like a match to a candle, I could feel our bodies responding to each other. We didn't move, letting the smoldering heat rise between us. She was the first to budge, moving her right hand from the small of my back to caress my buttocks. Her gentle touch only made me feel more rigid against the softness of her upper thigh. It must have been minutes, but it felt like an eternity before she gently pushed herself a few inches away from me, moved higher on her side, brought her hand to hold my shoulder, and slowly and shielded me in the heat of her warm vagina.

Nothing was said; nothing needed to be said. We were rocking to the gentle motion and the slow rhythm as Nickie straddled my hips. I could not see her face clearly in the semi-darkness, but I knew her eyes were closed. The strength of her tiny hands pinning me to the bed showed that she was enjoying our coupling on a whole different level. I gave up the effort and closed my eyes to enjoy the pleasure coursing through me fully. When her movements intensified and her breathing caught, I was happy to grab her waist as I thrust myself into her, matching our needs and urgency; then, a cascading wave of sensations made us cry out,

"I love you," in unison, and we reached our climax.

Nickie laid her head in the crook of my shoulder a moment later, and we kissed softly. I wrapped my arms around her, pulled the sheet over us, and slept deeply until the morning light.

Nickie

We packed our remaining items and ate a continental breakfast in the dining room the following day. We sat on the patio, holding hands, admiring the turquoise waves lapping against the shore. This soothing rhythm echoed the lazy afternoon memories we had just made—a dreamy escape that temporarily shielded us from the complexities of our lives. But reality seeped back in. The vacation was a quick fix—a temporary salve for deeper issues. I glanced at Ken, his sun-kissed skin glowing, gorgeous hair where the fiery strands of auburn had won their battle against the sedate browns. I recognized the apprehension in his eyes.

"This is my most beautiful and memorable vacation so far. Thanks, sweetie, for making it possible," I said.

"I wish it wouldn't end."

"I know. We need more than fleeting moments. We need a vision of our future."

"And some patience, I was thinking…"

The shuttle interrupted the conversation, making its presence known through screeching and a horn. We gathered our belongings, and Ken handed the suitcases to the driver.

"I want to spend every minute with you I can, including our flight home," was his answer when I expressed a delighted surprise at us being on the same flight to JFK from where he would take a connecting flight to Minneapolis.

My heart lurched at his words, and I had to push back the tears that threatened to spill down my face. I didn't trust myself to reply.

I hugged him tightly and whispered, "I love you."

We held hands through the flight, me leaning on his shoulder while making small talk, chiding ourselves for not taking more pictures, and laughing and recounting some of the more outlandish stories that Thierry and Helen told us. At JFK, I walked Ken to his gate, and we waited there until they announced boarding for his flight, just holding each other before I gave him a long, lingering kiss. My arms felt immeasurably empty when he pulled away and went to the boarding gate. I turned around with my carry-on, walked to the terminal airport exit, and got a yellow cab home. New York was winking at me once more.

"Anxiety"

I looked out the window, gazing at the city lights, but in my mind, I saw a sunny balcony and tasted sun-kissed skin and saltwater. The laughter, the tangled limbs—they were etched in memory. I traced the edge of a seashell souvenir from our trip. It seemed as out of place among the files and ledgers as I felt back in the office. After the first half-hour exchange of greetings and pleasantries this morning, catching up with everything piled up on my to-do list made it a busy and exhausting day. The silver lining was that my boss was in Aspen for the week, and there were no unproductive meetings to attend. By the end of the day tomorrow, I would be all caught up.

I set up the computer as soon as I arrived home. I heated up and ate the delicious minestrone I had bought for dinner at the restaurant by the bus station, but I left it unfinished when I heard a small ping from the chat box, which made me smile.

Chat 19—8/17/98

DK: Good evening, my love. How are you?

NC: Hello sweetie. Home safe. Miss you already. I can't believe vacation is over. Wish you were here. My day was very productive but otherwise uneventful. You?

DK: I miss you more than words can say. It's as if the distance stretches wider every day to see how far our hearts can reach. It's tough.

NC: I love you. We need a strategy. A famous French author named Antoine de Saint-Exupery once said "A goal without a plan is just a wish." I want more than that.

DK: When you first mentioned it, it took me by surprise, but you may be right. We should at least explore the big things.

NC: Like, ideally, where we would like to live? Your daughters' proximity, work preference, etc. We don't need anything precise, just an idea to make sure we are on the same page. For instance, if you were interested in coming to NY, you would find great theater possibilities.

DK: Would you consider moving?

NC: Sure, although Minneapolis would not be my first pick because of the cold winters.

DK: I wouldn't want to inflict that on you. I love you.

NC: I love you more!

Subj: ***Being back***
Date: 8/18/98 1:15:04 PM EDT

Dearest Nickie,

Good afternoon, my love. Is your day going well? I discovered an additional problem with the computer last night after our chat. We may not be able to connect this evening.

I don't know what to do with myself tonight. The director canceled rehearsal, and I can't access the Internet to speak with you. They asked me to be an extra in a movie they are filming here called Herman USA.

We should have made love on the beach in Barbados under the stars. The full moon had already set the stage for us. Before I forget, I received the postcard we sent to each other the day we left. I was instantly transported back there with you. Did you receive yours? It was such a great idea! I love you.

Till then,
Ken

Subj: ***Re: Being back***
Date: 8/18/98

Dearest Ken,

Did you say we can't chat tonight? I seem to be addicted to you as well. I haven't received the postcard yet; it'll probably be there tonight. Something good to look forward to! I'll write a longer letter soon.

Till then
Nickie

Subj: ***Another mail***
Date: 8/18/98

Dearest Ken,

Are your guests being careful when they use the computer? By the way, when are they leaving? New computers rarely have these many problems.

I wonder if something is conspiring to keep us apart. I will be miserable again; it sometimes happens when I am incredibly frustrated and cannot resolve it. I am not passive and struggle to accept things, yet I trust that everything happens for the best. It doesn't make it easier to deal with, and somehow, my day is spoiled. I am angry, unsure of the cause. I hope our communication system smooths out soon. I feel like a starving person at a banquet where I can smell the aroma of the food but can't touch it, only view it through a glass. That is how I have been feeling about us lately, and my mood suffers. I know it's not your fault; as much as technology helps, it can also hinder, but the result is a challenging sense of impotence.

I am sorry I sound dejected. I miss you terribly, and e-mails don't cut it. I'll be fine tomorrow. I get upset at anything keeping us apart. I love you. Ignore my bad mood. I wish we were on that Caribbean beach making love right now.

Till then,
Nickie

Subj: *Not pleased either*
Date: 8/18/98 2:47:16 PM EDT

Dearest Nickie,

Tim tells me they are being careful with the computer. I took the CPU apart, and we discovered the video driver card was defective. Gateway is sending me a new one, but it won't be here for 3-5 days. I miss you. Today, I considered asking how expensive your apartments were and how the job market was there.

Till then love
Ken

Subj: ***Loving in the Caribbean***
Date: 8/19/98 12:00:16 PM EDT

Dearest Nickie,

I have to learn to type faster. I could not work up the enthusiasm for the movie, so I didn't go last night; instead, I made some soup, went to bed at nine o'clock, and held you in my arms all night.

I keep losing the message. We sit on a blanket on the grassy edge of a beautiful white sand beach under tall, bowed palm trees. We built a fire, and the flames flutter in the evening breeze. The evening air is warm. You can feel its heat as it licks your skin; the setting sun is a burnt orange above the horizon, with bands of deep purple. I notice the sky, deep black with uncountable stars. The flames paint your soft skin with yellows, oranges, and amber as they dance.

Laughing, you pick up, and we run down the beach together; we run naked through the surf, scattering the gulls. Amidst their cries, I catch you silhouetted in the moonlight. I grab you, and we kiss, our fingers entwined.

By the way, how would you imagine your ideal life?

Till then, love
Ken

Subj: ***On my way***
Date: 8/19/98

Dearest Ken,

Reading your fantasy has suddenly made me ache for you. I love you. I know you have the girls tonight; say hello from me.

Regarding my ideal life, I don't envision anything outlandish, yet everything I see is important. Above all, I wish to be healthy and active well into my late 90s. Seeing my son successful and content with a loving family would bring me great joy. I would want to live this life with the love of my life in a place that would give us joy. Of course, It's important to me that my parents and siblings are also healthy and happy in their own ways. My partner/husband and I should find fulfillment in our chosen job/career/business, or passions while positively impacting others. Learning and reading are things I want to continue doing as I believe if we lived 100 lifetimes, we would still have so much more to learn.

Last but not least, I would like to travel the world, meet people, and experience different cultures until I am in my 90s. You can see, I want everything, at least all the essential things. How about you?

Till then
Nickie

Subj: ***Good morning***
Date: 8/20/98 7:40:45 AM EDT

Dearest Nickie

Good morning, my love. Last night with the girls was different; we went to Perkins for dinner. It's a casual eating-in kitchen place. A machine had a claw and the potential to win a small stuffed animal for 50 cents, but only if you could get it to the exit without dropping it. Chelsea and Claire threw a fit because I didn't want to give them more than 50 cents each. They became so upset that I took them to a toy store and bought a stuffed Garfield for each one. I may have future gamblers in the making.

We had thunderstorms last night, and it made for good sleeping. I did stay up long enough to watch the storm for a while. Lightning is beautiful, especially in the distance, where you see it trail up in the cloud, unlike the brilliant flash that comes straight down. It is like watching light dance. It helped me think about your question regarding my ideal life.

My vision is similar to yours in all the significant points. In that perfect life, we would be together and share my girls' lives as they grow into well-adjusted women. We would also have a cat and dog throughout. I would be active and happy and be able to make love to you at least into my 80s (the best part!) Are you smiling? Of course, I would continue my acting career and publish several poetry books. Be capable of always helping those in need. And, most importantly, always have your smile waiting for me when I get home. I love you.

Till then,
Ken

Subj: ***Good morning, darling***
Date: 8/20/98

Dearest Ken,

Your evening was "interesting." You learned something about what fascinates Chelsea and Claire. You know never to take them to Las Vegas or Atlantic City, or they'll clean you out! Seriously though, sometimes kids are unpredictable in what they find entertaining; they could get as fascinated by Nintendo as by an anthill. Their minds are very open, fascinated by many things.

I also slept well last night, although I woke up at 3:50. I had taken some Nyquil before bed. I woke up feeling much better; I hugged my body pillow very tightly, kept my eyes closed, and imagined it was you kissing my cheeks.

I wish I could have watched the storm with you. I fear thunder and lightning, but I would have been okay with your arms around me. I can even picture it now. How is your day thus far?

Yesterday afternoon, on the spur of the moment, I called you. I was so excited about surprising you, but no one was home. I would have loved to see your face as you realized it was me. I love you.

Till then,
Nickie

Subj: *Technology*
Date: 8/20/98 11:57:28 AM EDT

Dearest Nickie,

My love, I can only hope which cheeks! Bummer, my phone is my PC's built-in answering machine, and it's on when I am not on the Internet, but since the PC is down, I imagine it is the phone. I hadn't considered it. I can get a receiver and unplug the computer. Today is day 3 of 3 - 5. I hope my video card will be there when I get home.

> *Remember*
> *On this day,*
> *Smile for me,*
> *Whenever possible, laugh,*
> *Give warmth,*
> *For, unlike tomorrow,*
> *Today,*
> *Shall never be,*
> *Again.*

I'm taking this weekend off so that you know. I am losing my enthusiasm for work. The empty box came to return my defective board to Gateway. Hopefully, the replacement board will arrive today; I admit to a great deal of anxiousness. I miss you.

Till then, love
Ken

Subj: *Good morning*
Date: 8/21/98

Dearest Ken,

Losing your enthusiasm for work, you said? It doesn't sound at all like you. Is everything OK? I've burdened you enough with work concerns so, remember, I'm here to listen.

How are rehearsals going? Are you still wearing your "statement"? Sometimes, I picture you with Dockers pants, a polo shirt, and loafers, sort of yuppie-looking. I remember your nice muscular legs. In all my excitement, each time we met, I forgot to check your backside (I suppose I had better things, such as your lips, arms, and face, to occupy my field of vision and my thoughts at the time).

I will gladly indulge you occasionally if you teach me how to give you a nice back rub. I don't want to get too graphic since you are at work. I love you.

Till then
Nickie

Subj: ***Lunch?***
Date: 8/21/98 12:58:06 PM EDT

Dearest Nickie,

I felt this lack of enthusiasm before. It's like an invisible presence in my life, a shadowy figure I sometimes glance at from the corner of my eyes and can outrun for months or years. What I am saying doesn't make much sense, but it's not an overpowering feeling for now. Maybe, during our vacation, I realized there is another world to escape to instead of just duty and responsibilities—mere wishful thinking.

It is funny that you should mention Dockers; I bought a pair last week and a couple of cargo pants, so I don't have to carry a lot around in my back pockets. In both cases, they accent the roundness of my bottom.

I saved the second picture you sent to a floppy and brought it to work, so you are now in a window on my PC on my desk. I finally located the film from Milwaukee and am having it, and the one from Barbados developed; I can't wait! I love you.

Till then,
Ken

Subj: ***Good morning***
Date: 8/24/98 8:32:27 AM EDT

Dearest Nickie,

Good morning, my love. How are things on the renting front?

Good humor. A young friend asked if I would be the stripper at Stella's bachelorette party. Flattering at first (Stella is 19), but the girls implied their boyfriends wouldn't be upset if I were the stripper.

You look beautiful (and I would not have suspected your age if you had not told me). I will never tire of telling you or remembering the feel of your body against my skin, your weight in my arms, your taste, or the sound of your laughter. I love contemplating you. I hope your day goes well.

Till then, love
Ken

Subj: ***Re: Good morning***
Date: 8/24/98

Dearest Ken,

I know how you feel about comments like those from your young friends; something similar happened to me recently. My younger cousin Emilie, twenty-two years old, made me feel quite ancient. She looked at me and said, Nickie, you're over thirty. Aren't you, like, geriatric?

Do you have any particular concerns about getting older? For me, there are none yet, maybe because nothing in the mirror reflects my chronological age so far. Getting reading glasses for small prints made me realize that things are not static. I am not worried about career progression since I constantly think of new moves. Because I married and had my son so young, I grew up fast and embraced responsibility with a vengeance. Now that I am at a place where I can begin to relax, still young, and enjoy the silly things I didn't do, I worry I won't be able to be "insouciant" ever because I have squandered the opportunity. Falling in love with you makes me feel like a teenager again. It's about both finding love now and letting me recapture what I missed out on.

We are stuck between two worlds, with the younger generation seeing us as old, almost irrelevant, and our parents still treating us like clueless babies. The younger people don't bother me that much because I know their attitude is primarily grounded in ignorance. If they try to be rude, I have no patience for them. (Plus, culturally, I was raised to view older people with respect since they may be wiser, not with the derision the younger generation exhibits.) Getting frustrated is easy, but I usually smile and ignore the comments. Thank God we have found each other. I love you more than words can say.

Till then,
Nickie

The summer heat hit me as we exited the movie theater Saturday evening. Craig and Hyuen had dropped by early that afternoon and dragged me to what they called the "must-see" action movie of the summer—Direct Impact. With twilight fading on the horizon, the film's excitement lingered.

"Wow, that was intense! I mean, a comet the size of Texas hurtling toward Earth? Talk about a cosmic disaster!" Craig said excitedly.

"Absolutely. And the way they sowed it—the panic, the evacuation—felt so real. I kept thinking, what would I do if that were happening right now?" added Hyuen.

"Yeah, but did you notice how they focused on the human side? It wasn't just about the science but about people facing the situation together," I replied, pulling the car keys out of my purse.

"And Morgan Freeman as the president? Perfect choice. I'd follow him into space any day," said Craig, grinning.

"Me too," Hyuen and I replied in unison.

We ate at a tiny hole-in-the-wall Mexican restaurant three blocks away that we had decided on before the movie. I asked them to stay over, but they had morning plans with friends in Manhattan and wanted to return to the city that night.

The sporadic, rather than smooth, daily flow of communication we used to have grated on me. Sunday, however, was trying. After painting a small bathroom, I drove to Montauk, at the tip of Long Island. The Lighthouse stood tall against the blue sky, with its whitewashed walls and black lantern reminiscent of tales of shipwrecks. Weathered cliffs gazed over the ocean to where sky and water meet, inviting contemplation. It was stunning, seeming even more beautiful than when Ken and I visited. I had found a good parking spot for the car, walked half a block to the water with my sandals dangling through my fingers. Barefoot, I felt the warm, golden sand beneath my toes, the tang of salt hung in the air, invigorating and cleansing. My heart should have felt light amid such natural beauty, but it was as if I was outside myself observing all this. What I felt was melancholy.

I wondered about these gloomy thoughts. I had even skipped Wayne's daughter's birthday party this afternoon. Somehow, being around people other than Craig and Hyuen intensified my loneliness. My emotions were running wild. I was ecstatic when things were going well and in the dumps when things were unexpected. It wasn't at all like me.

By email, I shared my thoughts with Ken, relieved yet wary of burdening him. Not being near him was causing me disquiet and emotional turmoil.

Subj: ***Hello, my love***
Date: 8/24/98 8:59:26 AM EDT

Dearest Nickie,

My memory card has yet to arrive. I have rehearsal tonight, and I would like to chat before going. What have you been doing all weekend? Oh, I forgot our e-mails must have passed each other this morning. I love you.

Till then
Ken

Subj: ***Hope you understood me***
Date: 8/24/98

Dearest Ken,

I should not tell you everything that passes through my mind; it may scare you, but in my heart, you are a friend, boyfriend, and lover; I feel compelled to tell you everything. If I am overwhelming you with my thoughts, I am sorry. I may still be uneasy about your unexpected trip to Chicago.

Since we met, I have been the happiest I can remember in a long time. The thought that I may lose that happiness is causing me much anxiety. I don't understand why my emotions are so close to the surface. I always tease and never really believe women about PMS; it may be what I am dealing with. I don't appreciate creating excuses for my behavior, but I hope it's what's happening and will go away soon.

Till then,
Nickie

Subj: *Déjà-vu*
Date: 8/25/98

Dearest Ken,

I hope this finds you well, but I miss you terribly. You are a strong person not to feel the frustration plaguing me regarding our relationship. I have so much to share, talk about, and seek your opinion on, but I can't. I want us to get to know each other more intimately as individuals. I understand our situation is difficult, but not impossible. (I promise I won't tell you all my frustrations whenever they occur).

No one picks up when I call, including the answering machine. The computers, servers, and electricity are unreliable in your area. I wish there were another way to communicate (Maybe the fax machine or snail mail, ah ah). You are welcome to come to NY for another visit whenever you like. I am too emotional and could be rushing things by wanting to spend so much time with you, but I don't think anyone will fault me for wanting more personal communication than e-mail.

Till then,
Nickie

Subj: **Good morning**
Date: 8/26/98 7:00:12 AM EDT

Dearest Nickie,

I LOVE YOU!!!!!!

The mail server was down here at work yesterday. I have missed you terribly. Since Monday, I have been calling Gateway to find out where my video cards are, but they have not returned my calls. It is as frustrating for me as it has been for you. I race home every day, hoping today is the day I will have my board. It has been driving me crazy, affecting rehearsal, and we open on Friday. I think part of it is, well, this is stupid; I am playing a "GAY" artist, and there is no one I want to affirm my heterosexuality with except you. Practicing for the pictures I intend to send you elicited my dancing offer; sometimes, I get so focused I don't realize there is a world around me. I love you.

Any worries about getting older, you asked? They alternate in my mind. Most recently, it was not to get another chance at genuine love again. Meeting you has removed that doubt. Truth be told, I am also wondering if, at ninety, I'll still be able to satisfy you(smile); that's why I keep working out to remain in top shape! Sometimes, I worry whether Mary Lou and I are doing the right things for the girls separately so they'll grow up to be their best selves. Also, when they reach the difficult teen years, will I be able to handle them and provide the best guidance? I hope to fully subsidize their college education so they can start their adult lives devoid of any large education loans. I suppose every parent has those concerns, but they linger.

Please write to me about anything. I share the same frustrations. I never realized how much I had missed intimacy over the past six years until I began contemplating it with you. There is no one else I want to be intimate with; however, we are. You are always on my mind and in my heart. I wish I were there holding you now. I have considered chucking my job and everything else and coming out there. The girls hold me back, but truth be told, I'm not sure which attraction is stronger.

Co-workers can read over your shoulder at work, so I prefer not to share certain things. I love you and have missed you more than my humble vocabulary has words to express.

Till then,
Ken

Subj: ***Letters***
Date: 8/26/98 7:22:11 AM EDT

Dearest Nickie,

I just read your letters from the 24th. Sorry, I hadn't read all the letters before writing the last note. I love you. However, there is a commercial where the lady says, "Imagine what he is going to think when he finds out what he thought was PMS is your actual personality. (I laugh when I see the commercial; I hope you are at least smiling now.)

I have been working out a lot to counter my frustration level. Watch out; I am getting lumpy again; my chest has increased by 1/2 inch.

I will stop on my way home and buy a new phone.

Till then, love
Ken

Subj: *Good morning, dearest*
Date: 8 /26/98

Dearest Ken,

I love you to distraction. I'm feeling better now. Yesterday, Craig and Hyuen surprised me again. They brought me roses, chocolate, and a silk pouch of Chinese design. They wanted to cheer me up because they were worried about me. I almost cried afterward because it touched me so much.

I thank God for meeting you. By all means, please keep up those workout sessions. I want your arms to be powerful to keep supporting me in the shower. I hope I am not smothering you; I know I can be intense, and if you ever need breathing space, tell me. My sanity returned; I can only say I love you. I'll take the laptop home tonight, and if your board arrives, we can chat.

Till then,
Nickie

Subj: *Lunch*
Date: 8/26/98 3:01:53 PM EDT

Dearest Nickie,

Sorry, it's been so hectic today. I just got back to my mail, hanging with a customer while we reloaded her training equipment from scratch (I took a 10-minute call and turned it into 25 minutes). I love you. I hope your day has been pleasant so far; I find it difficult when I get too involved in dreaming while driving, but you give me quite the adrenaline rush. I love you. I've got to run now to check on my board. I will pick up a new phone for that line tonight!

Till then,
Ken

I muted the TV and placed the remote control on the nightstand, my heart racing with anticipation. Holding my breath, I picked up the receiver and dialed.

"Hi." My voice sounded too high to me.

"Hello, my love. I didn't believe my eyes when I saw your name on the caller ID."

"Believe it! I miss you so, I thought I'd surprise you."

"You can surprise me any day! The new phone I got is working. How are you? Did I tell you I love you already?"

"No, you get one demerit for that. But neither did I, so I guess we'll spend time in detention together!"

"Oh, goody!"

"I was thinking...I came up with some ideas. What if we create a system where we call and leave a voice message on the answering machine to say we are okay if we don't hear from each other for five days. Also, how about locking your bedroom door to ensure your friends' children are not messing with the computer and causing problems? You can give them access when you get home. This may seem extreme, but you would be sure it's the system and not someone misusing the machine."

"No, that seems... selfish; I don't want to deprive them of entertainment because I am not home."

"What if you didn't have the computer?"

"I know, but I don't feel right about it."

"Okay, a different idea. I am thinking of ways to ease our frustration. Let's schedule meetings every two months, with alternative dates, in case of problems. I'll be visiting you on weekends. You have traveled thus far, and I am the most anxious person, so I want to balance things out. Plus, I'll get to meet your girls in person. Staying with you isn't ideal because of your guests. I could stay at a hotel near your workplace to spend evenings or nights together, even if you're busy working on the weekend. I can't wait to attend one of your plays."

"You've been thinking about this."

"Knowing myself, even having a loose plan or system, will keep me focused and help me relax. Prioritizing each other is important, despite having friends, family, and a to-do list. What do you think?"

"I am more impulsive than you, but it's not a bad idea. You made one wrong assumption, though."

"What's that?"

"Once we are together, neither of us will ever leave that hotel room!" Ken's voice was filled with playful conviction.

"Is that a promise?"

"You bet! I love you."

"I love you more."

"Night, sweetie," I whispered.

"Night, my love; the tenderness in his voice sent a warm shiver down my spine.

Subj: *Good morning*
Date: 8/27/98 6:46:27 AM EDT

Dearest Nickie,

Hearing your voice last night was terrific. I went to sleep with more vibrant images of you. I couldn't resist giving you another hickey (the last one had faded). I am still smiling. I love you.

Till then, love
Ken

Subj: *Good morning, darling*
Date: 8/27/98

Dearest Ken,

The feelings are mutual. I have waited forever to hear your voice again, and I didn't stop smiling until sleep took hold of me. Talking to you made my heart peaceful and content. This morning, you were my first thought, as if I closed my eyes and reached out, I could pull you to me. I sensed you holding and kissing me, but before I could tell you I wanted another hickey, you read my mind and complied. I hope your day goes well. Your sexy voice will resonate in my ear all day.

Till then,
Nickie

Subj: ***Good morning***
Date: 8/28/98 6:56:19 AM EDT

Dearest Nickie,

Good morning, my love. The dress rehearsal went well last night; it should be a hilarious show. I called Gateway when I got home (and sat on hold for 74 minutes). They assured me they hadn't realized their shipping department had sent an empty box, and they would ship out a card the next day air, so I should be up and running soon.

It was an exciting day yesterday; I was swamped. Our new "skill" levels now allow for some quiet time for "study" instead, and call volume has picked up about 20%.

I will take my girls' clothes shopping again tonight for "a couple" things. I love you. Try not to overwork yourself today. I will write later.

Till then,
Ken

Subj: ***Good morning, darling***
Date: 8/28/98

Dearest Ken,

Yesterday was a great workday. I was calmer and more productive than I had been in a month. Talking to you the other night did me a world of good.

Good luck with the girls tonight. I remember those days with Craig; you may find it easier to make a list with them beforehand rather than go unprepared.

Till then,
Nickie

Subj: ***Good morning, love***
Date: 8/31/98 8:01:14 AM EDT

Dearest Nickie,

What a weekend it's been. The opening went great, and we may have a hit. There is already talk of doing it again at Kerin's this December.

Nelly threw Sara out of their place. I helped Sara, TJ, and Teddy move. So, it has been quite a weekend, besides being on an emotional roller coaster high with the play, downs with my friends, and missing you. What have you been up to?

Till then,
Ken

Subj: ***Good morning***
Date: 8/31/98

Dearest Ken,

I am OK, thanks, and my weekend was good. I only got part of this e-mail. The play is good news; I hope it's a hit, as you expect. I didn't realize you had the weekend off, and I thought it was the Renaissance fair weekend. My sister Macy called me last night to tell me that our mother will be in NY next Saturday evening; however, my dad is not coming, but it will be nice to see Mom.

I miss you,
Nickie

Subj: ***continued***
Date: 8/31/98 11:23:20 AM EDT

Dearest Nickie,

I am sorry for sending you a partial letter. My keyboard locked up, and I could either send the letter using the mouse or boot the P.C. to fix the keyboard; I sent the letter and then booted the PC.

I was in the middle of telling you about our dream picnic, but I want to read the letter you sent me. It was a lovely picnic. We listened to light classical music, had corn on the cob, deviled eggs, celery, carrots, baby tomatoes, and roasted chicken, played Frisbee with the dogs, and rode bareback through the lake's shallows. The geese have laid four more eggs, and Mother Goose is sitting them. It was a lazy day, and I loved how you wrapped your arms around me as we rode and rested your head on my back. I love you. Are you home today?

Till then, love
Ken

Subj: *Re: Thinking more about you.*
Date: 9/1/98

Dearest Ken,

I had to rush you my note this morning since I was going to court. I just came back home, and it's 3:30 p.m. The judge granted the tenants an additional two months to gather the money. In the meantime, there is nothing much I can do. I decided to put this house on the market.

It seems like a fun picnic we had, appropriate for those rare but perfect summer days. I miss you so much that I am unsure if I sometimes overreact in my perception of little things regarding you. Someday, we will have extended talks where I can tell you everything that surfaces whenever I think of you.

Till then,
Nickie

Subj: *Good morning, dearest*
Date: 9/ 1/98

Dearest Ken,

Did you have a show last night, or are they only on the weekend? Your recent letters seem distracted, as if you're preoccupied or not fully present (maybe because of work busy-ness). Calling you was tempting, but I don't want you to feel smothered. At what time of night does US West stop charging long-distance rates? In NY, AF&T doesn't charge extra for long-distance after 9 pm. I love you.

Till then,
Nickie

"What's Happening"

Subj: *Thinking about you.*
Date: 9/2/98

Dearest Ken,

Good morning, darling. Is your server still out? I have heard nothing since Monday. Is it busy at work? I'll be going to a meeting soon. I love you.

Till then,
Nickie

Subj: *Good morning*
Date: 9/4/98 7:54:37 AM EDT

Dearest Nickie,

We have mail!!. You didn't say whether you got the voicemail I left.

Gateway decided I needed a tech to do such a drastic fix, stripping my box to a shell and starting over. The extra parts came yesterday, and I was so focused on talking with you that I had it up and running in 30 minutes. The tech is due tomorrow. I love you (besides, I can't wait to kiss your _ _ _, give you those hickeys I owe you). I never told you how I lathered those hard-to-reach places in the shower,

Till then,
Ken

Chat 20—9/4/98

NC: Hi Ken, are you there?

DK: Sorry, I was out rounding up puppies

DK: 2 brown and white and five black, brown, and white collie puppies

NC: I was thinking of getting a dog. Too bad you are so far away.

DK: I might keep one of the brown and white. His tentative name is Hubert; the girls love him

They also picked out a black and white named Emma

Did you get the voicemail?

NC: yes, thanks; it was better than the first one

I didn't tell you, but my hairdresser got me mad again she cut ALL of my hair this time

DK: I just did the same

NC: my ears are sticking out. You should see the way I look.

DK: I would love to

NC: you are so sweet

DK: Were you mad at me on Monday?

NC: A little. I explained in my afternoon mail

DK: I thought as much. What did I do?

NC: Nothing. I was mad because I didn't know you were taking the weekend off

DK: Yes

NC: I had to rush the mail I sent you because I was going to court.

DK: My computer keyboard locked itself in the middle of the letter. Then I had to reboot. When it came up, I saw a note from you finished my letter to you, read your letter, and sent you another before the email went south, and it bothers me you didn't write back

Whose idea was the haircut?

NC: I get a trim every six weeks

DK: Funny, I saw Mike yesterday; he had been to the barber and told the barber to take a little off the sides. Mike now looks like a Mohican

could it be a country-wide conspiracy?

NC: a definite conspiracy

DK: I tried a mohawk when I was eight, but my hair is too Soft Looked like a rain-soaked rooster.

NC: I am trying to picture you at eight years old

by the way, I just resent that picture

DK: Did I tell you I saved one on floppy, took it to work, and it now serves as the bitmap on my desktop? Eve still bugs me; how did I do it? The truth is I don't know since I can't get one to stay on this desktop

NC: I love you a lot! Did I tell you recently?

DK: Not in three days. It's good to hear. I used the one of you sitting on the couch.

When I get my camera working again, I may have a surprise or two up my sleeves

NC: Did you miss me? Not what I want to hear, but the truth.

DK: Y E S!

NC: does that mean very?

kidding

DK: Duh! What did you want to hear? (I wasn't reading again)

NC: An accurate answer to my question.

DK: What would I gain by telling you what you want to hear? It's Not as if I was sitting next to you, trying to unbutton your blouse.

Of course, about now, I would be using my teeth, but that's another discussion

NC: I am very insecure nowadays, partly because you are so far away

My body was very naughty last weekend

I did a lot of walking, which helped very little. It's probably why I have been so volatile these previous two weeks.

DK: Sometimes I don't think too well; when this thing broke, I was frustrated. When email at work went down because of an upgrade that knocked them off the server, I was in a panic; somehow, I thought you knew I would get back as fast as I could. I thought you knew how I felt. I guess I was wrong, I am miserable without you. I don't know any other way to tell you. If I had died, I would still tell you I love you

NC: You tell me all the time that you love me, but because we are apart, whenever I go a day without hearing from you (unless I know why), I go into panic mode.

I doubt I'll ever not care if I don't hear from you.

DK: We learn to trust in small steps; distrust comes much faster, for it is defense.

NC: I don't mistrust you; I am afraid that you are going to stop loving me at any moment.

DK: Not a chance. I am not made that way, and it took a lot of years to get here

I Love You

NC: I love you

Promise me that you'll tell me if you ever stop loving me or want to write.

You will not just stop writing and disappear

DK: I promise if I should go blind, brain dead, crazy, or become mentally unbalanced (crazy), these conditions are necessary for me to stop caring, loving, and lusting after your body. You have my solemn vow to write and tell you off before I stop writing. I would sign it and have it notarized if I had a pen. Is it sufficient?

NC: Yes, it's adequate. Now, I will no longer panic when I unexpectedly don't hear from you

I am a notary, by the way. Ah ah

DK: If I were there, I would give you such a tongue-licking. I mean, lashing right now, oooh

NC: If I get such punishment, I promise to be bad more often

DK: Is your mother still coming tomorrow?

NC: yes, Saturday night

DK: Much as I hate to say it, I have to get up in 3 hours and get a nap. I love You.

NC: Good night, Darling; I love you.

Subj: ***Good morning, darling***
Date: 9/4/98

Dearest Ken,

It feels soooooooooooooooooo good to open AOL and see your letter waiting for me. I also received your voicemail last night. I'll never tire of your sexy voice and wonderful accent.

Will you go to the Renaissance fair this weekend? I came to work smiling this morning, and someone told me they had not seen me smile for a week! You have done quite an excellent job with the computer so far. Don't let the tech from Gateway mess it up. I love you. I can't wait to take that shower with you! If I close my eyes and concentrate, I can almost feel your soapy chest against my back, and of course, the hickeys are a MUST! Thanks for putting that smile back on my face.

Till then,
Nickie

Subj: *Weekend*
Date: 9/4/98 10:58:10 AM EDT

Dearest Nickie,

I am finishing with' Dr. Fell' tonight, tomorrow night, and Sunday afternoon. I am go-ing to the Renaissance Festival on Monday. I had cheap tickets, and because of Dr. Fell, I couldn't work the festival, but I enjoyed the atmosphere; sometimes, I feel as if I were born in the wrong century. It may be 9 to 9:30 before I get home tonight. I love you.

As long as this works, I plan to be a nuisance; talk to you later. (I don't know when you are having lunch, but I am going for Haagen Dazs's Rum Raisin!!!

Till then,
Ken

Subj: *Re: Weekend*
Date: 9/4/98

Dearest Ken,

You can never be a nuisance. You put a spring in my step. I wish I could join you in that Haagen Dasz- rum raisin ice cream!

As I write this, I am downloading the Internet phone 5.0 for the two-week trial period. We will close early today at 1:30 p.m., so I don't intend to go out to lunch (I felt so good this morning that I had a big breakfast). Once again, I have tentative plans with Craig and Hyuen for Sunday or Monday. I love you.

Till then,
Nickie

I parked my car in front of Netty's house, and while unbuckling my seatbelt, I couldn't help but admire her near-perfect landscaping. Lush green grass carpeted the yard, perfectly maintained and free of weeds. Colorful flower beds hugged the foundation, bursting with blooms—roses, daisies, and vibrant petunias. A giant oak tree provided shade, its leaves rustling in the breeze, while a vintage lamppost added a touch of nostalgia, planted at the beginning of a curved stone pathway leading from the driveway to the front door. Path lights illuminated it at night. *Excellent curb appeal*; I could see why Netty's house was always Mom's first stop when she visited for the summer.

Two short bursts of the bell and the front door opened, with Netty struggling to keep her enthusiastic terrier Hannah from rushing out the door.

"Hi!" I said, kissing her on the forehead and walking in.

"Mom, I am here," I said as she walked toward me. With a brilliant smile on her face, she engulfed me in the warmest hug.

"Nickie! It's good to see you. Let me look at you; it's been too long. A year feels like a lifetime."

"I know, Mom. It's so good to see you. But you can't both look at me and hug me," I said, laughing.

"That's what you think! Oh, it's so wonderful to see all of you!"

"I missed you too, Mom. I wish Dad could've come. It's not the same without him."

We walked to the kitchen with her holding my arm and Netty behind us, carrying an over-eager Hannah.

I was at the kitchen table with Mom as Netty made tea and placed some appetizing oatmeal and butter cookies on a plate for us.

"Your Dad, you know, he is fine. He wasn't up to traveling now, and I couldn't convince him otherwise. He is the same old self, stubborn as a mule, but enough about him. How's our recent college graduate? Is he conquering the world?"

"Craig is doing well. You know how talented he is. He has already landed a job and seems happy. He tells me he is well-liked at work."

"What's not to like? He is my favorite grandson, you know."

"You tell all the grandkids the same thing, Mom."

"Well, I love them all! And as long as they think they are my favorite; they are all happy! Craig is a tad special because he was with me the longest. And when will he visit? I want to celebrate his graduation correctly."

"He'll probably call you this evening and come by tomorrow."

"What about you? How's the job at the insurance company?" She asked, clasping my hand.

"Work has been a whirlwind. I'm navigating office politics, chasing deadlines."

"You've got your father's determination. But don't forget to breathe, my love. Life isn't just about work. You look good, just too skinny. How's your heart these days? Any special someone?"

"I am working on it, Mom; we'll discuss that when you come to my place."

Subj: *Weekend??*
Date: 9/7/98 7:11:41 AM EDT

Dearest Nickie,

How has your weekend been going? Did your mother come on Saturday? The play ran till 10 p.m. I thought I could be home in an hour, but by the time I got my make-up off and did a few minutes of glad-hand thing with the people, it was after 1:30 in the morning. I have run into a new snafu but got a tenuous workaround. I tried to write then, so I apologize if the note seems strange. I tried to write Sunday before leaving to pick up the girls, and the keyboard locked up.

How are Craig and Huyen doing? What else have you been doing? I work until two this afternoon, then go to the Renaissance fair till 6 p.m. I should be home between 8 and 8:30 p.m. I didn't want to risk losing the connection, so I stayed logged on to the Internet. I love you.

Till then, love
Ken

Subj: *Re: Weekend??*
Date: 9/7/98

Dearest Ken,

Good morning, darling; I presume the tech came and messed up a few things. You mentioned sending me some mail; this morning's letter is the first one I have received since Friday.

Craig and Huyen are fine. I am on my way out. We are going to the New Jersey shore for the day. It's not very sunny, and they predict a thunderstorm this afternoon. Have a great time at the fair. It's nice to feel you're in a different century when things were simpler. I love you. I'll log on if there is still time when I return. We'll be able to chat soon, if not tonight, at least tomorrow night. My mom is okay, and I spent all of yesterday afternoon and evening with her. I wish my dad had come too. I bought a new luggage set on sale last Saturday, so don't ask why—it was a good buy!

Till then,
Nickie

Subj: ***Good morning***
Date: 9/9/98 7:28:04 AM EDT

Dearest Nickie,

Sorry I missed you last night. I'm leaving early to check my eyes because I have trouble reading small print. I found a beautiful cloak at the Renaissance Fair for $245. It's made of three gray, maroon, and black wool blankets, with the maroon one doubling as a hood.

My sister called; Liam is doing better and getting his cast removed next eek. When will you be back in Milwaukee? I'm planning a four-day weekend. I sure miss you.

Till then, love
Ken

Subj: ***Good morning, dear***
Date: 9/9/98

Dearest Ken,

Good morning, darling. Sorry to hear about the continued problem with the computer. On the good side, when you fix everything, you will know enough to work for them!

I understand about the eyes; you probably need glasses. I went through that a year ago, as did my friends. People's eyes have timers.

The cloak sounds lovely; I can visualize the colors and picture you. Wouldn't wearing it over your winter coat solve the sleeve problem? If you like and want the look, go for it and enjoy.

Great news about Liam; I bet he can't wait to have the cast removed. I'll be back in Milwaukee for training from November 1 to the 4th. I'd love to spend your time off with you. No need to wait for my return to Milwaukee for work. (I need an excuse to use my brand-new luggage set.) I also plan to take another week of Mondays.

Till then,
Nickie

Subj: ***Good morning, dearest***
Date: 9/10/98

Dearest Ken,

Good morning, darling. How was your visit to the eye doctor? Yesterday, I bought a new silver frame for your picture; it looks better with the black-and-white photo.

Don't let work drive you crazy. Remember, I am here if you need an ear. Sending a big hug and a long, s-l-o-w kiss.

Till then,
Nickie

I pulled the computer cord from the jack and replaced the phone. I had just answered an email from my hiking group. There was a wine-tasting children's charity benefit in two weeks; Meg, the group organizer, wanted to get a headcount commitment. I will get back to her once I check my day-timer tomorrow in the office.

I jumped as the phone rang, and I picked it up without checking the caller ID.

"Hello love, how are you?" said Ken.

"Hi! What a pleasant surprise! I am okay, sweetie. How are you?" I replied, my eyes widening with joy.

"I was thinking of you. I tried a little while ago, but the line was busy."

"Yes, I was online; I just put the phone back. I debated calling you this morning because you mentioned feeling unwell on Friday and sounded distant." I nodded at the empty room, a concerned look on my face. "Are you okay? The constant yawning could be your body signaling a need for more rest. Can you take an additional two days off to relax quietly?"

"Yeah, I have been pushing it at work. It doesn't help that my girls were especially active this weekend. Claire got away with extra mischief since I was too tired to discipline her. Camille got her to behave, and she told me I looked exhausted. By the way, I would still like to see you in Milwaukee."

"Are you feeling better now? If Milwaukee works, I can fly in on Saturday, and we'll have two days before my training class starts. Can you let me know by Wednesday? I must return the papers for my training registration."

"I feel better. I need your input on something. I received a call from one of the more persistent headhunters. There is a senior IT position with Tropel Insurance he wants me to interview for. Excellent pay, greater responsibility. I would be the IT manager, not just the senior tech."

"That sounds good. Does Tropel have benefits? Pension plans? Are you fully vested in your 401k at your current job? It's early, but these should be considerations."

"Yes, we discussed all that: better pay, challenging work, and a chance to grow. The problem lies in the job being in Chicago. I would be closer to Billie and Liam, but I don't know how that would work out for my girls. I was also thinking of us. Would you ever consider moving to Chicago in the future?"

"Chicago? Wow, that's a big move! But hey, this is exactly the kind of thing we should chat about first so we don't miss out on a great opportunity. Remember when I mentioned we needed to think things through in Barbados? It was just so we would be prepared. Anyway, it's still early days—you haven't even had your first interview yet."

"The head hunter already faxed my resume to them. He said they called him back and wanted to schedule an interview."

"You have nothing to lose by attending the interview except for a few hours' drive. If you get it, we could make it work with some planning. I love you."

"I love you more. I know I am going to have beautiful dreams of us tonight! Oh! I just saw a flash of lightning outside. Love, I must bring the puppies to the barn."

"Get some rest, sweetie. You sound tired. I love you."

Subj: *Good morning - Mid-afternoon*
Date: 9/16/98 2:31:28 PM EDT

Dearest Nickie,

I just got my email back 1st. I LOVE YOU!!!! It was great to hear your voice; you always make me feel so wonderful. Sorry, I had to cut it short. I just got the last puppies in the barn as the thunderstorm hit. I took my eyeglass prescription in to have it filled out on Monday. Maybe it's psychological, but now my eyes bother me more than ever. I caught a cold and slept for 11 hours yesterday, leaving me with beautiful dreams of you. This morning, I connected to the Internet before I left for work. I left it turned on; unfortunately, I felt I was making headway and forgot about the time, so I was late again, but somehow, work wasn't that important.

I will write when I get home. I am leaving in about 45 minutes. I have the girls again tonight, so I will be away from 6 to 10:30 (your time).

Till then,
Ken

Subj: *Re: Mail*
Date: 9/16/98

Dearest Ken,

It's mind-boggling how much your messages transform my mood. Let's chat tonight after you drop off the girls. I miss you.

Till then,
Nickie

Subj: *Thinking of you*
Date: 9/17/98

Dearest Ken

Good morning, dearest. Before bed, I applied more of the "Dunes" men's cologne on my wrist last night. Imagining you instead of my pillow lying next to me was delightful.

I finally received that $50 rebate from the computer camera company. It's hard to believe that we haven't even used it yet. I loved the voicemail. My attempt to send you one was unsuccessful. You must tell me how you do it. I love you.

Till then,
Nickie

Ken

When I arrived home from dinner with the girls, I saw Nickie's message on the screen. It took three reboots, canceling the applications in my startup folder, and a shutdown to get the PC running again. By then, it was 11:30 p.m. my time and 12:30 a.m. her time. I assumed it was too late for her, so I chose a pleasant fantasy. *I love her so much!*

Subj: *Good morning love*
Date: 9/18/98

Dearest Ken,

Good luck with the computer tonight; it sure doesn't sound easy. I can try a few things regarding software, but hardware involving opening up the PC intimidates me. How can you detach the 300mhz processor from the old motherboard and connect it to the new one? That foot massage was excellent; we'll have to do that again soon. I miss you.

Till then,
Nickie

Subj: *Switching processors*
Date: 9/18/98 12:08:45 PM EDT

Dearest Nickie,

I have to use a soldering iron and carefully melt the solder connections on each leg around the processor, remove it from one board, clean the holes from the one I removed from the new board, and switch the processors. It's electronic heart surgery, indeed. I still need to get my glasses (It could be psychological); I could use them now. Hopefully, my processor didn't go bad with the motherboard. We should also be able to send video if I can get my camera working. I love you.

Till then,
Ken

Nickie

Unable to stay at my desk and having no appetite for food, I walked to Fifth Ave during lunch hour. It felt good to be amidst this sea of people—office workers, tourists, and locals—each with their purpose, the towering skyscrapers casting elongated shadows, shielding me from the late summer sun. Cracks and cigarette butts punctuated the gray sidewalk. Yellow taxis whizzed by, their horns blaring impatiently. I passed two food carts lining the curb of an intersection, wafting scents of pretzels, hot dogs, and roasted nuts. It must have been my empty stomach because the usually pleasant aroma made me nauseous. A little further on, a newspaper stand displayed bold headlines—political scandals, sports victories, and celebrity gossip. My eyes scanned without reading the front pages, catching glimpses of a world in flux. The pace and place kept me focused on the present, away from myself. Glancing upward, I caught sight of the iconic Chrysler Building; its art déco spire pierced the sky, hands down one of the most recognizable buildings in NYC, my office and current destination. I crossed the threshold, and I was back where I had started.

It's been over a week since we spoke, and I felt anxious. I got no response to my phone message last night. It felt like I was talking to the wind. It's unlikely his work server would be down for an entire week. His silence was disappointing. *Is he tired of me? Why does my mind jump to the worst conclusions?* I thought we agreed to leave a phone message if five days should elapse incommunicado. *Did he forget?* A week was not a long time granted, but it was all relative to how we communicated. *I need to occupy myself with something else, and I know just the thing. I need a new outfit for the children's charity dinner this weekend, something sexy but elegant. Shopping always works.*

Subj: *What is happening*
Date: 9/26/98 10:16:14 AM EDT

Dearest Nickie,

I didn't want to write until I knew what would happen this weekend, assuming you wouldn't want to speak to me, but that wouldn't be fair. I am sorry if I caused you any new worry by being silent the past week. I love you, miss you, desire you, and need you now more than ever, so it's a small wonder I didn't want to share my darkest secret.

When my marriage broke up six years ago, I went through a significant bout with depression and ended up in the hospital (I tried to kill myself). I got away from people (as much as possible). I may have alluded to my emotional struggles before, but was hesitant to specify. Recently, I thought I had life under control despite the burdens of caring for others, and I wanted to return to normalcy.

Last week, I went into another significant low. I am unsure if trying and maintaining a relationship is fair when I don't know if I will wake up tomorrow.

If you are still talking to me, I will write back; if I make it through tomorrow, I will at least allow you to tell me off.

Till then, I still love you,
(it's me I don't like) Ken

Subj: *Ken, I Loooooooove Youuuuuuuuu!!!!*
Date: 9/26/98

Dearest Ken,

Why did you not tell me, Darling? I LOVE YOU MORE THAN ANYTHING. What can I do to help? I would fly over to be with you, hold you against my heart, and make you feel better! Please do nothing foolish; It would devastate me! Will you be home tonight? Can I call and talk to you? I deeply care for you and will do anything to make you feel better.

Why are you depressed? Is it still your ex-wife? Your job? Your friends? PLEASE LET ME HELP! Your presence has brought me immense happiness. The thought of you far away and feeling down while I can't help is unbearable.

I will keep the computer on for the next hour; please, Darling, let me know when you get this note and if I can call you tonight. My hands tremble, and my heart palpitates with fear at the thought of anything going wrong with you.

Please answer soon. I am worried, and I LOVE YOU...

Until then,
Nickie

Subj: ***Another thing Darling***
Date: 9/26/98

Dearest Ken,

There is another thing I should have mentioned in my earlier reply to you. Don't worry about what is fair or unfair in maintaining a relationship. MY LOVE FOR YOU IS UN-CONDITIONAL. In good times or in bad, I wish to be there for and with you. When my heart told you it loved you, it meant it. I'll only leave if you say you no longer love or need me. But as long as there's a chance you want and love me, I'll stay by your side. You only need to ask; I'll do whatever it takes to make you happy. I love you.

Till then,
Nickie

Subj: ***Good morning, dearest***
Date: 9/27/98

Dearest Ken,

How are you, darling? I didn't call last night because I wasn't sure if it was okay, and I didn't want to make you feel worse. I can't pretend to understand what you are going through. I have been through very low periods, but nothing compared to the depression you seem to endure. I want to help but don't know how. I am sorry that my love is not enough to make you happy.

What triggered this recurrence of your state? In your last letter, you mentioned not liking yourself. Why is that? You are the most wonderful, loving, gentle, and kind person I know. You feel deeply for your fellow human beings and fondly for animals. How could you not love yourself? If I had half the qualities I see and feel in you, I would consider myself blessed. Look at all the people who love and worry about you. Would they feel that way towards someone who isn't a good person? I LOVE YOU. If anyone did or said something to make you feel bad, it's because they are bad, not you!

It frustrates me that I cannot comfort you at this time. Please think of all the people who love you and all the people you have made happy (Me being one of them) and realize that you are a good, caring, honest, concerned person.

I think of you constantly, and I miss you. Whenever you can, close your eyes and imagine my arms around you, your head on my heart, holding you, loving you, and thanking God for meeting you. I'll attend church today and pray to God to make you feel better.

Till then,
Nickie

Subj: ***Thinking of you***
Date: 9/28/98

Dearest Ken,

How are you? My worry grows as I am powerless to support you. I am in a quandary about what to do. I want to keep writing, and I want to call you to see if I can help. Unsure if it's best to let you be until you feel like talking again. I don't want to contribute to your sadness, as I'm unfamiliar with this situation and unsure of the appropriate action.

I want and should keep writing even if you don't answer me. I want to wrap my arms around you, hold you, and tell you I love you and everything will be all right. Please know that I am doing everything in my mind and want you to feel it. Yesterday at church, I prayed to God to help you through this low time, protect you, and accompany you everywhere, for I can't physically do that myself.

I love you unconditionally, and you are always with me in my mind. I miss you terribly.

Till then
Nickie

Subj: *Good morning*
Date: 9/29/98 6:56:56 AM EDT

Dearest Nickie,

Good morning, my love; I know my reclusiveness has been challenging. Strange as it seems, most people I know expressed no interest in my lack of interest or the problems I experienced conducting day-to-day affairs. It deepened my state to see the one-sidedness of my "friendships." I apologize for the worry, but thank you for your patience and concern. I wish I could have been there with you.

Although I am not yet 100%, I am doing better. Nafina is gearing up for next season and has three shows planned for next year: one in St. Paul, one in Madison, and one in Chicago. I am on the board of directors, and we meet tonight to read two B.J. Kean plays to begin the selection process. I am going to attend and pay attention.

It is strange to have a period where I have no dreams and push myself to get the needed things done, with no energy left to give to the daily things that in our lives become almost reflexive. It was terrific to hear your voice this morning when I woke. I nearly took the day off, and I knew I was doing better because I wanted to take the day off to spend it bedeviling you on the computer, not because it was so much work to get myself out the door. I love you.

Till then, Love
Ken

Subj: *Good morning, dearest*
Date: 9/29/98

Dearest Ken,

Good morning, darling. It's so good to get a note from you! I came to work late today (after being off yesterday). My mother is spending a couple of weeks with me and insists on my eating a "nutritious breakfast" before leaving the house (thus my being late.)

I am so glad to see that your spirits have improved. I have been worried since you told me what was going on. I was also quite frustrated at being unable to be with you. I am sorry that your friends weren't more supportive. Sometimes, people don't realize that being depressed is as debilitating as any physical ailment, and because they can't see it, they think it isn't real or it can quickly be fixed.

I don't want to dwell on the matter now that you feel better. However, I was curious about what caused this recurrence. Sometimes, simply knowing that there is someone who cares and is dependable can make all the difference.

I am glad you are going to that meeting tonight. It's the best outlet to keep your spirits upbeat. I love you; don't you ever forget that. I am pleased you are thinking of me again and want to fix your computer so you can talk to me. I don't know what else is happening in your life that is causing you trouble. You may need a change of environment, both work and living quarters. I am saying those things because they sometimes help. I wish we could sit down and have a heart-to-heart talk, but I cannot do that; I still want to discuss whatever is on your mind in any way we can accomplish it. Try to have a good day.

Till then,
Nickie

"Hard to Understand"

Subj: **Good morning**
Date: 10/2/98 7:18:55 AM EDT

Dearest Nickie,

Good morning, my love. Try as I might, I still am not dreaming as vividly as I was (at least, I do not remember my dreams), but I am having some beautiful daydreams as I prepare my thoughts for sleep. Work is tedious. I feel agitated when the phone rings, and my mind wanders; sometimes, I have to ask people to repeat themselves three times because what they say doesn't register. The next theater season worries me a little about whether I am up to the task. I feel like I am learning to walk for the first time, but I am very aware of falling this time. I love you.

I am going to Madison for Nafina after work today. I will be back tomorrow before 10. I have to check the stage and settle some promotional stuff.

Till then, love
Ken

Subj: *Good morning, darling*
Date: 10/2/98

Dearest Ken,

It may take a few more weeks to feel like your old self again. Don't worry if you are still not there. Be happy that you are getting better. I miss the enthusiasm I used to feel in your letters, but I will wait patiently. As they say, this too shall pass.

Although short, the trip to Madison is perfect for you. Changing environment, even briefly, helps when feeling down.

I went to a networking party last night. It went well. I met a few people and exchanged business cards.

I love you. I have been the same since we last met (maybe I gained five more pounds last week). My mother insists on feeding me as if food is going out of style (since I thoroughly enjoy her cooking, she does not have to do a lot of arms twisting to get me to eat more)! I'll be in Milwaukee for the weekend of October 31-November 1. Official meetings and training classes start Monday, November 2. If you are better by then and feel up to driving the 5 hours to get there, we could spend some time together then. I love you.

How are your daughters doing? Have you found a home for all the puppies yet? Are your house guests still there? Are you still considering Tropel's job offer? I miss you.

Till then
Nickie

I wondered if Ken took that trip to Madison on Monday morning. It may have been difficult for him, but staying involved with the theater was his best therapy. *Was he well enough to pick up his daughters?* Entertaining them would keep him in the moment, pooling him out of his dark state. Meanwhile, Mom would stay with me until Friday and return to Netty's house. I was worried about an upcoming test but didn't mention it to her. I hoped everything would be okay.

"Honey, can we talk for a moment?" Mom asked while stirring her coffee at the table.

"Sure, Mom. What's on your mind?" I said, looking up from my laptop.

"Well, sweetheart, you said we'd discuss it, but it's been a while since your divorce, and I can't help but notice that you haven't been dating or even considering remarriage since Larry. Is everything okay?"

"Mom, I appreciate your concern. It's just that... after my marriage ended, I needed time to heal. Then dating Larry, dealing with his jealousy and possessiveness, I've been focusing on myself, my career, and my happiness."

"I understand, dear. But don't you miss companionship? Someone to share your life with?"

"Of course I do. But I don't want to settle. I want something real, something meaningful. I loved Larry but wasn't in love with him."

"You deserve that, sweetheart. But don't close yourself off completely. There are good people out there. Maybe give it a chance? You seem rather quiet and reflective since I started my visit. You haven't laughed on the phone or gone out with friends. Having someone special in your life would be good, especially now that Craig has graduated and moved out."

"I know, Mom. It's just hard. Trusting again, opening up—it feels like stepping onto a tightrope without a safety net."

"But life is about taking risks, my love. You've got so much love to give. Don't let fear hold you back."

"You're right. I have been thinking about it and taking steps in that direction.

"That's my girl. And remember, you're not alone. Your sisters and I are here for you, cheering you on."

"Thanks, Mom. I love you."

"I love you too, sweetheart. I believe love will find you again when the time is right."

Despite my gratitude for God's blessings, I occasionally felt down and reflective for unknown reasons. It was probably clear because twice last week, my co-workers asked me why I was so subdued, and I didn't know what to tell them. I was not alone, but I felt lonely. Ken was battling his demons, and I neither knew what triggered them nor could I help significantly, *and the distance prevented me from learning more.* I needed to be cheerful, but that proved elusive.

Another six days of silence. My thoughts were on a different tangent than before. *Am I being stupid? Is this whole love fantasy one-sided? Are there really that many "computer" problems preventing us from communicating? Is his depression real?*

I stood outside the quaint bookstore admiring its charming facade; it was still bright out at 3 p.m., but the lighting in the store had a greater appeal than where I was standing and called me within. The book club sign on the glass door was inviting yet intimidating. I had passed by this place countless times, each time with a flutter of curiosity. Today, I took the plunge, my hand hesitating on the door handle before pushing it open.

The bell chimed and its melodic sound filled the room, announcing my entry. A few heads turned toward me. I passed a friendly clerk and followed the sign to the back of the store, where a door was ajar. Smelling coffee and old books was comforting, and the soft murmur of discussion was like music. I took a deep breath and approached the group, my heart racing.

"Hi, I'm Nickie," I said, my voice steadier than I felt.

Two faces, in particular, lit up with welcoming smiles. With fiery red hair and a stack of notes in hand, Jenna scooted over to make room. Beside her, Carlos, an older man whose glasses perched on the tip of his nose, offered a warm handshake.

"We're just discussing this month's read. Did you see it?" Jenna asked, sliding a copy of the book across the table.

I nodded, my nerves easing as I joined the conversation. I read the book two months ago, based on a recommendation from the NY Times bestsellers list, but they didn't need to know that. The hours flew by in a blur of passionate debate and laughter. Jenna and Carlos lingered as the meeting ended and our trio chatted about everything from favorite authors to travel dreams.

"Same time in two weeks?" Carlos asked, hope in his eyes.

"I wouldn't miss it," I replied, a genuine smile spreading across my face. *I think I made two new friends* I sensed as I left the store.

I had had a lovely time at the book club, but the minute I closed the doors of my apartment, the gloomy thoughts returned and were unsetting, so I wrote and told Ken as much.

Ken

The sun was setting, casting long shadows over the landscape; the fleeing day's warmth contrasted sharply with the chill settling in my heart. I tightened my coat, shielding myself from the world and the cool evening. My mind replayed the past month like a broken record, with each rotation bringing a deeper sense of helplessness.

I had been juggling the weight of my friends' problems—Tim's indecision, Michelle's relationship woes, Sara's career anxieties, Taylor's financial struggles, Bill's health concerns, and Pam's housing issues. Each name was a knot in the stress in my chest.

The play had been my escape, my nightly dive into a world where I wasn't Ken—burdened and weary—but someone else completely, someone unencumbered by the seriousness of real life. But the last curtain call had come and gone, and the applause now echoed hollowly in my memory.

My daughters had become unwitting contributors to the cacophony of demands. Their needs, though innocent, had piled onto the mountain of expectations until the weight was unbearable. Sleep had become a stranger, and food lost its taste. Home, once a sanctuary, now felt like a prison.

Three weeks, maybe four, blurred into continuous mental exhaustion. I was a ghost in my own life, moving without purpose, haunted by the absence of dreams. Dreams where I could find solace in thoughts of Nickie, who would fill my nights with hope.

But when even those dreams faded, leaving me in a void, I knew I needed help. The doctor's office was a blur, bringing no comfort.

As the pigeons took flight, scattering into the twilight, I promised myself I'd start untangling the knots tomorrow. I yearned for balance. But for tonight, I sat a little longer, alone with the pigeons and the fading light.

Subj: *What has happened to us?*
Date: 10/8/98

Dearest Ken,

Today is the first I have heard from you since last Friday. If you sent me any messages, I have not received them, and I am beside myself with longing and anxiety. I LOVE YOU, but I can no longer bear the long silences. I got your voicemail today but cannot understand most of it. What's happening? I spent my whole evening crying over the letter I sent you last night saying I wanted to walk away. I had to hide in my bedroom because I didn't want my mother to see me crying and worrying. She has been concerned that I have been too quiet and sad lately. If you get this, please answer me immediately, not five days from today. Are your feelings for me real? I can no longer stand days and days of silence. Can I call you tonight? Let me know. I love you so much.

I miss you
Nickie

Subj: *Message*
Date: 10/8/98 10:55:24 AM EDT

Dearest Nickie,

I read yesterday's email and found no mention of my messages sent on the 4th, 5th, or 6th. They didn't speak to you, or for whatever reason, you just wanted to say goodbye, so that was that.

I said I would let you vent. I am glad you did. I am trying to do better with my dark moments, but obviously, not to my satisfaction. I am sorry. You do injustice to yourself. If you no longer wish to talk, that is your right, but don't say that my feelings for you are not genuine.

Ken

Subj: *Confused and sad*
Date: 10/8/98

Dearest Ken,

I just listened several times to the voicemail you sent this morning. I finally could make out some words, but only part of the whole thing. Ken, I am so sad and confused that I can no longer function correctly. In your letter this morning, you said you wrote to me, yet I have received nothing, and I was desperate. I love you, but your silence has become torture. Not hearing from you for six days is more than I can bear. Did you forget we agreed to leave at least a phone message to acknowledge that we were okay? It makes me think you don't care and that I am bothering you.

You said in your voicemail that your friends' problems are overwhelming you and causing you to want to hide out. It may sound very selfish, but am I not one of your friends? And did you stop to think for a moment about the anguish I must be experiencing at not hearing from you and not knowing why? You may know what is happening, but I don't. I hang on to your letters for dear life, and when they don't come for days in a row, or they do come and don't give me any clues as to why they are so rare or don't address any of my questions, I get more frustrated and desperate. My only interest and concern are you; maybe it's my problem that I feel so strongly for you, but being far away and unable to see or talk to you is driving me crazy. I can't think straight from wanting to be with you, hold you, and tell you how much I love you.

I never know when to call you, even after asking multiple times. It leaves me think-ing that you don't want me to call. Often, I wanted to bring up a topic but held back, not wanting to seem pushy. If you didn't respond to my initial inquiries, I figured you weren't ready to discuss it. Ken, I love you to distraction, and I don't know if you realize how much what you do or don't do means to me. I am sorry if I caused you any pain with my letter of yesterday. Days of silence from you and anxiety over my hospital test led me to think that separating myself was the only path to sanity. I need clarity in everything I do; if it's impossible and I can't change it, I would rather walk away. The issue is that I love you and can't stop even if I try. I am a bit insecure and need more reassurance, being so far away. I have to find a solution.

Till then,
Nickie

P.S. I am writing again before getting an answer to the first letter, but I need to tell you those things and cannot wait.

Subj: ***Hard to understand***
Date: 10/8/98 2:23:31 PM EDT

Dearest Nickie,

Sorry if I was hard to understand; I am taking Trazadone to put me to sleep and Zoloft to level me out (I go down, no highs). I am glad your cancer test came out okay. Dr. Clifford said it might take a month for me to return to normal, and I will see him again in 30 days. A chemical imbalance causes depression in the brain, and lack of sleep, excess stress, or improper handling of stress can all trigger it. For several months now, between Tim, Michelle, Sara, Taylor, Bill, and Pam, I have felt like I have been running in place with one foot nailed down; it wasn't as bad when I was doing a play at night, I could get away from people. When the play ended, I couldn't bail fast enough to keep up with their personal, job, and housing problems. Then my girls came in, and it got to be too much. I wasn't sleeping or eating; I was afraid to go home. Three to four weeks of that, and the next thing I knew, I wasn't functioning. Aside from missing you, it was nothing you had said or done. Recovering from depression isn't always linear. When I couldn't dream about you, I knew I was in trouble and went to the doctor. I love you.

I am still picking plays for next year, meetings Tuesday and Thursday nights in St. Paul 6:30 - 9:00. I have the girls 6:15 - 8:15 Wed. Madison went well, but its stadium seating means the audience will be small (not over 200), and they want us to do an extra performance. I am still determining what will happen there; I have the girls the weekend of the 31st, so I won't make Milwaukee before 9:30 on the 1st. It's nice you are getting to spend some time with your mother. I won't tell you what I wrote when you said your mother was making you eat, and I thought about you on the table just in case your mother was reading over your shoulder. I will see if I have a copy of the letters from the 4th, 5th, and 6th; sometimes, they save to draft. But I write off the cuff and can't remember everything in them. I am sorry if I come across as distracted.

As far as I can remember, there was only one time I cut one of our conversations short, and that was because it had started to thunderstorm. The puppies were loose in the front yard; I had to put them in the barn, round up Tiffany, and get her in the barn with her puppies (Tiffany is a collie). Tim came to tell me it was pouring, but he couldn't help round up puppies. (not his job) I never stopped loving you; it scared me half to death when I couldn't at least dream of you.

I am not yet 100%, but I am better. I don't want to deal with everything at once; I drive around for a few hours to unwind after work. You can tell me anything. I wish I could be there when you do, rubbing your feet or sitting with you in my arms. Sorry this took so long; more later?

Till then, love
Ken

Subj: *Later*
Date: 10/8/98

Dearest Ken,

Thanks for your letter. Since you sent me a voicemail, your computer might be working again. I am glad to understand many things and finally put the pieces together. If, as you said, you can see me in Milwaukee, I am overjoyed, even for a brief time.

Till then,
Nickie

Subj: *Good morning*
Date: 10/9/98 7:55:36 AM EDT

Dearest Nickie,

I suggest writing to tell me if you don't get this letter, but it doesn't sound right. I love you.

I am sorry I didn't write last night. I arrived home at about 9:45, and the PC was working offline, so I shut it down to restart the modem and took the Trazadone at 10; it's signing on to Gateway instead of Netscape. To make a long story short, I fell asleep between 10 and 10:30.

Say hi to your mother and Craig if he's around. Yes, I took my last two days of vacation, Nov 1st and 2nd, because I knew you would be in Milwaukee. What made you think you had cancer? Have you lost weight and energy? How is work going? Stress can produce similar symptoms; take it from someone who has been there. I love you. I will write again later. I have a store where all its registers are down and opening in twenty minutes.

Till then,
Ken

Subj: ***Good morning, dearest***
Date: 10/9/98

Dearest Ken,

Good morning, darling. Last night, I had beautiful dreams/fantasies about you. It's been a while since I had such vivid dreams of us. I was disappointed when my alarm clock went off this morning. We weren't doing much more than kissing in most of them, but somehow, it was passionate. I love you.

After rereading your last letter yesterday, I realized you would get home late. It was enough for me to know what was happening and that our communication was back on track. I'll tell my mom you said hi. Craig is in Germany, and he'll be back on Sunday. He flew back about 1 1/2 weeks ago because he and Hyuen had broken up over the phone, and he wanted to discuss things with her. He told me they straightened things out and are back together.

Even with being very charitable, don't you think your friends might be taking advantage of your kindness? You cannot carry everyone's problems; God is not asking that. Helping when you can is Christian, but not when it becomes detrimental to your life. Charity begins at home, and you may consider that people often create their problems and are responsible for solving them; your name is Ken, not "Jesus Christ."

I had to undergo that test because the doctor thought I was bleeding internally, which he said could be due to benign or cancerous polyps. Thank God everything was clear, and I don't even have a benign polyp. He did say that there were some minor hemorrhoids, but he is still not satisfied that this caused the bleeding. Next week, he wants me to go back to the hospital for a test called an endoscopy. My brother-in-law told me that once, they did this test for him while looking for a bleeding ulcer. From what I understand, this one is not as involved as the test I did this week, so I don't even know why it can't be in his office.

I am ecstatic at the prospect of seeing you again. Expecting to get to Milwaukee on Sunday by 9:30. Is that AM or PM? I'll have training classes and meetings on Monday the 2nd, but we'll also have time to spend together that day, depending on when you plan to leave on Monday night. I'll stay at the Hyatt Regency Hotel this time and have requested a room alone. I feel so happy whenever I imagine being in your arms again.

Till then,
Nickie

Subj: ***Good morning***
Date: 10/10/98 5:55:07 AM EDT

Dearest Nickie;

Good morning, love. Last night, I had a house full of guests; when I got up for work this morning, I still had two people on the couches and one in the recliner. Every time I left the PC for something, I came back to see people watching movies on the DVD, and this afternoon, I heard Tom, Michelle, and Betty would go horseback riding. I will babysit six children from 1 to 8 years of age. Other than that, my evening was pretty dull. What have you been up to? I love you. (I am at work until 3:30.)

Till then,
Ken

Subj: ***Good afternoon***
Date: 10/10/98

Dearest Ken,

I just came home from being out all morning. I had met with the orthodontist and rushed afterward to pick up my mother. Netty had invited her today. She drives me up the wall. Nickie, you don't eat, Nickie, go out more, ah ah, she talks incessantly, but I miss her already.

After work yesterday, I met a few acquaintances for a drink, came home at about 8:45 p.m., stayed logged on until 10:30 p.m., and then went to bed. I have some more errands to run later this afternoon.

Ken, I am venturing into an area that is none of my business, but when are your guests leaving? I am concerned that you are being taken advantage of and creating a very unhealthy emotional environment. I find your lifestyle with your friends very hard to comprehend, but maybe because things are so different on the East and West Coasts, it would be almost impossible to imagine having people (not family) in your home for so long. How come they have free rein to come and go in your bedroom and use your stuff without asking permission? Even more puzzling, why do you allow it? Do you need to feel liked by people to the extent of ignoring your best interest to gain their approval?

Once again, forgive me for saying these things; I have seen people do that only when they have poor self-esteem and need approval from others. Don't get me wrong, I understand being Christian and charitable, but this goes way beyond that. Don't they have any family? Why are you saddled with caring for them if they do?

Would they extend the same generosity to you and your children if you were in the reverse situation? (Not that it should be the basis for helping others.) Somehow, I don't think so.

Darling, I hope you won't be offended by my saying those things, but my only concern is you. I care very much, and though I realize you don't need my help to live your life as you have been, I can't help but want to protect you and keep you from all harm. I sense great sensitivity from you for others, but the downside of an extreme is that you forget yourself. I cannot accept that I have waited so long to meet someone I could love as much as I love you. I find anything intolerable I perceive as threatening your well-being and happiness (call it self-interest if you must). Still, I love you, and that's all I care about, at the risk of seeming hard.

I am way out of bounds, but I am trying to know you best to match all my love for you and venturing into delicate areas.

Till then,
Nickie

Subj: *Golden rule*
Date: 10/10/98 4:21:30 PM EDT

Dearest Nickie,

The people playing on the computer were children, and I asked them to leave, but I was over my head with the number of children. However, the rule is to "treat others as you wish to be treated," not as they treat you. It's not always easy, but the right thing is not always easy. I have an appointment next week to look at a duplex in Cambridge. The price is reasonable, and if the house is in good shape, I may buy it and let everyone move in and pay rent.

I promised they could stay until they found a place they could afford. I always keep a promise. That is a sense of pride from which I derive much self-esteem. In addition, the duplex price is low enough that I could charge them less than $450 per month. And still pay the mortgage and taxes, thus solving everybody's problems. When they no longer need it, I can sell the house and worry about a profit. I still think it's wrong to make a profit from your friends.

I am not upset, but I believe God will provide. I love you.

Till then, love
Ken

P.S. I still can't think about you and food without getting sidetracked by you and the dining room table. (I wish I could make that smiley face.)

Subj: ***Good morning***
Date: 10/11/98

Dearest Ken,

Good morning, darling. I hope you had a lovely time with the kids last night. It was quite a handful to keep occupied and entertained. I love you. I am grateful my observations regarding your friends don't ruffle your feathers. Your answers, at times, make me feel like my favorite priest has admonished me for forgetting my Christian duties. (However, since you told me once you often get cast as a priest in your plays, it only seems fitting (smile).

I'll go to the 9 a.m. mass and take a short walk on my return. I have no other plans for the day. Next Friday, I plan to go to a dinner theater event with some acquaintances if we can get tickets. With a group of 6 going, we can get tickets at $25 a piece rather than $45. The play we intend to see is the British murder mystery sex farce Communicating Doors. It's off-Broadway.

Is your mother also living in Minnesota? Do you get to see her often? How is Liam doing these days? When is the next theater season starting for you? You are always on my mind.

Till then,
Nickie

Nickie

We were sitting side by side, Craig and I, on the plush sofa. There was no ceiling light, and only table lamps illuminated the room. I felt terrible seeing him slumped beside me, with genuine sadness on his face, staring at a page of the new album. The album contained photos of him, Hyuen, and me, collected throughout their two-year relationship. I was trying to console him, but I wasn't sure if I had any effect. It was hard to see your child hurting; it left you feeling helpless. Though already a man at twenty-one, he remained my little boy. I wished to see him happy and smiling.

"I know it hurts, sweetheart. Breakups are never easy."

"Mom, I thought Hyeun and I were forever. But now... it's all gone."

I remembered my heartbreaks. They shaped and even strengthened me.

"Craig, listen to me. You're allowed to feel this pain. It's okay. But often, healing takes time."

"I miss her, Mom."

As I flipped through the photo album pages, memories of vacations and laughter flooded back. Even my favorite photo of us, a duplicate of the framed one sitting on the wall unit, was in the album.

"I love Hyuen a lot, maybe not as much as you do, but I had hoped she would become my daughter-in-law someday; we got along well. When I was your age, I thought my world would end with every breakup. But it didn't. Life kept moving, and so did I."

"How?"

I moved closer to him and put one arm around his shoulder.

"First, let yourself grieve. Cry if you need to. Then, find distractions—things that make you smile. Remember the time we went to visit your grandparents on the islands? It rained the next afternoon. You were about 9 or 10 and ran out in the yard. I ran after you. We thought it was funny and danced in the rain during that summer storm."

"Yeah, I do."

Furious, your grandma insisted we come inside, or we'd catch a cold. When we finally came in, she was mad at us both, but we kissed her and had lots of fun. When you are sad, think of other good times, and you'll feel better."

"Yes, I remember now. Grandpa agreed with Grandma but winked at us behind her back. We had a lot of fun that day!"

I started humming the old tune we danced to in the rain, and Craig remembered the words. I couldn't help but feel a sense of satisfaction as a smile returned to his face while we sang along.

He'll be alright, I thought. New beginnings await.

Subj: ***Good morning***
Date: 10/13/98 12:29:47 PM EDT

Dearest Nickie,

People keep calling in on the crisis line, so I have had all three of my lines going most of the morning. I love you.

Last night, I bought an Appaloosa; he is still a colt but should be big enough to ride next spring. So, I must finish the corral and chase off the bunnies this weekend. I stopped in Cambridge long enough to drive past the house. Its brick facade gave it a timeless charm. From the outside, it looks small, but it may have potential.

The girls are excited about getting a horse, and Claire's birthday is next week. I am still trying to figure out what to get her.

Till then, love
Ken

Subj: ***Good morning***
Date: 10/15/98 8:26:40 AM EDT

Dearest Nickie,

Good morning, love. How did the tests go? When the tenants finally leave, aren't they legally responsible for the four months back rent they owe?

Camille went to a football game last night, and I reminded myself to thank her for all her hard work keeping Claire in line. Seeing a child of mine so consumed with her wants and desires is a little disheartening.

I have been putting off telling you I got a haircut I have been hoping it would grow out. Whatever happened to grow like a weed, ha. Anyway, I went to get a trim, and my regular barber wasn't there, and the new barber's idea of trim differed from mine. He won. Everybody thinks it looks okay, but not seeing my neck in several years, it seems like the top of my head has fallen into my eyebrows, which is embarrassing. It's been two weeks, and two more weeks will not help much. Forewarned is forearmed, they say. I love you.

How was your day off? Other than being hectic, what with tests and lawyers, did you have any time for yourself? Tell me more about the franchise. The idea went from possibility to airplanes without anything in between. Is it a good firm? Will you be au-tonomous? Will you be in your own office or someone else's? Are you excited about the prospects? Do you have any reservations? Did I tell you I loved you yet?

Till then,
Ken

Subj: ***Good afternoon***
Date: 10/15/98

Dearest Ken,

I intend to write this today even if I have to ignore everything else in the office. Things are getting very busy at work, but I am unmotivated. The test was quite an experience; the doctor didn't tell me he would sedate me until early morning, and I could find no one to go with me, so I opted to do it without the sedation. That was a mistake. I panicked and was gagging. The test only lasted 15 minutes but felt like an eternity. It was unpleasant, and I would advise no one to do it without sedation. This morning, I still had to take more aspirin, so sore my throat was from all the gagging. The doctor did not find an ulcer, so it's okay; he said there was stomach irritation but thinks it's nothing.

Last evening, I drove for 40 minutes to the lawyer's office, only to discover that my appointment was not recorded and he was absent. Thus, I am no further along now regarding which options to pursue with the courts.

Claire is quite a handful. Does she behave the same way with your ex-wife, or can she get away with doing certain things with you alone? Be firm and don't give in to tantrums, as she learns she can't always get her way. By all means, tell Camille often how much you appreciate her help with Claire. Chelsea sounds like a competent and caring daughter; surprising her with a token of appreciation might be a good idea.

Craig is back from Germany, so things between him and Hyeun did not work out. He is heartbroken, and I wish I could make him feel better.

It's my turn to tell you not to worry about the haircut. Even if you went bald, I wouldn't mind; it would just give me more accessible places to kiss and make your handsome features more visible. I'm sure there's enough hair left to feel. I love you.

The franchise is a nutrition company (they produce and sell vitamins, minerals, and other natural products). They approved me as a potential franchisee, but I am still in the information-gathering mode. When I meet with them, I'll have more complex data (demographics, average net bottom line, available locations, etc.) I wanted to simplify my life, and buying a business will not do that. but now, I need to find meaning in something. I feel very close to aimless. I am grateful to God for everything I have in my life, but he also made me who I am. I need passion, commitment, and a reason (besides all he has given me) to wake up and embrace the day. I need to have a goal and some control. From what I know, I would be autonomous but pay a franchise fee based on sales. They (The Company) will sign the location lease, and it makes sense to use most of their suppliers for quantity discounts.

I was glad to get your morning letter; it gave me the emotional boost I needed. I can't wait to hold you, kiss you, feel the warmth of your arms encircle me, feel your breath on my neck, your lips on mine. I miss you so much.

Till then,
Nickie

Subj: *Good morning,*
Date: 10/19/98 7:29:16 AM EDT

Dearest Nickie,

How was your weekend? I had the girls this weekend. We watched Lost in Space, went bowling, and checked out tack for the new horse at a store in Rogers and another in Blane; Chelsea's tastes lean slightly toward the garish. I love you.

I was off Friday. I caught the flu bug but am still not up to stuff. I checked out the duplex in Cambridge, but it needs a new roof, and there is considerable water damage to the second floor, so I will pass on it. I did find another house in Braim; I have yet to see it, but it sounds interesting: 5,000 square feet on 20 acres, hardwood floors, built in 1909, for $119,000. Real estate may be safer than the stock market. When the Euro comes out on January 2, they expect a big push for 60-90 days, and then it may drop big if the currency is not readily available, which is likely in France and Germany. Additionally, England is making a fuss about coin weights.

Bring warm clothing when you come to Wisconsin, much as I HATE to suggest covering works of art. We expect snow by Wednesday, and while I plan to heat things as much as the fire marshal will allow, I wouldn't want your strength snapped by a cold or, worse yet, the flu. I love you.

Till then, love
Ken

Subj: *Good morning, darling*
Date: 10/19/98

Dearest Ken,

I'm sorry about your cold; I hope it's better now. I met my new friends Friday evening at the theater. The play was excellent and quite funny. It made me think of you for many reasons, mainly because of your British accent. After the play, we went out for drinks. There were seven of us, and the conversation was lively. I arrived home at 3 a.m., so Saturday went to waste. I felt human again at about 5 p.m. On Sunday, my only activity was going for a two-hour walk. I took a different route in the park and followed a bike path. The trees are showing some yellow, red, and brown. It will take a couple of weeks before the foliage reaches its peak of beauty; next weekend, I'll take my camera to the park for some pictures.

We still have some 70-degree days around here mingled with the beauty and scent of autumn leaves. I'll make sure I bring warm clothes to Milwaukee. Thankfully, all the meetings are to take place at the hotel. When we are together, I fully expect us to generate enough heat to want to open the windows. I love you. I kissed your picture this morning (no one is around to think me crazy for it)! The phone number at the Hyatt Regency is (414) 276-xxxx, and the address is 333 West Kilbourn Ave. It's downtown Milwaukee and close to where I stayed in July. I will attend a welcome reception at the hotel on Sunday from 5 to 7 p.m. but should be in my room before you arrive. I can't wait to be with you again.

You sound like your old self, and I am so pleased. Enjoy the rest of the day.

Till then,
Nickie

Subj: *Are you out there?*
Date: 10/24/98

Dearest Ken,

How are you? Your last letter was upbeat, and I thought everything was going well. I am thinking of you.

Nickie

"On the Mend"

Nickie

Many days had passed, and I hated I was still counting them! I tried leaving a message on the phone, but his answering machine didn't pick up. Maybe it's full, but on the other end, why didn't he call me to do the same? Even at the height of his depression, he did not stay that long without writing. Did he have a relapse? That was possible. *Is he having second thoughts about coming to Milwaukee?*

Yesterday, I called Wendy, my friend Wayne's wife, and suggested dinner for this evening. I felt guilty for being absent at their daughter's birthday party and waiting to notify them until the last minute. Wendy was enthusiastic but declared that she could not secure a sitter on such short notice, but she would talk Wayne into going anyway, and I could stop at their house to catch up anytime.

We sat at an Italian restaurant less than a mile from their suburban home. The delicious scent of garlic, tomatoes, and fresh herbs wafted in the air, and the interior was cozy in its rustic charm, exposed brick walls adorned with vintage Italian posters. In the center, a wood-fired oven glowed, the heart of the restaurant, where pizzas were crafted with care and emerged with perfectly charred crusts. We had already ordered and waited for the food to arrive.

"Wayne, I'm sorry I missed Simone's birthday party. I've been... a bit lost in my world lately."

"It's alright. Wendy and I know you've had a lot on your mind. Speaking of which, how are things going with Ken?" he asked.

"It's complicated. I don't like how paranoid this relationship has made me. I never realized how vulnerable I could be. So much for my purported strength.'

"You are strong, Nickie. But even the strongest people have their moments of doubt. What's got you feeling this way?"

"With his job, art, friends, and children, I wonder if he genuinely has time for me. This is not a high-maintenance relationship! All it takes is a couple of weekly emails to keep me happy! In my experience, we find time to do what we want and make excuses for the rest."

"Have you talked to him about how you're feeling?"

"I have nothing to say that he doesn't already know. I shouldn't have constantly told him I loved him. Relationship wisdom is that we should always let the other person think they love us more than we do; otherwise, they take us for granted, and we become unimportant."

"Nickie, I have known you to only listen to your heart and your head; your instincts are usually spot on. These sayings, however, may have a good foundation; otherwise, they wouldn't have survived."

"The distance between us is the most significant problem. I know you initially thought it was a bad idea for me to be in a long-distance relationship. You insisted it wouldn't work and was a waste of time."

"What do I know? I said that based on what I had heard. I have no direct experience with it, and seeing how happy you have been lately, I refuse to believe that. Your love is strong enough to surmount any obstacles based on knowing you. Who hasn't had problems and things happen in their life? You realized you love him and made him a priority."

"I wouldn't let anything interfere with Ken or give him a reason to doubt my feelings. But that's me. Of course, he is not all to blame; I have free will and can walk away..."

"Nickie, love isn't about who loves who more or less. It's about being there for each other despite the distance or the silence. You're strong, and you're also human. It's okay to feel insecure sometimes. Just remember, you're not alone in this."

The waiter arrived with our food, and we spent the rest of the meal discussing his children and his plan to add to his already large house.

I hoped Ken was not playing with my heart, though it would not be in character for him. I had been hanging in, thinking it was worth all the inconvenience. I was neither a martyr nor aspired to be one; emotional pain was proving excruciating. *Am I asking for too much? Am I coming or going? I know one thing: no one loves him as much as I do.*

A few days after my dinner with Wayne, I felt much calmer. I reasoned that whatever was happening with Ken, I didn't cause it. I could only help him if he were ready. I would be there if he needed me, but I shouldn't be so distressed by something I couldn't influence.

Ken

The sterile white of the hospital room was blinding after the darkness of unconsciousness. There was a large window on one side, with thin, white blinds partially drawn to provide privacy while letting in natural light. Near the bed, a small bedside table held a pitcher of water and a plastic cup alongside a remote control for the room's television, which was mounted on the wall opposite the bed. The heart monitor was beeping rhythmically, the air carried a faint antiseptic scent, and the room was quiet except for the occasional sound of footsteps and the distant hum of activity from the nurses. I realized I was finally fully awake. I remembered whispering something to a nurse, and dropping back into slumber. My throat felt parched, and each breath was a raspy whisper against the oxygen mask clinging to my face. I tried to lift my hand, but it felt as heavy as the leaden skies over Lake Milacs on the day I fell ill.

Memories of that day trickled back—the excitement of acquiring the new horse, a sudden dizziness in the field, and nothing until now. The heat that had raged through my body had subsided to a dull ache. I turned my head, seeking, I don't know what, maybe a comforting presence, but found only the rhythmic pulsing of the machines keeping vigil over my fragile state. I recalled seeing a familiar face when I attempted to wake up, but I had no idea who it was.

As I lay there, the battle between illness and recovery waged within. I realized the road ahead would take days, but there was strength in my bones to carry me through this unexpected hurdle.

Subj: *Thinking of you*
Date: 10/26/98

Dearest Ken,

I wanted to turn on my computer this morning before leaving home, but I knew you didn't write, and confirming it would have made me skip work. I'm here at work, no better off.

I can't fault you for everything. I participated in this little world we constructed, but who can blame me for longing for a dream come true? It will be more challenging than I expected. Yesterday afternoon, I was trying to talk myself into going to the store to return a gift I bought you; I couldn't do it. It would have meant recognizing I would not hear from you anymore. I never got to the store, nor do I intend to go now. I love you, and that's the only reality I know.

Only write if you love me and genuinely desire a relationship. Even though I get angry with you sometimes, I know you are not the kind of person who would lead my heart on a merry chase for fun. In my mind, you are a generous person. I consider myself decent but don't have half the compassion you show others. A couple of times, I wasn't very nice regarding your friends, but to be truthful, most of it was jealousy; jealousy that you could give them all this care and time, when I felt deprived, unable to get a glimpse nor a hug from you.

I am slow in giving my heart, but once I do, try as I may, I can't turn off my feelings at the drop of a hat. If you don't care for me any longer, please don't write unless it's to tell me why. I don't know what else to say. You don't have to come to Milwaukee if that's the problem. Just don't be silent if you still care. I miss you.

Till then,
Nickie

Subj: *Percy Shelley*
Date: 10/26/98

Dearest Ken,

I arise from dreams of Thee in the first sleep of night –Percy Shelley.

I miss you.
Nickie

Subj: *Rationality at last!*
Date: 10/26/98

Dearest Ken.

I know I have been a pain today (this must be the 10th email I am sending you). I am sorry. You'll have reprieve tomorrow when I'm in Pittsburgh.

I just reread your last letter and my reply to you that day. It occurred to me you could have been home sick with the flu last week while I was making myself miserable with all kinds of imaginings. If you've been ill, you might consider me crazy for being so emotional and uncontrollable. Not having your love makes me behave like a complete idiot. I hope you are over the flu and feeling better now. I love you.

Till then,
Nickie

Subj: *Percy Shelley*
Date: 10/27/98 1:10:08 PM Eastern Standard Time

Dearest Nickie,

From fitful slumber, like the phoenix, I slowly rise, covered with the sweat of broken dreams. I am sorry not to have written for a while. I hope I have not caused too much worry; I was hospitalized and haven't gotten to read any emails yet. After paying for the horse last Wednesday, I fainted in the field and was then taken to Lake Milacs Hospital. My temperature spiked to 106. The flu became pneumonia; I am at work today, but I still feel like the horses have pummeled me. Sorry I haven't caught up on email, but I will try throughout the day. I am a bit skinnier than when we last met, but I needed to lose some weight. Currently, I am still planning on coming to Milwaukee on Sunday night. I will write after I catch up; I can't wait to see you. I love you. (If I look a little worse for the wear, don't worry too much; they sent me home last night. I was supposed to stay in bed for another week, but I have slept enough the past few days to last me a month.)

Till then, love
Ken

P.S. I will tell you about the house later.

Subj: ***Good evening, darling***
Date: 10/27/98

Dearest Ken,

I am so sorry to hear that you are unwell. Please follow the doctor's advice. If you do too much too soon, you may have a relapse, and I want you well. I just walked in from the airport (I was in Pittsburgh today; I will tell you about it tomorrow). I was worried sick and jumped to crazy conclusions about your silence. Ignore my stupid letters, except for the last one. I love you, and that is all that matters. You should know me well by now. I love you.

I will be off tomorrow trying to catch up with my lawyer. As I feared, while I was away today, the court gave my tenants an extension, and now I am supposed to appear in court next week when I'll be in Milwaukee. I hope the lawyer (a new one I am getting will go in my stead or get another date for me). I am overjoyed that you are okay and still love me. I'll write again 1st thing tomorrow morning. (The last letter I wrote, the only one that makes sense besides Percy Shelley, is called "Rationality... At last.") I am virtually hugging and kissing you.

Till then
Nickie

Subj: ***I love you***
Date: 10/28/98

Dearest Ken,

Good morning, dear. How are you feeling today? You must have been in pretty terrible shape to have passed out. I got home from the airport at about 11:15 p.m. and checked my mail for news of you. I am sorry about all the stupid things I may have said in last week-

end's emails. I lose my senses whenever I think of not having you anymore. Drop me a line today so I know you still love me, even if you read my stupid emails.

I look forward to Milwaukee and being with you again, but I'm worried about you. Perhaps you shouldn't take such a long drive right after being sick. What if something happens while you are driving? I would not forgive myself. Did the doctor give you the okay to return to work? Your company must have sick leave provisions. I am delighted to hear from you and know you are well; however, I am also concerned you think I am irrational.

I will refrain from preaching about taking on too many responsibilities and wearing yourself out. Be more cautious, take care of yourself when you feel tired, take plenty of vitamins, and get as much rest as possible. I can't wait to hold you and squeeze you in my arms again, feel your body against mine, and give you a million little kisses (besides a few thousand big ones)

Till then,
Nickie

Subj: *Good evening, darling*
Date: 10/28/98 10:23:40 AM Eastern Standard Time

Dearest Nickie,

I made it to work. I still sleep more than I am used to. It may be the medicine. The dogs were happy to see me (two puppies joined me in bed last night). The horse is coming Saturday at noon, and Larry (the rancher I bought the horse from assures me the horse will be fine for 2 or 3 days.) Sorry, I still haven't had time to catch up on the mail. When I got home, I made a peanut butter sandwich, poured a glass of milk, took my pill, laid down for a minute, and woke up with two puppies at 1:30 this morning. I may skip a few after reading your letter this morning. I don't know how you were hurt so badly, but hopefully, you can trust me again with time. Your time with friends is valuable, and I am always available. However, my imagination can only reach so far in longing for you. We can handle it until we find an answer to the distance thing. I love you. I have a lot of work on my desk and 32 people on hold; I have to go for now, but I'll be back!!!!! (Get the hint)

Till then, love
Ken

Subj: *Good morning, darling*
Date: 10/29/98 11:50:58 AM Eastern Standard Time

Dearest Nickie,

Good morning, my love. Sorry I am so late. I walked into a mess this morning, and I am leaving early. I have a doctor's appointment at 1:00 and will go at noon. I am doing better, thank you, (but if I eat more soup, I think I will start to slouch when I walk. I love you. I have a Nafina meeting tonight if I can stay awake, but I will try to write before I go. I love you.

Till then, love
Ken

Subj: *Good morning, darling*
Date: 10/29/98

Dearest Ken,

Sleeping is the best thing for a fast recovery. I want you to reconsider coming to Milwaukee. I don't want anything to happen to you, and I would rather we postpone our meeting than have you do something detrimental to your health.

You are probably still swamped with work and can't spend too much time in email, but when we meet in Milwaukee, I would like to hear more about the horse and the house you are considering purchasing. I smiled when you told me about waking up from sleep to find two puppies sleeping with you. I had a quick mental image of the entire scene and thought it was sweet. I wish I had been there to take a picture of the three of you lost in the land of dreams. Whenever I think of you, I get this warm, gentle glow around my heart, which feels so good. I love you a lot.

Till then,
Nickie

Subj: *Hugs, kisses, and smiles to you too! :) :) I love you*
Date: 10//30/98

Dearest Ken,

Thank you for the cute card (hug, kiss, smile). It's an excellent start to the day. I previously gave you this information, but a reminder that I'll be at the Hyatt Regency at 333 West

Kilbourn Ave in Downtown Milwaukee. Unless you should feel too weak to travel or I hear differently, I am looking forward to seeing you on Sunday evening around 9:30. I love you. Are the puppies still sneaking into bed with you? You should inform them that they infringe on my territory and that I don't take kindly to that. I know you have the girls this weekend, and I won't have my laptop with me in Milwaukee, but I promise that if you can't make it and I don't hear from you, I won't get hysterical again. I miss you.

Until then,
Nickie

Subj: ***Hugs, kisses, and a smile to you***
Date: 10/30/98 2:57:07 PM Eastern Standard Time

Dearest Nickie,

The Dr. and I are at odds. Yesterday, my temp was 104, and the Dr. sent me home. I got home at about 6:45 and went straight to bed; I woke at 3:15 this morning. I missed my meeting last night but was pretty bored sitting around the house, so I am working a half day today (The doctor told me to stay in bed till Wednesday). I still am planning on Sunday. I am not coughing, my temperature remains elevated, and my blood pressure is up a little, so I will be a good boy tonight. The girls must settle for a quiet weekend, but I am determined. I want to hold you again. I love you. How did it go in court with the new attorney?

Till then, love
Ken

Subj: ***Good morning, dearest***
Date: 11/4/98 12:40:04 PM Eastern Standard Time

Dearest Nickie,

I am off to see the doctor. I hope this message finds you safely home. I am sorry we did not connect this past weekend. I would feel terrible if I were to cause your illness. You are always in my heart and my dreams. I love you.

Till then,
Ken

Subj: *Good afternoon, dearest*
Date: 11/4/98

Dearest Ken,

My heart still skips a beat whenever I receive your letters. You sound in good spirits. I missed you more this past weekend (because of the proximity of our locations). I felt guilty about not trying to dissuade you from coming, but glad that, in the end, you listened to your body. I wouldn't have gotten the flu from being with you, so that wasn't a concern. I closed my eyes and thought about you during the flight back. I imagined we were together the whole weekend; we snuggled and slept in each other's arms, how your lips felt on mine, how we fed each other from room service, how much fun we had showering together, and how pleasurable and warm it felt to feel our bodies becoming one! I hope these words describe our reality again soon.

I immensely enjoyed talking to you yesterday. I wasn't nervous for the first time since we've known each other. It almost felt as if we were chatting cozily on the sofa, nudged in each other's arms, and making plans. I love you. Don't do too much, even if the doctor gives you the okay. It'll take at least two weeks of solid food and nights of sleep before you will feel like your old self again. Go easy with the horse as well. Let me know what you decide to name him. Take pictures, and bring them with you the next time we meet. I also want to see photos of your daughters. Put that on your list for our next meeting.

Till then,
Nickie

Subj: *Good morning*
Date: 11/5/98 8:30:24 AM Eastern Standard Time

Dearest Nickie,

You must know my doctor. I am on half-days this week, and he wants me to eat more. Anyway, I have another appointment on Friday, and the short version is that I will be okay. I am glad you are safe at home. Are you back at work? I want to get my camera working again so I can see you. Dreaming of you is taking new heights of distraction (sometimes I think I got sick to spend more time in bed with you.) I love you.

Till then, love
Ken

Subj: *Good morning, darling*
Date: 11/5/98

Dearest Ken,

Since your doctor and I are telling you the same thing, it's the best course of action; if we could also get your mother involved, you would not dare disobey our collective wisdom. I am glad you are dreaming of us again, and I find myself a lot more open in the fantasies I am allowing myself to dwell in. Please fix your camera. I am curious to see how you look with shorter hair.

To be back at work today is not exciting. The franchise seems more attractive now if only I could solve the problem of working seven days a week. Our headquarters may have finally decided on a replacement for my boss. I'll keep an open mind. Be a good boy, and don't overwork. I miss you.

Till then,
Nickie

Subj: *Hi*
Date: 11/6/98

Dearest Ken,

Good morning, darling. I woke up with my allergies on full blast. I have not stopped sneezing for more than 5 minutes. I took an antihistamine a little while ago, but it will be an hour before I see its effect.

How is the horse doing? Are your girls good to you while you are sick? Do you know what play your theater season will open with? I love you. Have you had the chance to wear your new cloak yet? I can't wait to see you in it.

I was awake for about an hour in the middle of the night and spent all of it thinking about you. What would be the most pleasurable way to wake you up? (I have come up with a couple of juicy ones!) Please follow the doctor's orders.

Till then,
Nickie

Subj: *The weekend*
Date: 11/8/98

Dearest Ken,

Good morning, darling. How have you been the last two days? Recuperating well? I love you. Are you working 1/2 day this weekend or resting more?

I spent the day hiking in Rockefeller State Park with my new friends (6). I went to Manhattan first, and then we took the train north for an hour. It was very sunny. We talked a lot and got lost in all the different trails but found our way. Overall, it was a lovely day, and I am glad I could persuade myself to do that instead of my usual chores. I went almost straight to bed when I returned home and woke up a few hours ago. We have a baby shower for someone in my office on Tuesday, and I am going to the stores to get a gift today. Any luck so far with the camera? I love you and miss you.

Till then,
 Nickie

Subj: *The weekend*
Date: 11/8/98 9:20:30 AM Eastern Standard Time

Dearest Nickie,

Dr. Clifford stuffed me in the hospital; he said he wanted to make sure I got some rest, and the nurse let me borrow her laptop. The doctor should be by on rounds sometime between 9 and 11, and if the nurse tells him I have stayed in bed and my blood pressure and temperature are acceptable, I can go home. I feel good now, so I will probably be home later today. I love you.

When I read your letter, the last line on the first page ended with "We are having a baby." I don't mind telling you my first thought was I had been out longer than I thought. It bummed me because I had missed out on the best part of "having a baby" (I mean before the actual birth of the baby); then I went to page 2 and saw the word "shower." Say, isn't someone having a birthday soon?

Till then,
Ken

Subj: ***Doctor's orders***
Date: 11/8/98

Dearest Ken,

I approve of your doctor's actions. You are not following his dictates, and he must feel he has no alternative. I hate to sound like a mother, but I will anyway. If you obeyed him, you would surely be well past this.

Frankly, you worry me, and I strongly request that you rest, eat well, and stay in bed. There is nothing that cannot wait if you are sick! I love you, Ken; if you don't do this for yourself, do it for those who love and care for you. Stay in bed! If you get bored, read a book, ask someone who lives with you to go to the store and get you a couple of videos, do a puzzle, learn the lines of a new play, write poetry, or think of making love to me, think of me making your wildest fantasies come true! (I particularly insist on that one!) Anything! But stay off your feet until the doctor says it's okay. If I were close to you, I would box your ears to make my point and then tie you to the bed until I judge you fit to get out. I am sure you must be concerned about work, but since you are under the doctor's care, they must know you will return as soon as possible.

I smiled at what you said regarding the baby. Forgetting making the baby's creation would be like waking up, receiving congratulations, holding the World Series Cup, and having no recollection of any games or even being part of the team! If this ever happens to us, we would have no choice but to request a play-by-play reenactment of the baby "making" part to ensure our lucidness. I love you. Yes, Darling, I will have a birthday on Tuesday, and I'll try to imagine I am as young as that brand-new baby! I hope I will wake up someday, and your face will be the first loving thing I see on such a day.

Till then,
Nickie

Subj: ***Monday***
Date: 11/9/98 11:20:29 AM Eastern Standard Time

Dearest Nickie,

I am working half-days till I get the okay. Dr. Clifford let me go home yesterday, but not before 4:30. I tried to take care of myself, but the problem is the medication they want me to take to help me sleep doesn't work well with the medication they gave me to help my blood pressure. Combine that with two small children who are also sick, Alissa especially, and I think we trade off. Anyway, the Dr. says I need rest the most, so I take the pills for sleep, but I have borderline high blood pressure, 143/90+; it's been like that for 20 years, no big deal, but now that I am taking the Tratden I hover around 154/102-106 and that Dr. Clifford says is a big deal. But as soon as this stuff clears my lungs, we will see if I can start sleeping without it, and my blood pressure should normalize. I love you.

Sorry I am so late. Working from 10 a.m. to 2 p.m. Thank you. Happy Pre B.day, trying to be cute; I wanted you to know I remembered.

Till then,
Ken

I received an e-card from Ken today, and what he wrote went straight to the depth of my heart.

My Love,

You inspire my soul, ignite my heart, haunt my dreams, and crowd my thoughts. My arms ache in your absence, and my smile waits for your return. I hope your birthday meets you with lots of joy and lingers until we are together again.

I love you. Happy Birthday.
Ken

Subj: ***Dearest***
Date: 11/10/98

Dearest Ken,

Good morning, darling. Thanks for the lovely cards. I had to download a small program to view the second one. I just got to work and took my time dressing today (since it's my birthday). You are in my heart and constantly in my thoughts; I won't feel alone today. I kissed your picture, which helped, but I would have liked to feel your arms around me in a hug and long embrace. I love you.

Till then,
Nickie

Subj: *Re: Internet Phone Message*
Date: 11/11/98

Dearest Ken,

Thank you for your good wishes and for singing to me. I love you. I want to figure out why I can't send a voice mail from the Internet phone. I am sorry to hear about your accident with the car. God is keeping you safe. How are you feeling today? I presume you are home since they would not have fixed the car so fast. I'm off work, luckily, as it poured all night and continues to do so. I have some work reading and two action videos my son forgot to take with him. I missed you yesterday, but you were in my heart. Thanks again for the lovely e-cards. I finally played the one with the robot and the cake; it was charming. Please be careful driving.

Till then,
Nickie

Subj: *Lonely Friday*
Date: 11/13/98 12:47:24 PM Eastern Standard Time

Dearest Nickie,

Good morning, my love. I am a little congested, but my blood pressure is down, and the doctor thinks I will be fine in another week or so. My temperature is back down under 100. Dr. Clifford said not to worry about it; my body was still fighting the infection and considered it normal.

I had work to catch up on for Nafina last night; sorry, I didn't get home until 10:41, and I thought writing might be a little late. I miss you. Sometimes I feel useless. I spend so much time sleeping that I must stay awake for a month to catch up. I love you.

Till then,
Ken

Subj: *Morning*

Date: 11/16/98 7:24:14 AM Eastern Standard Time

Dearest Nickie,

Good morning. I am getting back to work regularly. The girls were out yesterday and full of energy. I went to bed when I got home at 5:30 and didn't wake until this morning at 3:30. What were you doing this weekend? Are you still gorgeous? How are you feeling? I love you.

Till then,
Ken

Subj: *Dearest*

Date: 11/16/98

Dearest Ken,

You sound in good spirits. Don't fight your need for rest, even 12 hours.

My weekend was quite busy, but it was good. I was out both Friday and Saturday evenings. The dinner party at Craig's friends turned out very nicely.

Things were upbeat at the office today. I had several projects, including overseeing the appraisal of the company's equipment, furniture, and fixtures for the transition. I also had to make a presentation in the afternoon that included my boss. I am still considering the nutrition company and doing my due diligence on all the information.

I love you. I hope I am still beautiful to you; I don't have anyone around these days to tell me anything, but I am exercising, eating well, and staying in shape, so you will continue to find me appealing. Once things normalize, check if you can take a few days off at year-end. Combining it with the weekend, you could visit New York. Is your hair back to its regular length? Have you named the horse yet? Have a good evening.

Till then,
Nickie

"Happy Thanksgiving"

Subj: *Dearest*

Date: 11/17/98 6:37:46 AM Eastern Standard Time

Dearest Nickie,

Good morning, my love. I had the most beautiful dream of you last night. I took a nap after work and got up around 1 a.m. to watch the meteor shower, and the aurora borealis was out. The meteors looked as if they were taking target practice through the halos the sun produced reflecting off the polar ice caps.

My hair has yet to grow out (it may take a couple of years to reach its former length). Your weekend sounds excellent. I am glad you had some time with your son. I love you.

Till then,
Ken

Subj: ***Working and dreaming***
Date: 11/18/98

Dearest Ken,

You sound significantly better these days. There are days when I almost feel happy, and I know I can occasionally go for a few hours without feeling lonely. I try to keep busy and no longer isolate myself, but it's like putting a Band-Aid on a deep wound. I'll be off from work from the 26th to December 6th. I have the family over for Thanksgiving dinner, and I plan to attend a function with my friends the following weekend. Again, it feels like I am outside myself watching a film, going through the motions with complete emotional detachment. I am ashamed of how I feel because everything is right in my life; I have my health, job, child, and family, but I still feel empty inside. I look at couples with a lot of longing. This past year and a half have seen me the loneliest I have ever been, and sometimes, I wonder if I'll be strong enough to keep loneliness and anxiety from becoming despair.

I know my happiness is my responsibility and no one else's. Still, it's as if I have all the numbers in a combination, but I can't remember the sequence of right turns and left turns necessary to open the safe. I love you more than I have ever loved anyone, but in the last few months, I have wondered if we'll ever be more than a dream. It's a dream I can't give up. Why aren't our plans getting any traction? I can't imagine loving or wanting to be with anyone other than you. Why would God bring us together to make me experience this pain of not having you nearby?

You are lucky to indulge your passion for the theater. I wish I could find sustained enthusiasm for anything besides you these days. I miss you in every way, emotionally as well as physically. My body aches for yours like we have made love a million times.

Till then,
Nickie

Subj: ***Good morning***
Date: 11/19/98 8:48:29 AM Eastern Standard Time

Dearest Nickie,

Good morning, my love. One of these days, I will learn to press 'enter.' Someone told me the email would not time out if I only pressed enter every so often. I was writing to you, and the words were flowing, spiked with this movie of epic proportions of us in my mind. While I was lost in your arms, my screen timed out. Sometimes, that is very frustrating because there are times when my dreams allow me to wax poetic, which expresses what I see in my mind with greater color, but like the dream that inspires the poem, the dream fades if the words are lost. You can recall it, but some vibrancy, flavor, and subtleties are lost in forcing the details back into place. I love you. I was writing you an excellent letter about your aching loneliness, time, space, and other metaphysical things, the gist of which was a minute apart is forever, and Milwaukee, NY, and Barbados were just yesterday. I love you.

Till then,
Ken

Subj: ***Good evening, Darling***
Date: 11/19/98

Dearest Ken,

As you can see, this week, I have been writing to you after work rather than in the morning. The pace of things has picked up considerably, and I must postpone my letter until almost everyone is gone and my phone stops ringing.

It's a pity you lost the first draft of your letter. Even in the one I received, you were very eloquent, and I couldn't help but smile. You came through as well-rested and in a great frame of mind. It's been a long time since I sensed those feelings in your letters. You were very much the person I fell in love with; I wish I could express myself as well as you.

I always appreciate your letters; they brighten my day. I sometimes feel like there could be more acknowledgment and reassurance about how our physical distance affects me. I know you love me and are doing your best with work and other commitments, but I worry about us. I think it's because we haven't been working together as a team to find solutions. Instead, we've been approaching things individually. We need a unified plan to make our dreams a reality.

I'd like us to discuss specific topics to ensure we are on the same page and can work towards solutions together. First, we must address the technical difficulties with your computer, modem, and phone line. Second, we should confirm that these issues are technical and not caused by others' misuse. Third, we need to clarify your responsibility for helping others, especially if it's to your detriment. Fourth, we should discuss coordinating our travel or meet-up plans without interfering with your time with your daughters. Fifth, I'd like to confirm that I will visit every other month, as it's more feasible for me. (I can make my first visit at the end of the month. I plan to be off work.) Last, I want us to talk about my concerns regarding your silences or uncertainties, not when I am emotional but with calm and a clear head. I hope we can work through these issues together. What are your thoughts?

Are you still considering buying that house, or is it on the back burner? How are your daughters? Have you found suitable homes for the puppies? Let me know how your meeting for the new play went. I haven't been sleeping well these past few nights.

Till then,
Nickie

Ken

The highway was deserted, a ribbon of asphalt illuminated by the car's headlights, save for the occasional truck or late-night traveler. The radio played softly, a mix of late-night jazz.

I let my mind wander about Nickie's afternoon email. I had read it multiple times, not for the usual reasons when her words would set my heart and body on fire but because it gave me cause to pause. She was thorough and methodical—just like an accountant should be. That was not my way. I thought we had been handling things well. Her list had thrown me slightly off guard. I imagined her sitting at her desk, glasses perched on her nose, typing out each point.

I chuckled. She was right about the technical difficulties; we had encountered our fair share of glitches. It was like our love was running on a faulty internet cable. My computer was new, but maybe I had gotten a lemon. I doubted Gateway would reimburse me, but I should approach them about returning the whole thing and getting a replacement. Missing that, I needed to think of a permanent workaround.

She had reservations about Tim and Michelle; I doubted they would intentionally misuse the computer. What would they gain by it? After all, it was one of their primary sources of entertainment during the day, as neither one had a new job yet. Did they even know how much this thing cost? Perhaps it was a mistake. The computer was more delicate than the television. I made a mental note to observe them more.

I didn't view my tendency to help people as detrimental; I had always been the fixer, who stayed late at work to troubleshoot, volunteered for extra shifts, and helped when my friends were in a bind. Although I admitted people were not always grateful, I saw it as my Christian duty to help. Was it affecting our relationship that much? Maybe she thought I prioritized others over her. I didn't, but she might not see it that way.

Balancing time with my daughters was essential, and Nickie didn't have a problem there; however, she had a point. We had to ensure our time together wouldn't interfere with my girls' custodial visits.

Her plan to visit every other month was reasonable, and I agreed. Had I been clear on that? I might have to juggle a few things with work to accommodate this first visit at month-end but it's possible. I smiled, imagining her stepping off the plane, her eyes lighting up, waiting at the gate. It would be a welcome routine, reminding us that distance couldn't dampen our love.

I sighed and leaned over the dashboard to turn off the radio. The music had ended, and a talk show was about to start. I could only continue to reassure her, affirming my love. I sensed fragility there. She never mentioned any past emotional trauma, and I tried my best to show her I loved her. What was I missing? Maybe I should surprise her with a letter, pen on paper, once again expressing how much she means to me.

Moments later, I parked in the driveway; the porch lights a beacon of home. I walked to the farmhouse. I only needed to communicate my thoughts on her letter to her before I got distracted or forgot. The whole thing had not been too hard to think about. Maybe she had a point: putting something down on paper and going at it methodically wasn't as overwhelming as one would think otherwise. I smiled. Our styles were different, but we complemented each other well. I should tell her again.

My dream of a quiet house, a quick note to Nickie, and a fast journey to pleasant dreams evaporated as I opened the door to the sound of World War III, an argument between Tim and Michelle while both the baby and Alissa were crying at the top of their lungs. I retreated to my bedroom but came out five minutes later, grabbed Alex from his crib, took Alissa's hand, and bundled them up for a moonlight stroll around the glistening moat that mirrored the night sky. Neither Michelle nor Tim stopped their argument for a second as I cooed and removed the kids.

Subj: *Good morning*
Date: 11/20/98 8:19:23 AM Eastern Standard Time

Dearest Nickie,

Good morning, my love. As hectic as things are at the office, do you think the new owner will replace you in the spring? Last night, I scented my pillowcases again with your perfume, as I couldn't immediately fall asleep. I was a little late this morning; I didn't want to leave. I love you.

I have the people from the mortgage company talking to the realtor about the house in Braim. It would be an excellent investment. Instead of a garage, there is an old carriage house in the back. The house has a circular drive and 1.9 acres of land, 80-100 ft evergreens, and maple trees. I will think more about it when and if the i's and t's get dotted and crossed.

Tim and Michelle are working on their relationship. Tim has moved home to his parent's house but will come over in the evenings to spend time with Michelle and the kids two or three nights a week. I have agreed to let Michelle take my car tonight; she and Tim are going out on a date, and I will watch the kids.

I had a minor scare. My mother stopped talking to anyone for two weeks, and my sister asked me to check on her. My mother wouldn't answer the door, but someone turned the television on between my second and third stops last night, so at least I can say she is among the living. She did that once before for no apparent reason.

My reading for the play went well. I did the opening monologue from "Love's Labor Lost," and then they asked me to do a cold reading for Frank (the faith healer). The directors laughed in the appropriate places, and all three applauded when I finished (which was unusual). Then they took my picture. I will know more on Saturday.

The girls are doing fine, fiddling more than usual but happy. Chelsea loves the horse and named it Apache. Camille involves herself in her schoolwork, and Claire constantly gives her sisters a lousy time, but she is only trying to get their attention. I am still trying to find homes for two puppies. Five dogs would be a little excessive, but it may come to that.

Till then, love
Ken

!!!!!! I LOVE YOU!!!!!!

Subj: ***Loving you***
Date: 11/20/98

Dearest Ken,

Feeling the "Joie de vivre" (zest for life) come through your letters again is good. I know I have already told you in my last three letters, but I still marvel at it! (some of it should rub off on me soon).

Are you considering purchasing the house for personal use, or is it purely an investment rental? Your description painted such a fabulous picture that I felt transported there for a moment, seeing it through your eyes. You have a fantastic way of making me experience whatever you are describing.

I am glad your friends are getting things straightened out. It's good not only for them and their kids but also for your emotional well-being. I hope your mom is ok. Did you do anything to get her angry? Sometimes, parents become eccentric and unpredictable as they age. As long as we can satisfy ourselves that they are physically okay, it is best to let them have their temporary space.

I am supposed to meet one of my three best friends for dinner and a "talk." I feel very fortunate to know all three of them. I love you more than words can express.

Till then,
Nickie

Subj: **_Good morning_**
Date: 11/21/98 7:02:12 AM Eastern Standard Time

Dearest Nickie,

Good morning, my love; it feels so wonderful to wake up with you in my arms and your fresh taste on my tongue. How was your evening with your friend and your "talk"? I love you.

Last night, we had gentle snow. There was not a cloud in the sky, for the stars were incredibly bright. I let the horse run in the pasture later than usual. Apache is becoming friendly now, galloping and neighing when you walk up the fence. We walked under the stars and talked for an hour before I put him in the barn for the night. When I entered the house, I started a fire and watched the flames, lost in thoughts of holding you;

I mean to buy the house as an investment. I thought about moving Tim and Michelle into it and collecting a small rent for a while. Recently, I've gone out to plan the necessary mending (the house needs some work, but the carriage house needs extensive repairs). The house is 90 years old and elegant, with 12-foot ceilings, stained glass windows, hardwood floors, pillars, scrollwork arched doorways, and marble fireplaces. (not a shower in the place).

Till then,
Ken

Subj: **_Without you_**
Date: 11/21/98

Dearest Ken,

Dinner went well with my friend Wayne and his wife, Wendy; hanging out with them is always good. They've been married a while and seem to have figured things out. Their oldest daughter will attend Craig's old High School, and they had a few questions I was happy to help with. Of course, they are usually available when I need a friendly ear. It's more often these days. I had anticipated our Milwaukee meeting too much, and because it didn't happen, I feel lonelier; of course, you getting sick was out of your control. However, I am a tad disappointed that you neglected to send the physical birthday card you promised. I also didn't get your thoughts on the issues I mentioned in my letter of 11/19.

I constantly review all the qualities that make me love you more and minimize everything else, so my unhappiness in this is also partly my fault.

Missing you,
Nickie

Subj: *re: without you*
Date: 11/21/98 11:57:27 AM Eastern Standard Time

Dearest Nickie,

I still need to finish reading your letter, but I must address something; I didn't forget. I sent your card on 11/08/98, complete with a new picture, a picture of the new horse, and a new poem. You never bore me, and I told you in the Email greeting cards I sent they were not your actual card; that one was coming in the mail. Why didn't you mention it earlier?

I expected you in late November or early December to make up for the missed Milwaukee connection., but I didn't let it get me down when I failed to hear anything more concrete about it. I planned to mention that I would visit NY on New Year's Eve since I don't have any vacation left this year, so I need to wait to borrow from next year.

I thought I addressed all the points in your letter of 11/19, but now I realize it was the evening of Michelle and Tim's big argument, and in my eagerness to spare the children the noise, I left the house without having answered you. It's great that you can visit at the end of the month. I am sorry; we'll discuss all the points you raised in that letter on the phone tonight if there are no line issues. I love you.

Till then,
Ken

Subj: *Happy now*
Date: 11/21/98

Dearest Ken,

I am going grocery shopping for Thanksgiving dinner. I am so excited about visiting you in just over a week. Finalizing things over the phone would have been easier, but I don't know the airline schedules. I will get more information when I call for reservations. A flight on Monday the 30th would be good. Which hotel should I stay in to make it easier for us to spend time together? (I want to minimize disruption to your routine.) I love you. Once again, I am sorry for accusing you of not keeping your promise with the card. I should have told you I didn't receive it. Please send me the poem in one of your next emails; I can't wait to read it.

Till then,
Nickie

Subj: ***Good morning***
Date: 11/22/98 6:41:28 AM Eastern Standard Time

Dearest Nickie,

Good morning, my love. November 30th would be fine. How was your day yesterday? Did you run all of your errands? I went to callbacks for Faith Healer, and I may have the lead, a character named Frank. I love you.

"Empty Rooms"
I sit in a room,
Filled with blurred images,
And rebounding verbal vibrations,
All indistinguishable,
Yet I see you,
Vivid and clear,
Many things I wish to say,
But the words,
They don't come out.
I sit in an empty room.
Just be,
Ken

I am sorry you didn't receive your card. I have another picture of Apache, Chelsea, and Claire, but I must take another picture of myself. The only ones I have now are from my nephew's birthday party (I look big in them, maybe too much cake), and my hair looks so much different now.

Till then,
Ken

Subj: *Good morning, darling*
Date: 11/22/98

Dearest Ken,

Thanks for the lovely poem; your feelings mirror mine, and if I could have put the words together, I would have said the same thing.

Please don't resend the pictures; We'll look at them when we meet. I'd rather they don't go awry again.

When I visit, can we see the house you plan to purchase? It sounds so lovely. Somehow, they don't build new homes with the same elegance of the past. The other day, when you told me about babysitting and playing with Alisa and her Barbie dolls, I pictured it, and it melted my heart. Did I tell you how much I love you? You are such a good person that sometimes I feel God made a mistake in bringing us together. Have a great day. Mine always goes well whenever I hear from you.

Till then,
Nickie

Subj: *Monday morning*
Date: 11/23/98

Dearest Ken,

Good morning, darling. How was your Sunday? Yesterday was very productive; I cleaned my apartment in one session, did the laundry, learned a new financial program, and found time to watch television. The thought of seeing you soon gave me an incredible energy boost. I even dreamed of you last night but can't remember the details.

Till then,
Nickie

Subj: 11/30
Date: 11/23/98 6:22:08 PM Eastern Standard Time

Dearest Nickie,

I apologize for being so slow in replying. I had another doctor's visit today. The virus has gotten into the muscles in my back and neck. I had difficulty getting dressed this morning, so I returned to the doctor. She gave me a new prescription. I have to go back on Monday at 3:00 p.m.

It is expensive, but a downtown hotel might be the best. The Marriott is the hotel's name, and it is in the same building as my office. Plenty to occupy you during the day, and we can find something together for your evenings. I am trying again to get the camera working. I wonder if I can last another week without seeing you again. (Now, I am being selfish; of course, I can wait, but if I don't have to, I don't want to.) I am putting on weight again, and they say that's good. I got the part in Faith Healer and start rehearsal on Thursday. (They wanted to start tomorrow night, but I convinced them to hold off till after the holiday) and I have the girls on Wednesdays. I love you.

How is the franchise location hunting going? Any recent developments with your tenants?

Till then,
Ken

Subj: *I love you*
Date: 11/25/98

Dearest Ken,

Good morning, darling. Apologies for not writing yesterday. I never made it to work and didn't have my laptop. I went to court in the morning and expected it to be brief. I got out of there at 3:45 p.m. I was so stressed and infuriated that I decided against going to the office.

How are you feeling today? Are your back muscles still troubling you? Anytime you are unwell, I want to take care of you. Gaining some weight will speed up your recovery. I enjoyed talking to you and hearing your incredible voice the other night. I can't wait for us to be together again. I miss you so much.

Till then,
Nickie

Subj: *Happy Thanksgiving!*
Date: 11/26/98

Dearest Ken,

Good morning, and Happy Thanksgiving! Are you spending the day with family or with friends? Did you get my card? Get plenty of rest, and eat all the turkey and anything else you can get your hands (mouth) on. It's one day when we don't have to think about the waistline. I am already cooking up a storm for the family's arrival this afternoon.

Were you able to make reservations with Northwest for New Year's Eve? Is the fare reasonable? Can you take the first week of the year off? New Year's Eve is a hard day to get a flight. Let me know when you have confirmation; I'll switch some days off from the last week of this year to coincide with your visit. I want to get us tickets to a few Broadway shows. They have a special this week until Saturday. I'll make an itinerary of things to do/places to visit while you are here. Do you have other interests (besides watching the ball at midnight on New Year's Eve)? Any specific museums, buildings, or sites? If so, I'll find out the schedules.

Till then,
Nickie

Nickie

I stood in the kitchen, the smell of roasted turkey mingling with the sweet scent of pumpkin pie. Laughter echoed from the living room where my family gathered, joy that seemed to bounce off me without leaving a mark. I smiled, a well-practiced curve of the lips that didn't quite reach my eyes as I arranged the glazed carrots on a platter.

The place was warm despite the late November chill clinging to the windows. I watched Craig, my nieces, and nephews play board games, absorbed in fierce competition. Macy caught my eye, raising a glass in silent toast, and I raised mine.

I made a mental note to contact Jenna and Carlos. I wanted their opinion on a book for next month's club meeting. The thought of attending a children's fundraiser with my hiking friends was comforting, even if it became a performance where I played the contented woman everyone expected to see.

My brother-in-law Adrien entered the kitchen, snatched a napkin and two cookies wordlessly, and returned to the living room. My eyes followed him as he handed the cookies to Macy. She kissed his cheek. I sighed and longed for the warmth of shared experiences and the comfort of a hand holding mine.

Craig had turned on the music to show off the multi-disc CD player he had given me for Mother's Day. Netty jumped to her feet, already swaying, and urged her reluctant husband to dance. As the evening wore on, I got into the spirit of our Thanksgiving party and soon realized that my sadness had dissipated amid family fun. We shouldn't waste these precious occasions because we'll never have them again. Despite my earlier thoughts, I resolved to seek moments of genuine joy, no matter how fleeting. I had accepted that I couldn't stop loving Ken; the heart wanted what it wanted, and I surrendered to it. I couldn't control anything and made peace with that. I was not at fault when, occasionally, Ken didn't write or call. It was difficult, but I had no choice. And maybe, just maybe, I would find the strength to release the yearning and embrace my life, imperfections and all.

"Déjà-vu"

Subj: ***Good morning, my love***
Date: 12/1/98 7:53:36 AM Eastern Standard Time

Dearest Nickie,

Good morning, my love. I went to Chicago to visit my sister for Thanksgiving and returned to Minneapolis at 4:45 this morning. Before I left, the doctor said I was improving, but I could have told him. I thought of you often this past weekend and missed you terribly. I tried to connect my sister's computer to show her your picture. Still, after we got her modem and the new hard drive installed, we discovered she needed more RAM to support the additional windows. I love you.

I am still bummed out that you couldn't get a flight out for the 30th/. During the holiday season, I would work 12 hours a day until Christmas, meaning that if you had come for three days, we would have only been able to spend 3 hours together; I can see why you decided against booking the trip. I promise you'll have ALL of my time when I am in NY. I could not leave the office on Christmas weekend, so I put in for New Year's Eve and the subsequent week off.

We had a traditional Thanksgiving dinner. Sweet potatoes are my favorite, and I thought of you as I sat down at the dining table with my plate and envisioned you there.

How was your Thanksgiving? Did your mother help with the preparations? What did you eat for the celebration? What I ate was not on my plate but was gourmet? I love you.

Till then,
Ken

Subj: ***Nothing special***
Date: 12/1/98 1:26:49 PM Eastern Standard Time

Dearest Nickie,

Good afternoon, my love. How are you spending your vacation? I imagine checking the PC is the last (or at least pretty far down the list) thing on your mind.

I hope your weather is as lovely as it is here. I miss you. During lunch, I strolled through the lobby, took in the Christmas decorations, and thought of you (I got a little nervous around Victoria's Secret again; I don't know what it is.) I will write later.

Till then, love
Ken

Subj: ***Morning***
Date: 12/1/98

Dearest Ken,

It's nice to hear that you were with your sister on Thanksgiving. Keep getting adequate rest to maintain your progress in the future.

Thanksgiving was full of laughter and warmth. I hosted 14 people, and it went well. Smell of roasted turkey and baked pies filled the air. I even got compliments on the food from my most critical sister, Macy. There were no heated family discussions, but we enjoyed catching up and creating lasting memories. I fielded some questions about my dating life; I figured I would surprise them and introduce you to Craig and the rest of them when you came for New Year's Eve. I also want us to coordinate our stories, as I doubt they would understand about online dating.

The weather has been nice, and I have resumed my 2-hour walks. However, I still have trouble keeping my mood even, from missing you. I hope things keep going well for you.

Till then,
Nickie

Subj: ***Hello again***
Date: 12/1/98

Dearest Ken,

Was I a bit short in my earlier letter? I had been worried last weekend, thinking you might be back in the hospital. I was relieved to hear you were with your sister but disappointed not to know you would be gone.

How is everything else? I thought last weekend was your time with your daughters. Did you go to Chicago with them? You are correct in being careful with the real estate situation; banks like nothing better than to see people overextend themselves. Sometimes, they make things so easy that it is tough to say no.

Please check the airlines for that date, as I suggested. Coming back would not be a problem, but you must reserve the flight to New York. I watched the Christmas tree light up at Rockefeller Center. The city is adorned with twinkling lights, creating a magical atmosphere. You can hear holiday shoppers' joyful laughter and excited chatter. The tree will still be up when you come. I'll put one up at home this year so we can cuddle and listen to music (it's been a while since I had one). Even after Christmas, being together will make it the best holiday season in a long time. I love you.

Till then,
Nickie

Subj: *Good afternoon*
Date: 12/1/98 3:18:52 AM Eastern Standard Time

Dearest Nickie,

I received your messages an hour ago; a system update is causing delays in specific programs. Since you were on vacation, I thought you had left all the work-related things at the office. I am on standby for 12/31 on NW. The only sight I am looking forward to seeing in NY is you. It's glaring to me that I miss you more every day, and I want to discuss something with you, but we'll talk about it when I see you in NY. I love you.

The play is going well, and I had another audition for Jacobs Wives with TRP last Tuesday evening. I want to land at least one play there as I would like to do voice-overs (radio commercials and background voices on TV commercials); they hire most of the actors out of TRP. Additionally, it is expected to demand a mid to upper 6-figure income doing voice-overs part-time.

Unfortunately, Mary Lou won't let the girls out of state with me yet. So, they could not visit with Billie and Liam, but we will trade pictures back and forth via snail mail. We tried to roll Thanksgiving and Christmas up into one visit this year.

How was your walk? How does the tree look? Do you ice skate? I heard there is a great ice rink in Central Park.

Till then, love
Ken

Ken

I drove straight to work this morning from seeing Billie and Liam. I realized that the more I examined Nickie's list of 11/19, the more I agreed we needed to find permanent solutions to those inconveniences before they became significant issues in the relationship. An independent opinion would help; I could meet with my therapist to see if I was handling things correctly. I knew one thing: I didn't want to distress Nickie further, and I concluded it might be time to consider moving. I asked Billie to check with her contacts again to see what opportunities might be in Chicago; she was happy at the possibility of having me closer to her and my favorite nephew. I didn't have the heart to tell her there was only a remote possibility that I would move there; Chicago would be a prime consideration only if Nickie would be interested. I emailed two head hunters during lunch, asking about contacts in the Big Apple and potential offers in my field. NY would be my top location consideration as Nickie would not have to move and upend her life since she had her real estate holdings and soon-to-be franchise business to think about. I knew she loved me, but would she think it too early for me to propose? Aside from her answer, my primary concern was my girls; what would Mary Lou be amenable to? Would she let me have them for holidays and part of the summer if I'm not here during the school year? Since Claire was a handful, I would probably have to get a separate place until Nickie and I decided to get a larger home together for that possibility. Mary Lou was so unpredictable in that respect that I didn't even know if she would consider changing our custody agreement. I would contact my old divorce lawyer to explore the possibilities and find the best way to approach Mary Lou if I got positive feedback from the headhunters. If I relocated, I could rent the farm to Tim and Michelle and fly back to Minneapolis once or twice a year to check on it.

The traffic slowed once I reached my exit; I realized I had already gone through one detour and had a few barricades ahead. I spotted an officer arranging highway cones and inquired about the commotion. He informed me of a fire and requested that I move along. I thought it was a shame until I approached the entry to my land and noticed that the caution tapes had ended at my property. My heart started pounding as two more police officers stopped me. I informed them that this was my driveway and I was returning home from a trip. The officers waved me in, their stoic expressions revealing nothing of what lay ahead.

I drove toward the clearing and a sense of unease crept over me. The sight that greeted me almost stopped my heart. My farmhouse and barn were reduced to smoking cinders, and the air filled with an acrid smell. My eyes welled up as I pulled the car to a stop and opened the door. My legs felt weak, and I stumbled; overcome with emotion, I sank to my knees and wept. It was too much to bear.

A policewoman who noticed approached me and told me everyone from the house was okay, but the horses ran away and caused some damage. The town caught them; they would return them once they assessed the fines and completed the paperwork.

A voice I didn't recognize as mine asked:

"What, what happened?"

"Based on our report, sir, two couples, Tim, Michelle, Sara, and Taylor, were having a barbecue near the house with their kids. The adults were drinking, and since it was rather chilly, they moved indoors for a bit, leaving the grill on. They were careless in securing the top. It was slightly windy, and a spark flew and ignited a piece of paper that blew off and ignited a dish towel they were using. When they realized what had happened in their stupor, one side of the barn was on fire. The two horses spooked, ran off half a mile and ended up on the highway, causing a six-car pile-up. The couples ran after the horses before they realized the barn fire had spread to the house, and the kids were inside. They turned around and were able to retrieve them safely. Tim and Michelle called the fire department, but by the time they arrived fifteen minutes later, the house and all his belongings had burned to the ground."

I could hardly hear her. The weight of the situation pressed down on me, causing my chest to tighten with anxiety. The reality of losing my home and the uncertainty of my future engulfed me, making it difficult to think clearly. I couldn't stop thinking about being homeless and not seeing my daughters. I realized I no longer had a home to renovate or sell to be with Nickie. I didn't have a change of clothes to my name except what I had taken to Billie's for the weekend. At some point, I must have risen. I had sat all night in the car, staring at the ashes of my home. Desperation welled inside me. On auto-pilot, I called my job from the nearest convenience store fifteen miles away to tell them what happened and that I wouldn't be in the next day. I called my sister; Billie listened patiently, her voice filled with empathy, and she asked me to live with her in Chicago. *How can I do that when my job and children are in Minnesota? What am I going to do?* My hands trembled as I clutched my credit card and counted the meager 80-dollar cash in my wallet. My bank card wasn't there.

I checked into a modest motel on my route home. I would stay there for the next two days. I practically lived at the convenience store five minutes away, using the public phone and the most recent Yellow Pages to make a million calls to the police, my insurance company, work, and Mary Lou to explain the fire and why I could not pick up my girls.

"You're lying, Ken! It's is just another one of your stories to get out of your responsibilities," Mary Lou said after a few seconds of silence.

"Mary Lou, I'm not lying. I—"

"No! I've heard enough. You always do this. You leave me to deal with everything. The girls, the house, the bills—everything!" she interrupted.

"I understand you're upset, but it's not like that. I—"

"Upset? Do you think I'm just upset? You've never taken responsibility for anything. You left me to fend for myself, running to the hospital and pretending you were hurt! And now, you expect me to believe you?"

"You know that's not true, Mary Lou. You hurt me; you are the one who called the ambulance! Please, let's not - I'm trying to explain if you'd listen—"

"Listen to what? More excuses? I hate I have to rely on you for anything. You've never been there when we needed you, and you're not here now!"

I could see my reflection in the convenience store's window. My shoulders were slumped, weighed down by the accusations and the emotional toll of the conversation. I ran a hand through my hair and rubbed the back of my neck from stress and frustration. Even though she could not see me, my movements were slow and somewhat hesitant, from weariness and the desire to avoid further conflict.

"Mary Lou, please. Let's try to be civil, for the girls' sake. I'm doing the best I can."

"Oh, your best? That's a laugh. I'd hate to see you at your worst! I hate you. We're better off without you."

I wondered if she was right, if I was a loser unable to save my marriage and now had no home for my daughters or a place to sleep.

The bell jingled as I entered the convenience store. Ralph, the portly owner, greeted me with his perpetual smile.

"Morning, Ken. What can I get for ya?"

"Just a cup of coffee, Ralph."

It wasn't the coffee I needed. It was a moment of solace, a break from the chaos in my head and outside.

"You look like you've been through hell, my friend. Everything okay?"

I automatically shook my head, and then I realized there was genuine concern in Ralph's eyes, his brows furrowed, etching lines into his forehead. I hesitated, then blurted out the words, seeking release from the immensity of my sadness.

"The farm... It's gone. The horses escaped, causing a pileup on the highway. It's all over the local news."

"I heard the report on the radio driving here this morning, but I didn't know it was your place."

"Ken, that's a tough break. You've been coming here for years, always with a smile. How are you holding up?"

"It's been hard, Ralph. I lost everything, and it's just... overwhelming."

"You are one of the good ones, Ken. It's not right what happened to you."

"I guess I'm just trying to figure out where to go from here. I have no place to stay at the moment."

"You're not alone in this. You've been more than a customer."

"I appreciate it, Ralph. I didn't expect... I mean, I wasn't looking for sympathy."

"It's not about sympathy, Ken. It's about doing what's right. You would've done the same for any of us. You can use the store's address to receive mail if needed."

"Ralph, I can't thank you enough. It's going to make things ten times easier."

Ralph entered the backroom and returned with a new blanket and two sweatshirts with the "Minnesota" logo. These were brand new tourist store merchandise, and he offered them to me. I could feel myself blushing to the roots of my hair from embarrassment and regretted that I had said anything.

"Oh, Ralph, I... I can't accept these."

"Of course, you can. These have been sitting in the back for ages. If you're worried about charity, then don't. Consider it a loan if that sits better with you."

"A loan, then. Until I'm back on my feet."

I thanked him, at once embarrassed and touched. This gesture was the kindest thing anyone had done for me in a while, considering that the very people who destroyed all my material possessions did not even try to contact me to at least see how I was doing or express regret at the events. I thanked Ralph and left.

I spent the next two weeks sleeping in my car near my burned-out house, waking up to the chirping of birds and the crisp morning breeze before heading for work. Every other day, I charged a night's stay at the motel to shower, shave, brush my teeth, wash my change of clothes, the t-shirts, and sweatshirts in the bathroom sink. Once I received my next paycheck, I would check into the motel for a two-week stay and buy another set of clothes, underwear, and necessities.

I received correspondence regarding my daughters' visitation rights from Mary Lou's lawyer. The day after, I received a legal notice from a lawyer representing the six people involved in the highway pile-up caused by the runaway horses. My spirits couldn't sink lower, but now they did, and each day grew more challenging to navigate. My mood tumbled into a funnel of darkness; I was powerless. Despite the sympathy from my co-workers, I found myself lost in sadness, gazing blankly into space. Eve would stop by my cubicle daily with tea or water, but I suspected she was checking to see if I was alright. As the work piled up undone and unanswered, my manager asked me to seek help. I was clueless and stared at her, not understanding. I was confused, and it wasn't until HR referred me to a psychologist that I realized the gravity of my situation. The psychologist admitted me to the hospital for careful observation and daily counseling sessions.

A month later, they discharged me, and I returned to work in slightly better condition. I was at least able to function and carry out my duties. I was also heavily medicated with anti-depressants. I knew there were possibly thirty or forty unopened emails in my work computer folder marked "Nickie's mail."

It broke my heart more that I wasn't talking to her. But what could I say to her? What did I have to offer now? I couldn't provide for myself, let alone my daughters. Every day was a struggle to keep functioning one hour after the next. I used to request every overtime opportunity to afford extra cash to buy a few things to spoil and delight my daughters. I could not see them now since I was behind in their support. An investigator came by, but I refused to press charges against Tim, Michelle, Sara, and Taylor, grateful that none of them or their children were hurt.

I had regained access to my bank account, found a buyer for the horses at a discount, and ended up with a loss after settling room and boards for the animals with the city. The Minneapolis Police SCID offices convinced me it was the best course of action to halt the exponential fees I was incurring. I had maxed out my credit cards, so I drained the small amount left in my savings.

Eve stopped by my desk, trying to cheer me up with a few silly jokes, but I felt a sharp pinch in my heart as my thoughts turned to Nickie. I berated myself anew for the pain my silence probably caused her and my failure to have the mental strength to let her know what was happening. I stared at my "Nickie" email folder, not ready to respond, but able now, for the first time, to face the words she had written since we last spoke on December 1st of last year.

Subj: *Saying hello*
Date: 12/3/98

Dearest Ken,

Did you have a rehearsal last night? I hope TRP hires you for Jacob's wives; if that can get you a foot in the door for doing those voice-overs, it would be fantastic. It's hard to imagine them not considering you with a voice as sexy and warm as yours. I love you.

It's a shame you couldn't take the girls to Chicago. There is always next year; maybe Mary Lou will see the light eventually.

My walks are going great. It's 50 degrees today, and I was out with only a sweat-shirt. I took my car for service this morning; it's laughable they did the 21,000-mile service (my odometer is only reading 20,350 miles); the vehicle is four years old. I will get a tree next week. I want it to stay fresh for Christmas or when you get here. Unfortunately, I don't ice skate, but I can learn; there is a rink in Central Park and Rockefeller Center where the main Christmas tree is.

I hope you can get on that flight on 12/31. I can't wait to be in your arms again. The week flew by quickly; Netty was also off and had invited me to go away with her to a resort in New Jersey. I considered it but did not find the four-hour drive appealing.

Will you be rehearsing every day? Try not to overdo anything.

Till then,
Nickie

Subj: *Good morning*
Date: 12/7/98

Dearest Ken,

Good morning, darling. Did you work, or did you spend the weekend with your daughters? How is rehearsal coming along? Any news on the other play and the TRP voice-over possibility? What's happening with the house purchase? How is Apache coming along? I love you.

Till then,
Nickie

Subj: *Miss hearing from you*
Date: 12/9/98

Dearest Ken,

Good morning, darling. Is everything OK? I love you. Are you simply busy? Work, play, and house hunting must consume all your time. Still, I miss you.

Till then,
Nickie

Subj: *Why the silence?*
Date: 12/11/98

Dearest Ken,

Good morning, darling. An entire week has passed with no word. I reread your last letter several times this week and cannot find anything that would indicate anything wrong. Are your daughters ok? I miss you. I have nothing else to say except that I am thinking of you. Take care of yourself.

Till then,
Nickie

Subj: *Good morning, Ken*
Date: 12/13/98

Dearest Ken,

I left a message on your line Saturday morning, hoping it would prompt you to write.

Did you think about not coming to New York and feel bad about telling me so? I'd rather be disappointed than not hear from you at all.

It's not endearing to beg you to write to me., but it's my mind talking, and my heart is not listening. I love you

Till then,
Nickie

Subj: *Where are you, my Darling?*
Date: 12/14/98

Dearest Ken,

Good morning, dearest. I am considering seeing a psychologist for advice on how to cope with my sense of emptiness. Let me know how you are. I will love you no matter what, even if it's one-sided.

Till then,
Nickie

Subj: *Good afternoon, Dearest*
Date: 12/15/98

Dearest Ken,

Are you even opening my emails? Are you alright? Thirteen days without a word from you, it's a record. The only possible reason for your not writing is that you are traveling. Would you be away for so long? I miss you.

Till then,
Nickie

Subj: *I love you*
Date: 12/16/98

Dearest Ken,

Thank God I only bet with myself. I bet I could stay the whole day without writing to you. (I lost!). I apologize for being such a pest (I know I should stop bothering you). You don't want to talk to me, but my heart hasn't accepted it yet. So please be patient with me. I have loved you for months and cannot stop telling you so overnight. I have not cried since last night. (I consider this significant progress!) I love you. I wish I knew what went wrong.

I bought a Christmas tree and will decorate it between now and Sunday. (You are why I bought it; I haven't had one in 6 or 7 years). I will spend evenings cuddling under the tree with you. (I know, not physically, but you will be in my heart.) You can take your love away, but you can't stop me from loving you! You must think I am crazy.

I'll say bye for now, Darling. If your daughters ever ask about me, tell them I send my love even if they never got a chance to meet me. Take care of yourself. I'll write again tomorrow. I love you.

Till then,
Nickie

Subj: *Thursday morning*
Date: 12/17/98

Dearest Ken,

Good morning, darling. It is possible that if you keep ignoring me, I'll stop writing. In the meantime, it would be much faster if you told me to stop writing and why. What's happening in your life? Unless you are unwell, I can't imagine why you would ignore me for so long (two weeks already).

If you feel bad about hurting my feelings, your silence is worse than anything you could say. It means that you have no concerns at all about my feelings. Even if you met someone else, not acknowledging that does not seem like what you would do.

I will eventually leave you alone, and for the hundredth time, I am sorry about being such a pest. I still love you very much.

Did you finish Christmas shopping? What are you getting them?

Till then,
Nickie

Subj: ***Nothing special***
Date: 12/18/98

Dearest Ken,

Good morning, darling. How are you? I dreamed about you. It's a testimony to Ray Charles's song "I Can't Stop Loving You." The lyrics reflect my feelings perfectly.

Till then,
Nickie

Subj: ***Feeling so lonely without you***
Date: 12/18/98

Dearest Ken,

I could use a hug, kiss, and your arms around me. I am very lonely. I strive to concentrate on work and other tasks, yet my mind continuously drifts back to you.

What's going on? Won't you at least tell me? Ignoring me is easiest, but you claimed to love me once. Don't you realize the pain you are causing me? I love you. I can't go on like that; please tell me why. Can you feel the tears on my cheeks? I need you so much.

Till then,
Nickie

Subj: ***Saturday night goodbye***
Date: 12/19/98

Ken,

I just called you; there was a click like a hang-up on the line. Frankly, there was no reason to be so rude. I have been acting like a stupid, lovesick idiot, refusing to get the message, instead deluding myself that you were maybe sick or otherwise called away. I have been waiting to hear from you for two whole weeks. You have my phone number, my address, and, of course, my email. You could have gotten in touch in any of those ways.

It's my fault for having thought so much of you. It could also be a bit of pride in refusing to admit that you could engage in such cowardly behavior, not writing without explanation, hoping I would stop when you did not write back. I thought so much of you.

The depth of my disappointment only equals the depth of my love. It's funny, but I don't have one tear right now. It could be the shock of the truth. I did not want to believe that of you. Even this afternoon, I called to share my joy after decorating my Christmas tree (for you) and tell you how I missed you. I did not deserve this treatment.

I never claimed to be remarkably skilled in choosing my loves, but I thought I had more than an average capacity to judge character. How wrong I was! How hard did you laugh when you told me you were coming to NY on New Year's Eve? I may be stupid, but I know the answer.

Nickie

Subj: ***I don't hate you, despite everything. I love you.***
Date: 12/21/98

Dearest Ken,

I sent you this irate letter Saturday night. I am still hurt and angry but want to correct my statement. I don't hate you; I could not hate you if I tried. I don't know if you hung up the phone on me Saturday or I misheard. Call it blind trust, but I can't reconcile that behavior with you. Although you dumped me, I still need to believe certain things.

Do you believe my heart still trembles with hope every morning when I turn on my computer? Hoping to see mail from you. These two weeks at home will be an emotional hell because I won't even have work to distract me from the thought of you. I know you will not be here, but I could not bring myself to remove your gifts from under the tree.

You must think me pathetic for being so weak and unable to accept your blatant rejection. I must have sensed this kind of weakness; that's probably why I never let myself fall in love so entirely with anyone. I feel as if I have broken the dam that was keeping my feelings harnessed, and now my love for you is rampant, unable to be contained no matter what. I hope you won't be too hard on me even if I act stupidly; you once loved your ex-wife deeply and were hurt when she took her love away. It's how I feel about losing your love, maybe even worse because I don't know why. Despite our limited physical connection, my love for you was sincere. The relationship was genuine, and you were the one thing that kept me going, the light of my day. You have no idea HOW MUCH I LOVED YOU and still DO, to my detriment.

Remember this? From your first letter: 'I am not perfect, and I'll not claim to be, but I can still get to heaven if you come to take my hand and walk with me.'

I still feel the same; that›s why it struck a chord then. I know my love is pure, and I am not confusing it with lust or anything. I kicked myself for not coming to Minneapolis two weeks ago, even if that meant spending only hours with you. That's more than I have now.)

Ken, all color is gone from my life. I don't know how much longer I'll be able to function without you. I love you and always will.

Nickie

Subj: ***Promises***
Date: 12/23/98

Dearest Ken,

I remembered a promise you made to me in the summer. I asked you to promise to let me know if you ever intend to stop writing. It was hard getting you to promise that, but you did. I know you take great pride in always keeping your word, so this may remind you to tell me why you stopped loving me and why you haven't written despite my begging you to.

Till then,
Nickie

Subj: ***Merry Christmas***
Date: 12/24/98

Dearest Ken,

I will hold your picture in my arms tonight and the memory of our love in my heart. Merry Christmas, dearest! Nothing will ever change my love for you.

Till then,
Nickie

"Baby Steps"

Nickie

Rising from the cool wooden floor, I rolled up the vibrant green yoga mat and stretched my tired muscles. The soothing scent of lavender filled the air, lingering from the calming, essential oil diffuser nearby. With a sense of accomplishment, I tucked the mat into the hallway closet. I was proud of myself and of my consistency. I had kept up with my new twice-weekly yoga classes and did the exercises at home on most of my off days. It was a blessing in multiple ways. We had several late-season snowstorms this year, and they had curtailed my walking and jogging activities, not wanting to risk slipping on icy pavements or in the park. I grabbed the pen and the piece of paper with scribbled notes resting at my favorite spot around the kitchen table, picked up the phone receiver from the wall, and dialed Francine's number. She picked up on the third ring, by which time I had already blocked off 'Vaca' for the last week of July, excitement in my fingertips.

"Hi, Francine! Pack your bags. Our trip to Turks and Caicos is all set for a month from today!"

"Wow, that was fast! I'm glad I could carve out the time on my schedule. It'll be a blast."

"Absolutely! It's another all-inclusive resort. And guess what? I've booked us for scuba diving lessons and parasailing!"

"Scuba diving sounds fun, but parasailing? When did you turn into Evel Knievel? Whatever happened to Miss Sensible?"

"Come on, it'll be an adventure! But don't worry, I'm bringing three books. If you'd rather not join me, you can read on the beach, but I must get out of my comfort zone." Plus, no matter my feelings, the world keeps on turning.

"Have you heard from Ken?"

I felt a dull pain in my chest but kept a smile while holding the receiver.

"No, nothing. It's been eight months. As the saying goes, just because someone doesn't love you the way you want, doesn't mean they don't love you with all they have."

"You're handling it so well. By the way, Linda told me Eric, the accountant, aka 'comedian,' was quite smitten with you at the party a few months ago. He's been asking for your number."

"Eric, huh? He's nice, but I don't see him as boyfriend material. Plus, I'm not ready for that step yet."

"He's successful and a nice guy. You might consider him as a friend for now?"

"Maybe you're right. A friend could be good, but my heart is still taken. I don't want to string anyone along."

"3 Years Later"

Ken

I left the bank with a smile on my lips. I did it; I made my last car payment. It was so wonderful that I had to do it in person. I raised my head and looked at the midday sun. The sky was a magnificent blue, two wisps of white clouds trailing in the distance. I felt like jumping with joy, but I contained my enthusiasm and just smiled at a random couple walking by. Yesterday was equally satisfying. Dr. Paul diagnosed me as depression-free. I only needed to schedule a quarterly session to ensure I was still on track; I could call whenever required. I told him not to hold his breath, though. It hadn't been easy for the first year and a half, but with courage and persistence I didn't know I possessed, I kept coming week after week until, to my surprise, I felt better. I met Camille to tour the University of St Thomas, my alma mater; she was adamant about going there, and I was eager to show her around.

I was about to leave the house when the phone rang.

"Ken, hey, I'm in a bind. I'm at Maddy's place, out of gas, and I forgot my credit card. Can you pick me up?"

"Ed, you know I'd be there in a heartbeat, but it's a 120-mile journey during rush hour; I've got a play rehearsal tonight. I can't miss it, and there's no way I'd make it back in time."

"I get that, but I don't want to ask Maddy for help. I'll look like an idiot."

"Ed, we've been through this already."

"I know, but—"

"She's your girlfriend. She cares about you. Trust me, it's okay to rely on others sometimes, and now that it's happened twice, you know you won't forget again."

"Alright, I'll ask her. Thanks, Ken."

"Anytime, buddy. Break a leg with Maddy, and I'll do the same at rehearsal."

My old self would have twisted himself into a pretzel, trying to do everything, likely fall short, and disappoint at least one person. I realized it wasn't an emergency, and Ed should have been more careful; I had already helped him once in the past, it was now up to him.

Instead of feeling guilty and miserable, I was proud to stand my ground and not cave in. The only fly in my ointment was when my mind drifted toward thoughts of Nickie and the chance for happiness I may have missed. I finally understood her empowerment instead of the enablement concept. I could have helped Michelle and Tim more effectively by providing rent money for a couple of months and helping them write resumes and job applications to speed up resolving their situation. Their motivation to recover would have been higher, and I would still have my farm and be living with Nickie in NY. But what was done was done; I held no ill will toward my old friends.

Through therapy, I realized that my behavior may have originated from a desire to seek approval, which began during my college years. Being considerably younger than my peers, I felt the need to be accepted. My marital difficulties no doubt contributed to the problem. But I left it all behind and was determined to concentrate on the future.

I started the car and drove, my subconscious taking me home. I arrived and parked in the driveway of my small but cheerful little house, a hair short of being called a bungalow. Despite being a rental, I grew to love it during the last few months. The cerulean blue of the siding, the white shutters framing the windows, the light gray roof, and the brilliant, overflowing flower boxes at the base of every window made it a welcoming site that I eagerly entered every day of the week.

I had resumed acting a year ago, and the joy it brought me was sometimes palpable. Every time the plays received a standing ovation, Nickie was the only person I thought of sharing the moment with. I hope she forgave me for the pain my absence must have caused her. I love her; at least on that score, time had stood still. Walking to the front door, I found shears I had neglected to return to the garage. I picked them up and assembled a lovely bouquet. I picked up an empty vase, filled it with water, and placed it back in its place—a warm and beautiful welcome into the house. I made green tea, sat at my kitchen desk, and opened my brand-new laptop.

Nickie

I locked the front door to the store, then fixed the center display on a large table showcasing the latest products and promotions. I visually inspected the shelves lining the walls, each stocked with various health and nutrition products. The aisles are wide enough to navigate, with clear signage to different sections. They delivered the new shipment shortly after opening for business this morning, and since store traffic was light, I restocked the essential items. Lizzie, my only employee, should have no issues when she opens tomorrow. I stored the morning receipts in the safe; she would have to make the bank run. I was anxious about being away for a week but needed relaxation. Just like all newlyweds, I deserved a honeymoon as planned.

The Three Village Inn banquet manager had just returned my call to indicate their power was back on and all would proceed as expected. Many parts of New York had not returned to normal after the blackout. John was at the airport picking up his children for the ceremony the next day. I spoke to Craig earlier, and he said he would drive in tomorrow with the professional photographer and his friend Juan from college. I closed early, and I was going to head home. We would have a barbecue on the back deck for the kids this afternoon; later, he would go out with his son Dean and a couple of work buddies for a bachelor party. I would spend the evening with Crystal, Audrey, and a couple of friends for our "bachelorette "evening. We had everything set. I wanted to check my email for missed messages during my offline day without power. I turned on my laptop and went straight to my email account. There appeared to be about sixty new emails, and as I reached for my purse, I clicked on the first piece of mail to skim, making sure it was nothing vital. I didn't recognize the address, but as I read the first words, my fingers froze on the mouse, my heart catapulted in my chest, and I knew I held my breath as my eyes read with disbelief:

Dearest Nickie,

I...

Sonnet 116

Let me not to the marriage of true minds
Admit impediments. Love is not love
Which alters when it alteration finds,
Or bends with the remover to remove.
O no! it is an ever-fixed mark
That looks on tempests and is never shaken;
It is the star to every wand'ring bark,
Whose worth's unknown, although his height be taken.
Love's not Time's fool, though rosy lips and cheeks
Within his bending sickle's compass come;
Love alters not with his brief hours and weeks,
But bears it out even to the edge of doom.
If this be error and upon me prov'd,
I never writ, nor no man ever lov'd.
William Shakespeare